The Air Raid Book Club

The Brilliant Life of Hattie Honeywell

ALSO BY ANNIE LYONS

The Brilliant Life of Eudora Honeysett

The Air Raid Book Club

A Novel

Annie Lyons

HARPER LARGE PRINT
An Imprint of HarperCollinsPublishers

THE AIR RAID BOOK CLUB. Copyright © 2023 by Annie Lyons. All rights reserved. Printed in the United States of America. No part of this book may be used or reproduced in any manner whatsoever without written permission except in the case of brief quotations embodied in critical articles and reviews. For information, address HarperCollins Publishers, 195 Broadway, New York, NY 10007.

HarperCollins books may be purchased for educational, business, or sales promotional use. For information, please email the Special Markets Department at SPsales@harpercollins.com.

FIRST HARPER LARGE PRINT EDITION

ISBN: 978-0-06-332283-7

Library of Congress Cataloging-in-Publication Data is available upon request.

23 24 25 26 27 LBC 5 4 3 2 1

For Helen, my much-missed tip-top friend,
with endless love and thanks

Once "in the blood," it is often said, bookselling is a disease from which one never quite recovers.

—Thomas Joy, *The Truth About Bookselling*

Reading brings us unknown friends.

—Honoré de Balzac

The Air Raid Book Club

Prologue

London, 1911

Gertie Bingham was standing in the queue at Piddock the Butcher's contemplating offal when she experienced a thrill of longing a little like falling in love. She recognized this sensation immediately, as it was only the second time she'd experienced it in her life. Some people thought falling in love happened over time, unraveling like a spool of thread, but for Gertie, it was instantaneous. A thunderbolt through the heart. Unexpected. Immediate. Everlasting.

Her eyes traveled from the trays of burgundy sheep hearts and slabs of plum-colored pig's liver to the shop opposite and more specifically the "For Lease" sign within it. Gertie let out an involuntary yelp of excitement. The woman before her in the queue, a Miss Crow, whose name befitted her beady-eyed appearance, issued a loud tut.

"Sorry," cried Gertie, abandoning her place and heading for the door. "It's just that I've found it. I've found it!"

The "it" in question was a milliner's. "Buckingham Milliners, Elegant Millinery for Ladies of Discernment," to be precise. Beechwood High Street boasted not one but two milliners, along with a butcher, a baker, and, indeed, a candlestick maker, although this establishment went under the broader umbrella term of "ironmongers." Gertie despaired at the paucity of interesting shops on offer. Having grown up in the center of London, she found married life in this southeast corner of the capital rather humdrum at times. She longed for a theater or a concert hall or, best of all, a bookshop to add a little cultural distraction. The shops were very pleasant, of course, but largely functional. There was a tailor, a chemist, and a confectioner run by Mrs. Perkins, who Gertie had to admit made the best homemade toffee she'd ever tasted. She also enjoyed visiting Travers's Greengrocers, run by Gerald and his wife, Beryl, and Mr. Piddock was an excellent butcher, but Gertie longed for more, and on this bright June morning, it seemed that it might be in her sights.

She hurried up the hill to the public library where her husband, Harry, worked, impatient to give him the good news. Gertie burst through the heavy mahogany doors, receiving a sharp reproach from the senior librarian, Miss Snipp, who glared at the intruder over the top of her pince-nez.

"May I remind you that this is a library, Mrs. Bingham," she hissed. "Not one of your raucous suffragette gatherings."

"Sorry," whispered Gertie. "I wanted to speak to Harry if he's available."

Miss Snipp opened her mouth, ready to scold such presumption, when the door to the head librarian's office swung open and Harry appeared, carrying a cup and saucer and a copy of a P. G. Wodehouse novel. He didn't notice Gertie at first, and she was reminded of that deliciously heady sensation she'd experienced when they first met. To the casual observer, Harry Bingham's appearance could most generously be described as awkward. He looked like a man whose arms and legs had grown too long for his body, giving him the haphazard air of a foal who was learning to walk. His tie was invariably askew and his hands covered in ink stains, but this simply made Gertie love him more. In fact, it had been one of the key factors that drew her to this rumpled, charming man when he walked into her father's bookshop all those years ago.

Gertie Bingham was fortunate enough to be born into a family of forward thinkers. Her father, Arthur Arnold, had established Arnold's Booksellers in Cecil Court, London, with his brother, Thomas, at the end of the last century. For Arthur and his wife, Lilian, there was never any distinction made between the education of Gertie and her younger brother, Jack. One of the first books her mother had taught her to read was *Original Stories from Real Life*, by Mary Wollstonecraft. Lilian Arnold was a staunch suffragette, and so Gertie was raised with a keen mind and a bloodhound's instinct for sniffing out injustice. This was all well and good in the confines of her home life, where debate and discussion were commonplace. However, when her mother decided to send her to an all-girls school, she was often out of step with her peers, who were shocked to learn that she didn't long for a life of domesticity and submissiveness.

"Why on earth have I been given a brain if not to use it?" she would complain to her mother.

"Patience, my love. Not everyone sees the world as you do."

But Gertie had little patience. She was always in a hurry, eager to read the next book, absorb a new idea and release it into the world like a butterfly from a net. Her mother suggested that she attend university, but Gertie didn't have time. She wanted to be living, to be out in the world. So she asked her father for a job at the bookshop, and it was there that the stars aligned and she met Harry.

"Gertie, I've got a new recruit for you," said her uncle Thomas one day. "Would you show him the ropes, please?"

Gertie glanced up from the index cards she was filing and knew that she was staring into the startlingly blue eyes of the man she would marry.

"Harry Bingham, Gertrude Arnold."

"Call me Gertie," she said, standing up and holding out her hand.

A flush of scarlet spread up from Harry's collar as he accepted. "Pleased to make your acquaintance," he said, pulling his hand away as soon as it was polite to do so and pushing at his large round spectacles, which had slipped down his nose. They gave him an owlish appearance, and this paired with his tall, ungainly frame only made Gertie like him more. He was a shy apprentice, but Gertie discovered that as soon as they began to discuss books, all traces of bashfulness were banished. They bonded over a mutual love of Charles Dickens and Emily Brontë. It wasn't long before days working together became evenings at the theater and weekend promenades in the park. Gertie sometimes mused that falling in love with Harry had been as easy as the songs told you it was.

They were married a few years later and moved south of the river when Harry qualified as a librarian. The newly married Binghams had assumed that their snug little house would soon echo with the sound of infants, but years of heartbreaking disappointment resigned them to the fact that this wasn't to be. Ever the practical stoic, Gertie continued with life as she knew best, and when she spied the "For Lease" sign in Buckingham Milliners on the high street, her impatient mind saw a solution and an exciting new future for them both.

"A bookshop?" said Harry as she linked an arm through his and led him on a lunchtime walk around the rose garden next to the library.

"Why not? We could run it with our eyes closed, and besides, wouldn't you like to work in a place where you don't have to whisper all the time or get snapped at by Snipp?"

"Now, Gertie, Miss Snipp isn't that bad."

"Yes, but she's not a patch on your wife," said Gertie, leading him behind an oak tree out of sight and planting a kiss on his lips.

Harry smiled and kissed her again. "Where would I be without you, Gertie Bingham?"

"Tragically alone and terribly brokenhearted," she said.

They applied in person to Miss Maud and Miss Violet Buckingham, the sisters who had run Buckingham Milliners ever since their father died thirty years previously. The pair seemed very taken with the young couple who stood before them, complimenting Gertie on her "elegantly demure" choice of hat.

"Oh, aren't they a darling couple, Maud?"

"Absolutely darling, Vi."

"And what will your business be, dear hearts?"

"Books," said Gertie.

"Ah, books. How wonderful. Isn't that wonderful, Vi?"

"Wonderful," confirmed Violet.

It was indeed wonderful, as Violet and Maud not only agreed to sign over the lease but also became long-term customers of the Binghams. Gertie always delighted in sending any newly published romances to the two retirees in Suffolk. She imagined the pair of them, happy in a cozy cottage surrounded by a garden filled with the lavender, delphinium, and plump, fragrant roses befitting two devoted romantics.

On the day they opened the doors of their new venture, Gertie inhaled the rich scent of new books, more intoxicating than French champagne, and couldn't imagine wanting to be anywhere else in the world. Harry took her hand and kissed it.

"Welcome to Bingham Books, my love."

Part One

London
1938

Chapter 1

Our deeds still travel with us from afar,
And what we have been makes us what we are.

—George Eliot, *Middlemarch*

Gertie arrived at the shop early that morning. She didn't sleep much past five these days. It was a nuisance, but there it was. Hemingway, the mild-mannered yellow Labrador, was at her side as usual. He had become something of a local celebrity since joining their staff four years ago. Gertie noticed that he had the ability to raise a smile from even the most austere of customers, and several mothers had been known to make a detour during shopping trips so that their eager children could pat his bearlike head.

Little had changed in the town of Beechwood since Harry and Gertie first opened the doors of Bingham Books all those years ago. The Tweedy family still ran the bakery, and Mr. Piddock the butcher had retired only last year, handing over his impeccably sharpened knives to his son Harold, who, according to local gossip Miss Crow, left too much sinew in his leg of beef. Gertie glanced along the high street now. Her shoulders dipped at the sight of the honey-colored lettering of Perkins's Confectioners. Harry had bought a bag of cinder toffee from Mrs. Perkins every week without fail for them to share during evenings beside the radio.

"Come on, Hemingway. Good boy," said Gertie, ushering the dog inside the shop, grateful as ever for his distracting presence.

The sun's early rays cast a spotlight through the window, as motes of dust danced and swirled like fireflies. Gertie paused to inhale the exquisite possibility of unopened books as she had done every morning for nearly thirty years. This place had brought her such joy for so long. She and Harry had built something wonderful. Their own world full of ideas and stories. At one stage in her life she thought she'd change the world in some dynamically public way, but she soon realized that she could do the same with books. They were powerful. They forged ideas and inspired history.

That joy was beginning to diminish now, however. She gazed toward the doorway at the back of the shop and imagined Harry standing there, arms full of books, smiling at her. Instinctively she reached down to stroke one of Hemingway's velvet ears as the memory pinched her heart. The dog stared up at her with mournful eyes.

It had been the medical condition that won Harry his exemption from the Great War that had also caused his death two years ago. Gertie counted herself lucky when Harry was granted exemption on medical grounds, although Miss Crow had not missed the opportunity to dismiss him as a "shirker" to anyone who would listen. If Harry was hurt by these comments, he didn't show it. His quiet service as a volunteer air-raid warden made Gertie burn with pride. But life has a way of catching up with you eventually, and the respiratory illness, which Harry had endured since childhood, meant that his body wasn't able to fight the tuberculosis that finally stole his life. Gertie still couldn't believe it. How could he be gone? They still had so much life to live.

"It's not the same without him, is it?" said Gertie, her voice seeming too loud in this hallowed space, as if she were bellowing in church. Hemingway sighed in agreement as Gertie brushed away a tear. "Well. No use in dwelling on things you can't change. Come along. We're down to our last volume of Wodehouse, and Harry wouldn't like that one jot."

By the time Betty, the assistant bookseller she'd employed after Harry died, arrived, Gertie had dusted, tidied, and restocked the shelves ready for opening.

"I must say it looks spick-and-span in here, Mrs. B," said Betty, shouldering off her coat. "Shall I make us some tea?"

"Thank you, dear. I'm absolutely parched."

Betty reappeared a short while later carrying two mismatched cups and saucers. "Here we are. By the way, I'm still mulling over next month's book club title and wondered if you had any thoughts."

Gertie gave a casual wave of her hand. "I'm sure whatever you decide will be splendid."

"Well, I'm quite keen on *Middlemarch*."

"Good idea," said Gertie. "I can't remember the last time we chose a George Eliot novel."

"Unfortunately Miss Snipp isn't so sure."

"Is she campaigning for another Thomas Hardy book by any chance?"

Betty nodded. "I don't mean to speak out of turn, Mrs. Bingham, because he's a wonderful writer, but we only read *Tess of the d'Urbervilles* two months ago, and forgive me for saying this, but some of the members didn't care for the way Miss Snipp conducted the meeting."

This didn't surprise Gertie. Miss Snipp's communication style could most accurately be described as abrupt bordering on downright rude. When they first met, Gertie had assumed that Miss Snipp simply didn't like her. However, she soon came to realize that she disliked almost everybody, apart from Harry, but then, everyone had loved Harry. "I see. And what is she proposing you read next?"

"*Jude the Obscure.*"

Gertie winced. "Heaven help us all."

"Mr. Reynolds was so upset by what happened to Tess, I'm not sure he could take it."

"I'll speak to Miss Snipp."

Betty exhaled. "I would be grateful, Mrs. Bingham. I'm already concerned about our membership. I know we have our postal members, but last month's meeting was very poorly attended. Mr. Reynolds said that it used to be standing room only when you and Mr. Bingham were in charge. I don't want to let you down."

Gertie gave her a reassuring smile. "Oh, Betty. You're not letting me down. The world has changed and people are all rather distracted at the moment. I'll speak to Miss Snipp, but please, don't give it a second thought. Bingham's Book Club is the least of our worries." Gertie couldn't say what she really felt: that *her* world had changed and she was rather distracted, and the book club was the least of *her* worries because she couldn't bring herself to think about it. She hadn't attended a single meeting since Harry died. In fact, Gertie had intentionally absented herself because of the simple fact that she couldn't bear to attend without him.

They had set up Bingham's Book Club together and run it as a partnership, relishing the monthly challenge of selecting the perfect book and chairing the most stimulating discussions. Mr. Reynolds had been right. People had traveled from the surrounding towns to take part. They had even attracted authors who were willing to come and discuss their works, achieving something of a literary coup when Dorothy L. Sayers agreed to attend what turned out to be a particularly lively meeting.

That seemed like a distant memory to Gertie now. Gone was the spark of excitement that used to fizz in her brain as she and Harry carefully chose the book club title. She could barely conjure up the impetus to read these days and certainly lacked enthusiasm for anything new or original. This was the reason she had delegated the role to Betty. She was an avid reader with far more youthful zest than Gertie could muster.

Not only was Betty a welcome addition to Bingham Books's staff, but she also served as a pleasant antidote to Miss Snipp, who had spent her life forging a successful career in both books and complaining. It had been

Harry, naturally, who insisted they employ her after she retired from the library.

"Her bibliographic knowledge is encyclopedic, Gertie," he said. "There is no one better qualified to source books for our customers." He had been right of course, but still, Gertie was relieved that she worked only two mornings these days and was largely confined to the makeshift office in the corner of the stockroom.

Her heart sank as Miss Snipp appeared at the door, her face as sour as if she were sucking a sherbet lemon. Gertie decided to try to adopt Harry's amiable attitude while also feeling decidedly queasy at the conversation that lay ahead.

"Good morning, Miss Snipp," said Gertie with as much cheer as she could muster. "I trust you are well?"

"Not especially," she replied with a frown. "My gippy hip has been playing me up dreadfully."

"I'm terribly sorry to hear that," said Gertie. "Have you tried Epsom salts?"

"Of course. It's this wretched damp weather," she said accusingly, as if Gertie were somehow to blame.

"Ah yes, well, there's not much we can do about that."

"Hmm. I suppose not. Now, Mrs. Bingham. May I have a moment of your time?"

"Of course."

Miss Snipp repositioned her glasses on her nose. "It's about the book club."

"Oh yes," said Gertie with a rising sense of dread.

Miss Snipp folded her arms. "I am afraid I'm going to have to resign my position as chairwoman."

"Chairwoman?" said Gertie in surprise.

Miss Snipp nodded. "It is simply too much for me at my age, and frankly the individuals who attend the meetings these days seem wholly undeserving of my efforts."

"I'm sorry to hear that."

Miss Snipp gazed into the distance and shook her head. "They fail to appreciate the magnitude of some of our greatest writers. They are beyond my help."

"Oh dear."

"Indeed. So I think it would be best if Miss Godwin took the reins."

"I see. Well, if you think that's best."

Miss Snipp glanced up sharply. "I must say you're taking this very lightly, Mrs. Bingham."

Gertie sighed with what she hoped was sufficient gravitas. "Believe me, Miss Snipp, it saddens me greatly, but I fully support your decision."

Miss Snipp regarded her over the top of her half-moon spectacles. "Well. I best get on," she said, hobbling toward the back of the shop.

"Good morning, Miss Snipp!" cried Betty as they met in the doorway.

"Is it?" she muttered, before disappearing into the back room.

"Is she all right?" asked Betty, approaching the counter.

"She's perfectly fine. She's just delegated her book club responsibilities over to you, so George Eliot it is this month. I hope that meets with your approval?"

"I won't let you down, Mrs. B."

Gertie patted her hand. "I know you won't, dear."

The day seemed to drag like a spoon through treacle until midmorning, when Barnaby Salmon, the young bespectacled publisher's representative, appeared. The fact that Betty always stood up straighter, smoothed her dress, and patted her hair whenever he entered the shop was not lost on Gertie, nor was the fact that Mr. Salmon always made sure his appointments fell whenever Betty was working.

"Good morning," said Gertie.

Barnaby tipped his hat in greeting. "Good morning, Mrs. Bingham, Miss Godwin."

"Mr. Salmon," said Betty, seeming to grow inches taller under his gaze.

Gertie turned to the young man. "Now, Mr. Salmon, do you think I could leave you in Miss Godwin's capable hands this morning? She has been assuming more responsibility of late, and I'm keen to encourage her endeavors."

Mr. Salmon looked as if he'd been offered the keys to the kingdom. "Of course, Mrs. Bingham. It would be my great pleasure." He turned to Betty. "I have a wonderful new book by Mr. George Orwell which I know you're going to like, Miss Godwin."

"How marvelous," said Betty with a sparkle in her eye.

Gertie smiled. She enjoyed watching their charming bibliophilic romance unfold. It transported her back to the days when she and Harry first met. Such joyful memories. How she missed his disheveled presence.

She was grateful that Betty readily accepted extra responsibility whenever it was offered to her. She told herself that it was important to encourage the younger generation, but deep down Gertie knew she was retreating. Bookselling had been her world, but without Harry, it had lost its magical luster. Every aspect of her life had in fact. His absence was Gertie's most constant companion. She found herself laying out two cups and saucers for tea, or she would hear something of note or concern on the radio and turn to discuss it with him, or a customer would ask for a book recommendation and she would immediately think of Harry. He had instinctively known what every type of customer would enjoy reading, from the small boy who loved pirates to the elderly retired gentleman with a passion for Shakespeare. Gertie had an instinct for this too of course, but Harry was a natural. She had been the one to deal with publishers, and he had been the one to nurture the customers. There were still people who came into the shop now and asked to speak to him two years on and who always seemed deeply distressed when she told them that he had died. She knew how they felt. Sometimes she would run her hands along the spines of the books on the shelves because Gertie saw Harry in every book, in each page, in every word. It offered some comfort but also a sharp tug of sorrow. Gertie loved their shop, but she loved it most with Harry in it.

"Did you hear me, Mrs. B?"

Gertie blinked away her daydream. "Sorry, dear. What did you say?"

Betty chuckled. "You were in a proper brown study there, Mrs. B. I was just telling you that Mr. Salmon is leaving now. Would you like to check the order? I thought we could make a big thing of the new George Orwell book. I'll do a window display, if you like?"

Gertie glanced over the docket, grateful to have someone else making the decisions for her. "This looks splendid. Thank you both."

Mr. Salmon gave a polite bow. "Thank you, Mrs. Bingham. Miss Godwin, I'll see you on Saturday?"

Betty held his gaze. "I'm looking forward to it."

"Good day, ladies," he said, pausing in the doorway to tilt his head toward Betty in farewell.

"Saturday?" said Gertie after he'd gone.

Betty nodded. "He's asked me to the pictures. We're going to see the new James Stewart film. Usually, I'd be giddy about him, but I don't really give two hoots now."

"I'm delighted for you, my dear."

Betty gave a happy sigh. "It's just marvelous to find someone who loves the same things you do, isn't it? Barnaby and I—"

"Oh, it's Barnaby now, is it?"

Betty looked coy. "Well, Mr. Salmon is a bit formal, isn't it? It's not the 1900s. We were just saying how we can't think of anything better than bookselling. It really is a salve to the soul. I mean, take P. G. Wodehouse. The fascists take over Europe, and he creates Roderick Spode to make them look like nincompoops."

As Gertie listened to Betty expound her theory on how every author from Charlotte Brontë to Charles Dickens had improved life, an idea crept into her mind. Betty and Barnaby were the new generation. They had the passion that she so dearly lacked these days. Maybe it was time to hand over the mantle like Mr. Piddock had done with his business.

Gertie had been mulling this idea over the past few months, but now it seemed obvious. It was time to move on, to move away even. She rather fancied Rye or perhaps Hastings. She was approaching sixty, and despite what Mr. Chamberlain said, it looked as if the country could well be on the path to war again. Gertie wanted to be tucked up safely away from London by the time anything happened. She couldn't face another war in London. She wasn't sure if she could face another war full stop. Most of all, she wanted to escape the constant reminder that Harry was gone and the painful reality of a life without him.

Chapter 2

The past and the present are within my field
of inquiry, but what a man may do in the
future is a hard question to answer.

—Sir Arthur Conan Doyle, *The Hound of the Baskervilles*

Thomas Arnold was something of a character in the book world. At the age of seventy-eight, he still ran Arnold's Booksellers, declaring himself to be the oldest bookseller in London. He was fit as a flea, putting this down to his daily swim in the Serpentine and the fact that "I had the good sense never to marry."

Thomas had established Arnold's with his brother, Arthur, in the previous century, surviving the pitfalls and dramas of the past fifty or so years to emerge as one of the most successful bookshops in the land. He was known for having an explosive temper and a kind heart. The gentleman publishers of London either held him in high regard or viewed him as a blessed nuisance. Writers and artists beat a path to his door in the hope of being invited to one of his legendary literary lunches. Whichever side of the fence you perched, Thomas Arnold was lauded as both a great eccentric and the most astute of businessmen. This was perhaps most succinctly illustrated by the telegram he had sent to Hitler in 1932, asking if he could buy the books he was planning to burn.

"Such a criminal waste!" he had told Gertie and Harry during one of their monthly Sunday promenades around Greenwich Park.

Needless to say, Gertie adored her uncle. Since she'd lost her brother, father, and mother, he was her last living relative and assumed the role with aplomb. Their monthly walks were sacrosanct to Gertie, even more so after Harry died. They would talk business, books, and about the family they missed.

"You do know that if I'd had a daughter, I would have wanted her to be just like you," he said as they climbed the steep hill to the top of the park, ready to have their efforts rewarded by the astonishing view of London, which unfurled before them like an old master's canvas.

"You are a dear," said Gertie, pausing to catch her breath.

"Of course, I'm a miserable old beggar, so I would have made a dreadful father. And then there's the issue that I can't stand children. Never have. Never will."

"You've always been lovely to me."

"Ah, but you're different, Gertie. You're a treasure."

They paused on a park bench to take in the spectacular view, as streaks of golden sunshine framed the skyline to perfection. Beyond the rolling hill, Queen's House, and the military college, the River Thames stretched its meandering passage toward St. Paul's Cathedral and beyond. It was as if the entire city were laid out before them. "As Dr. Johnson and I agree, if a man is tired of London, he is tired of life," said Thomas. "Take note, dear niece. I'd like that epigram on my gravestone."

"I refuse to discuss your demise," said Gertie. "You're the only family I've got left."

Thomas took her hand and kissed it. "Dear heart, I didn't mean to upset you. Forgive a foolish old man."

"It's all right. I'm just a little out of sorts today."

"What is it, Gertie? You look pale. Are you not sleeping?"

Uncle Thomas was obsessed with sleep. He believed that every man, woman, and child needed exactly eight hours' sleep every night. No more, no less.

"I'm fine," she said. "A little tired but no more than

usual." This was a lie, of course, but where was the sense in worrying him about the fact that she often lay awake fretting, her mind twisting in an endless thicket of sorrow? Some nights she would sleep and then wake with a momentary frisson of joy, before rolling over in bed to be confronted with the empty space where Harry had once been. Most mornings, she was relieved that Hemingway was there to give her the impetus to move.

"And business is still brisk?"

"Oh yes. Ticking along nicely."

"Then what is it, my child?"

Gertie cleared her throat. "I'm thinking of selling the business and moving to the coast. I'm wondering about East Sussex."

"I see." Thomas stared toward the river. Gertie was used to her uncle's raging outbursts and explosive reactions. She braced herself for a storm, but he remained taciturn, eyes fixed forward.

She took a deep breath and continued. "I think it's time for me to retire. Harry and I ran the shop together, and now that he's gone, I'm not sure I want to carry on alone. I'd like to be somewhere peaceful. I think Hemingway would enjoy walks on the beach, and of course you could always come to stay. It would do you good to escape London every now and then."

"Is that what you're doing then?" asked Thomas. "Escaping London?" He sounded almost hurt.

"I don't know. I'm weary, Uncle Thomas. And I miss Harry. I don't know how to live my life without him." Tears pricked her eyes.

Thomas pulled out a green silk handkerchief and offered it to her. "Oh, my dear girl. I'm sorry. I do understand. It's merely that I'd miss you. I'm being selfish. Forgive my petulance."

Gertie accepted the handkerchief and dabbed at her eyes. "I'd still see you. I can come to London for visits."

He patted her hand and cast his gaze across the city. "I can't blame you for wanting to escape London, Gertie. The prospect of another war fills me with dread."

"Do you think it's likely?"

Thomas shrugged. "Someone needs to stand up to that madman. It's shocking what's happening to the Jews in Germany. Businesses wrecked and looted, synagogues set on fire, men rounded up like animals. It's monstrous."

Gertie nodded. "It's dreadful. I wish there was more I could do to help."

Thomas turned to her. "You must do what's best for you, my dear. And if that's retirement, then so be it."

Gertie sighed. "Part of me feels as if I'm giving up. I never thought I'd end up like this. I used to have so much more fight in my youth."

Thomas chuckled. "You certainly were a spirited youngster. It was a job for your mother and father to keep up with you. You had so many ideas and opinions. Enough to change the world."

"You know as well as I do how life knocks that out of a person."

"My darling Gertrude, you are fifty-nine, not eighty-nine."

"So you think I should stay?"

"All I would say is don't make any rash decisions you might regret. There's a storm coming. I'm sure of it. We might just need the likes of Gertie Bingham to stand up and fight."

"I'm not sure I can do it on my own."

"I'm here, Gertie."

"I know. And I'm grateful." She leaned over to kiss him on the cheek before linking an arm through his. "Now. Tell me your book trade gossip."

Thomas's eyes glittered. "Well, let's just say there's a certain female author whose husband is filing for divorce after she was discovered in a compromising situation with a famous Shakespearean actor."

The rain was beginning to fall as Gertie let herself back in through the front door later that afternoon. She shook off her umbrella and left it in the porch.

"It's coming down in stair rods," she told Hemingway, who trundled out to greet her. She planted a kiss on the top of his great furry head. "Have you had a good day, my darling?" People would think her daft, but she knew that this gentle giant was one of the few beings who kept her going these days. The thought of moving to that cottage idyll with him, sitting out their days by the coast, taking slow walks together, and gazing out to sea was very appealing.

"I could take up writing," she said as she lit a fire in the living room. Hemingway cocked his head to one side as if hanging on her every word. "Give Georgette Heyer a run for her money."

Gertie smiled at the idea. It was a romantic notion in every sense of the word, but what was the alternative? Stay here in the oppressive silence of a house that was far too big for her, or move somewhere more tranquil, where she could gather her thoughts and not be reminded of Harry's absence all the time?

She set about making tea, putting the kettle to boil on the stove and retrieving a cup and saucer from the dresser.

"Here you are, my boy," she said to the dog, tipping food into his bowl. Hemingway sniffed at it before gazing up at her with a heavy sigh. "I know exactly how you feel," she said, scratching the top of his head. "I'm not the slightest bit hungry either."

She was about to make her tea when there was a knock at the door. Hemingway gave a half-hearted growl. "I think you may need to brush up on your guard dog skills," she told him, glancing at the clock. It was nearly six and pitch-black outside. Gertie made her way to the living room and peered through the net curtain. Her face relaxed as she recognized the caller.

"Now, Mr. Ashford, I've told you before. I don't entertain gentleman callers after dark," she said as she opened the front door. Charles Ashford was her husband's oldest friend. They had met at school, and when Harry began his book career, Charles had entered the world of banking. His time as an officer in the Great War had altered his opinion of humanity, and he returned a changed man. He left the world of finance to take up a post with the International Committee of the Red Cross, before continuing to work for a number of other humanitarian organizations. Harry always maintained that Charles was one of the truest, kindest people you could ever hope to meet.

Gertie's heart lifted when she saw this affable man

standing on her doorstep. His hair was thinning at the temples, but his face was as open and kind as it had always been. He made her think of Harry in the best possible way, reminding Gertie of the treasured times when they'd formed a happy band of three in their youth. They spent many joyful evenings at the theater or out for dinner together. Charles was always vastly amused at Gertie's attempts to pair him off with any woman who batted her eyelids his way.

"I prefer my own company," he would always say. "Or yours or Harry's. I'm too selfish to be a good husband."

Charles's usual genial demeanor was serious tonight, though. "Sorry to call so late, Gertie. May I come in? I need to talk to you."

"Of course," she said leading him toward the living room. "Is everything all right?"

"Not really," he said as Hemingway lumbered in, his tail wagging as soon as he saw their visitor. Charles patted his head. "Hello, old chap."

"I'm just making some tea. Would you like a cup?"

"I don't suppose you've got any whisky, have you?" In the half-light of the living room, Charles looked gaunt and drawn.

"I think I've still got a bottle of Harry's somewhere,"

said Gertie. She opened the drinks cabinet and poured two glasses. "Come and sit down. You look as if you've had a fright. Whatever is it?"

They sat side by side on the sofa. Gertie took a sip of her drink, welcoming its sharp heat.

Charles swirled the amber liquid around his glass before taking a large gulp. "I daresay you've heard about what's happening to the Jews in Germany?"

Gertie shivered. "Yes, of course. Terrible business."

"I'm going over to help them."

Gertie stared at him. "Help them. But how?"

Charles took another sip of whisky. "There's a delegation going to speak to Chamberlain and the home secretary next week. They want to rescue as many children as possible. The British government is almost certainly going to allow them to come here."

"Goodness, Charles. But won't it be dangerous for you to go out there?" Gertie couldn't bear the thought of losing another person she loved.

Charles was stone-faced. "Not as dangerous as it will be for the poor blighters if we leave them in the clutches of Hitler and his henchmen."

Gertie nodded. "Of course. Will you be gone long?"

"As long as it takes."

She laid a hand on his arm. "Thank heavens for

people like you, Charles. How will you find homes for them?"

He shot her a sideward glance. "I'm asking everyone I know to take in a child."

Gertie stared at him for a moment, unsure of what to say. "But, Charles, I'm about to retire." She knew this sounded hollow, selfish even. Here was this man, about to risk his life for a group of strangers, and here she was, fixated on her own fanciful needs.

Charles's eyes didn't leave her face for a second. "Do you know what I thought when Harry introduced you to me all those years ago?"

"'Does this woman ever stop talking?'" suggested Gertie with eyebrows raised.

Charles laughed. "Well yes, but above all, I thought how lucky he was to have found someone with such fire in her belly and fight in her soul."

Gertie stared into her whisky glass. "I'm too old to fight, Charles."

"No one is too old to fight, Gertie, and you are far too young to be giving up."

Gertie frowned. "Who said I was giving up? I'm merely planning the next step in my life." Her mind cast back to the conversation earlier with her uncle.

Don't make any rash decisions you might regret . . .

"Let's just say I never had Gertie Bingham down as a woman who would sit idle in retirement while the world needed her," said Charles.

Gertie caught sight of the photograph of her and Harry on their wedding day. They had been giggling when the photographer took the picture. You could see the sparkle in their eyes. They couldn't wait to get started on their life together. "I'm tired, Charles. I've had enough of all this."

Charles followed her gaze. "You miss him, don't you?"

Gertie was surprised how quickly the tears formed. "Of course. He was the very best of men."

Charles took her hand and kissed it. "And you are the very best of women. Which is why I'm asking you to do this."

Gertie brushed away a tear. "What kind of place is this for a child?"

Charles glanced around the room at the shelves lined with books, the glowing hearth, and the dog, snoring gently at Gertie's feet. "The very best place I can imagine," he said. He took another sip of whisky. "All I would ask is that you give it some serious thought. The world is on the brink of something terrible. The question is do we stand by and watch, or do we stand up and help?"

Gertie stared at the fire. She knew he was right, and if she were thirty years younger, she'd have jumped at the chance. But as the world darkened around her, Gertie felt her own existence contract. She didn't feel strong or capable or stubbornly opinionated as she had in her youth. She was bruised by life and unsure if she had the strength of will to offer hope to anyone, least of all herself.

Chapter 3

You are part of my existence, part of myself.
You have been in every line I have ever read.

—Charles Dickens, *Great Expectations*

And what did you say your business was, Mr. Higgins?"

The burly man stroked his abundant beard. He reminded Gertie of a bear. "I'm a horticulturalist and seedsman by trade, Mrs. Bingham," he told her. "But I like to think of myself in broad terms as a naturalist."

"Ah," said Gertie. "Like our famous former local resident, Mr. Darwin." She pulled a copy of *On the Origin of Species* from the shelf and held it out for him to see.

"Oh yes. A great man," said Mr. Higgins with a faraway look in his eyes.

"And I suppose you will be selling everything the amateur horticulturalist requires?"

Mr. Higgins's ruddy face grew serious. "Oh no, dear lady. My real passion is taxidermy."

"Taxidermy?"

He nodded. "I'm an expert in the art. People are very keen to preserve their deceased pets, you see."

Hemingway gave an involuntary whine from his prone position behind the counter. "I see," said Gertie, dearly wishing Harry could hear this. She imagined his eyes twinkling with mischief at the turn the conversation had taken.

"I also sell dry shampoo powder for dogs," he added cheerfully. "Here, have a free sample." He pulled a dark brown vial from his pocket and offered it to Gertie.

"Thank you," said Gertie, accepting the bottle with a rictus grin.

Mr. Higgins touched the brim of his hat. "I best be off. I'll wait to hear from Miss Crisp, shall I?"

"Yes, if you would be so kind. Thank you for taking the time to call in."

Gertie exhaled as soon as he left. "Well, that's certainly food for thought, eh, boy?" she said, glancing down at Hemingway. "I'm not sure what the local residents would make of a taxidermist, but then it took them a while to get used to me."

This was certainly true. "Bohemian" had been one of the more charitable words Gertie had heard muttered when she and Harry first established Bingham Books. People would eye her with suspicion as if she might at any moment curse them with a spell that would fill their minds with new ideas. It never ceased to amaze Gertie that, despite living less than ten miles from where she grew up, people's worldview was often as different as if they lived on the moon. They came 'round in the end, but some, like the redoubtable Miss Crow, still gave the shop a wide berth.

Gertie glanced up as the bell above the door rang and an elderly woman entered, using a stick for support. Mrs. Constantine was a poised, dignified lady who reminded Gertie of Queen Mary. She always wore a choker of pearls with her hair swept into an elegant chignon. On spotting Mrs. Constantine, Hemingway made the considerable effort to lift himself to his feet and approach her, tail wagging.

"Ah, my dear Mr. Hemingway. I've got a treat for you," she said, holding out a bag containing some juicy pieces of chicken. "I can't eat a whole breast on my own, so I like to share it with a friend," she told him, watching with satisfaction as he devoured the offering in seconds.

"That canine is thoroughly spoiled," said Gertie.

"He deserves it," said Mrs. Constantine, "don't you, Mr. Hemingway?" The dog gave an affirmative bark. "And so clever too. Like Hercule Poirot himself. Which reminds me, has my book arrived, Mrs. Bingham?"

"It has," said Gertie, retrieving a copy of *Appointment with Death* from the shelf. "I think you'll enjoy this one. I thought it was better than *Death on the Nile*."

"High praise indeed, my dear," said Mrs. Constantine, holding up the book to admire. "Such a fine writer. She always keeps me guessing. I've never got it right once!"

Gertie smiled. Mrs. Constantine was one of the customers she would miss. She had moved to the area alone nearly twenty years ago. There was a rumor that she had been a member of the Russian aristocracy, forced to flee Moscow following the revolution. Gertie always thought that hers would be a story she'd love to read. "That's the mark of an excellent crime writer," she said.

"It was your dear Harry who put me onto the great Mrs. Christie in the first place," said Mrs. Constantine.

"He had a knack for matching readers with the perfect book," said Gertie, eyes glittering at the memory.

The old lady studied her face. "How long has it been, my dear?"

Some people would have found this question meddlesome, but Gertie had known Mrs. Constantine long enough to realize that it came from a place of heartfelt concern. "Two years. It's a long time."

Mrs. Constantine shook her head. "That's a matter of minutes when you have loved and lost. Trust me, I know this. We women have many crosses to bear. Don't bear them too heavily, my dear."

Gertie knew she was right. Still, grief haunted her like the ghosts of Christmas past, present, and future combined, and she had no idea how to banish it.

On the stroke of 11:30, the bell above the door signaled the arrival of Miss Alfreda Crisp. Gertie liked Miss Crisp. She was a young, ambitious woman whose father had established his estate agency business shortly before the war, when his wife was expecting their first child. He then found himself in the inconvenient position of having a succession of daughters. Undeterred, Crisp and Daughters became one of the foremost estate and letting agents in the area, staffed by the amiable Mr. Crisp and three of his five girls. Alfreda was the youngest and had a youthful vigor that Gertie greatly admired. She had vowed to do everything she could to find the right tenants to take over "your splendid bookselling establishment."

"Good morning, Mrs. Bingham," said the young woman with a keen, efficient smile. "May I ask how your interview with Mr. Higgins went?"

Gertie hesitated. She dearly wished she'd been able to consult Harry, to check that what she felt in her heart was an accurate representation of the facts. "Well, he's an absolutely charming man."

"Oh, absolutely," echoed Miss Crisp. "Quite charming."

"But if I'm completely honest, I had hoped to find someone to continue to run the shop as it is."

"As a bookshop?"

"Precisely."

Miss Crisp's face fell. "I'm most dreadfully sorry, Mrs. Bingham, but I fear that may be a challenge given the current climate. Taking over an existing business, even one as successful as this, is a tall order, especially when we have no idea where the country will be in six months' time."

"But what am I to do?" cried Gertie with a rising desperation that she immediately regretted.

Miss Crisp raised her eyebrows. "I'll keep trying, of course. You never know, but I feel it's my duty to be honest."

"Of course," said Gertie, embarrassed she had let her feelings show.

"Please be assured that I will continue to work my hardest for you."

"Thank you, my dear."

Miss Crisp gave her the sympathetic look that Gertie had become used to over the past couple of years. It was the one people offered whenever they remembered that she was a widow. *Widow.* Such a dark, depressing word. So final.

"Don't give up hope, Mrs. Bingham," Miss Crisp said before she left.

"I think it might be a bit late for that, don't you, Hemingway?" said Gertie. The dog looked up at her and yawned. "I agree. Grief is terribly dreary." She glanced at the clock. "Come on. We'd better close up. Betty will be arriving soon for the book club meeting. It's Dickens today." Hemingway emitted another loud yawn. "For a literary dog, you're very disrespectful, you know."

"What ho, Mrs. B," cried Betty, charging through the door like a comet.

"Hello, dear. Hemingway and I were just shutting up shop, ready to get out of your way."

"Please don't rush on my account. In fact, you're welcome to stay for the discussion, if you'd like? *Great Expectations* is such a terrific read."

"It is indeed," said Gertie. "But we always visit Harry on Mondays."

Betty put a hand to her forehead. "Of course you do. Forgive me, Mrs. B. I'm an absolute dunderhead sometimes."

Gertie waved away her concerns. "Are you expecting a good turnout?"

"I'm not sure. Mr. Reynolds has a bad head cold, and Mrs. Constantine has a prior engagement. I'm hoping Miss Pettigrew might come, although it's difficult to convince her to read anything apart from Georgette Heyer. So really that leaves—"

"Good afternoon," said Miss Snipp in a dull tone as she appeared in the doorway. "Where is everyone?"

"Some of our regular members were unable to attend," said Betty.

"Oh dearie dearie me," said Miss Snipp. "I feared this might happen now that Mr. Bingham's no longer with us, God rest his soul."

Gertie's back stiffened with indignation. *Do not rise to it, Gertie.* She imagined Harry resting a consoling hand on her arm and busied herself by counting that day's takings.

The shop door opened again, and this time a small, mouselike woman wearing a cherry-red beret stood blinking at them as if amazed by her own entrance.

"Miss Pettigrew, you came! I'm so pleased to see you," cried Betty with an overexuberance that caused Miss Snipp to frown. "Come in and I'll fetch some chairs from the storeroom. We'll be a small but perfect discussion group."

Betty sat them beside the poetry section and took out her copy of the book.

"So," she said. "What did you think of the novel?"

Gertie watched Betty with a heavy heart as she did her best to cajole a stone-faced Miss Snipp and a bemused-looking Miss Pettigrew.

Miss Snipp gave a heavy sigh. "I must say I have always found it rather feeble."

"Oh," said Betty. "How so?"

"I didn't engage with these characters. Pip is a coward, and Estella is a Jezebel."

Gertie noticed a rare flicker of irritation in Betty's expression. "Yes, but what about the story? It's jolly dramatic, and Pip's character goes through so many twists and turns, and of course there's Miss Havisham and the love story with Estella. And what about the ending?"

"Excuse me, dear?" said Miss Pettigrew.

"Yes?" said Betty, looking visibly relieved by the interruption.

"When are we going to discuss *Oliver Twist*?"

Miss Snipp rolled her eyes to the heavens.

"*Oliver Twist*?" said Betty.

Miss Pettigrew nodded. "You said we were reading Dickens, so I chose *Oliver Twist*. I do love the Artful Dodger. Such a naughty boy."

Betty glanced over at Gertie, who winced sympathetically.

"Well," said Miss Snipp with obvious satisfaction. "That's that then."

Betty looked panicked before a flash of inspiration came to her. "No. No, it's all right. We can just talk about Dickens. Miss Pettigrew, tell us about *Oliver Twist.*"

Gertie gave Betty an encouraging smile before taking her leave. She knew she was being cowardly by retreating, but she felt she had no choice. Gertie couldn't allow herself to invest in the book club, and indeed the bookshop, if she was planning to step away from it. She gathered her belongings and gave Betty a cheery wave before creeping out the door, leading the dog along the high street and up the hill toward the cemetery.

She caught sight of the Beechwood town sign with its galloping white horse and beech tree insignia and wondered how it might feel to leave a place that had been her home for so long. It was a charming little town. The shopkeepers took pride in keeping their shop fronts gleaming, shining out beneath brightly colored canvas awnings.

Two small boys were standing with their noses pressed up to the window of Stevens the Chemist's, with its intriguing rainbow display of liquid-filled conical bottles, waiting for their mother to reappear. They turned as Gertie passed.

"Hullo, Mrs. Bingham. Hullo, Hemingway the dog," said the larger of the two boys. "Please may we pat him?"

Gertie was used to these interactions. Hemingway's dignitary status in their little town meant that she often had to stop so that both children and adults could stroke him.

"Of course," said Gertie, watching as the boys showered love and affection on the appreciative dog.

"Look. He's smiling," squeaked the smaller of the two boys before kissing the top of Hemingway's head. "You're the best dog in the world."

Gertie glanced up at the large square clock hanging outside Robinson the Cobbler's. "Well, if you'll excuse me, young gentlemen. Hemingway and I have a prior engagement."

She felt weary to her bones as she climbed the hill to the cemetery. When she reached the gates, Gertie paused to catch her breath and take in the view. As a final resting place, it was rather splendid, lined with carefully tended gardens and enveloped on all sides by towering beech and horse chestnut trees. Their branches were mostly bare, but a few stray leaves clung resolutely to the trees, fluttering like orange-and-red flags against a sapphire sky. Gertie closed her eyes and turned her face upward to feel the precious warmth of the sun on her face. She'd always disliked autumn, much preferring the fierce hope of summer when the world seemed so alive, gardens bursting with color, parks and beaches crowded with joyful humanity. The world began to disappear underground in autumn, decaying and decomposing before her eyes. It had been Harry's favorite time of year, of course.

"But everything's dying," Gertie would complain.

Harry would hold out his hand and lead her into the garden. "No, my darling," he would say, pointing to a tightly furled bud on the magnolia tree. "Everything's sleeping. Resting until the spring when the world begins anew."

Gertie opened her eyes and picked her way to his grave. "The trouble is," she said as they reached it, "you died in autumn, but you'll never begin anew, my love." She pulled out her handkerchief and gave the letters on his headstone a clean while Hemingway sat in obedient silence.

HARRY BINGHAM,
DEVOTED HUSBAND TO GERTIE AND
BELOVED SON OF WILBERFORCE AND VERONICA,
AT REST 25 OCTOBER 1936

Gertie had been very certain about the wording, much to the surprise of Mr. Wagstaff the undertaker, a thin man with an even thinner mustache.

"May I suggest a more formal approach?" he had said. "It is usual to at least use full given names to add a sense of gravitas."

"You may, but I shall reject your suggestion," said Gertie firmly. "My husband was Harry to everyone who knew him. His death has provided me with all the gravitas I require. And given that I shall be the only one to tend and visit his grave, I think I should be able to choose the words which will greet me, don't you?"

Mr. Wagstaff had stared at Gertie appalled, as if expecting her to apologize for such an outburst. He was to be sorely disappointed when Gertie stood up and fixed him with a determined look. "I am assuming this is all you require. Good day."

"I certainly gave him what for," she said, as she extracted the old flowers from the vase on Harry's grave, replacing them with the roses she'd cut from the garden that morning. "There you are, my darling. A surprise bunch for you, thanks to the mild weather."

Hemingway moved forward to sniff at the arrangement before nuzzling Gertie with his nose. She stroked his ears and put her arms around his head, cuddling him to her as tears formed in her eyes. The dog leaned instinctively toward her.

"What are we going to do, eh, boy?" she whispered into his fur.

A dancing breeze whipped up around them, so that Gertie had to clutch her hat as some of the last leaves scattered across the graveyard like confetti. A couple of pages of old newspaper caught by the wind whipped and dived in the air, causing Hemingway to bark in excitement. He leapt up with surprising enthusiasm, scampering after them as if they were giant versions of the butterflies he liked to chase with little success. This time, however, he caught one of the large sheets in his teeth and paused in astonishment at his surprise victory, before growling and shaking it in his jaws as though it were prey that needed to be tamed.

"What have you got there, you silly dog?" said Gertie in amusement, reaching down to wrest it from him. Hemingway gave a reluctant growl. "Hemingway," warned Gertie.

The dog looked away as if assessing his options before dropping the half-chewed pages at her feet.

"Thank you, I think," said Gertie, wrinkling her nose and picking it up with the tips of her gloved fingers. "We don't really want you ingesting newspaper, now do we? Remember what happened when you ate those licorice twists complete with paper bag?"

Hemingway bowed his head as if he did remember that particular trip to the vet.

"Come on. Let's go home," she said. She was about to fold the newspaper into a neat parcel ready to put on the fire later when she spotted the word "Help!" The letters surrounding it had been ripped by Hemingway's eager jaws, but as Gertie smoothed them, the startling text leapt out at her.

HUMANITY TO
THE RESCUE OF GERMAN JEWRY
HELP!
BEFORE IT IS TOO LATE

She stared at the words for a moment before glancing back at Harry's grave, the oval pink rosebuds nodding in the breeze. Gertie Bingham wasn't a superstitious woman, but she did believe in being in the right place at the right time. Call it fate or luck, it had been a feature that had underpinned most of her life. Whether it be her first meeting with Harry or the moment she spied the shop on the high street, Gertie had always followed her heart. It had occasionally gotten her into trouble but had invariably led her to where she needed to be.

As she stood now, clutching the newspaper, taking in these words, she knew what she needed to do. Moreover, she knew that Harry would agree with her. Gertie felt foolish that it hadn't been immediately obvious to her. She folded the newspaper carefully and slid it into her coat pocket. "Come along, Hemingway. We've got business to attend to. Goodbye, my darling. See you next week," she said, hurrying toward the gates as the wind picked up.

She quickened her pace with Hemingway trotting alongside her. By the time they reached home, a squally shower was nipping at their heels. Gertie hurried in through the door, brushing away the droplets of rain from her hair as Hemingway shook off his coat. Gertie hastily lit the fire and reached for the telephone. She waited to be put through and relaxed when she heard the voice answer.

"Purberry 4532?"

"Charles? It's Gertie."

"Gertie. It's good to hear from you. Are you well?"

"Yes. Thank you. And I've been thinking about our conversation the other night."

Charles cleared his throat. "I have too. I'm sorry I put you on the spot, Gertie. You've had a ghastly couple of years. It was wrong of me to ask that of you.

You don't need a stranger in your house. You should be enjoying your well-deserved retirement."

"No, Charles. I'm glad you did. You've made me realize some important things. Things I'd lost sight of."

"And have you come to a conclusion?"

"I have. I've made up my mind. I want to help. I'll take in a child and give them a home and do my best for them. It's the least I can do."

"Are you sure?"

Gertie glanced at Harry's face, smiling out from their wedding photograph, eyes sparkling, full of hope. "I've never been surer."

Chapter 4

1939

There was once a wealthy man who had a kind
and beautiful wife. They loved each other very
much but had no children. They desperately
longed for a child, and every day and night the
wife prayed and prayed but to no avail.

—"The Juniper Tree," *Grimm's Folk Tales* (author's trans.)

Gertie stepped through a grubby brick archway,
pausing at the top of the girder bridge to take in
the hubbub of Liverpool Street station. She tried to picture what it would be like for a child, arriving alone,
viewing all this for the first time. The ornate pillars that
lifted your eye toward the glazed roof and sky above
would have offered a note of optimism if it weren't for
the fact that any light was obscured by a thick coating

of soot. In truth, the whole station was dark and dirty. Gertie stared forlornly at the steep, grimy steps leading to the concourse, where a constant stream of passengers hurried toward whichever steam train was preparing to leave. The din and clamor of the closed-in space merely added to its dingy atmosphere. She could only imagine that the poor children, having endured a long and tiring journey after leaving their homes and families behind, would be utterly terrified.

Gertie made her way slowly down the steps, using the rail for support. She found the bustle of London overwhelming now. Gone were the days when she would have relished an excursion to London: a browse in an art gallery, afternoon tea with a friend, and, of course, a trip to Cecil Court to visit Uncle Thomas.

She stepped onto the concourse and approached the mahogany kiosk selling newspapers and paperback books. Gertie smiled to herself as she recalled her uncle's explosive reaction on the day he'd discovered that Allen Lane would be introducing paperback books into the world.

"It is an affront to the very fabric of our civilized society, Gertie. Nothing more, nothing less. They will never catch on, and Mr. Lane will be left with egg on his face. Egg, I tell you."

Uncle Thomas held firm until the publisher offered

him a very favorable deal to trial a few of these monstrous volumes. He was a businessman, after all. He continued to sell both formats to his customers but took great pleasure in the fact that hardback books were still the main meat of his business.

"I tried to tell Mr. Lane, but these publishers think they know it all," he would say to anyone who would listen, patently ignoring the fact that this innovation had changed the reading world forever.

Gertie cast her gaze around the concourse. She spied a banner displaying the words "Movement for the Care of Children from Germany," with a table set up beneath it where several individuals were sitting, clipboards at the ready. She recognized one of them as Agnes Wellington, the woman who had come to vet her house a few weeks earlier. Gertie felt as nervous now as she had back then, when Agnes walked from room to room, regarding everything with a critical eye.

"You live here alone?"

"Well, there's Hemingway," said Gertie, gesturing toward the dog, who had already disgraced himself by greeting Miss Wellington with a succession of deafening barks.

"Hmm," said Agnes, climbing the stairs. "No children?"

"Er, no," said Gertie, following her to the landing.

"You've never had children?"

The question felt like an accusation. "No," said Gertie, her voice almost a whisper.

"And which of these rooms would be the child's?"

Gertie led her to a bedroom overlooking the garden. "I thought it would be nice for him or her to have a view. I'll redecorate and air everything, of course," she said, pulling back the curtains, sending up a vast cloud of dust in the process.

"Have you thought about the practicalities of looking after a child? Would you be able to care for a baby, for example, or a toddler?"

Gertie's mouth went dry. "I hadn't really thought about that."

Agnes raised an eyebrow. "It's probably time you did."

"Yes. Yes, of course," said Gertie. "I'm sorry. I suppose I was thinking about an older child, maybe fourteen or fifteen years old? I run a bookshop, so it would be lovely if he or she liked to read." She didn't think this was the time to mention she was trying to sell the business. From the look on this woman's face, her disapproval of Gertie had already reached its zenith.

Sure enough, Agnes gave a reproachful grunt. "Well, you won't get a choice about that. These children are in desperate need. The question is, Mrs. Bingham, can you meet that need?"

"I think so."

"Thinking is not good enough. Knowing is what we need."

"All right then. I know so."

"Very well. We'll be in touch."

Gertie had telephoned Charles the second Agnes left in a high state of anxiety. "Who did you see?" he asked.

"Agnes Wellington."

He chuckled. "Oh, don't give it a thought. Agnes can be a little heavy-handed, but she's got a good heart."

"She keeps it well hidden. She scared me half to death."

"Don't worry, Gertie. You're doing a good turn. She merely has a duty to the children, but admittedly, she does take the responsibility very seriously." He laughed again. "I wish I could have seen your face."

"Horrible man. You're lucky I'm so fond of you."

"I can assure you the feeling is mutual."

Good morning, Miss Wellington," said Gertie, approaching the desk now. "I'm Gertie Bingham. We met a few weeks ago."

Agnes glanced up from her clipboard. She was wearing a cloche hat that was a little too large for her and a serious expression. She gave no hint that she recognized Gertie as she scrutinized her list. "Bingham.

Bingham. Ah yes, here we are. Gertrude Bingham. You'll be collecting Hedy Fischer. The train should be here any minute. Please wait by the barrier until they call your name."

"Thank you," said Gertie with a certain amount of relief. "I can't wait to meet her, but I must confess, I am rather nervous."

Agnes raised an eyebrow. "Rest assured, these poor children will be far more nervous than you."

"Of course," stuttered Gertie. "Well. I'll just wait over there."

Agnes pursed her lips as if to say, *You do that.*

All that Gertie knew about Hedy Fischer was that she was fifteen years old and came from Munich. Once she had this information, Gertie had taken the preparations for her arrival very seriously. She enlisted the help of Betty, barely past Hedy's age herself, to ensure that everything was as it should be. Betty chose the buttercup-yellow paint and helped Gertie to redecorate the bedroom. They also washed the curtains, beat out the rug, and eliminated every last speck of dust. They took great care to select a few books from the shop that they thought Hedy might enjoy and that might help with her English. *The Secret Garden*, *Pride and Prejudice*, and *Mary Poppins* all made the cut. After Gertie placed them carefully on the mantelpiece, she and Betty stood back to admire their handiwork.

"Do you think she'll be happy here?" asked Gertie.

Betty threw her a sideways glance. "If she's not, she can come and live at my house. I'd happily swap. My brother, Sam, is a pig!"

"Betty!" said Gertie, chuckling. "Thank you for your help, my dear."

"It's my absolute pleasure, Mrs. Bingham. And I mean it. Hedy is very lucky to be coming to live with you."

Gertie patted her shoulder and dearly hoped she was right.

She watched now as the steam train transformed from a smoke-curled dot in the distance to a billowing behemoth, hissing to a halt alongside the platform. The noise was terrific, and yet Gertie could still hear the sounds of children: a babble of chatter, an anguished shout, a few plaintive sobs. There were a lot of other expectant-looking individuals, mostly women, waiting behind the barrier alongside her. They watched as the station staff moved forward to open the doors and a handful of adults emerged, each leading a little group of children toward them. Gertie was immediately struck by the variety of ages. They ranged from babies in arms to boys and girls who almost looked like adults. They bore every expression Gertie could imagine. Some looked excited as if they were off on an adventure; others seemed terrified, eyes darting left and right as they took in the noisy chaos. Some were crying, mouths open wide, wailing with a sorrow that made Gertie's heart break.

"Poor wee mites," said a woman in the crowd, echoing everyone's thoughts, because it was pitiful. They all looked so lost and alone. A freshly stoked fire of indignation flared up somewhere in Gertie's soul. Who would do such a thing to this poor, wretched group of children? To children, for pity's sake? Forcing them to leave their homes and their parents and come to a strange land without knowing what might happen. What kind of evil did this to children?

As they were led through a side exit to a waiting area, Gertie spotted a familiar figure carrying a small boy who couldn't have been older than four or five.

"Charles!" cried Gertie.

He turned and waved before passing the child to another volunteer and hurrying over to her.

Gertie flung her arms around his neck. "I'm so glad to see you. I didn't realize you'd be traveling with this particular group. How was the journey?"

Charles's face was ashen, his chin pricked with

stubble, his eyes ringed with gray shadows. "It's a relief to be here finally."

Gertie could tell this was only half the story. "Was it difficult leaving Germany?"

Charles ran a hand over his chin. "Let's just say it was easier once we arrived in Holland. The people there were very kind. They gave the children chocolate." He glanced over his shoulder. "I should get back. What's the name of the child you're collecting?"

"Hedy. Hedy Fischer."

Charles nodded. "I'll find her."

Gertie watched him disappear out of sight. She had known this man for most of her life, and yet, when she glimpsed him in this world, he took on an enigmatic quality.

"Charles Ashford is a man I know better than myself," Harry used to say. "And yet there are times when he's a complete mystery to me. And I like him all the better for it."

Agnes and her army of clipboard volunteers had already leapt into action and were introducing the smaller children to their new families. Most of them looked bewildered as they were led away to new lives with these strangers. One small boy, suitcase in hand, caught Gertie's eye, his frowning face a picture of resilience. She gave him an encouraging smile as he passed her.

"God save the King!" he cried in a squeaky German accent, causing those around him to chuckle.

Moments later, Charles tapped Gertie on the arm. She felt a flurry of nerves as she turned. "Gertie Bingham. This is Hedy Fischer," he said as casually as if introducing two people at a party.

The girl standing before her with a rucksack on her back was almost the same height as Gertie. She had shoulder-length wavy brown hair and eyes the color of molasses. She wore a navy-blue wool coat with a rose-colored scarf and looked as wary as a kitten in a corner.

Gertie held out a gloved hand. "My name is Gertie Bingham, and I'm very pleased to meet you," she said, noticing that Hedy's hands were trembling as she accepted with a polite nod.

"Here is your paperwork, Mrs. Bingham," said Agnes, appearing alongside them. "You can collect Hedy's luggage over there. Her suitcase has a label with the same number as the one on her coat and rucksack. Then you're free to go."

"Thank you," said Gertie.

"Welche Nummer haben Sie?" asked Charles as they reached the neat rows of suitcases lined up against one wall.

"Neunundfünfzig," said Hedy in a faltering voice, holding up her label for inspection.

"Fifty-nine. Right ho," said Charles.

As he headed off to search through the luggage, Gertie was momentarily thrown into a panic. How on earth was she going to be able to communicate without him? She scrabbled around in her brain for a smattering of schoolgirl German. "Neunundfünfzig," she ventured, gesturing at Hedy's label. "Ich bin neunundfünfzig Jahre alt." Hedy's eyebrows lifted in obvious surprise at the fact that this stranger was readily sharing her age.

"Here we are," said Charles, returning with an olive-colored suitcase. "Will you be all right getting back home? I could find you a taxi."

"Oh no. We'll be quite all right, thank you, Charles," said Gertie in a breezy tone that she hoped concealed her apprehension.

"Are you sure? What about the suitcase? It's rather heavy."

"I carry," said Hedy, moving forward to pick it up.

"There we are then. Hedy is strong as an ox. We're going to be top hole, aren't we?" said Gertie with forced cheer. Hedy's brow furrowed with confusion.

Charles laughed. "'Top hole' is Gertie-speak for 'excellent,' in case you were wondering, Hedy. Ausgezeichnet!"

The girl nodded uncertainly. Gertie felt her stomach lurch with fresh consternation.

She had been determined to keep everything light and cheery for both their sakes, but now she appeared to be baffling the poor girl. Added to this, the thought of the journey across London was making her skittish with nerves. Gertie knew that Charles would accompany them if she asked him, but she could see how tired he was. *Come along, Gertie. You can't shirk your responsibility now.*

"I'll telephone you, Gertie," said Charles, leaning down to kiss her cheek. "Thank you for doing this. Truly."

Gertie nodded, taking fresh courage from her friend's words.

Charles turned to Hedy. "Schön Sie kennenzulernen, Fräulein Fischer."

"Sie auch," said Hedy in a small voice.

He touched the brim of his hat before disappearing into the crowd as Gertie fought the urge to call after him. She glanced at Hedy, who was staring at her with expectation. "Right," said Gertie, the sudden weight of responsibility making her dizzy. "Time to go home."

Gertie Bingham had always prided herself on being a capable woman. Despite growing tired of London's chaos, she knew perfectly well how to travel across it, and yet she was woefully out of practice. They were immediately out of step with the streams of people, who all seemed to be moving in the same direction like a stubborn shoal of mackerel, refusing to let them pass. Of course their progress was hampered somewhat by Hedy. It wasn't just her luggage, which took up the space of another person, but also the child's reticence when confronted with everything from the escalators to the screeching Tube trains, which flew in from both sides of the platform. At one stage a man walked straight into her, and instead of apologizing, he shouted: "Oi, watch where you're going!"

"Now hang on a minute," cried Gertie with an outrage that surprised her. "How dare you jostle this poor girl after all she's been through."

But the man had already disappeared into the crowd. Hedy's neck flushed scarlet.

"It's all right, dear," said Gertie. "London is very busy. It makes people forget their manners sometimes."

Hedy didn't respond, keeping her head down as a train pulled into the station.

"Here, let me help you with that, miss," said a young man from inside the train, gesturing toward Hedy's suitcase. She glanced at Gertie for guidance.

"Oh, thank you," said Gertie. It was standing room only in the carriage, but two men moved forward to offer their seats, and Gertie graciously accepted. "There you see, Hedy. There are kind people in the world."

Hedy didn't answer. Gertie had always been nervous during long bouts of silence and now felt compelled to fill it with idle chatter. "Mein Deutsch is nicht gut," she said cheerfully.

A man in the seat opposite wearing a bowler hat and reading a copy of *The Telegraph* lowered his newspaper to scowl at the sound of this offensive language. Gertie blushed at her foolishness.

"Perhaps it's better for you if I speak in English. It will help you learn."

Hedy stared as Gertie embarked on a strange, one-sided conversation.

"I run a bookshop. Do you like books?" Hedy gave a small nod. "Good. That's good. I bought some books for your room that I thought you might like. Betty, she's my assistant bookseller, helped me choose them. You'll like Betty. She's very friendly and not much older than you." Hedy blinked at her. "And then there's Hemingway. He's my dog. We live in a small house, but we have a lovely garden. Do you like gardens? I do. I like to grow lots of flowers. Dahlias are my favorites. Do you like dahlias? In the summer, I'll cut some for your room. I also grow vegetables. Potatoes, onions, runner beans, that sort of thing. I used to grow carrots, but they were always getting ravaged by carrot fly. They're such a nuisance. And I like to grow brassicas, but you have to cover them, otherwise the pigeons strip them bare. They're terrors."

Gertie noticed Hedy mouth the word "brassica" and recalled the earlier confusion from their conversation with Charles. "Oh, sorry, brassicas are cabbages really. And cauliflowers. Also brussels sprouts, broccoli, spring greens . . ." The furrow in Hedy's brow deepened as she tried to comprehend why this strange woman was listing vegetables. Gertie knew she was talking absolute codswallop but couldn't seem to stop. Had she actually just told this girl about dahlias and carrot fly? She heard the man behind the *Telegraph* tut and clamped her mouth shut until they arrived at their stop.

Gertie ushered Hedy through the crowds to the overground station, where they would catch their connecting train. The concourse was a sea of men in bowler hats returning from their day's work. Gertie had to fight the urge to plonk herself down in the middle of them for a rest. She could see that Hedy was struggling too, her face a picture of fretting weariness.

"Come along," said Gertie. "Take my arm. Our train is ready on platform one." Hedy looked reluctant but did as she was told. Gertie experienced a small thrill of victory on discovering two empty seats and flopped down into the one nearest the aisle after managing to lift Hedy's suitcase onto the shelf above their heads.

"You must sit by the window," said Gertie. "So you can see London in all its glory."

When the train pulled out of the station, Hedy sat up taller in her seat, transfixed by the River Thames, glittering in the early-evening sunshine with St. Paul's Cathedral a beacon in the distance, as Gertie pointed out the sights. Hedy remained silent, keeping her eyes fixed on the images flashing by as London's industry gave way to residential brick terraces with neat gardens. Gertie was grateful to slide into a peaceful daydream, closing her eyes for a moment, wondering and worrying what the future might hold. She couldn't quite believe this girl was now in her charge. She squinted through half-closed eyes and noticed Hedy staring out the window, biting at her lip as if she couldn't quite believe it either.

As they emerged from the station a while later and made the short walk home, Gertie felt a tingle of pride for her neighborhood. She caught sight of Mr. Travers, Beechwood's retired greengrocer, who tipped his hat to them both. Gertie offered a cheery wave in reply.

"I think you'll like Beechwood. Everyone is very friendly," she said, dismissing thoughts of Miss Snipp's antagonism and Miss Crow's petty gossiping for the time being. She glanced at Hedy, but the girl's eyes remained fixed forward as if she were in a trance. *Hardly surprising,* thought Gertie. *The poor child must be exhausted.*

As they rounded the corner onto her street and walked up the garden path to the front door, Gertie's body flooded with relief. She had always loved her little house, with its bottle-green door and roses in the garden. She hoped Hedy would find it as inviting as she did. Gertie stood back to usher her inside. "Welcome to your new home," she said, trying to read her expression as Hedy gazed around in bewilderment.

They were interrupted by Hemingway bounding out from the living room to greet them. Gertie grabbed his collar as Hedy took a step back.

"Now, Hemingway. That is not how we greet guests." She reached out a hand to Hedy. "Don't worry, dear. He's just a big bear really."

Hedy stared at the dog for a moment before dropping to her knees and wrapping her arms around his furry body, receiving a frantic tail wag in reply. "I love dogs," she murmured into his fur.

"I think you may have a new friend, Hemingway," said Gertie, buoyed by their meeting. "Would you like to see your new room before I make us some tea?"

"Please," said Hedy.

Gertie told herself that Hedy's monosyllabic responses were only to be expected. The child had left her home and arrived in a strange land after the most arduous of journeys. *Press on, Gertie,* she thought, echoing her mother's words whenever life threw up a challenge. *You'll find a way.*

"Follow me," she said, leading Hedy up the stairs to the freshly painted bedroom. She switched on the bedside lamp, delighted at how cozy and inviting it looked, bathed in a warm apricot glow. "Here we are," she said, placing Hedy's suitcase on the bed.

Hedy gazed around the room without comment, so Gertie pressed on.

"I hope you'll be very comfortable. Betty and I tried to choose nice colors. Oh, and these are the books I told you about," she added, gesturing toward the mantelpiece. When there was still no reply, Gertie made an attempt at levity. "We bashed the rug to within an inch of its life."

Hedy frowned in confusion.

"To get rid of the dust," she explained, feeling the color rise in her cheeks. *For heaven's sake, Gertie. Stop talking.*

"Ah," said Hedy finally. "Thank you."

Gertie hadn't expected Hedy to dance the cancan in gratitude, but she had hoped for something a little more effusive. She told herself that a thank-you would suffice for now. "I'll go and make us that tea," she said. "Why don't you unpack your things and come downstairs when you're ready." Gertie moved toward the door.

"Excuse me?" said Hedy.

"Yes?"

"I am very tired. I think I sleep now."

It was posed as a statement rather than a question. "Of course," said Gertie. "But what about supper? I was going to toast us some crumpets."

Either Hedy didn't care for crumpets or she didn't know what they were, as she answered without hesitation. "I am not hungry."

"Oh," said Gertie. "Well, if you're sure."

Hedy nodded. "But please wait," she said, reaching into her backpack. Hedy pulled out an envelope and a small brown paper-wrapped parcel tied with red string. She handed both to Gertie. "My mother send a letter and ein Geschenk—a gift for you."

Gertie unwrapped the parcel and pulled out a plum-colored hardback book. "*Kinder und Haus Märchen?*" she read, looking to Hedy for help with her pronunciation.

"*Maer-chen,*" corrected Hedy. "Gesammelt durch die Brüder Grimm."

"Oh. It's a book of Grimm's folktales. How wonderful."

Hedy nodded. "My mother thought you like, as she likes books too."

Gertie held the volume to her chest. "Thank you. That is really very kind. I might suggest to Betty that she chooses this for our next book club. Perhaps you would like to go along, although we'll probably have to read it in English."

Gertie gave a brief chuckle. Hedy said nothing and clasped her hands together, watching Gertie, clearly willing her to leave.

"Well, good night then," said Gertie, backing toward the door.

"Good night," said Hedy, turning away.

As Gertie set about making tea and toasting crumpets for one, she could hear Hedy moving around upstairs. It felt odd after the years of echoing silence since Harry died and even odder to have this stranger in her home. "Tomorrow will be better," she told Hemingway, who yawned in reply. She carried her tray into the living room, setting it down on the tea table in front of the fire, and sank gratefully into her armchair. She watched the flames skip and dance for a moment before pulling out the letter Hedy had given her. It was written in an elegant hand and perfect English.

Freising, 2 March 1939

Dear Mrs. Bingham,

I am writing to thank you for agreeing to take my daughter, Hedy, into your care. She is clever and kind, occasionally headstrong, and always full of opinions, but I know she will work hard at whatever task is set for her. She is a good girl with a good heart. I don't know if you are a mother, Mrs. Bingham, but I do know from your actions that you are a kind woman, so I think you will understand when I say how hard it has been to send our daughter away. We are in a very difficult situation at the moment, but I remain optimistic that there will be better days ahead.

I will of course continue to write to Hedy at your home address. We are hopeful that we may be able to join her in England soon.

Thank you again for your selfless kindness. It is people like you who make me believe that there is still good in the world.

Yours,
Else Fischer

Gertie stared at the fire, feeling as if her entire body were cast from lead. She closed her eyes for a moment, the steady breathing of Hemingway at her feet lulling her off to sleep. She woke a while later to find both the tea and crumpets had gone cold and the dog had disappeared. The house was silent as she rose stiffly from her chair and climbed the stairs. The door to Hedy's room was ajar, and she spied the girl, still dressed, lying fast asleep on her bed with Hemingway on the floor beside her, keeping guard. Hedy's brow was furrowed, as though her worries had followed into her dreams. Gertie watched the girl's troubled face for a moment and was aware of a long-forgotten but strangely familiar sense of purpose rekindling within her. If Else Fischer couldn't be here for the time being, Gertie must assume that role. She picked up a blanket from the chair in the corner of the room and laid it carefully across Hedy's sleeping form.

"Sleep well," she whispered, before tiptoeing from the room.

Chapter 5

I declare, after all, there is no enjoyment
like reading! How much sooner one tires of
anything than of a book! When I have a house
of my own, I shall be miserable if I have not an
excellent library.

—Jane Austen, *Pride and Prejudice*

G ertie was certain she'd made a terrible mistake. Her quiet, ordered life had been turned on its head, and she didn't like it one bit. She would wake during the night to the creak of floorboards, shoulders stiffening with fear, convinced there was an intruder in the next room before she remembered. Or she would enter the living room, ready to flop into her armchair with a cup of tea after a long day, and find Hedy curled up asleep there. The child seemed to have a unique ability to nap like a cat at all hours of the day. Some mornings she didn't appear before Gertie left for the bookshop. Having had no experience of fifteen-year-old girls, aside from the distant memory of being one herself, Gertie had no idea if this was normal behavior. In desperation, she turned to Betty for advice.

"Oh yes, I used to sleep for days and days when I was that age. It drove my mother potty," said Betty as they restocked the poetry section.

"Well, that's a relief. I was worried I was boring her. She's very quiet."

"How is her English?"

"Better than my German, but we never progress past the usual pleasantries," said Gertie, sliding a slim volume of Shakespeare's sonnets onto the shelf. "'How did you sleep?' 'Would you like tea?' 'What a lovely day,' and so on. I can't seem to get much more than a polite nod out of her."

"It's early days, Mrs. B. It must be a terrific shock being ripped away from your family and friends. She's probably just homesick."

Gertie sighed. "I'm sure you're right. I just worry that I don't offer enough excitement for a young girl like her."

"Well, I'm sure that's not true, but here's an idea. Barnaby and I are going for a drive into Kent at the weekend. She could come with us. I'll ask my brother,

Sam, along too. Provided you give your permission of course?"

Gertie was caught off guard. Truth be told, she would welcome a break from awkward, monosyllabic exchanges. On the other hand, would it be entirely proper to let this young girl go out for the day with Betty and two young men? In the end, Gertie decided that there was no one more trustworthy than her bookselling assistant.

"It would be nice for her to spend some time with people nearer her own age," she reasoned.

"That's settled then. We'll pick her up at eleven."

"Thank you, dear. I'm delighted that things are going well for you and Mr. Salmon, by the way. He's a fine young man."

Betty's eyes sparkled. "I'm glad you think so too, Mrs. B."

On Sunday morning, Gertie tapped against Hedy's door at a little after eight o'clock. "Good morning, dear. I'm making breakfast for us. Something to set you up for the day before you head off with Betty."

There was a grunt from the other side of the door.

"It will be ready in about half an hour."

Half an hour came and went, and Hedy failed to appear. Gertie stood at the bottom of the stairs.

"Breakfast time!" she cried with barely masked impatience.

A minute or so later she heard Hedy stomping down the stairs. She was wearing her dressing gown and a scowl as she sat down at the table. Gertie placed the plate in front of her.

"Kippers," she said. "They're an English delicacy."

Hedy stared at the plate in bewilderment. "I am not hungry," she muttered.

"You have to eat," said Gertie. "And we can't waste food."

She picked up her knife and fork and began to attack the rubbery fish. As she placed a forkful into her mouth, her eyes widened. She'd forgotten how horribly bony they were. It was as if her mouth were full of smoked shoe leather.

"Excuse me," she said, rising to her feet and hurrying from the room. When she returned, Hedy's plate was empty, and Hemingway was looking very pleased with himself.

"Delicious," said Hedy with an innocent expression.

"I tried to feed her kippers, Charles," she wailed into the telephone after Hedy had left. "I don't even like kippers. What is wrong with me?"

"Nothing, Gertie. You're trying your best. Perhaps

you're trying a little too hard. It will take a while for you to get used to having another person in the house, and it's difficult for Hedy too."

"I know. I know. I'm sorry. I need to give it time, but you know how impatient I am."

"Are you, Gertie Bingham?" teased Charles. "I had no idea."

Gertie laughed. "That's enough about me. How are you?"

"Busy. I'm going back to Germany next week to help bring over another trainload of children."

"You're a good man, Charles Ashford."

"And you're a good woman, Gertie Bingham. Give it time with Hedy. You're still getting to know each other. It's been a while since you've had to share your living quarters with anyone. You'll be firm friends in no time."

"I hope you're right."

"Trust me. I know you."

Gertie sensed he was right about that part at least. She had always felt as if Charles Ashford knew her better than she knew herself. It was as if he could see into people's souls. Her brother, Jack, had summed it up perfectly when Gertie introduced them amid the opulent luxury of the Savoy's River Restaurant many moons ago.

"It's strange, but I feel as if I already know you," he said as they shook hands. "Or rather, you already know me."

They had been there to celebrate Gertie's twenty-fourth birthday. Her parents had been out of town at the funeral of a distant relative, so Jack had been sent to chaperone Gertie. She had swallowed down her irritation and persuaded her father to let her invite Charles to make up a four with Harry.

The evening hadn't been the rip-roaring success that Gertie hoped. Encouraged by her mother, she had worn an uncharacteristically showy cream silk gown decorated with cascading lilac wisteria and sage-green foliage. She had felt like an empress as they swept in through the entrance of the Savoy and then immediately peeved when Harry didn't tell her that she looked like one. He was too busy tugging at the collar of the evening suit he'd borrowed from Charles's brother with obvious discomfort and proclaiming astonishment at how expensive everything was.

At the end of the evening, when Harry went to fetch their coats and Jack predictably disappeared to the American Bar after spotting an old chum, Charles turned to ask if she'd enjoyed her evening. Gertie had looked into his engaging blue eyes and bared her soul: the fact that she was still very young, that Harry seemed so uncomfortable in this world, and her worry that life was moving a little too fast toward the inevitability of marriage. She was almost breathless when she finished. Charles had smiled with careful kindness as he spoke.

"My dear Gertie, I can't tell you what you should do, but I do know this."

Gertie straightened her shoulders, ready to listen.

"Firstly, and I confess I'm a little envious of this fact, I can't remember ever meeting a couple who fit so perfectly together. And secondly, I can honestly say, hand on heart, that there is no kinder, truer, finer man anywhere than Harry Bingham."

"Gosh, that was a hairy moment. I thought they'd lost your shawl, Gertie," said Harry, returning from the cloakroom.

As their eyes met, Gertie realized two things: she would never find a man who loved her as much as he, and Charles Ashford would always tell her the truth.

"I do trust you, Charles," she told him now on the phone. "And I'll do my best to be patient."

"You'll be marvelous, Gertie. You always are."

Later that afternoon, Gertie went into Hedy's room to dust. She was impressed by the way her guest had made her bed with neatly folded corners, pillows plumped, and the eiderdown smoothed. It was clear that Else Fischer had taught her daughter well. Gertie was also pleased to see the upside-down copy of *Pride and Prejudice* by her bedside, although she couldn't resist marking Hedy's place with a ribbon from the dressing table before closing it again. Gertie's vision of hell was a shelf-lined room full of books with cracked spines.

She was working her way around the cornices with her feather duster when she spotted the photograph. As the man staring back at her had the same clear gaze as Hedy, Gertie guessed it had to be her father in his youth. She noticed his thick mustache, strong jaw, and chin tilted forward in a confident pose but also spied a glittering kindness behind his eyes. What disturbed her, however, was the fact that he was wearing an army uniform. A German army uniform.

Gertie sank onto the bed, photograph in hand. She may be a naïve fool, but it had never occurred to her that Hedy's father would have been a soldier in the Great War. That he may well have fought and killed English soldiers. English soldiers like her brother, Jack. Gertie stared into his eyes. He didn't look like a murderer. If it weren't for the Pickelhaube helmet and bayonet by his side, he looked like the kind of man who would offer you a seat on a train or help you with your luggage. An ordinary man. A husband. A father. History liked to cast people as heroes or villains, but Gertie knew from experience that life was less definite. It tossed humans from event to event like pebbles in the sea. All you could do was deal with the world that surrounded you. To fight or flee, to protect the ones you loved and try to survive. It was all anyone could do. She ran her duster over the outer edges of the frame, replaced it on the nightstand, and crept from the room, pulling the door shut behind her.

When Hedy returned later that afternoon, it was Sam who escorted her to the door. Gertie spied the car pulling up outside the house and rose to her feet, nearly tripping over Hemingway, who was in a great hurry to greet their visitors.

"Good afternoon, Mrs. Bingham," said Sam, tipping his hat. Gertie had met Betty's brother once before when he called in to the bookshop. He had an affable quality and a boyish appearance, which reminded Gertie a little of Jack. "I'm returning Fräulein Fischer to your care."

He bowed to Hedy. Gertie noticed a rosy flush to her cheeks that hadn't been there this morning. "Vielen Dank, Herr Godwin," she said, stepping over the threshold.

"Bitte schön," he replied with a grin.

"Did you have a good trip?" asked Gertie.

Sam turned to Hedy. "Well, Miss Fischer. What did you think?"

"It was spiffing," declared Hedy triumphantly.

Sam and Gertie laughed. "We've been helping Hedy with her English, not that she needs it really," he said.

"Come along, Samuel," called Betty from the car. "Don't make Mrs. B stand on the doorstep all day."

Sam grimaced. "She called me Samuel. That means trouble." He gave a gallant bow. "Schön dich kennenzulernen, Hedy. Good to see you again, Mrs. Bingham."

"And you, Sam. Thank you for your kindness today. Hedy, did you remember to thank Betty?"

The trace of a frown flitted across Hedy's face. "Of course."

"Toodle pip," said Sam. "Hopefully see you next week at the pictures."

"Goodbye, Sam," said Hedy with a smile.

"A trip to the pictures?" asked Gertie as they waved them off.

"Yes," said Hedy, the smile disappearing from her face. "Betty ask me."

"Oh. That's lovely."

"Yes." Hedy was already making her way up the stairs.

"I'd love to hear about your day," said Gertie. "Perhaps over some tea?"

Hedy didn't turn 'round. "No, thank you. I'm very tired." She continued up the stairs with Hemingway following close on her heels.

Gertie stood at the bottom of the stairs for a moment, the shadow of loneliness descending. She longed to follow after Hedy, to ask about the trip, to share in her joy, but something prevented her. Gertie knew she wasn't enough for Hedy. She was a frumpy old woman who cooked kippers and couldn't remember how to have fun. Why would this young girl want to spend time with her? Charles asserted that it would take time for them to become friends, but Gertie couldn't imagine this ever happening. Besides, there was a good chance that Hedy's family would join her in England, and then her role as host would be done. Perhaps it was for the best that their relationship remained fleeting. Like ships that pass in the night.

An atmosphere as closed in as a London smog settled on the house that evening. Gertie sat alone in the living room without even Hemingway for company. Hedy didn't come down from her room, despite Gertie's assertions that she needed to eat. The girl was stubborn. Headstrong, as her mother had warned in her letter. Gertie recognized a girl like this from her dim and distant past but couldn't say she relished sharing a house with her.

Hedy didn't even wish her a good night, and so Gertie went to bed feeling out of sorts. Not even the emergency Wodehouse volume she kept by the side of her bed for days like these could console her this evening. All tales of Bertie's capers were shoved out of the way by feverish thoughts that Gertie had made a mistake. She found herself praying that Else Fischer's efforts to bring her family to England to join their daughter would come to pass sooner rather than later.

Eventually, Gertie fell asleep but was awoken at a little after one by a fearful shriek piercing the darkness. At first she thought it was foxes in the garden, but it was followed by a despairing voice calling out and she realized it was coming from Hedy's room. Gertie stepped into her slippers and wrapped her dressing gown around herself before emerging onto the landing and peering through the half-open door. The full moon cast a milky light through a gap in the curtains onto Hedy's anxious face. The girl was mumbling to herself, tossing and turning restlessly in her sleep. Hemingway, who now seemed to have assumed a full-time role as Hedy's protector, was awake, eyes fixed on her, ready to attack any foe who might spill from her dreams. Hedy's moans grew louder until she cried out.

"Nein, nein, nein! Lass meinen Bruder gehen!"

Gertie recognized the words from her schoolgirl German.

Let my brother go!

Hemingway barked, and Hedy woke with a start, rubbing her eyes. She reached down to wrap her arms around the dog's huge head as she sobbed.

"Hemingway, du bist mein bester Freund. Danke. Danke!"

You're my best friend.

Gertie crept back to her room. The stark echo of this language reminded her that she had a German living under her roof. Germans were their enemies, and yet this was a child. A child in pain. Gertie was used to hearing German screeched by Hitler in the snippets of his speeches broadcast on the radio, but this was different. Hedy was no more a part of the Germany of jackboots and fascism than Gertie was. Gertie tossed and turned for the rest of the night, ashamed that she had allowed some deep-rooted intolerance to rise to the surface. She eventually fell asleep around five and woke a couple of hours later with an unexpected sense of purpose.

At eight o'clock, Gertie knocked on Hedy's door.

"Would you like to come to the bookshop today? Betty is running the book club meeting later and they're discussing *Pride and Prejudice*. You could perhaps share your thoughts on the story." There was a blanket of silence on the other side of the door. Gertie froze, realizing she'd inadvertently acknowledged the fact that she'd been in Hedy's room. "I was dusting the other day and noticed you'd been reading it, you see," she added with a wince.

The next sound Gertie heard was a half-hearted groan and the sound of two feet landing on the floor. Moments later, Hedy opened the door a fraction. "Yes," she said. "I would like. Danke."

Gertie's shoulders relaxed a little. "Splendid. I'll make us some breakfast."

"Please, Mrs. Bingham?"

"Yes?"

"No kippers today."

Gertie saw the twinkle of mischief in her eyes. "Oh, but I thought you said they were delicious."

Hedy shrugged. "We should save for special times."

Gertie pursed her lips into a smile. "Tea and toast it is then."

I must say your new houseguest is charming," said Mrs. Constantine, glancing over to where Betty and

Hedy were setting up chairs for the book club meeting. "You are a good woman to offer her shelter, Mrs. Bingham. It was the kindness of strangers which saved me when I first came to this country."

"I can't help thinking she'd be better off with a proper family," said Gertie as she wrapped Mrs. Constantine's latest Agatha Christie novel in brown paper.

"A proper family, you say? And what is that exactly?" Mrs. Constantine gazed at Gertie, her eyes as shiny as sapphires.

"Oh, I don't know. Somewhere with a mother and father, some siblings perhaps."

Mrs. Constantine shot Gertie a wry look. "Sometimes the thing you're looking for is right in front of your nose."

Gertie stared at her in astonishment. "I would never presume to act as a mother to Hedy and I know she'd hate it," she said, recalling the look Hedy had given her when she'd politely suggested she take her elbows off the table at breakfast.

"My dear Mrs. Bingham, no one is asking you to take on that role. All anyone needs, particularly in these dark times, is human kindness."

Gertie glanced at Betty and Hedy, who were giggling together. "I know you're right, but I can't help thinking that Hedy needs to be around people her own age."

"Well, why not enroll her at St. Ursula's? I know a young girl who came from Poland and went there for a time. The headmistress is a wonderful woman."

Gertie's eyes widened. "Mrs. Constantine, you're brilliant. I know Mrs. Huffingham. I'll telephone her later."

The old lady nodded her approval, scooped up the paper parcel, and swept toward the back of the shop. "Now then, girls," she said. "I am very much looking forward to our discussions. I consider myself to be as obstinate and headstrong as Miss Elizabeth Darcy."

Gertie watched as the others arrived. Miss Snipp was thankfully absent today because of an appointment with the doctor regarding her bunion. Miss Pettigrew was in attendance again and had apparently read the right book this time, and Mr. Reynolds had recovered from his head cold and was telling a bemused Hedy about his collection of eighteenth-century Prussian fusilier caps.

"Fantastically ornate artifacts," he said, shaking his head in awe. "Like an archbishop's miter."

"I'll leave you to it then, Betty," called Gertie, gathering her belongings. "Come along, Hemingway."

The dog glanced at Gertie from his position at Hedy's feet before returning to his afternoon snooze.

"He can stay with me," said Hedy.

"Oh," said Gertie, caught off guard. "Are you sure?" Hedy nodded.

"And I can walk them home, Mrs. B. Don't worry. We'll be fine," said Betty.

"Right," said Gertie. "Thank you. See you later then." Gertie took her leave with the sound of their chatter and laughter echoing in her ears.

"I just feel rather surplus to requirements," she told Harry later as she placed the delicate posy of pale lemon primroses on his grave. "Hedy seems to engage with everyone but me. I don't know how to talk to her. Oh, Harry, all this would be so much easier if you were here. You'd know exactly what to say, you'd jolly us all along, and . . ." Her voice trailed off as the pain of the past rose up to meet her. "It makes me think I wouldn't have been much of a mother after all." The tears sprung from nowhere as she recalled the endless failed pregnancies, and the last one in particular.

She had kept it secret from everyone including Harry. It had frightened her a little, this secret, and she wanted to be sure that everything was all right before she told him. Gertie had become well-versed in recognizing the signs that she was expecting. She always seemed to develop a voracious appetite, while exhaustion would roll over her in a great wave. During one pregnancy she'd experienced an uncontrollable craving for hot buttered crumpets. Another time, she had developed an inexplicable urge to sniff the bindings of hardback books.

On this occasion, Gertie was experiencing mild nausea and seemed to have developed a penchant for licorice, so it wasn't immediately obvious, but she knew. She recognized the sensation of her body changing in readiness for the new life growing inside her like a seed in warm earth. She pictured the miniature being in exactly this way too. A tiny seed germinating into budding life. All she had to do was provide the nutrients and shelter for it to do just that. Of course, this was where the problem lay.

"It's nature at its cruelest," Harry would say as they mourned another lost child. "You would make the most wonderful mother. But as long as we have each other, I have all I need."

Dear Harry. He made Gertie so happy, but despite his soft words and gentle kindness, she blamed herself. So this time, she was taking extra special care, treating herself like a mother hen on her nest, staying close to the coop. One day, she went to the shops as usual and,

after lunch, took her habitual afternoon nap. She retrieved the copy of *A Room with a View*, which Harry
had recently brought home for her from the library, and
started to read. Quickly her eyelids grew heavy, and she
set it to one side, allowing delicious sleep to wash over
her. She woke hours later to the sound of the front door
opening.

"What ho!" cried Harry.

Gertie sat up abruptly in bed as a sharp cramp
stabbed at her abdomen. "Dyspepsia," she muttered
to herself. "It's just dyspepsia." She cursed herself for
sleeping so long. Gertie had wanted to be waiting for
him when he came home, sitting at the kitchen table,
ready to share her precious secret. She swung her feet
onto the floor, wincing against the pain as she stood up.
"I'll be down in a moment," she called.

"Right ho."

Gertie made her way to the bathroom. The pain
intensified along with her sorrow. She knew what
this meant before she even saw the blood. Gertie had
failed again. She had failed Harry, and she had failed
herself. She would never be a mother, never rejoice as
their house echoed with the peals of children's laughter, never delight in watching as their faces lit up when
Harry read them stories. It was this that wounded her

the most. The idea of these phantom children who would never know their love.

Gertie palmed away her tears and rested a hand on Harry's headstone. "It just wasn't meant to be, was it, my darling?"

Gertie had been home a good while before Hedy and Betty returned with Hemingway. She heard them laughing as they walked up the garden path and went to the hall to meet them. Hemingway, perhaps feeling guilty at abandoning his mistress earlier, hurried forward to greet her, his tail whirling with excitement.

"How was the meeting?" asked Gertie.

"Oh, Mrs. B, we had the most marvelous discussion—didn't we, Hedy?" said Betty.

Hedy nodded. "I would like to go again."

"Wonderful," said Gertie. "I've just made some tea. Would you both like a cup?"

"Thank you, but I better not," said Betty. "Mother will be expecting me." She made her way back down the path with a wave. "Toodle pip both."

"Bye, Betty. And thank you," said Gertie, closing the door and turning to Hedy. "Would you like some tea?" she added hopefully.

"No," said Hedy. "Thank you. I think I go to my room now."

"Wait." Gertie touched Hedy on the shoulder. The girl froze and Gertie drew back. "I just wanted to tell you that I telephoned the local girls' school this afternoon and spoke to the headmistress. They have a place if you'd like to go?"

Hedy spun around, her eyes wild and bright. "Wirklich?"

Gertie nodded. "Really. You can start next week."

Hedy blinked at her. "Thank you," she said, her voice almost a whisper. "I miss school. My mother forbid me from going because a girl who was my friend spat at me." Hedy stared at the floor. "It is hard to understand."

"Yes. It is," said Gertie, encouraged by her shared confidence. "That must have been very upsetting for you and your family."

Hedy studied her face for a moment as if searching for an answer. "Would you like to see a photograph of them?"

"I would like that very much," said Gertie. "Perhaps we could have that cup of tea and you could show me."

Hedy gave a brief nod before disappearing upstairs. By the time she returned, Gertie had made the tea and carried the tray into the living room. Hedy held out the photograph with tender pride, and Gertie accepted it with care. It was a sepia family portrait much like any other, except there was a joyful informality about this one that reminded Gertie of the times she and Harry had posed for photographs. Hedy and her family smiled out at Gertie from where they sat on a long velvet sofa, elbows touching companionably. A sleek black Labrador stood beside them.

Hedy sat next to Gertie, her face animated as she spoke. "This is my mother, Else. She is musician. She played for the Munich orchestra." Gertie was saddened by Hedy's use of the past tense. "She is also very good at sewing. She make all my clothes." Hedy smoothed down the fabric of her bottle-green skirt as she said this.

"She sounds very talented," said Gertie. "And this is your father?"

Hedy nodded. "Johann. He was music teacher and is excellent singer. And this is my brother, Arno. He was studying to be . . ." Her voice trailed off as she searched for the right word. "Architekt?"

"Architect?" said Gertie. "A person who does the drawings for buildings?"

"Yes. Architect," said Hedy.

"And how old is Arno?"

"Nineteen years old."

"He's a handsome young man," said Gertie, gazing at this boy with his wild hair and laughing eyes.

"He knows this," said Hedy, her expression vivid with amusement. "Many girls like him."

"And who is this beautiful dog?"

"Mischa," said Hedy. "I miss her very much."

Hemingway approached, sniffing and licking the back of her hand as if sensing that she needed him. Hedy bent down to kiss the top of his head.

Gertie was struck by how carefree they looked. They were a family who clearly enjoyed one another's company. She could see that Hedy had inherited her beauty from her mother and that Arno was like her father, with dark curly hair and sparkling eyes. Hedy's breath deepened as if she longed to pull them through the photograph into her arms. "Let's hope that your family can join you in England soon," said Gertie.

"I hope also," Hedy said. She pointed toward Gertie's wedding photograph, perched on the mantelpiece. "Was that your husband?"

"Yes. That's Harry and me. He died," said Gertie, her voice seeming too loud in the silence.

"I am sorry," said Hedy.

Gertie nodded as they sat side by side staring into the distance. Both alone. Both missing the ones who couldn't be with them. Neither of them had chosen this situation, and yet here they were, flung together. Two lonely strangers, clinging to the same life raft as the storm raged around them.

"I'll pour us some tea," said Gertie.

Chapter 6

You have not lived today until you have
done something for someone who can
never repay you.

—John Bunyan

"Come along, Hedy," called Gertie with a note of exasperation. "You don't want to be late on your first day."

Hedy appeared on the landing wearing a starched white blouse teamed with a dark navy pinafore and a petulant frown. "I never wear uniform in my German school," she said, plodding down the stairs. "Soldiers wear uniforms, not schoolgirls."

"Well, you look jolly smart," said Gertie, trying to keep her tone light and encouraging. She hadn't realized how opinionated fifteen-year-old girls could be. Or how their moods could change like a coin flipping from heads to tails. Gertie had decided that the best course of action was to stay calm and steer a steady ship until Hedy's parents arrived. After that, she could hand her over safe in the knowledge that she had done her best.

"It is, how do we say, kratzig?" said Hedy, pulling at her collar.

"Itchy?"

"Yes. Very itchy."

"You're probably just a bit hot and bothered. You'll get used to it. Wait a moment, though." Gertie spotted a bobble of fluff on Hedy's back and reached out a finger to brush it off. The girl ducked away with a scowl. Gertie took a deep breath. Else Fischer couldn't arrive soon enough. "Right. Spit spot, as Mary Poppins would say."

Hedy rolled her eyes before trooping out the door after Gertie.

The redbrick exterior of St. Ursula's School for Girls was as bright and smart as the cheerful swarms of girls who thronged its polished marble corridors. Gertie could see the excitement in Hedy's face as they climbed the steps into the vast echoing entrance hall, where Dorothy Huffingham greeted them as if they'd known one another all their lives.

"I think you'll enjoy your time here, Hedy. We certainly expect you to excel in German class. Now, if you will follow me, I'll give you the grand tour and then take you to your form." As she led them around the school, Gertie glimpsed classrooms of girls reciting French and spied an energetic hockey match through the window. "We encourage our girls to undertake academic and extracurricular activities," said Mrs. Huffingham. "To my mind, both are important for the development of a young woman's brain. I also don't believe that we should be limited by dint of the fact that we are the so-called fairer sex."

Gertie dearly wished that this woman had been teaching when she was a child. She and the school she ran seemed to positively fizz with hopeful ideas and possibility.

Gertie's own memory of school had been somewhat colored by the circumstances under which she was forced to attend. The early part of her education had been served by a governess, an austere yet well-informed woman called Miss Gibb, whose nostrils flared like a racehorse's whenever Gertie did something to displease her. In Gertie's memory they were perpetually flared. One day, Miss Gibb's patience snapped.

"I'm sorry, Mrs. Arnold, but your daughter's insolence is simply too much to bear. She questions everything I say. I am left with no alternative but to hand in my notice."

Gertie, who had been listening at the door, hid behind the large cherrywood hallstand as Miss Gibb emerged. After she'd gone, Gertie dashed up the stairs to tell Jack the good news. "I've got rid of Old Gibface," she cried, dancing around the room with glee.

"Golly. I bet Mama's as angry as a hornet."

"Gertrude," said her mother, appearing in the doorway.

Gertie jumped. Her mother never called her Gertrude. Her father used her full name on a semiregular basis, usually when she brought a book to the dinner table or fed Gladstone, their ancient overweight spaniel, tidbits from her plate. Gertie could tell that Lilian had heard her daughter's words. She seemed to glow with incandescent rage. "Yes, Mama?" asked Gertie, trying to look as cheerful and innocent as possible.

Lilian's voice was brisk and clipped. "As you no longer have a governess, I have telephoned St. Margaret's School for Girls. You will start there tomorrow."

"St. Margaret's? Oh, Mama, please no!"

Lilian held up her hand. "It is decided, Gertie. You have a magnificent curiosity, my child, and it is time for you to be schooled with your peers so that you may develop that curiosity."

"But I like learning at home."

Lilian's face softened slightly. "You've outgrown the nest, Gertie. You need to be challenged, and the teachers and girls there will challenge you. It won't be easy, but it will transform you. I promise."

Jack whispered behind his hand. "Bet you wish you'd been nicer to Old Gibface now."

They stopped outside a door marked "5B."

"Here we are. This is your form, Hedy." Mrs. Huffingham pushed open the door.

The twenty or so girls rose from behind their desks as one. "Good morning, Mrs. Huffingham," they chorused.

"Good morning, girls. Good morning, Miss Peacock," she said to the teacher. "This is Hedy Fischer, who will be joining your form."

Miss Peacock, a slight young woman with a gentle expression and the daintiest nose Gertie had ever seen, moved forward to greet her. "Welcome, Hedy. Come in. I've asked Audrey to look after you."

Audrey wore round gold spectacles and two neat plaits and was several inches taller than her diminutive teacher. She stepped toward them with a friendly wave.

Hedy joined her new friend without a backward glance, while Gertie did her best to dismiss her bruised pride. *What did you expect?* she told herself. *You're not her mother. Besides, she's exactly where she needs to be.*

"Don't worry, Mrs. Bingham," said Mrs. Huffingham, as they walked back along the corridor. "We'll take good care of Hedy."

"Thank you," said Gertie. "She hasn't been to school for a good while. Her mother was too afraid to send her."

The headmistress shook her head. "A terrible business. We will do all we can to make her feel welcome for the time she's with us. Girls generally leave education at sixteen, so she'll need to find some employment when the time comes."

"I'm hoping that her family will have joined her by then," said Gertie, trying not to look too eager at the prospect.

Mrs. Huffingham nodded. "In the meantime we will follow your lead and do our very best for her."

"Thank you," said Gertie, unsure if she was worthy of such praise.

If Hedy was enjoying school, she certainly didn't share her feelings. On the first evening, Gertie had tried to engage her in conversation about her day, to quiz her a little on what she was learning and how she was getting along with the other girls.

"Audrey seems like a nice girl," said Gertie over a supper of pork chops and boiled potatoes.

"Yes. She is," said Hedy, pushing a cube of meat around her plate with a fork.

"And your form tutor? Miss Peacock?"

"She is nice."

"That's good. What about your subjects?"

"I am best in class at German," said Hedy.

"I daresay you could teach the class if you wanted to."

"Yes," said Hedy. "The German teacher is not very good."

"Hedy!" cried Gertie scandalized.

Hedy shrugged. "I am German. She is not." She put down her knife and fork. "Can I go to my room now?"

Gertie glanced at her half-eaten dinner. "You've hardly touched your food."

"I do not like Schweinekoteletts. Can I give to Hemingway?"

Gertie sighed as both the dog and the girl gazed at her with eager eyes. She couldn't entertain the idea of a battle. There was too much turbulence in the world at the moment without starting a row about pork chops. "All right then, but if you do not like my food then perhaps you should cook something you like for both of us."

"I cook all the time in Munich. I like to bake best, so perhaps I make something one day. And now I can go?"

Gertie put down her knife and fork in defeat. "You may."

A few weeks later, Gertie returned home after a brisk day's business at the bookshop. Despite an uncertain future and the dreadful weather, people were still planning their fortnight's holiday to the seaside and seemed to be stocking up on books for this purpose. Margaret Mitchell's *Gone with the Wind* and Georgette Heyer's *Regency Buck* were both proving particularly popular, while John Steinbeck's *The Grapes of Wrath* had been a big hit at that month's book club, according to Betty. Gertie let herself in through the front door, looking forward to flopping in her armchair with a cup of tea and perhaps an early-evening program on the radio. She was surprised, therefore, to be confronted by the clamorous melody of "The Lambeth Walk" spilling from the living room at some volume accompanied by the singing and laughter of girls' voices. Gertie froze. It had been an age since the gramophone had last been in use. Harry's gramophone.

On Friday evenings, if the week had been a good one, she and Harry would treat themselves to a fish supper. Afterward, Harry would wind up the gramophone, place a record on the turntable with care, drop the stylus, and offer her his hand.

"Would madam care to dance?"

They weren't particularly accomplished dancers. Gertie lacked rhythm and Harry was too clumsy to be able to dance with any skill, but they seemed to fit well together, shuffling around the living room, laughing as they went. Gertie couldn't recall ever feeling as safe and happy as she did when she was in Harry's arms.

The sound of careless laughter and raucous singing coming from the living room felt like an affront to this precious memory. Gertie's body fizzed with indignant anger as she pushed open the living room door. A girl, whom Gertie recognized as Audrey, was teaching Hedy the Lambeth Walk while another girl offered encouragement.

"Any time you Lambeth way, any evening, any day, you find us all, doing the Lambeth Walk, oi!" sang Hedy, pulling her elbow into a triumphant thumbs-up.

"That's it, Hedy. You've got it!" cried Audrey, before they all dissolved into laughter with Hemingway turning delighted barking circles in their midst.

The sight would have gladdened most people's hearts, but Gertie was not in the mood to have her heart gladdened today. "What is the meaning of this?" she shouted.

The girls turned in alarm. Instinctively Hemingway sank to his haunches in an obedient sit. Hedy frowned but offered no response, so Gertie strode over to the gramophone, wrenched the stylus from the record, and folded her arms.

"I asked you a question," she said, surprised by her rage.

Hedy mirrored Gertie by folding her arms as Audrey stepped forward. "We're most dreadfully sorry, Mrs. Bingham. We thought it was all right." She glanced toward Hedy, who had clearly given this impression.

"Perhaps we should go," said the other girl, hastily retrieving the record from the player and reaching for her satchel and coat.

"Yes. All right," said Audrey, following her lead. "Sorry again, Mrs. Bingham. See you tomorrow, Hedy."

Hedy was still frowning but managed to offer her friends a half-hearted wave in reply. After they'd left, Gertie turned to her. "Well. Do you have anything to say?"

Hedy gave an exasperated sigh. "Sorry. Pardon. Je m'excuse. I did not know that playing records in England was bad. You say I can read any books, so why is music forbidden?"

Gertie was struck dumb. Hedy was right, of course. She knew it was an overreaction, but Harry's loss was still too sharp and painful. She needed to preserve his memory at all costs. "You should have asked first. It's presumption of the highest order, young lady."

"I say sorry. I don't know what more you want," cried Hedy, the color rising in her cheeks.

"I would like you to show some respect," said Gertie. "I have offered you a place to stay and think you should be more grateful."

"Thank you very, very much," said Hedy with a mocking curtsy.

"There is no need to be rude," said Gertie.

"Why not?" said Hedy. "I know you don't want me here, that I have spoiled your quiet life. Well, don't worry. I had letter from my mother today, and they will be coming very soon."

"Well, that sounds like good news for both of us." Gertie regretted the words as soon as they escaped from her mouth. She thought she'd left that keen anger behind in her youth, but it seemed to have followed her into middle age and beyond.

They stared at each other for a moment as if both aware they had gone too far. Hemingway gave a piteous whine.

Gertie sighed. "Look, Hedy. I should never have said that. I was cross. Let me make us some tea."

"I don't want more tea!" cried Hedy. "Why do English people make tea all the time? It doesn't make things better and it tastes horrible!"

Gertie knew it was ridiculous to be affronted by this insult to her nation's favorite drink, but for some reason it touched a nerve. "Go to your room!" she cried.

"I go!" shouted Hedy, storming from the room and stomping up the stairs. "And I don't want any supper!"

"I wasn't going to make anything for you anyway," called Gertie, realizing how petulant she sounded. She took a deep breath. Her body was still trembling. Hemingway blinked at his mistress, his eyes darting toward the door. "Oh, go along then, Hemingway. Don't stay on my account."

He scooted after Hedy, leaving Gertie feeling more alone than ever. She thumbed away the tears that sprang to her eyes.

"You are being ridiculous," she told herself. "Why do you care what this girl thinks? She's just a child, for heaven's sake, and she's missing her family. Don't take on so."

Gertie did her best to shake off this feeling as she set about preparing supper. She carried her bread and cheese into the living room, deciding to listen to the news while she ate. She sat up straighter when, on the stroke of six o'clock, the announcer spoke: *Here is the Second News, and this is Alvar Lidell reading it.* He went on to tell her in clipped, precise tones that the prime minister was promising a full investigation into the sinking of HMS *Thetis* in Liverpool. This was followed by a report about the ongoing success of the King and Queen's trip to the United States. Apparently, His Majesty had *risen to the challenge* when offered a hot dog by the First Lady, Mrs. Eleanor Roosevelt, during a visit to the White House.

Gertie heard a floorboard creak behind her and spied Hedy listening at the door with Hemingway beside her. She could see the longing in her expression, the desperation for news of home and family.

"Don't stand there making a draft," said Gertie. "You can come in and listen properly if you would like."

Hedy crept in and sat on the stool nearest the gramophone with Hemingway lying at her feet. She scratched the dog's head as they listened together in silence. "Will there be a war?" she asked, stealing a glance toward Gertie as the broadcast ended.

Gertie folded her hands in her lap, wishing she could provide an answer. In truth, she didn't know but sensed she needed to offer something. "I hope not. I don't think anyone wants war."

"I think Hitler does," said Hedy, staring at the rug. "And I think he will not rest until he gets it."

Gertie was surprised by her insight. She didn't sound like a child anymore. "Then we must pray that Hitler can be stopped."

"Do you believe in God?"

The question caught her off guard. It was an unusual one for a child to ask an adult, but it was exactly the kind of thing she used to ask her mother. She considered how Lilian might have answered. Gertie's parents had raised their children in the Christian tradition, but there had been little attentiveness to their faith aside from church at Christmas and Easter. "Not especially. Do you?"

"We are Jewish, but we are not practicing," said Hedy. "It is hard to believe in a God who allows his people to suffer."

"Yes," said Gertie. "I suppose it is."

Hedy looked up. "I am sorry for what I say earlier, Mrs. Bingham."

"It's all right, dear. So am I. We all say things we don't mean sometimes. And you know, I think it's high time you called me Gertie, don't you? Mrs. Bingham is so formal."

Hedy gave a small nod.

"And, Hedy?"

"Yes?"

"There's bread and cheese in the kitchen if you're hungry. Help yourself."

"Thank you, Mrs. B— Gertie."

Gertie watched as Hemingway settled himself on the rug and let out a huge sigh. "My thoughts precisely," she told him.

A few days later, Gertie returned home to an empty house. It was a little after four thirty, and she was surprised that Hedy hadn't returned home from school.

"Where's your best friend, eh, boy?" she asked Hemingway, who seemed as bewildered by her lateness as Gertie. "She's probably dawdling and chatting with Audrey."

Shortly before five o'clock, there was a knock at the door. Gertie moved forward to open it. "There you are! We thought you'd got lost. Oh." She paused in her greeting at the sight of a shamefaced Hedy standing beside Miss Crow, whose face was puce with indignation.

In Gertie's experience, human beings often mellowed with age. This had not been the case with Philomena Crow. She had become even more damning in her judgment and keen to offer this judgment to anyone who crossed her path. Gertie often wondered if she and Miss Snipp could perhaps be distant cousins or even twins, separated at birth.

"Good afternoon, Mrs. Bingham." She managed to utter these words in an accusing tone, as if Gertie were responsible for all the ills of the world. She was holding a bamboo-handled dark brown umbrella that reminded Gertie of a truncheon.

"Good afternoon, Miss Crow. Is everything all right?"

"No. Everything is not all right," said the woman in a forceful tone. Gertie noticed Mrs. Herbert's net curtains twitch in the front room of the house across the road.

"Perhaps we could continue this conversation indoors. Can I offer you some tea?"

"No, thank you," said the woman, stepping in front of Hedy onto the threshold. "This won't take long."

"Very well. Come along, Hedy. Let's go into the living room."

Miss Crow refused her offer of a seat, preferring to stand as she held court. "This child knocked on my door this afternoon with an impudent request," she said, pointing an accusing finger at Hedy.

"Is this true, Hedy?" asked Gertie.

"Of course it's true," cried Miss Crow. "Are you accusing me of lying?"

"No, not at all. I just want to know the full story." She turned to Hedy. "Did you knock on Miss Crow's door?"

Hedy gave a barely discernible nod.

"And why did you do that?"

"She wants me to take in the rest of her family," said Miss Crow. "She knocked on my neighbor's door as well. And goodness knows how many others. Is it not enough that we've taken in all these children without having their parents here too? There's barely enough houses and jobs to go 'round as it is without us having to give them away to these people."

Gertie rose slowly to her feet as a ball of rage started to uncurl inside her. "'These people'?" she said. "What exactly do you mean by that?"

Miss Crow narrowed her eyes. "You know."

"No," said Gertie. "I do not know. That is why I asked." Her voice, like her anger, was sharp and clear like cut glass.

"Well, if you don't know, you're more of a fool than I thought. I wondered what on earth you were doing taking in a German after the Great War, but now you seem to want to offer refuge to half the Jews in Europe."

Fury poured lavalike through Gertie's veins. "And what, may I ask, would be wrong with that? Would you rather we stood by while an entire race of people is persecuted?" Gertie could feel Hedy's eyes on her. It spurred her on.

"Look," said Miss Crow, shifting her weight a little. "The Jews have my sympathy, really they do, but I don't see why it's our problem. We can't open our borders to everyone. We only live on an island, don't forget."

"No man is an island, Miss Crow."

The woman flared her nostrils. "Oh, you think you're so superior, don't you, Mrs. Bingham? With your books and your ideas. Well, I'm here to tell you that you're no better than the rest of us."

Gertie moved forward with such purpose that Miss Crow took a step backward. "How dare you?" she said. "How dare you enter my house, call me a fool, and insult my guest in this way. How can you be so unkind to a child who is merely asking for help? Call me a fool if you will, but at least I'm not heartless."

Miss Crow stared at her for a moment, as if ruminating on her next move, before turning on her heel, hurrying from the room with a mumbled "Well, I never," and slamming the front door behind her.

"Good riddance," muttered Gertie, balling her hands into fists to stop them from shaking.

"I only want to help my family. To get them out of Germany," sobbed Hedy. "I'm sorry, Gertie."

Gertie longed to reach out and offer a reassuring embrace, but something hindered her. Instead, she reached into her pocket and pulled out a clean handkerchief. "Here," she said, handing it to Hedy. "Dry your eyes. Don't let Miss Crow upset you. Come and sit down. Why didn't you talk to me about this?"

"I want to try and find a way on my own," said Hedy, her shoulders stiff with determination as Gertie took a seat next to her on the sofa.

Gertie smiled. "You may find this hard to believe, but I was a little like you when I was younger."

Hedy gazed at her. "Really?"

Gertie nodded. "So sure of myself. So determined."

Hedy cast her eyes downward. "Sorry."

"No," said Gertie. "Don't be sorry. It's a good quality. You just need to use it in the right way."

"How?" she asked, moving a little closer to Gertie.

"Well, for a start, you can't go knocking on strangers' doors asking for help. It's not safe. Did you knock on other doors apart from Miss Crow's?"

Hedy nodded. "Yes. Some people were kind, but others . . ." Her voice trailed off.

"What happened?"

Hedy stared into the distance. "One man call me a dirty Jew."

The furnace of Gertie's anger was stoked once more. "I'm sorry, Hedy."

Hedy shrugged. "I am used to this. It happen all the time in Germany."

But not here, thought Gertie. *It's not supposed to happen here. It's not supposed to happen anywhere.* In that moment, Gertie knew exactly what she needed to do. She would use her fire and fury and turn them into something good. "We're going to make a plan to get your family out."

"Really?" said Hedy.

"Of course. Leave it with me. But you have to promise that you will stop knocking on strangers' doors. And come to me for help next time."

"I promise."

Gertie gave Hedy's hand the briefest of pats. "Good. I know just the person to ask."

Chapter 7

I must lose myself in action,
lest I wither in despair.

—Alfred, Lord Tennyson

For Gertie, stepping through the doorway into the hallowed calm of Arnold's Booksellers was always like being transported back in time. Virtually nothing had changed. The ceiling-to-floor mahogany shelves lined with clothbound books in shades of chestnut, mulberry, and jade. The sliding ladders, which enabled booksellers to retrieve volumes from the uppermost shelves and which brought to mind one unfortunate incident, when she caught a young man peering up her skirt as she fetched him a particular book. Gertie chuckled to herself as she recalled her uncle Thomas chasing him out of the shop, brandishing a copy of *Les Misérables*, which at more than one thousand pages had the potential to be something of a deadly weapon.

She was delighted to see Mr. Nightingale, who had worked with her uncle ever since her father died, at the orders desk situated in the middle of the shop floor. Thomas Arnold was adamant that all customers should channel their requests via this desk and should be actively discouraged from browsing.

"This is not a public library," he would fume. "If a customer wants a recommendation, then we will furnish him with one. Otherwise, he needs to make up his mind before he enters our premises. You do not handle the apples before the greengrocer sells them to you, do you?"

When Gertie told him that she allowed browsing in her bookshop, he shook his head. "I hope you know what you're doing, dear heart. To my mind, it can only lead to lunatic behavior. People do not thrive when they have choice. It addles their brains."

"Good morning, Mr. Nightingale," said Gertie, approaching the desk.

He glanced up from his orders ledger and uttered her name as if offering a blessing. "Mrs. Bingham. How wonderful to see you."

"And you. Is Uncle Thomas in the stockroom?"

Mr. Nightingale gave a wry smile. "He's on the roof with Mr. Picket."

"On the roof? Whatever is he doing up there?"

"Let's just say that it's another of your uncle's grand ideas."

Gertie laughed. "Don't tell me. I'll go up and see for myself."

She climbed the stairs at the back of the shop, leading to the first floor, where the most valuable antiquarian tomes were housed in glass-fronted bookcases. Pushing open a door, Gertie climbed another winding staircase up to the apartment where her uncle lived with yet more books and a large marmalade cat called Dickens. The cat greeted her with an insistent meow, casting a forlorn gaze toward his empty bowl.

"Hello, boy," she said, scratching him under the chin. "He's forgotten to feed you again, hasn't he?" She riffled through the cupboards and found a packet of Spratt's Cat Food, which she sprinkled into his bowl. "Now, where is your master?"

A loud crash that sounded like someone dropping several hardback books onto a wooden floor directed Gertie toward the door leading to the sleeping quarters. She pushed it open and peered around to be confronted with a pair of tweed-covered legs standing on a ladder leading up to the roof.

"What ho, Uncle," called Gertie. "What on earth are you up to?"

Thomas Arnold's head appeared through the hatch. His face lit up when he saw her. "Gertie! Good to see you. Would you be a dear and pass me those books, please?"

Gertie approached the scattered volumes and picked one up. She was astonished to see that they were all copies of *Mein Kampf.* "What are you doing with these?"

"Mr. Picket and I are making preparations in case the worst happens," he said, taking an armful from her. "We're covering the roof with them for protection."

"You're covering the roof of the bookshop with copies of *Mein Kampf* to protect you from air raids?"

"Yes," said Thomas, nodding. "Unless you can think of a better use for them?"

Gertie smiled. "I cannot."

Thomas disappeared with the rest of the books. "That's the last of them, Mr. Picket," he called. "Jolly good job." He climbed down the ladder, straightened his polka-dot bow tie, and smoothed his dusty white hair. "Now then, Gertie. You said you wanted my help.

Let's discuss it over tea, shall we? Mrs. Havers baked one of her heavenly malt loaves yesterday."

Gertie brought her uncle up to date on developments with Hedy and explained how she longed to help this girl. She omitted to mention her lingering hope of retiring and that if she identified a suitable situation for Hedy and her family, this might yet be possible. Perhaps this was because she was finding it increasingly difficult to imagine this herself. It was a ship on the horizon, moving further into the distance with every day that passed.

Thomas Arnold listened carefully, his fingers steepled together, face grim with concentration. Dickens strolled across his path, and he plucked him onto his lap, absentmindedly stroking the cat's rich orange fur as Gertie spoke.

"So you see, I made a list of people I thought I could ask for help, and you were at the top of it."

"I'm sorry I can't offer refuge here," said Uncle Thomas. "I don't have the space, but I could perhaps offer the brother a position in the bookshop. He's studying to be an architect, you say?"

Gertie nodded. "That would be wonderful. Any ideas who might be able to help Hedy's parents?"

Uncle Thomas chewed the inside of his lip for a moment before waggling a finger. "Let me make a telephone call." He checked for a number before dialing. "Dicky Rose, please," he said. Gertie stared in surprise as her uncle embarked on a long, friendly conversation with one of the richest men in the country. "Dicky? Tom Arnold. I need to ask you a favor, old boy."

Half an hour later, Gertie felt like somersaulting with joy as her uncle secured posts as a gardener and seamstress for Hedy's parents, as well as a cottage on Rose's estate. "Her father is a music teacher, Uncle Thomas," she said. "I'm not sure how much experience he has of gardening."

Thomas shrugged. "I'm sure he'll adapt. Dicky won't mind. He's already taken in a group of boys. He and his wife are happy to help."

She leaned forward to kiss him on the cheek. "Thank you," she said. "I knew you were the one to ask."

He kissed her hand as he led her to the door. "It's good to see you still fighting, Gertie."

Yes, she thought as she hurried home to give Hedy the good news. *It feels good too.*

As summer took hold, the world held its breath. People did their best to continue as normal, to picnic in the park or take day trips to the seaside, but a cloud of toxic uncertainty hung over Europe. No one could be sure what Hitler would do next.

Gertie and Hedy tried to steer an even path through the doubt. Their plan was afoot. Once her uncle had arranged positions for Hedy's family, Gertie turned her attention to ensuring that their paperwork was in order. She anticipated their biggest hurdle would be gaining permits from the Nazis. As it transpired, making three Jews someone else's problem was positively encouraged provided they left all their money in the German banks. As Else Fischer wrote in her letter delivering the good news, "We do not care if they take the clothes from our backs as long as we can be reunited with our daughter." Hedy translated the words for Gertie with tears in her eyes.

It was something of a surprise, therefore, that the main obstacle in securing passage for the Fischer family came from the British government. The reply to Gertie's letter was curt, to say the least.

"We regret to inform that we are unable to assist in your request."

"We'll see about that," she told Hemingway with a frown.

Gertie dusted off her best suit, a scratchy damson-colored affair that was too hot for the time of year but seemed like the correct kind of armor when dealing with officialdom. She also wore her mother's cameo brooch for courage. Gertie didn't mention the letter or her plan to Hedy. This felt personal. It was as if her principles were being challenged and Gertie was the only one who could stand up for them.

She left Betty in charge of the bookshop, much to Miss Snipp's annoyance, and caught the train to London. Gertie checked the address on the letter, swallowing down her nerves as she made the short walk to the government offices. The imposing white building shone in the morning sunshine, giving off an air of imperial confidence with its Union Jack flag fluttering in the breeze. Gertie took a deep breath as she pushed open the glossy black door.

The receptionist sat at a heavy oak desk flanked on all sides by dark wood-paneled walls, which gave the hall a suffocating atmosphere. She peered at Gertie over the top of her gold-rimmed spectacles. "May I help you?"

Gertie cleared her throat. "I'd like to see Mr. Wiggins, please."

"Do you have an appointment?"

"No, but I have a letter." She held it out for the woman to see.

The receptionist frowned. "It clearly states that Mr. Wiggins is unable to help you."

"Please," said Gertie. "I'm trying to unite a Jewish girl with her family."

The woman's face softened slightly. "Give me a moment." Gertie's spirits rose as she disappeared into Mr. Wiggins's office. She reappeared moments later. "I'm sorry. He's very busy this morning."

Gertie glanced over toward the office. The door was ajar. Something stirred inside her. *Deeds not words, Gertie.* She dashed forward before she had a chance to change her mind.

"You can't go in there," called the woman after her.

But Gertie had already slipped through the gap and pulled the door shut behind her.

"What is the meaning of this?" cried the man behind the desk.

Gertie faltered. Now that she had taken action, she wasn't quite sure what to do next. "I'm sorry," she stammered. "I had to come. I sent you a letter about a Jewish girl who is staying with me. Her family is trying to leave Germany. They have visas and positions here. All they need is the British government's permission."

"Mr. Wiggins? Are you all right in there?" called the receptionist, rattling at the door. "Should I call the police?"

Mr. Wiggins looked Gertie up and down before replying. "That won't be necessary, Miss Meredith." He turned to Gertie. "Please. Take a seat."

She did as he asked. Mr. Wiggins had the pale and weary appearance of a man who couldn't quite believe the hand life had dealt him. He gestured toward a pile of documents that reached the height of his shoulder. "Do you know what these are?"

Gertie thought the question unusual but decided it best to answer honestly. "No."

"They are applications from Jewish families and individuals requesting to come to Britain."

"I see."

"And these have arrived only today."

"But surely—" began Gertie before Mr. Wiggins cut her off with a raised hand.

"And there will be the same number or possibly more tomorrow. And the day after. And so on."

"But surely this means that they need our help."

"I'm sorry, Mrs. . . . ?"

"Bingham. Gertie Bingham."

"Yes. Mrs. Bingham. I'm sorry, but we can't give carte blanche to everyone."

Gertie cast her eyes behind Mr. Wiggins to the portrait of King George VI gazing benevolently at her. She remembered a photograph she'd seen of him laughing with the little princesses. "Do you have a family, Mr. Wiggins?"

A flicker of irritation darted across the man's face. "Yes, of course, but I'm not sure what that has to do with—"

It was Gertie's turn to cut him off. "I am asking because I wonder how you would feel if you were sent away with no hope of seeing them again."

Mr. Wiggins frowned. "The British government has and is still offering refuge to thousands of Jewish children."

Gertie sat bolt upright in her chair. "But what about their parents? What about their siblings? Do they not have a right to live free from persecution too?"

"Please do not raise your voice in this office, Mrs. Bingham."

Gertie was on her feet now. "When should I raise my voice then, Mr. Wiggins? When people start to be killed because of their race or religion? Because I can guarantee that this is already happening."

"I am going to have to ask you to leave."

An adjoining door toward the back of Mr. Wiggins's office opened. A pristine man appeared, wearing an Egyptian-blue suit and mauve silk tie with matching handkerchief tucked in his breast pocket. He exuded the air of private school and privilege. "Is everything all right, Mr. Wiggins? Miss Meredith said there had been something of a kerfuffle." He flashed a brilliant smile at Gertie. It gave her the courage to speak before Mr. Wiggins could deliver his version of events.

"I apologize if I have caused a scene," she said. "But I am trying to help a young Jewish girl's family escape Nazi Germany. They have visas and offers of work in this country."

The man held her gaze. "Could I see the application please, Mr. Wiggins?"

Mr. Wiggins's face tensed. "Of course." He turned to Gertie. "What are the names, madam?"

She held out the letter for him to take.

"Fischer," he said, approaching a filing cabinet and searching through before pulling out a buff-colored folder. He handed it to the other man.

His superior's face lit up as he read through the papers. "Well, this family has Dicky Rose as a guarantor."

"Yes, sir," said Mr. Wiggins. "But the present government policy states—"

"Oh, Wiggins, for heaven's sake. Have some compassion. This fine woman . . ." He raised his eyebrows at Gertie.

"Gertie Bingham," she confirmed.

"Mrs. Bingham," he continued, "has come to us with visas from Germany and a guarantee from *the* Richard Rose. I think we can make an exception."

"Oh, thank you," said Gertie. "I'm so very grateful."

The man gave a polite bow. "Not at all. I was at Oxford with Dicky. Splendid chap. See to the paperwork for Mrs. Bingham, will you, Mr. Wiggins?"

"Of course, sir," said the man with a tight expression.

"A pleasure to meet you," said his superior before disappearing.

"Thank you," cried Gertie after him.

"Well," said Mr. Wiggins after he'd gone. "Let me sort that out for you." He paused to glance at the towering pile of papers waiting to be processed. "What a shame none of these are as well connected, eh?"

Gertie left the offices a while later with Mr. Wiggins's words echoing in her ears. She was delighted that Hedy's family would be saved but knew he was right. His superior had rubber-stamped the application only because of a connection with the Rose family. It didn't have anything to do with the Fischer family's situation. As she glanced back at the Union Jack flag flying over the government building, Gertie's cheeks burned with shame.

Within a fortnight, Hedy's mother wrote to confirm that they had booked their tickets. They would leave Germany in three weeks, at the beginning of September, and arrive at Croydon Aerodrome a few days later.

"Thank you, Gertie," said Hedy, placing a hand on her heart. "I will wash dishes until my parents arrive."

"I'm just happy you're going to be reunited." Deep down, of course, Gertie's overriding feeling was one of relief, and she sensed that Hedy felt the same. Gertie was too old to navigate the choppy waters of a fifteen-year-old's whims, and Hedy certainly needed a livelier living companion. Once the Fischers arrived, she would be happy to return Hedy to the familial fold safe in the knowledge that she had done her best for the child.

"Oh, Mrs. B," said Betty one afternoon while Barnaby was visiting the shop. "We're taking a trip to the seaside this weekend with Sam and Hedy, if it's all right with you?"

"I think that's a splendid idea," said Gertie, her mind already conjuring up a peaceful house and a morning spent hoeing her vegetable patch before relaxing in the garden with a copy of *The Good Earth*, which was Betty's latest book club choice. Gertie had picked up a copy on a whim and was very much admiring Pearl S. Buck's writing. "It's supposed to be warm this weekend. It'll be lovely by the sea."

"You should come, shouldn't she, Barnaby?"

Barnaby glanced up from his orders book. "Oh yes,

Mrs. Bingham. It would be delightful if you could join us."

"I'm not sure . . ." said Gertie, alarmed at the thought of her tranquil Sunday disappearing into the distance.

"Oh, go on, Mrs. B. It'll be too hot in London, and Hedy's parents will be whisking her away soon. It'll be a last hoorah."

Gertie wavered. Betty could be very persuasive, and the idea of a cooling sea breeze was tempting. It felt like a lifetime since she'd even seen the sea. She recalled Sunday trips with Harry, the way he would roll up his trousers and wade into the ocean, invariably returning soaked as a wave surprised him. Then they would spread out their red-and-blue-checked picnic rug and feast on the lunch inside the wicker hamper, which had been a wedding gift from Charles. Treasured times. Distant memories now. Perhaps it was the time to revisit them. "In that case, I accept, but only if you let me make the picnic."

Whenever Gertie thought back to that trip, it truly felt like the last day of summer. Everything about it was golden. Gertie rose early to prepare their picnic: ham sandwiches, boiled eggs, a homemade Victoria sponge cake filled with her own plum jam, and apples from the tree in the garden. She packed it all in the wicker hamper along with a flask of tea and bottles of ginger beer.

At ten o'clock on the dot, Sam knocked at the door and Hedy flew to answer it.

"Well, gosh, don't you look lovely," she heard him say as she carried the picnic basket from the kitchen. "Good morning, Mrs. B. Let me take that from you."

"Thank you, Sam." Gertie caught sight of Hedy as they walked to the car. She was wearing a beautiful yellow polka-dot tea dress that gathered at her bust and flared out from the waist. "You do look pretty, my dear. Your parents will be amazed at how grown up you are."

Sam held the door open for Gertie so that she could take her place in the front while Hedy sat in the back with Betty and Barnaby. As they set off, Gertie gazed up at the whispering trees, letting the dappled sunlight kiss her face through fluttering leaves. She listened to the youngsters talk. Their carefree chatter of who was the better actress, Greta Garbo or Vivien Leigh, and whether the sea would be warm enough for a swim was a welcome refuge from the turmoil in Europe.

Betty squealed when she first glimpsed the sea, and moments later, they were making their way toward the vast, sweeping beach. It was busy with holiday-makers and day-trippers, but they soon found a spot to spread out the large green picnic blanket that Betty had brought with her.

"Who's for a swim before lunch?" said Sam. "Mrs. B?"

"You youngsters go ahead. I'll watch."

"You could come for a paddle," said Betty.

"Very well," said Gertie, peeling off her shoes and stockings, their youthful enthusiasm inspiring a burst of energy within her.

The youngsters ran pell-mell into the sea, while Gertie picked her way with care. Hedy glanced over her shoulder and, noticing she was falling behind, turned back to offer an arm.

"Thank you, dear," said Gertie, accepting with a grateful smile. She gazed up at the near-cloudless sky and inhaled. The world seemed perfect. How could anything bad happen under a sky this blue and with an ocean this infinite? "Oh, I do like to be beside the seaside," sang Gertie, wiggling her toes as the waves washed over them, the refreshing chill reminding her of what it was to be alive. "Oh, I do like to be beside the seeeea."

Hedy laughed. "What is this song? You must teach me."

Sam had jogged back to join them, and he and Gertie sang together. "Oh, I do like to stroll along the prom-prom-prom where the brass band plays tiddly-om-pom-pom."

They all laughed, and Hedy splashed Sam playfully. Gertie detected the blossoming of a romance and smiled. She was fond of Sam and hoped that Hedy's parents would approve.

"Right. You two go and have your swim and I'll lay out the picnic."

"I can't eat another morsel," groaned Sam as he flopped back onto a towel later.

"Hardly a surprise, Samuel," said Betty. "I've never seen anyone scoff so many boiled eggs in one go. Thank you, Mrs. B. That was top-notch."

"I'm glad you enjoyed it," said Gertie, pouring herself more tea from the flask and relishing the unusual sensation of playing mother. She enjoyed sitting back and listening to them talk. Hedy's English was almost perfect now. Gertie was astonished at how quickly she'd mastered the nuances of the language. She was even able to tease Sam, who seemed to particularly relish making her laugh.

"Join me for a walk, Betty?" asked Barnaby, standing up and offering her his hand.

"All right. Who's for an ice cream when we come back?"

There were positive murmurs from everyone even though they were still full from lunch.

Gertie closed her eyes, listening to the crash of the waves, the seagulls shrieking as they spiraled across the sky, and allowed herself to daydream about moving to the coast again. Perhaps it could still be a reality once Hedy was gone. She must have dozed off for a short while, because when she woke, Betty was standing in front of them wearing a mile-wide grin.

"Where are our penny ices?" asked Sam.

"Never mind that," said Betty. "Barnaby has just proposed, and I've said yes!"

"Oh, but that's wonderful!" cried Gertie as they all rose to offer handshakes and congratulatory hugs. They toasted the happy couple with the last two bottles of ginger beer and more slices of cake. "I must say how much I approve of any marriage that is forged over the counter of a bookshop," she said. "I met my own dear husband in my father's shop."

"That's so romantic," said Betty, gazing up at her fiancé, who placed a hand on her shoulder.

"It was rather wonderful," said Gertie. "We were very happy . . ." Her voice trailed off as the longing of memory overwhelmed her.

Hedy raised her glass first to Gertie and then to Betty and Barnaby. "To finding true love in a bookshop," she said. Gertie lifted her glass in reply.

"This has been a spiffing day," murmured Betty as they drove home later that afternoon. "I am the happiest girl in the world." Barnaby squeezed her hand.

"And I want you to be one of my bridesmaids, Hedy. Maybe your mother would make my dress. It could be her first commission!"

"I know she will be honored," said Hedy. "I can't wait for you to meet my family."

This morning the British ambassador in Berlin handed the German government a final note stating that, unless we heard from them by eleven o'clock that they were prepared at once to withdraw their troops from Poland, a state of war would exist between us. I have to tell you now that no such undertaking has been received, and that consequently this country is at war with Germany.

Hedy stared at Gertie, words tumbling from her as she tried to make sense of it all. "What does this mean? We are at war? What about my family? Will they still come?"

Gertie wanted to tell her that it would be all right, that there was still hope, but she could sense it slipping from their grasp. It was stifling in the living room. Despite throwing open all the doors and windows, the heat of the day spread furnace-like through the house. It felt to Gertie as if the walls were closing in. "I'm sorry, Hedy, but I don't think it will be possible now."

"But perhaps they knew this might happen? Perhaps they have already left? Perhaps they are on their way?"

Gertie didn't know what to say. She watched as Hedy paced the floor in desperation, eyes wide with panic. As Chamberlain reached the end of his broadcast, assuring them that he was *certain that the right will prevail,* she let out a scream. Gertie had never heard a sound like it. Raw. Anguished. Hopeless.

She rose to her feet. "Now, Hedy, your mother wouldn't want to see you like this."

"What do you know of my mother?" shouted Hedy, turning on her, eyes blazing with fury. "You do not know my mother."

"No, but I know she loves you and wouldn't want you to be upset. I don't want you to be upset, so please . . ." Gertie opened her arms.

"You're not my mother," cried Hedy as anger gave way to sorrow. "I want my mother! I want my family!" She began to sob hysterically before rushing from the room.

Gertie thought about following her, but her feet seemed glued to the spot. She couldn't believe it. They were at war again. Where would any of them find the strength to get through this?

She rose from her chair, longing to escape this suffocating misery. Walking to the back door, Gertie gazed out toward the garden. The birds still chattered in the trees; the flowers still bent their heads in the late-summer breeze. It seemed inconceivable that they could be at war when the world was as peaceful and calm as this.

As the first air-raid siren pierced the sunlit peace, she heard Hedy cry out like a wounded animal, echoing the hopelessness of the world as darkness engulfed it once more.

France, 1917

Captain Charles Ashford signed his name at the bottom of the handwritten note to Mrs. Percy Rose, blotted it, and placed it on top of the pile of forty other letters he had written to forty other new widows that day. He stared at the flickering candle, which illuminated the bare brick walls of the bomb-damaged farmhouse where he and his men had sought refuge. Most of them were asleep, exhausted after days of attacks and counterattacks. His commanding officer had declared the operation to be a success: "It marks a new phase, Ashford. We now know how to break quickly and deeply into enemy lines with minimal casualties. We just need better communication to crack it next time. With a fair wind, we'll be home by Christmas."

"Yes, sir," Charles had said, although he begged to differ and felt sure that the families of the thousands of dead or missing soldiers would agree with him. He couldn't imagine being home by Christmas. He couldn't even remember what Christmas was like. All Charles could see stretching before him was an endless conflict, more young men senselessly losing their lives, more new widows, more children being raised without fathers. When he signed up, he had done so out of duty for King and country. These were the rallying cries. But after years of watching young men—boys, really—crying for their mothers as they lay dying, of soldiers who had become close friends blown to pieces before his eyes, Charles struggled to imagine a world beyond the daily horror of war.

He contemplated his own death every day. In many ways, he was ready for it. In dark moments, he even longed for it. An end to all this. The blessed kiss of death. He wasn't superstitious, wasn't one of those chaps who carried 'round a rabbit's foot or a lump of coal for luck. He knew that if your time was up, your time was up. It had happened to Jack Arnold. Gertie wrote to tell him the news only last month. Dear Gertie. He could imagine her distress and the way she would try to console her parents. Such a close family. And of course she had Harry. Good old Harry. Charles pulled out his leather wallet and gazed at the photograph of Harry and Gertie on their wedding day, with Charles and Jack standing proudly on either side of them. Such precious times. He felt tears stab behind his eyes. He couldn't fathom what it would be like to go back. Perhaps that told its own story. Maybe his time *was* nearly up. He took another sheet of paper and dipped his pen in the ink.

5 December 1917

My dear Gertie,

Thank you for your letter. I had to write as soon as I could to tell you how sorry I was to hear about Jack.

Charles paused as he fumbled for the right words.

He was such a fine man and a good brother to you. I remember with fondness those happy afternoons we all spent together, punting in Oxford. It still makes me laugh when I recall the time he tried to jump from one boat into another and ended up in the Cherwell!

Charles wiped at the corner of his eye. Even though most of the men were asleep, it would not do to allow emotion into this world.

I hope treasured memories of days like these will offer you some comfort in the weeks and months ahead.
    I am in good health and

Charles broke off, frustrated by his hollow platitudes. These memories wouldn't bring back Jack. Those were the facts. The plain truth. Perhaps it was time for Charles to tell a truth of his own.

He dipped his pen again and paused before replacing it in the inkwell and rubbing at his temples. How to express this? How to tell Gertie what he really wanted her to hear? What would she think? What would Harry think? His oldest, dearest friends. His racing mind wrestled for clarity: *I have to tell you something in case, by some misfortune, I do not return. I think it's only fair that you know the truth.*

The truth. There was that word again. So easy to write and yet so difficult to express. *What is the truth, Charles?* He looked at the wedding photograph again, stroking it with his thumb.

"I love you," whispered Charles. "I will always love

you, and no other will ever come close to you." He pressed the photograph to his lips before sliding it back into his wallet and picking up the pen again, ready to write. If he died out here, he needed Gertie to know his true feelings.

"Tea, sir."

Charles looked up from his letter as the weary soldier placed a tin mug before him. "Thank you, Sergeant."

"Shall I take these letters for you, Captain?"

Charles glanced down at his unfinished letter to Gertie. He paused for a moment before scribbling hastily.

I am in good health and hope for brighter times when Harry, you, and I will be reunited in person. Do send him my very best. You are always in my thoughts.

I am yours ever,
Charles

"Thank you, Sergeant," he said, placing Gertie's letter with the others and handing them over.

Part Two

London
1940

Chapter 8

My Best Friend is a person who will give me
a book I have not read.

—Abraham Lincoln

Gerald Travers frowned at the bare brick wall as if expecting Hitler himself to emerge from within before giving it an authoritative tap and cocking his head to listen. He stepped back with a satisfied nod.

"Safe as houses, Mrs. Bingham," he said, glancing around the dimly lit, shelf-lined room, which up until today had served largely as the storeroom and orders office. "I'm more than happy to rubber-stamp this as a public air-raid shelter."

"Thank you, Mr. Travers," said Gertie. "We'll be glad to offer refuge should the need arise. I'm sure we can make it more welcoming with a few chairs and cushions. At least there's plenty to entertain us," she added, nodding toward the book-stacked shelves.

Gerald gave a considered nod. He reminded Gertie a little of Alderman Ptolemy, the tortoise character from the Beatrix Potter stories who moved with slow deliberation and was also partial to the lettuce that grew in his abundant garden. "Hitler's too busy trampling his way across Europe at the moment, but it won't be long before he's knocking on our door. And we'll be ready for him," said Gerald, tapping the side of his nose.

Gertie smiled. She had known him for years. Everyone knew Gerald and his wife, Beryl. They had run the local greengrocer's and they'd taken a special shine to Gertie one day when she admired their homegrown cauliflowers and confessed a dream of trying to grow them in her own garden. Beryl immediately took it upon herself to play fairy godmother to Gertie's horticultural ambitions. She brought her not just cauliflower seedlings but dwarf beans, tomatoes, marrows, and trays of sprouting seed potatoes. Under Beryl and Gerald's tutelage, Gertie fell in love with gardening, gifting the couple with jars of pickles, jams, and preserved fruits in grateful thanks. Gertie still remembered the day Beryl became too sick to work, because Gerald pulled down the shutters on the greengrocer's and never raised them again. He would often come into the shop to buy a book to read to Beryl while she lay in bed.

"Something amusing and diverting, please, Mrs. Bingham," he would say. Gertie had sent him home with a steady stream of Wodehouse and *Three Men in a Boat* of course too. He returned them all to Gertie after Beryl died. "You can sell them from your secondhand selection with my blessing, Mrs. Bingham. I don't have any need for them now."

Gertie considered Gerald to be a gentleman in every sense of the word. She remembered him coming to visit her at home shortly after Harry died. He stood on her doorstep, clutching a paper bag and gazing at her with the look of someone who had also lost their life's love.

"Cox's Orange Pippins," he said, pressing the bag into her hands. "Mr. Bingham's favorite, if I'm not mistaken."

It was no surprise to Gertie that this pillar of their community, who also acted as caretaker for the village hall, had taken on the role of senior Air Raid Precautions warden as soon as war was declared.

"I'm grateful to you for taking the time to visit, Mr. Travers," she said, following him back onto the shop floor. "I know how busy you must be."

"It's no bother, Mrs. Bingham," said Gerald. "No bother at all. I'm glad to be occupied, especially in the evenings. The house can get a bit, well, you know . . ."

"Yes." She did indeed know. At least she used to. The gaping silence of her house after Harry died had made her breathless at times. She used to take Hemingway on long, rambling walks for hours at a time, desperate to avoid the oppressive quiet.

It was different with Hedy staying. Nothing like when Harry was alive, of course, but Gertie had realized that she slept a little easier at night. Waking to an empty house had given her scant impetus to get out of bed, but now, Hedy needed to be roused and coaxed to get ready for school. It was often a challenge, as fifteen-year-old girls apparently relished their sleep, but it gave Gertie a reason to be up and on, and she was grateful for it.

After war was declared and the numbing realization that her family was to remain in Germany at the mercy of the Nazis sank in, Hedy retreated like a wounded bird. She left her room only for meals or to go to school, and Hemingway rarely left her side. Worst of all was the fact that there were no letters now. As soon as the war began, communication from Germany was only possible via Red Cross telegrams of just twenty-five words. The first arrived a few days after the Fischers' failed attempt to leave Germany.

We are in good health. Do not worry. You are
a dear daughter. Papa, Arno, and I send our love.
Stay cheerful. Mama.

With this final confirmation that her family would not be coming to England, Hedy withdrew, ghostlike, as if she couldn't believe the reality of her life now. Gertie was reminded of herself during the weeks and months following Harry's death, when she had been gripped with fear by his absence and yet unable to believe he was gone. Desperate to rouse Hedy from the doldrums, she tried to offer solace in the only way she knew.

"*Jane Eyre*," she said, sliding her own treasured volume across the kitchen table toward Hedy one evening. "It brought me comfort when I needed it most. It still does, in truth."

Hedy lifted her gaze toward Gertie and then looked back to the slim green book. She opened the cover and read the inscription. "This was from your husband?"

Gertie swallowed. "It was. He gave it to me the day we were married." Her eyes sparkled as she was drawn back to the memory. "I remember it was a hot day. I wore this heavy ivory gown with scratchy lace sleeves and a long train, and I had a headdress decorated with orange blossom which made my head itch." She shook her head with amusement, almost forgetting that Hedy was listening. "All I wanted to do was marry Harry so that we could get on with our lives together. The photographer was a jolly fellow called Mr. Archibald who had this splendid handlebar mustache which made him look like a cheerful walrus. I was desperately trying to smile for the portrait but couldn't think what to do with my face. My brother, Jack, was behaving like a dolt, pulling faces behind him. Mother scolded him but only gently, as was her way." She chuckled. "He said that I looked as if I was posing for a death portrait."

"This sounds like something Arno would say to me," said Hedy. "Always teasing."

Gertie smiled. "And then Charles appeared. He was Harry's best friend, you see. I was so pleased and relieved to see him that my face was transformed. Then Mr. Archibald took the perfect photo, and forever afterward Harry would joke that his blushing bride was grinning from ear to ear not because her mind was filled with thoughts of her beloved but because she'd just spotted her husband's best friend in the distance."

Hedy laughed.

"And so he was the one who delivered this book from Harry," said Gertie, gesturing toward the volume.

Hedy read the inscription out loud. "*Reader, she married me and made me the happiest man alive. Ever yours, Harry, June 1906.*" She closed the cover, running a tender hand across the gilt type. "Thank you for letting me borrow it."

Gertie nodded, a sudden swell of longing sweeping through her body. She could see them all posing for a portrait after the ceremony: Harry smiling down at her, Charles and Jack joking behind them, Gertie's maiden aunt scolding her father and Uncle Thomas for being too raucous, and her mother seizing her hand and kissing it. It had been the happiest day, and she dearly wished she could go back. To bask in that moment again. To feel that love and joy around her once more. She rose to her feet, keen to escape the melancholy. "I hope you enjoy it, dear," she said. "Now if you'll excuse me. It's high time I pruned my roses."

A few days later, Gertie returned from the bookshop to find Hedy in the kitchen, the teacups and saucers laid out, kettle boiled.

Her face lit up when she saw Gertie. "I finished *Jane Eyre*," she said. "She is the best heroine I have ever read. She even learns to speak German." Hedy cast her eyes toward the table. "I have made tea and . . ." She lifted a tea towel to reveal a tray of caramel-colored biscuits. "They are like Lebkuchen we have at home. I hope they taste good. I thought we could have tea and talk about the book, if you would like?"

Gertie shouldered off her coat with a smile. "I would like."

Harry had always said that the best things in life invariably start with a book, and as Gertie and Hedy shared their love of stories over tea and biscuits during the following weeks and months, she was reminded how wise her husband had been. Gertie offered Brontë and Wodehouse, while Hedy brought Droste-Hülshoff and Hesse. Once they had shared their favorites, they moved on to new authors. Together, they discovered Edna Ferber, Winifred Holtby, Aldous Huxley, and plenty more besides. Gertie noted with satisfaction that they not only had similar tastes but that Hedy discussed stories, characters, and literature with a passion that Gertie recognized but hadn't felt for a good few years. Since Harry's death, to be precise. She had fallen out of love with reading for a time, and now Hedy was helping to reignite that joy.

When she wasn't at school or reading, Hedy would write. Sam had enlisted with the RAF, and she would compose long letters to him, her face coming alive whenever she received a reply. Gertie also noticed the scribbled stories, penned on scraps of paper, some fragments in German and some in English. It made her smile. There was comfort in words. A world of much-needed strength and hope too. Gertie bought Hedy a midnight-blue leather notebook and gifted her Harry's bright red Parker Duofold pen.

"If it's good enough for Arthur Conan Doyle, it's good enough for me," he'd always say.

Hedy accepted both with a look of grateful wonder. "I promise I will take care of Harry's pen."

"I know you will," said Gertie with satisfaction. "You can be Bingham Books's first writer in residence."

"I'll write a story that would make you both proud."

Gertie felt her heart rise and dip all at once, as it sounded exactly like the kind of thing a child would say to her parents. She patted Hedy's shoulder. "I can't wait to read it."

"**I've got** one, Mrs. B!" cried Betty, bursting in through the door, holding up an egg like a trophy. "Oh sorry, Mr. Travers. I didn't see you there."

"Don't mind me, Miss Godwin. Mrs. Bingham and I were just shoring up the old defenses."

Betty's eyes lit up. "You've signed it off?"

He nodded. "It'll be a boon on the high street when the Jerries get here."

"*If* they get here," said Betty. "I'm proud as punch

to be one of your wardens, Mr. Travers, but I don't need to do much except hand out gas masks and shout at people to 'put that light out!'"

"Be careful what you wish for," said Gerald, exchanging a glance with Gertie. It was the look of a generation who was relieved that there had been little fighting during the first few months of this war. The thought of burying more dead when they were still reeling from the horrors of the last conflict was almost too much to bear. Betty's generation couldn't recall this, of course. They were eager to defeat fascism, to stand up and fight. Gertie applauded their spirit, but every time she heard of another young man joining up, dread pooled in her stomach like tar. Hitler was spreading his tentacles of power through Europe, and it wouldn't be long before his attention turned to Britain. It was as if they were poised, staring into the terrifying darkness, fearful of the moment the monster would strike.

For the time being, life felt like a dress rehearsal for what lay ahead. The government had introduced rationing, which, if you listened to the likes of Miss Crow, was a "travesty of justice," but to Gertie seemed like a small price to pay to keep the country fed. The nightly blackouts were seen by most as an irksome necessity but, to Gertie's delight, had fueled a greater thirst for reading. She could barely keep *Gone with the Wind* in stock, and her sales of Jane Austen and Charles Dickens titles were booming.

"Jolly good work on the egg front, by the way," she said to Betty. "I've saved up my butter ration."

"What about sugar?"

"I read somewhere that you could use carrots to sweeten a cake."

Betty pulled a face. "Sounds a bit odd."

"I have sugar," said Mr. Travers.

Betty turned to him. "Are you sure? We're making a birthday cake for Hedy, you see."

"Of course," he said. "The young lady must have a cake after everything she's endured. I've got a meeting with the WVS now, but I can bring it to your house later, Mrs. Bingham."

"Then we must give you something in return," said Gertie.

"Oh no, there's really no need," said Gerald.

"Here," said Betty, plucking a book from the shelf and handing it to him.

"*The Grapes of Wrath*," read Gerald.

"It's very popular at the moment. We chose it for the book club last year, and Mr. Reynolds said it was one of the best books he'd ever read," said Betty. "I think you'll enjoy it."

Gerald turned it over in his hands. "Might be nice

to have something to read on my nights off. Blackout evenings do drag on a bit. Thank you."

"It's a shame we've had to suspend Bingham's Book Club for the time being," said Betty. "Otherwise, you could join."

Gerald sighed. "Hitler's got a lot to answer for. Right, I best be off. Don't want to keep Mrs. Fortescue waiting."

"Heavens no," said Gertie. She knew Margery Fortescue by reputation. She had been widowed for a few years and liked to host supper parties and recitals in the drawing room of the mansion house where she lived with her daughter, Cynthia. It was just outside the boundaries of the town, nudging the picturesque Kent countryside.

"Fancies herself as lady of the manor," Miss Crow had been heard to comment on more than one occasion. "Lady La-Di-Da more like."

Gertie wasn't one to believe the idle chitchat of Philomena Crow but had encountered the formidable Margery Fortescue in person on one occasion. It had been a quiet day in the shop, not long after Harry died. Gertie was in the stockroom when she heard the bell above the door ring. She smoothed her dress and made her way to the front. A woman in her thirties with small round glasses, wearing a plum-colored beret, was standing in the middle of the shop holding a copy of *The Arabian Nights* in her hands. It was a beautiful edition, rich purple cloth with an elaborate gold leaf design laced over the spine. The woman had her eyes closed and was inhaling its scent as if drawing the stories into an embrace. Gertie paused. She didn't want to intrude. She understood the sanctity of this moment. She enacted it almost daily herself, like a priest practicing some sacred ritual. The poor woman didn't have long to enjoy this precious peace, however, as the shop door flew open and Margery Fortescue stood before them, frowning with arms folded.

"Cynthia Fortescue! What is the meaning of this?" she thundered. The younger woman's eyes shot open, but she remained frozen to the spot, clutching the book as if it might save her from the impending onslaught. "Cynthia!"

Cynthia turned 'round, shoulders hunched. "Sorry, Mother," she said. "I was just browsing."

"May I be of assistance?" asked Gertie, breezing into their midst as if she had only just encountered them in her shop.

"No," said Margery. "We are leaving. Cynthia. Put that book down."

Cynthia's face fell as if she had been told to part from

her beloved forever. She traced a finger over the spine of the volume before offering it to Gertie.

"Keep it," said Gertie.

Cynthia's eyes grew wide.

"No," said her mother, snatching the book from her daughter's grasp and placing it on the counter. "We do not need your charity, and Cynthia should not be rewarded for sneaking off to this"—she threw a disapproving gaze across the bookshelves—"emporium. Now come along, Cynthia. We have an appointment at the hairdresser's. Good day."

Gertie watched them leave, offering a sympathetic smile to Cynthia as she glanced back toward the shop, a look of longing on her small studious face.

"I hope Mr. Travers knows what he's dealing with. Mrs. Fortescue can be terrifying," said Gertie after he'd gone.

"What a dear man for offering us his sugar ration, though," said Betty.

Gertie nodded. "It'll be a lovely surprise for Hedy. Is Sam still able to get weekend leave?"

"I don't think Hermann Göring could stop him."

"And Barnaby?"

"Not this time unfortunately."

"I'm sorry, dear," said Gertie.

Betty gave a stoic shrug. "England expects."

Gertie reached out to squeeze her arm. She wasn't a religious woman, but every night she prayed that this war would be short, that their young men would be spared. However, as Hitler marched his relentless progress across Europe, this wish felt increasingly unlikely.

Gertie was laying out the breakfast things when the telegram arrived. Hemingway barked as soon as the boy rang the doorbell, and then she heard Hedy racing down the stairs to answer.

She appeared in the kitchen moments later, clutching the telegram to her heart. "My mother wishes me a happy birthday," she said, her face a mixture of longing and delight.

Gertie sensed the need to prevent Hedy from brooding. "Well, what jolly good luck it arrived on the day. Happy birthday, dear. I've got something for you too." She nodded toward a brown paper package on the table.

"*Villette*," said Hedy, pulling a small blue volume from the paper. "Thank you, Gertie."

"I know how much you enjoyed *Jane Eyre*, so I thought you might like to try another by Charlotte Brontë."

"And these flowers are beautiful," said Hedy,

stroking a finger over the delicate blush petals of the round pink buds.

"Peonies," said Gertie, satisfied. "They've bloomed just in time for your birthday. So do you have any plans for today?"

"Betty is coming later, and we might go to the cinema."

"Sounds like a super idea," said Gertie, ticklish with excitement about the surprise that lay ahead. Thanks to Betty's egg and Mr. Travers's sugar, she'd managed to bake a passable chocolate cake filled with homemade cherry jam, which she was hiding in a cake tin in the pantry, ready for when Sam arrived.

At a little after two o'clock, there was a knock at the door. "Hedy," called Gertie. "Will you let Betty in please, dear."

"All right," said Hedy.

Gertie emerged from the kitchen and stood to watch as she opened the front door.

"Happy birthday!" cried Betty, throwing her hands into the air before standing to one side as Sam, dressed in RAF uniform, poked his head around the door-frame.

"Surprise!"

"Sam!" cried Hedy, darting forward and throwing

her arms around his neck. Gertie and Betty grinned at each other. "You look so smart," she told him.

"About time someone spruced him up," said Betty, elbowing her brother in the ribs.

"You do look very dapper, Sam," said Gertie, a sudden recollection of Jack leaving for war all those years ago catching in her throat. "Shall we go into the living room and celebrate this young lady's birthday properly?"

After tea and the cake, which everyone declared a success, Sam reached into his pocket and pulled out a small square parcel. Hedy unwrapped it to reveal a ruby-red velvet box containing a silver locket. "I've put in the photo from the day at the Hop Farm," he said with a chuckle. "When Betty sat on that wasp."

"It wasn't funny, it was awfully painful," said his sister.

Hedy unhooked the chain.

"Here. Let me help you with that," said Sam, moving toward her. He looped it around her neck and secured the clasp.

Hedy's cheeks flushed a little as she placed a hand on the locket. "Thank you, Sam," she whispered.

Gertie knew enough to see when two people were falling in love. Her heart stirred in a swirl of joy and sorrow for what lay ahead for them both.

There was another knock at the door. Sam glanced at his sister. "I think this one might be for you, Betty."

Betty frowned. "What do you mean?"

Gertie approached the window and glanced through the curtains. "He's right. It's definitely for you."

Betty flew to the door. Gertie, Hedy, and Sam eyed one another as they listened.

"Oh!" cried Betty. "Oh, it's you! Wonderful, wonderful you." She returned moments later clutching Barnaby's hand. "This rotter told me he couldn't get leave," she cried, her eyes brimming with tears. Barnaby pulled her close and kissed the top of her head.

"Not too late for the party, am I?" he said. "Happy birthday, Hedy."

"Thank you, Barnaby. I'm so glad you're here."

"Well, I don't know about you, but I think this calls for some music," said Sam. "All right if we fire up the gramophone, Mrs. B?"

"It's not a proper party without music," said Gertie, sharing a smile with Hedy.

"I'm going to teach you the Charleston, Hedy," said Sam. "Come on you two." He turned to Barnaby and Betty. "No time to rest."

Gertie watched in delight as the youngsters swiveled and pivoted their way around the floor, laughing as they went. It felt good to have these moments of joy in times of despair. She noticed the way that Hedy and Sam looked at each other. Hedy seemed too young to be falling in love, and yet she couldn't think of a better man for her than Sam. It brought to mind joyful reminiscences of when she and Harry first fell in love. Those stolen glances. The dip of longing when you parted. The thrill of the moment when you met again. There was comfort in these memories, but stabs of painful longing too.

Her reverie was interrupted by a knock at the door. "No one is expecting another surprise visitor today, are they?" asked Gertie, moving forward to answer it.

"Perhaps it's the prime minister," said Betty, laughing. "He's heard about that delicious cake and wants a slice."

The smile on Gertie's lips disappeared as soon as she saw the policeman. He looked younger than Hedy as he clutched at his notebook with nervous fingers, a sheen of sweat on his upper lip. "Good afternoon, Constable. Is everything all right?"

"Mrs. Bingham?" he said, glancing down at the notebook. "Mrs. Gertrude Bingham?"

"Yes. I am she."

He took a deep breath. "PC Wilberforce. We understand you have a German national living with you. Is that correct?"

"Yes," said Gertie, irritated. "She is a young Jewish girl who was forced to flee her homeland because of the Nazis."

"Oh," said the officer.

"Look, what is this about, young man?" she demanded, surprising herself with the ferocity of her tone. "What do you want with Hedy?"

He swallowed and stared down at his notebook as if it might offer the answer, before looking back at her ruefully. "I've come to arrest her," he said. "On the orders of Winston Churchill himself."

Chapter 9

I would rather be a rebel than a slave.

—Emmeline Pankhurst

Gertie stared up at the royal coat of arms embla-
zoned on the back wall of the magistrates' court
through narrowed eyes as anger pulsed through her
veins like electricity. She had been in a perpetual state
of fury ever since they'd tried to arrest Hedy. Gertie
had escorted her to the police station and told the sergeant on duty in no uncertain terms that Hedy would
not be taken away until she had been given a proper
hearing. He was a kindly man called Fred Mayfield
who had a daughter of around Hedy's age and who
occasionally dropped into the bookshop to buy her a
Mills and Boon novel. He made a phone call, arranged
for an appeal hearing the following month, and sent
Gertie and Hedy home.

Gertie was relieved but remained outraged by this turn of events. Galvanized into action, she persuaded everyone she knew to write to *The Times* on Hedy's behalf. A week later, a young female journalist appeared at the bookshop, asking to interview her.

"How do you react to the story that the prime minister ordered the police to, and I quote, 'collar the lot'?"

"I would ask if the prime minister has ever had cause to flee his home due to the tyranny of the government," said Gertie without missing a beat.

The journalist raised her eyebrows. "May I quote you, Mrs. Bingham?"

Gertie looked her in the eye. "Yes, dear. You may."

This wasn't the first time Gertie had found herself challenging the political might of Winston Churchill. In 1905, encouraged by her mother and Mrs. Pankhurst's rallying "Deeds Not Words" cry, Gertie had been mobilized into action. Her first act of rebellion was not entirely successful.

"Gertrude. Could you come here for a moment please?"

Gertie glanced up from the orders ledger to see her father standing uncomfortably beside a small, elderly woman, dressed in black, who was dabbing at her eyes with a handkerchief. As Gertie approached, she could hear the woman's plaintive moan. "The great

Alfred, Lord Tennyson! How could they? It sullies his very name."

"Father?" said Gertie.

Arthur Arnold's face was grave. "Do you know the meaning of this?" he asked, holding out the book.

Gertie took it and gazed down at the "Votes for Women" inscription on the front page. She looked up at him with a bright, innocent smile. "I think it has something to do with the campaign for women to gain the vote."

The diminutive customer was incensed. "It is an abomination!" she cried. "These women are monsters without a shred of decency in their bones. They should be horsewhipped, I tell you. Horsewhipped!"

Gertie and her father stared at the woman in astonishment as she jabbed a gloved finger to emphasize her point.

"We have managed quite well enough with our fathers, husbands, and brothers representing our views. We do not need this to change. I'm sure as a devoted father you agree?" she said, turning to Arthur.

He glanced at his daughter before giving a polite cough. "Dear lady, I am afraid I do not. It has long been my assertion that my wife and daughter share a fearsome intellect that far outweighs my own. They are not only equals but betters to my mind. Now, I apologize that the book you purchased has been defaced in this way and am prepared to offer you a replacement copy or a full refund."

"Well," huffed the woman, preparing to begin a fresh rant.

"A replacement or a refund," repeated Arthur. "Which would you prefer?"

The woman jutted out her chin and glared at Gertie. "A refund, and I shall never darken the door of this establishment again."

Later that evening over dinner, Arthur turned to his wife and daughter with a sigh. "Dear hearts, I would never ask you to diminish your ardent beliefs for what is right, but please, I beg you, give me a little warning before you drive us out of business."

Gertie planted a kiss on his cheek. "Sorry, Father."

Lilian slid a copy of The Tenant of Wildfell Hall toward her daughter. "It won't be easy," she said. "Seismic change never is. But it will be worth it in the end. Never lose that indignant spark, Gertie."

Lilian's words had helped to heighten Gertie's courage. Her next act of political insurrection took place at the public meeting she attended, clutching the book her mother had given her. As Winston Churchill began to speak, Gertie had risen to her feet, her body tingling with purpose as she heard the tuts and mutterings of

"Not another one." She took a deep breath and looked the speaker in the eye.

"Mr. Churchill," she said as he turned to regard her with one eyebrow raised. "Mr. Churchill. I ask not *if* but *when* you and your Liberal Party will support women's right to vote?"

Charles telephoned Gertie a few days later. "Did you know you're quoted in *The Times*?"

"Am I, by Jove?" said Gertie mildly. "Well, fancy that."

"Criticizing the prime minister no less."

"We are still allowed to do that even though there's a war on, aren't we? A democracy is a democracy even in times of conflict surely."

"I couldn't agree more. I telephoned to congratulate you in fact." He paused. "Harry would be proud of you."

"He used to scold me when I got angry."

"Ah, but when you channel that anger into something important, you can change the world."

She asked Charles to accompany them to the tribunal hearing. She was emboldened by the public support for Hedy and the other internees but still needed a friend by her side. She glanced at him as they sat in the courtroom waiting for the magistrate. Dear Charles. There was so much about him that reminded her of treasured times with Harry. The way his mouth drew upward as if a smile were never far from his lips, the laughter lines at the corners of his eyes, the kindness in his gaze. It transported her back to suppers with just the three of them or, on occasion, with Jack. Gertie was starting to realize that the weight of longing was lifting slightly. She could look back without that familiar twist of sorrow.

"All rise for the Honorable Geoffrey Barkly Hurr."

As the magistrate took his place underneath the royal coat of arms, Gertie took heart from the fact that he reminded her a little of Uncle Thomas. He peered at the documents in front of him before clearing his throat and addressing the court. "This is a tribunal hearing regarding one Hedy Fischer, aged sixteen years old. Our task today is to determine whether we should reclassify her as a Class C alien, which would mean internment is not required. She is currently categorized as a Class B alien, which demands internment as an emergency measure following the escalation of the war in Europe. Is that correct, Mr. Baxter?"

A man sitting at a table to the right of Gertie and Charles, whom she hadn't noticed until now, rose to his feet. "It is, sir."

"And could you tell me why the government feels it necessary to have Miss Fischer interned. She is a Jewish refugee, isn't she?"

"Yes, sir. The issue for the government is one of national security."

Gertie let out an indignant grunt.

The magistrate raised an eyebrow. "Could I have silence."

Gertie felt Charles's eyes boring into her. She kept her gaze fixed on the coat of arms. The lion glared at her wild-eyed. She glared back.

"As I was saying," continued Mr. Baxter. "Since the escalation of the war in Europe there are concerns that Miss Fischer could potentially be involved in espionage."

"Poppycock!" cried Gertie.

The magistrate fixed her with a grave look. "Madam, I will not have interruptions in this court. You will either be silent or be removed."

"I'm sorry, sir," said Gertie. "But I know Hedy Fischer and I know she's not a spy."

Mr. Barkly Hurr turned to Mr. Baxter. "Do you have testimonies for this young woman?"

Mr. Baxter sifted through his file. "Yes, sir. There's quite a few. From a Mrs. Constantine, Miss Snipp, Mr. Travers and Mrs. Huffingham, the headmistress of the local girls' school Miss Fischer attended for a while. And then there's the small matter of the newspaper article and public outcry which followed it . . ." His voice trailed off as he slid a copy of *The Times* toward the magistrate.

Mr. Barkly Hurr scanned the article with eyebrows raised before turning to Gertie. "You are the woman who criticized our prime minister."

Gertie looked him squarely in the eye. "I am. I think his decision to intern all foreign nationals is wrong. And the public agrees with me."

"My dear Mrs. Bingham. In Germany, the public appears to be agreeing with a madman. That is not necessarily a measure of what is correct."

"Yes, sir, but we live in a democracy, where we are permitted to speak freely, and surely that's what we're fighting for. The right of people to speak and act and live their lives regardless of race. That's what this case is about. Hedy came to this country to escape persecution. What kind of nation are we if we imprison her because of her nationality? What kind of hypocrisy is that?" Gertie was aware that everyone in the courtroom was staring at her now. The silence was all-encompassing.

Mr. Barkly Hurr gave an approving nod before turning to Hedy. "And you, young lady," he said. "Would you be so kind as to explain why you came to this country?"

Hedy's neck flushed scarlet. Gertie gave her hand a

reassuring squeeze, and Hedy shot her a grateful look before she began to speak. Her voice was small, but there was something compelling about the way she spoke. The courtroom leaned in to listen.

"It started when Hitler came to power. I was still allowed to go to school for a while, but then everything changed. People shouted names at us. I still had non-Jewish friends, but their parents would not let them speak to me anymore. Some children followed us and threw stones. My mother was scared and would not let me go to school." She swallowed. "Then came the night when they attacked the shops and burned the synagogues. My father was sent to Dachau, and my mother hid my brother because she was worried they would take him too. When my father came back, he spent every day searching for a way for us to leave Germany. He got me a place on a train, and I came here, to live with Mrs. Bingham."

The magistrate gave a grave nod. "And what of your parents? And your brother? Do you know of their whereabouts?"

Hedy held his gaze for a moment before shaking her head and casting her eyes downward. Mr. Barkly Hurr glanced toward the heavens as if pleading for divine intervention before addressing the court. "I am satisfied on the strength of the evidence presented here today that Hedy Fischer should be released with immediate effect and reclassified as a Class C alien with no further need for internment or investigation." He turned to Hedy and Gertie. "Young lady, I wish you well, and Mrs. Bingham, I think you should consider standing for public office."

Gertie shared a smile with Hedy. "It's kind of you to say, but I'm afraid we have a bookshop to run."

Chapter 10

There is no happiness like that of being loved
by your fellow creatures, and feeling that your
presence is an addition to their comfort.

—Charlotte Brontë, *Jane Eyre*

I t was Gerald who gave Gertie the idea. He stood at
the counter one day, his usually languid demeanor
seeming positively animated.

"That *Grapes of Wrath*. What a book," he said, eyes
glittering in wonder. "It whisked me away entirely. I
haven't enjoyed reading so much in years. Got anything else by Mr. Steinbeck?"

"Follow me, Mr. Travers," said Gertie, leading him
to the fiction shelves.

"I've been recommending it to all the other ARP
wardens," he told her, as she placed copies of *Tortilla
Flat* and *Of Mice and Men* into his hands. "Just the

ticket for when the raids start. Something to take our minds off it all."

It was as if a hundred tiny fireworks exploded in Gertie's mind. She rushed through to the stockroom where Hedy and Betty were unpacking boxes and Miss Snipp was frowning at a customer letter. "We need to relaunch the book club," she said.

"Beg pardon, Mrs. B?" said Betty.

"The book club. Bingham's Book Club."

"Forgive me for stating the obvious," said Miss Snipp, peering over the top of her spectacles. "But have you forgotten that there's a war on? You can't stage book clubs and social gatherings if people need to run to the air-raid shelter every five minutes."

Gertie threw up her hands and laughed. "Miss Snipp, you're a genius! That's it. That's what we'll call it."

Miss Snipp turned to Betty and Hedy. "She's experiencing a rush of blood to the head, if I'm not mistaken. It happens to women of a certain age. We should fetch the smelling salts."

Gertie ignored her. "The Air Raid Book Club," she cried, sweeping her hand through the air as if writing the words in lights.

"Ooh," said Betty. "I like that name. How would it work?"

Gertie considered the question. "Well, we select a

book every month for people to read during the air raids, and we read it too so we can discuss it with anyone who uses the public shelter."

"That's a splendid idea," said Betty.

Hedy nodded. "I like this very much, Gertie."

"Good, because we three are going to choose the books between us, and then Miss Snipp can order a dozen or so to start with. Perhaps we could advertise it to our postal customers in case they'd like to take part?"

"As if we haven't got enough to do already," said Miss Snipp with a deep sigh. "You'll be setting us up as a book wholesaler next."

"I can help you, Miss Snipp," said Hedy.

Miss Snipp's hangdog expression lifted. "Thank you, dear," she said, before firing a withering glance toward Gertie. "At least someone understands the burden imposed upon me."

Gertie folded her lips to suppress amusement as she caught Hedy's eye. She had been working in the bookshop for the past few months and had proved to be a godsend, not least in appeasing the unappeasable Miss Snipp. The customers loved her, and as Hedy was now too old to attend school and needed employment, it was the perfect fit. It also offered her some distraction from fretting about her family and a little normality after what Gertie now dismissed as "that internment nonsense."

"So what should we choose for our first book?" asked Betty.

"*Jane Eyre*," said Hedy, smiling at Gertie. "We have to start with *Jane Eyre*."

September proved to be blissfully warm that year as if summer were offering a final burst of glory before the season turned. Gertie's garden was in its zenith. Plant stems drooped heavy with fat red tomatoes, onion sets nudged their papery bulbs up through the earth, the branches of the trees bowed with russet-and-green apples. She made her way across the dewy grass to gather windfalls and pick any ripe fruit. In light of the fact that oats were unrationed, she and Hedy had become rather partial to porridge with a liberal sprinkling of fresh blackberries. Gertie paused to admire the marrow, snaking its prickly stalks across the Anderson shelter, which now felt like a permanent fixture in the garden. Charles had helped her build it just after the war started. They had spent a happy morning digging deep trenches so that they could bury the corrugated construction before placing makeshift bunk beds inside and covering the whole thing with soil.

"It looks like a mud igloo," said Gertie, wiping her hands on a cloth as they stood back to admire their handiwork.

"You'll be safe as houses," said Charles with satisfaction.

Gertie peered inside. "There's enough room for six people. Hedy, Hemingway, and I are going to rattle around in there."

"You could always invite the neighbors," said Charles, nodding over his shoulder to where the woman who lived next door was pretending to hang out washing while earwigging on their conversation.

"Good morning, Mrs. Gosling," called Gertie. "Lovely day, isn't it?"

The woman grunted in reply. "What's all this then?"

"It's an air-raid shelter," said Gertie. "You'd be very welcome to share it when the time comes."

"Will your gentleman friend be using it too?" she asked, shooting a disapproving glance in Charles's direction.

"Oh, I should think so," said Gertie. "We'll be having raucous soirees. We'd love it if you could join us."

The woman stared from Gertie to Charles, who had turned away to stifle his laughter. She spun on her heel, bundled her basket under her arm, and fled back inside. "Scandalous!" she muttered before slamming the door.

"Gertie Bingham. You're dreadful."

"I know. But I've always thought it's important

to feed people's imaginations," she said. "It's why I became a bookseller."

Gertie's basket was nearly full with blackberries and loganberries now. She was about to go back inside to prepare breakfast when she heard the sound of a child crying from Mrs. Gosling's garden. She peered over the fence and was surprised to see a small boy, his mouth a wide O of despair.

"Hello," said Gertie softly, not wanting to alarm him. "Whatever is the matter?"

The boy stopped crying and stared up at her with huge wet eyes. He glanced back toward the house. "I'm not allowed to talk to strange ladies."

"Oh dear," said Gertie. "That is a bind, because I'm a very strange lady indeed."

"Gertie, are you out there?" called Hedy from the kitchen. "Have we had any post?"

"Yes, dear, I'm in the garden. And no, no post yet." This was always Hedy's first question when she woke. They were learning to live with the knife-edge existence of waiting for news of Sam or Hedy's family. "Come and see who I've found in the garden."

Hedy appeared beside Gertie. "Hello there," she said. "And what's your name?"

"He's not allowed to talk to strange ladies," said Gertie.

"Billy! Billy, where are you?" cried a furious voice from the boy's house.

Billy stared at them with fearful eyes. "It's all right. He's in the garden," called Gertie.

Billy's mother appeared at the back door looking frantic. She was wearing a housecoat with her hair drawn up in a scarf. Her face was pale, and there was a smut of soot on her cheek. She strode across the garden, scowling. "Billy," she said, seizing him by the shoulders. "What have I told you about wandering off?"

The little boy began to cry again. "I'm sorry, Mama."

"It's entirely my fault," said Gertie. "I spoke to Billy. He was just being polite."

The woman looked as if she might start to cry too. She knelt in front of her son and pulled his small body to hers. Hedy and Gertie exchanged glances as Billy reached a hand 'round to pat his mother consolingly on the back. She pulled away from the embrace and wiped his eyes, kissing the top of his head. "It's all right, Billy. Everything is all right. But we have to be brave, remember? Very, very brave."

Billy nodded earnestly. "Okay, Mama."

"Good boy. You run along inside and play. I found your jigsaws and put them in your room."

"Thank you, Mama."

She stood up and put a hand to her head. "I'm sorry,"

she said. "I must look a fright. We had to move in a bit of a hurry and everything is such a mess. I'm Elizabeth Chambers and that's my son, Billy, but you probably knew that already." She offered a weary smile.

"Delighted to meet you. I'm Gertie Bingham, and this is Hedy Fischer. I was wondering who might move in after Mrs. Gosling went to live with her sister in Devon. Please let us know if there's anything we can do to help."

Elizabeth Chambers gave a brief nod. "Thank you. That's very kind. Well, I must be getting on. I seem to have hundreds of boxes still to unpack."

"Of course," said Gertie, sensing her need to be away.

Gertie and Hedy had adopted a series of codes for letters and telegrams to help reduce the daily sense of anticipation. A day without correspondence was "no news is good news," a day with one communication was "tea and biscuits," and a day with news from both Sam and the Fischers was "champagne cocktails at the Café de Paris."

"Tea and biscuits today, Gertie," said Hedy as she carried in a letter from Sam like a hallowed artifact.

"That's two days in a row after that telegram from your brother yesterday."

Hedy nodded. Gertie was impressed by her stoicism. The letters from Sam were cheery and full of news, whereas the telegrams from her family were alarmingly sparce. They would never speak about it, of course, but each communication merely served to confirm that the sender was still alive. It was an unbearable but unavoidable fact. If the letters stopped coming, it would be hard to keep up the pretense that "no news is good news" for long. Several families in the area had already lost sons. Old Mr. Harris, a customer with a penchant for Celtic history, had heard that one of his grandsons had been killed at Dunkirk, while Mrs. Herbert across the road had received word that her husband was missing. These horrors seemed remote in some ways: fighting in a faraway land was like a distant rumble of thunder, and yet Gertie felt sure that lightning would strike soon.

Gertie and Hedy were busy restocking the shelves when Betty arrived that morning. She uttered an uncharacteristically muted greeting before shouldering off her coat and muttering that she needed to press on with the orders.

Hedy and Gertie exchanged looks as they heard Betty drop a pile of books with a loud "Blast!"

They approached the storeroom. "Are you all right, dear?" asked Gertie.

Betty brushed away a tear as she turned. "Sorry. I'll be fine in a jiffy."

Hedy put her arm around her shoulders. "What is it, Betty? What's wrong?"

She regarded them both sorrowfully. "I haven't had a letter from Barnaby for a week."

"Oh, dear heart," said Gertie. "He probably hasn't had time to write."

Betty considered this. "He had been writing every day, but maybe you're right. When did you last hear from Sam?" she asked Hedy.

"Oh, not since last week," said Hedy, throwing Gertie a meaningful look. "Remember, no news is good news."

"Thank you," said Betty. "Thank you both. I know you're right. Sorry for being such a grump."

"You have nothing to apologize for," said Gertie.

Business was brisk that morning. "We're going to need to stock up on Brontë and Dickens," Gertie told Betty. "And best check our stocks of crime and romances. Hercule Poirot seems to be a particular favorite at the moment. And Sherlock Holmes."

"Right ho, Mrs. B."

At a little past eleven the gentle peace of the browsing bookshop customers was interrupted by the arrival of Miss Snipp's twin nieces, Rosaline and Sylvie Finch.

They were as chatty as sparrows and often finished each other's sentences as if they were sharing the same thoughts. As soon as Miss Snipp saw them enter, she turned abruptly toward the back of the shop.

"Hullo, Aunt Snipp," cried Rosaline, waving to her hastily retreating back.

"And goodbye, Aunt Snipp," added Sylvie, nudging her sister, who giggled.

"Good morning, girls," said Gertie, looking up from the counter. "What did you think of *Jane Eyre?*"

The pair exchanged glances. "We didn't really think Jane should have gone back to Mr. Rochester. He was far too cross," said Sylvie.

"Terribly cross," agreed Rosaline. "Although that St. John chap was a complete bore, so she couldn't stay with him either."

"True," said Sylvie. "But Jane's a good egg, and Mother said she'd never seen us so quiet during the blackouts, so she's sent us in to ask what's next."

Gertie held out a buttercup-yellow volume with red and black type.

"*Rebecca*," read Rosaline, running a finger over the cover.

"A new novel. Daphne du Maurier," echoed Sylvie in wonder.

"It's completely gripping," said Betty, joining them

at the counter. "Kept me up all night, and the twist is splendid. I think you'll enjoy it."

The two girls shared an excited look before turning back to Gertie. "We'll take it, thank you, Mrs. Bingham."

"Just the one copy?"

Sylvie nodded. "Oh yes. We like to sit beside each other and read so we can share the story as we go."

Gertie smiled. "I look forward to hearing what you think."

The shop quieted to a trickle of customers in the afternoon. "I expect people are making the most of the last days of summer," said Betty, gazing out the window. "They're probably all sitting in their gardens."

Gertie was about to suggest that they close early when the wail of an air-raid siren punctured the quiet. Hemingway barked in alarm as they looked at one another in surprise.

"This is it," whispered Betty with barely concealed excitement. "It's happening."

"Come on, girls," said Gertie. "Let's get to the shelter. Hemingway!"

As they hurried to the back of the shop the bell above the door rang, and Gertie turned to see an anxious Elizabeth Chambers leading Billy by the hand. "May we join you?" she asked as if suggesting tea in the garden.

"Of course," said Gertie. "Follow us."

"I like books," said Billy, trotting happily beside his mother. He caught sight of Hemingway's wagging tail. "And dogs."

Once inside the shelter, Gertie lit a candle and glanced around at the bare brick walls. "It's a little sparse in here, but we'll be snug as bugs in no time," she said, taking comfort from the book-ladened shelves above their heads.

"Are the Germans coming now?" asked Billy, stroking Hemingway's soft ears as the hum of aircraft began overhead.

Everyone exchanged glances. No one knew what was happening. They had been expecting this for the longest time and yet, somehow, felt woefully unprepared. "Perhaps it's a drill?" suggested Betty, but this idea was quickly overturned as they heard the first terrifying explosions.

"Are those bombs?" asked Billy, eyes wide with fear.

Elizabeth Chambers swallowed. She looked more frightened than her son. "I think so, Billy, but our brave soldiers will stop them from falling," she said, clasping his small hands in hers.

"I'm scared," he said, his face crumpling with the imminent threat of tears.

Gertie spotted a book on the shelf behind his

head. "Have you ever read the story of Winnie-the-Pooh?" she asked, reaching for it. Billy shook his head. "Well, he's a bear who has lots of friends including Piglet, Tigger, and Christopher Robin, and sometimes Piglet in particular is very scared, but his friends always make him feel better."

"I would like to hear that story," said Billy with a grave nod.

Gertie opened the cover. "Very well then."

The first raid lasted for over an hour. Gertie sensed them all leaning in to listen as she read. There was untold comfort in these words uttered out loud, in the story of a little boy and his bear playing with their friends in the forest. They could pretend it was all for Billy's benefit when really they were grateful for a distraction from the horrors outside. As the all clear sounded, Gertie finished the chapter she was reading and closed the book. "Did you enjoy that, Billy?"

He gave a thoughtful nod. "Yes, and I think that if we see the Germans like Woozles and learn not to be afraid of them, everything will be all right."

"You're a very clever boy," said Hedy.

"Can we read more stories like this if the Germans come again?" he asked.

"Perhaps," said Hedy, glancing at Gertie, "we should have a book club for children too."

"What a splendid idea," said Gertie. "And perhaps this young man could help us choose the books."

"Would you pay me?" asked Billy.

"Billy!" cried Elizabeth. "I'm so sorry, Mrs. Bingham."

Gertie laughed. "Not at all. I admire your entrepreneurial spirit, Billy. I tell you what, why don't you keep that copy of *Winnie-the-Pooh* as your first payment?"

"You don't need to do that, Mrs. Bingham," said Elizabeth.

"I know," said Gertie. "But I'd like to."

"Thank you," said Billy. "When I'm older, I want to join the RAF so I can protect you all."

"My chap is in the RAF," Betty told him. "And so is Hedy's."

"Gosh," said Billy, his eyes bright with awe. "They must be very brave."

"They are," said Betty, nudging Hedy.

"Betty, dear," said Gertie. "Why don't you use the shop telephone to call your mother and let her know you're all right."

"Oh yes, hell's teeth. She'll be beside herself. Thanks, Mrs. B," said Betty, disappearing to the back of the shop.

"I'm very grateful to you, Mrs. Bingham," said Elizabeth. "It's not been easy." Her voice wavered slightly.

"Call me Gertie," she said, touching her on the arm. "And you're both welcome here or in the shelter at home anytime. I'll make sure I leave the side gate open for you."

Elizabeth nodded with gratitude.

"Mama, it looks like the sky is on fire," called Billy, pressing his nose up against the shop window.

Acrid smoke filled their nostrils as Gertie opened the door and they spilled out onto the street. She glanced up and down the high street. Thankfully, this little corner of London remained untouched, the closed-up shops all defiantly intact, the clock above Robinson's still ticking. Her eyes were drawn toward the horizon above the center of London. "Oh my goodness." The others followed her gaze in silence. The entire sky over London was a glowing furnace.

"It's started," murmured Elizabeth.

"You should get home," said Gertie.

"Goodbye, Gertie Bingham and Hedy Fischer," called Billy over his shoulder as Elizabeth took his hand. "Remember, don't be afraid of the Woozles. I'll come and help you with the book club soon."

Hedy and Gertie stood for a moment staring back toward London and the horror left by the first raid. "I'm scared, Gertie," whispered Hedy.

Gertie rested an arm against hers. "So am I, dear."

"I worry about Sam and Barnaby."

"I know." Gertie glanced back toward the bookshop. "All we can do is offer an escape to ourselves and one another."

Hedy nodded.

"Come on. Let's find Betty and go home."

Hedy and Gertie squinted in the half-light of the bookshop as they walked back inside. Betty was standing stock-still in the doorway to the shelter, her face pale and expressionless as if carved from alabaster. She seemed to be in a trance, staring straight past them. Hedy shot Gertie a worried look.

"Betty," said Gertie, "are you all right?"

Betty turned her gaze on Gertie as if seeing her for the first time. "I spoke to Mother," she said.

Gertie's first thought was that something had happened to Sam. Hedy clearly thought the same, as she gave a shuddering gasp. "What is it?" she whispered.

Betty's eyes were wide with disbelief. "He's dead."

"No," cried Hedy, clutching a hand to her mouth.

"Who's dead, Betty?" asked Gertie, resting a hand on Hedy's arm.

"Barnaby," said Betty, blinking at them both as tears formed in her eyes. "His father telephoned this afternoon. He was killed on Sunday. Barnaby is dead."

"Oh, my dear," said Gertie as she and Hedy rushed forward to fold her into a sobbing embrace.

And so it begins, thought Gertie as she held the girls tight in a fruitless attempt to comfort and console. *The next round of senseless deaths. Another generation who will mourn endlessly for the ones who never came home, who never got to live the lives they yearned for. How can this be happening again, and when will it end?*

Chapter 11

Reflect upon your present blessings—of
which every man has many—not on your past
misfortunes, of which all men have some.

—Charles Dickens, *Sketches by Boz*

"May I speak with Miss Godwin, please?"

Gertie glanced up from the counter to see Miss Pettigrew standing before her, a twist of worry creasing her elderly brow. She was a tiny lady with a delicate frame and an aroma of lavender that followed wherever she went. "I'm afraid that Miss Godwin doesn't work here anymore, Miss Pettigrew."

"Oh dear," said Miss Pettigrew, wringing her hands together. "That is sad."

"It is. Very sad," said Gertie, recalling the conversation when Betty had visited her at home a month after Barnaby's death.

———

"I'm sorry, Mrs. B, but I've decided not to come back to the bookshop," she said. "I'm taking a permanent ARP post, you see."

"That's brave of you, dear," said Gertie.

Betty shrugged. "I don't know what else to do, to be honest. I just know I can't be in the bookshop. It reminds me too much of . . ." She clutched a hand to her mouth. "Sorry."

Gertie took her hand. "I felt the same after Harry died," she said. "I shut up the shop for a month. I could barely put one foot in front of another, and I stopped reading for a good while."

Betty gazed at her. "How do you feel now?"

Gertie considered the question. So much had changed over the past four years. "I miss him every day," she said. "But the pain becomes bearable somehow. You will feel wretched for a while and always miss Barnaby, but you will find a way to go on. I promise." They sat in silence for a while, listening to the tick of the hall clock, Hemingway snoring on the rug, Hedy humming to herself in the kitchen as she prepared tea for them. Life going on, carrying them with it. Onward. Ever onward.

"But whatever am I to do?" asked Miss Pettigrew, pulling Gertie back to the present.

"I can help you," offered Gertie.

The woman shook her head. "It has to be Miss Godwin," she said, her voice trembling as she spoke. "She's the only one who knows, you see."

"Knows what?" asked Gertie.

"Oh, Miss Pettigrew, there you are," said Hedy, appearing from the back of the shop. "I was wondering when I might see you. Betty gave me your list."

Miss Pettigrew stared at Hedy agog. "My Georgette Heyer list?"

Hedy nodded. "Precisely." She fished a notebook from her pocket and leafed through the pages. "And I can see that the next book is *The Spanish Bride*. Would you like me to fetch you a copy?"

"Oh yes, please, dear. Thank you so much."

"She reads everything Georgette Heyer writes," explained Hedy later. "But she can never remember what she's read, so Betty kept a list. She passed it on to me before she left."

Gertie smiled. "Where would I be without you girls?"

It was now clear that Hitler had his deadly sights on London. The bombing was relentless. Every night and sometimes during the day, the planes appeared, littering the city and its outskirts with a carpet of fire. Gertie and Hedy got used to spending night after night in the shelter with the Chamberses and Hemingway. Gertie made it as cozy as possible. She would bring a flask of tea and whatever sweet treats her rations allowed that week. Elizabeth Chambers and Gertie would often play cards while Hedy read to Billy. The little boy always brought his sweets to share, although he saved the Fry's Chocolate Creams for Hedy because he knew they were her favorite.

One night, Hedy was reading Billy's latest children's book club choice, *Peter and Wendy*, to him.

"I don't ever want to grow up," said Billy. "I want to be like Peter and stay a child with Mama and you and Gertie Bingham and Hemingway forever."

"I know what you mean," said Hedy, turning her gaze toward the framed photograph on the wooden shelf behind their heads. She had taken to always bringing the picture of her family into the shelter with her.

"Who are those people?" he asked.

"That's my family. My mama, papa, brother, Arno, and dog, Mischa." Hedy reached out a hand to Hemingway as she said this, receiving a friendly lick in reply.

"But I thought Gertie Bingham was your mother," he said.

"No. She is my friend," said Hedy.

Gertie's heart sang. *Friend.* That's exactly what they'd become.

"Why aren't your family here with you?"

"Billy, don't be a nosey parker," warned his mother.

"It's all right," said Hedy. She turned to Billy. "My family is in Germany. We are Jewish, and Hitler does not like Jews."

"He's a bad man," said Billy, frowning.

"Yes," said Hedy. "He is a very bad man. My parents were able to send me to England to stay with Gertie."

"Hooray for Gertie Bingham!" said Billy, throwing up his arms in celebration.

"Hooray for Gertie Bingham indeed," said Hedy, grinning at her friend.

"But why can't your family come here too?"

Hedy pressed her lips together. Gertie could see she was fighting back tears. "Because the bad man won't let them."

Billy folded his arms. "We should send Gertie Bingham over to rescue them."

"Do you know, Billy?" said Hedy, thumbing away a tear. "I think you're absolutely right."

"Now then, young man," said Elizabeth. "That's quite enough talk for tonight. It's time for bed."

"Can Hedy tuck me in, please?"

"Come along then," said Hedy. "Have you got Edward Bear?"

Billy held up a startled-looking orange teddy bear wearing a green scarf. "Here he is."

"Good boy," said Hedy, pulling the covers up to his chin.

"Can I have one more story, please, Hedy Fischer?"

"William," warned his mother.

"Just a short one, Mama. I'm not quite sleepy enough yet."

Hedy laughed. "Well, there is a story in my head at the moment about two fantastically brave children called Gertie and Arno."

"Like Gertie Bingham and your brother?"

"Same names, but these are children, and they have magical powers."

"What kind of magical powers?"

Hedy's eyes shone as she spoke. "Gertie can escape into any book if she needs to and transport her and Arno to other worlds."

"Gosh. And Arno?"

"Arno has the most brilliant mathematical mind and can do any sum at lightning speed."

"I would like to hear a story about them," said Billy, yawning.

"How about I write it and then tell you another time when you're not so tired?"

Billy nodded as his eyelids drooped. "And Mama could draw the pictures. She's even better at drawing than E. H. Shepard."

"I don't think that's strictly true," said his mother.

"It is," whispered Billy to Hedy before wrapping his arms tightly around her neck. "I'm glad Gertie Bingham rescued you."

"Me too," said Hedy, flashing a smile at Gertie. "Good night, Billy."

"Good night, Hedy Fischer," he murmured before falling asleep.

"I'm sorry for Billy's questions," said Elizabeth, as Gertie poured them cocoa from a flask.

"I don't mind," said Hedy. "I think it is better to be honest."

Elizabeth gazed at her. "You are a very brave young woman."

Hedy's eyes glinted in the lamplight. "I think we are all brave now."

Her words echoed in the silence of the shelter as they listened to the roar of battle outside. Gertie was sure that the bombs were getting nearer. A house three streets over from hers had been destroyed only last week. The Germans often scattered so-called bread baskets of incendiaries as they passed over, leaving flaming pyres in their wake. The townspeople's existence was a surreal combination of horror mixed with the mundane. They went about their business, queuing for rations, listening to the radio, taking strolls in the park, and yet everything was edged with fearful anticipation.

"Everyone knows there's a bomb with your name on it," Gertie heard Miss Crow remark to anyone who would listen as she stood behind her in the butcher's queue one day. Every time the siren wailed, Gertie's heart plunged. *This could be the one. Maybe tonight we won't be so lucky.*

Yet Gertie had surprised herself in the way she was able to live with this fear. She had thought it would be impossible to face another war without Harry to spur her on. She knew she had Hedy to thank in many ways. Together, they were doing their part in the bookshop. Despite Miss Snipp's misgivings, the Air Raid Book Club was proving to be something of a hit. They now had a devoted number of grateful members and had enjoyed animated discussions in the shelter on *Rebecca* and *Frankenstein* over the past couple of months. Although she wasn't able to stop the raids or soften people's losses, Gertie was proud that they were helping in their own way.

Hedy had fallen asleep with her cocoa mug still in her hands. Gertie pried it from her fingers and set it on the side table, placing a blanket over her. "Billy is a splendid little chap," she said to Elizabeth.

Elizabeth stared into the middle distance. "He finds it hard without a father."

"I'm sorry," said Gertie. "It must be hard for you too."

Elizabeth nodded. She opened her mouth as if trying to decide whether to elaborate before folding her lips together. "Well, I suppose we best try to get some sleep." She gazed at Billy's sleeping form, his lips pursed in a perfect curve, a tiny frown on his soft brow. "Good night, Mrs. Bingham."

"Good night, dear," said Gertie. She sat for a while longer in the quiet of the shelter, its closed-in atmosphere offering an unexpected sense of security. The steady breathing of her companions, Hemingway's gentle snoring, and the distant thud of bombs were a familiar background. She lay down and closed her eyes, wondering at how strange it was to find peace among the horror, but perhaps that was the only way to survive in life.

Gertie paused to admire the holly wreath tied with scarlet ribbon that Hedy had hung from the bookshop

door the day before. The window was filled with copies of *A Christmas Carol*, their book club choice for
December. Hedy had carefully copied a selection of
the delightful John Leech illustrations onto the backs
of some old rolls of wallpaper and hung them behind
the piles of books. Gertie decided that Mr. Dickens
would be proud of their festive display.

She unlocked the door and made her way inside.
The reassuringly musty scent of books lifted her heart.
It seemed strange that only a year ago she had been
ready to leave this haven behind. Its walls had echoed
with Harry's absence, every book a stark reminder
that he was gone. Gertie ran her hands along their soft
spines. Harry was still here, but instead of filling her
with sorrow, she was comforted. She had found a way
to carry on, to build on what they'd created. Gertie
wished that Harry were there to see it, but she sensed
in her heart that he knew. The bookshop had saved
her. She could never imagine turning her back on the
place now.

By the time Miss Snipp and Hedy arrived, the shop
was teeming with customers. The mood was one of
cautious optimism as people seemed determined to
enjoy the festive season regardless.

"I've heard a rumor that the Jerries are going to
call a truce over Christmas," said Mrs. Wise, who was

buying an illustrated edition of *Alice's Adventures in Wonderland* for her granddaughter.

"Try telling that to the people of Manchester," said her husband, glancing up from a book on animal husbandry. "They've got it worse than us at the moment."

Gertie was surprised when halfway through the morning Miss Crow made an appearance. She eyed the shelves with suspicion.

"Good morning, Miss Crow," said Gertie. "How may we help you?"

"I'd like to buy a book," she said in a faltering voice. "For my nephew's son."

"I see. Well, perhaps Hedy could help you. She's our children's specialist."

Hedy glanced up from the shelf she was dusting. "Of course. How old is the boy?"

"He's five," said Miss Crow. She stared at the floor. "He's just lost his father."

"I'm very sorry to hear that," said Gertie.

Miss Crow gave a brief nod as Hedy retrieved three volumes from the shelf. "I know a little boy who is the same age who enjoyed these very much." Miss Crow looked at each one in turn before settling on a copy of *Treasure Island*.

"An excellent choice," said Gertie. "I'm sure he'll enjoy you reading it to him."

"Well, I don't know . . ." began Miss Crow.

"Philomena?" said Miss Snipp, appearing from the back of the shop.

Miss Crow froze. "Hello, Eleanora," she said with a frosty edge to her voice.

Miss Snipp clasped her hands together. "I haven't seen you for a good while. I was sorry to hear about your nephew."

Miss Crow avoided her gaze. "Yes, well. It's the world we live in." She took her purchase from Gertie. "Thank you, Mrs. Bingham," she said, tucking the book in her basket. She was just about to leave when the air-raid siren sounded.

"Come along, everyone," called Gertie, ushering them toward the back of the shop. "Into the shelter. This way. Miss Crow?"

The woman frowned before turning to follow her. "Oh, very well."

The crowded shelter immediately reminded Gertie of when Bingham's Book Club really had been standing room only. "Is everyone all right?" she asked, ushering Miss Crow inside and closing the door behind them.

"Not really," said Miss Snipp, glaring at her nieces who, in the absence of spare chairs, had decided to perch on the edge of her orders desk.

"Oh, Auntie Snipp, don't be such a crosspatch. It's nearly Christmas."

"Try telling that to Hitler," said her aunt as the hum of planes overhead built to a crescendo.

"Why don't we discuss *A Christmas Carol.* Who's read it?" asked Gertie. Half the assembled company raised their hands. "Splendid. What did you think?"

"Well, as you know, dear lady, my passion is military history, but I rather enjoyed it," said Mr. Reynolds, leaning on his silver-topped walking stick. "I'm hoping Hitler gets a visit from the three spirits and learns to change his ways too." There were murmurs of agreement around the shelter.

"Do you remember reading it at school?" said Miss Snipp to Miss Crow. The latter had her back to the company and appeared not to hear. "Philomena?"

Miss Crow inhaled deeply. "I do not wish to discuss it."

The others in the shelter seemed to hold their breath in almost delighted silence at the unfolding drama.

"What else did people enjoy about the book?" asked Gertie, throwing a panicked look toward Hedy.

"Tiny Tim was my favorite character," said Hedy.

"Adorable little chap," said Sylvie.

"Charming," echoed Rosaline.

"He is a metaphor for the deprivation of the poorest elements of London society, which was a theme that greatly preoccupied Dickens," said a voice. They all turned in surprise to see Cynthia Fortescue blinking out at them from the corner of the shelter, her cheeks crimson, her eyes saucer-wide, as if the sound of her own voice had surprised her too.

"That's a fascinating insight," said Gertie.

Cynthia gave a shy smile before shrinking back into the half-light.

"Would you read a little from the book, please, Gertie?" asked Hedy after a particularly loud explosion made them all jump. "I'm sure everyone would like to hear it, even if they already know the story."

There were positive murmurs around the shelter. Gertie took in their expressions. Some looked worried, others scared, others as if they were praying.

"How about I read the passage where Scrooge visits his old employer, Fezziwig, with the first spirit?"

"That's the bit with the party," said Rosaline with a sigh. "How I love a party."

"Me too," said Sylvie while their aunt rolled her eyes and tutted.

As Gertie began to read, some of the gathering inclined their heads, as if by moving toward the story they could escape into it. They were there in Fezziwig's snug warehouse, transformed now into a ballroom with music and partygoers, dancing and games. They feasted on cake and roasted meats, ate mince pies and drank beer. Gertie glanced up and noticed their expressions had changed. Their creased brows were now soothed to gentle contemplation as Gertie told them of Fezziwig and how "the happiness he gives, is quite as great as if it cost a fortune."

"What a splendid chap," said Mr. Reynolds.

When the all clear sounded, they emerged from the shelter with breathless relief. Gertie turned to speak to Miss Crow, but she was already disappearing out the door and up the street.

"I didn't realize you knew each other," she remarked to Miss Snipp.

She nodded. "We were at school together. We were the very best of friends . . ." Her voice trailed off as she stared into the middle distance.

"Are you all right, Miss Snipp?"

The woman snapped her gaze back to Gertie. "Yes, yes. I'm fine. Right well. No time to dawdle. We've had enough distractions today as it is," she said as if the Luftwaffe had been sent merely to disrupt her day.

"See you for Christmas, dear Aunt Snipp," said Rosaline with a fluttering wave.

"Yes, goodbye, Aunt Snipp," called Sylvie, clutching her sister's arm as they left in a flurry of giggles.

"Hmm," muttered Miss Snipp, disappearing back to her domain.

"Well, we live to fight another day, Mrs. Bingham," said Mr. Reynolds, doffing his hat to her before he left. "And God bless us, everyone!"

Chapter 12

Swerve me? The path to my fixed purpose
is laid with iron rails, whereon my soul is
grooved to run.

—Herman Melville, *Moby-Dick*

Christmas Day arrived crisp and clear without the usual peal of church bells but with a welcome lull in the bombing. Gertie had barely marked the festivities after Harry died and neither she nor Hedy had felt the inclination to celebrate the year before, but this year was different. Everything had changed and Gertie was compelled to make an effort, whilst Hedy was keen to embrace new traditions. Else Fischer was a Christian, and so Hedy had been used to observing certain traditions such as putting up a tree and singing carols. They decorated the house with holly from the garden and hung the glass baubles and tinsel, which

Gertie had found in an old box on top of the wardrobe, on the tree.

"It's perfect, Gertie," said Hedy, standing back to admire their handiwork. Gertie knew she was thinking of home. The telegrams still arrived most weeks, but twenty-five words could only say so much. They had hoped that Sam might have been granted leave over Christmas, but he had written the week before to report that it was impossible. Gertie wasn't surprised. Whenever she heard the planes droning overhead, her thoughts immediately flew to Sam and his fellow airmen, and a silent prayer flew with them.

She was unused to entertaining in great numbers, and yet today she would be serving dinner for six. Charles was coming and Mrs. Constantine, and after a conversation with Elizabeth Chambers, she had invited her and Billy too. Uncle Thomas had graciously declined her invitation on the basis that he "disliked Christmas intensely," preferring the company of Dickens in both book and cat form.

Gertie couldn't remember the last time she'd cooked for so many people. She was glad that her vegetable crops had been successful that year. She had plenty of potatoes and carrots, and even managed to acquire a chicken to roast.

Charles was the first to arrive. "Something smells

good, Gertie," he said as she took his coat and led him into the living room. He greeted Hedy like an old friend, and the two sat chatting companionably while Christmas carols echoed softly from the gramophone.

Mrs. Constantine arrived next. She handed over a bottle of sherry with a wink. "Something to keep out the cold."

Gertie was pouring glasses for them all when a knock at the door signaled the arrival of Billy and his mother. The little boy stood on the doorstep holding up a model spitfire for her to admire. "Happy Christmas, Gertie Bingham."

"Happy Christmas, young man. Was that a gift from Father Christmas by any chance?"

Billy nodded in delight. "And I got a bar of chocolate, a walnut, and an orange. But it was funny because the orange didn't have any peel on it."

"That's because I used it in the mixture for this," whispered Elizabeth, handing over a blue-striped basin with a cloth-tied top.

Gertie laughed. "Thank you, dear. It was good of you to make the pudding."

As they sat down for dinner, Gertie looked around at the faces of the people in this unusual gathering. If you had told her two years previously that she would be celebrating Christmas with an exiled

Russian aristocrat, a Jewish refugee, and a five-year-old boy, she would never have believed it. And yet, she couldn't imagine anywhere she'd rather be. Of course, she dearly wished that Harry were by her side, along with her parents and brother, but that was no longer the reality, and in this topsy-turvy war-ravaged world, you had to hold on to the ones who were still with you. Each person sitting at this table was without someone dear to them. Charles had lost his best friend, Billy and Elizabeth were without the boy's father, Mrs. Constantine had no family at all, and Hedy—dear Hedy—she was caught in that dreadful no-man's-land of constantly waiting and hoping for news. As she watched her laugh at something Billy said, while Charles and Mrs. Constantine discussed Russian literature and Elizabeth reached out a hand to tousle her son's hair, Gertie realized she was happy. There was no telling what tonight or tomorrow would bring, but in the glow of this moment, she felt nothing but joy.

She rose to her feet and held up her glass. "I would like to propose a toast," she said. "To friends and loved ones old and new, absent and present, but forever in our hearts. Happy Christmas."

"Happy Christmas!" they chorused.

The moment was interrupted by a knock at the door.

"Excuse me," said Gertie. The woman standing on the doorstep was a stranger, but there was something about her dark brown eyes that seemed familiar to Gertie. She was dressed in a smart red wool coat with matching hat and a fur stole over her shoulders.

"I'm most terribly sorry to bother you," she said, "but I was wondering if you knew of the whereabouts of Elizabeth Chambers."

"Mother?" said Elizabeth, appearing at Gertie's shoulder. "What on earth are you doing here?"

"Oh, Elizabeth, I had to see you."

"Grandmama!" cried Billy, bolting down the hallway into her arms. "I got a model spitfire!"

"Oh, my dear heart," said the woman, clutching him to her as tears formed in her eyes. "I'm so happy to see you."

"Would you care to come in?" asked Gertie.

"Oh, well, that would be rather—"

"No. It's all right. We can say what we need to on the doorstep," said Elizabeth, folding her arms.

"Oh, Mummy, please, can Grandmama stay?"

Elizabeth stared at her son's pleading face and sighed. "As long as we're not intruding on Gertie."

"Not at all, my dear. Your mother would be most welcome."

Elizabeth turned to her son. "Billy, why don't you show Grandmama what you got for Christmas."

"Actually, I have something for you in the car." She glanced over her shoulder, gesturing to the chauffeur, who retrieved a large box from the back seat and brought it over.

Billy's eyes grew wide. "Is that for me?"

His grandmother nodded. "Shall we take it inside?" She held out a hand to Gertie. "Lady Mary Wilcox."

The woman had such a regal air that Gertie had to fight the urge to curtsy. "Delighted to meet you. I'm Gertie Bingham. Would you care for some tea?"

"That would be most kind."

Despite her aristocratic pedigree, Gertie was tickled to see Lady Mary crawling on her hands and knees with her grandson when she returned with the tea. Much to Billy's delight, his grandmother had brought him a tin hat and a wooden rifle. "I am Sergeant Billy Chambers," he said to them all. "And I will protect you from the Jerries."

"Oh, how wonderful. Thank you, Sergeant Chambers," said Lady Mary, placing a hand on her heart.

Gertie noticed Elizabeth standing on the sidelines, watching them with a reserved expression. "Tea, dear?" she asked.

"Thank you," said Elizabeth, taking it from her.

"It's lovely to see Billy having fun," said Gertie.

"Yes. It's just a shame he can't see his grandmother more often," said Elizabeth with a note of bitterness. "Excuse me." She disappeared from the room.

Gertie was about to follow when she caught sight of the time. "Gather 'round, everyone," she said. "The King's speech is about to start."

They sat in silence. Even Billy was quiet, swooping his spitfire through the air as they listened: *We must hold fast to the spirit which binds us together now. We shall need this spirit in each of our own lives as men and women, and shall need it even more among the nations of the world. We must go on thinking less about ourselves and more for one another, for so, and so only, can we hope to make the world a better place and life a worthier thing.* Gertie caught Hedy's eye and they shared a smile.

When it was over, Lady Mary rose to her feet. "I should go now."

"Oh, please stay, Grandmama," said Billy.

She cupped his face in her hands and kissed the top of his head. "I'll see you again soon, dear heart," she said. "It was a pleasure to meet you all. God bless."

Gertie followed her out to the hall as Elizabeth emerged from the kitchen. Mother and daughter stared at each other for a moment. Lady Mary moved toward her daughter with her hand outstretched, but Elizabeth took a step back. "Please don't be angry with me, Elizabeth."

Elizabeth regarded her coldly. "How is Father?"

Lady Mary's eyes misted. "It's hard for him, you know."

"It's hard for all of us." She stared at her mother for a moment before turning away. "Thank you for Billy's gift. Goodbye," she said, disappearing back into the living room.

Lady Mary sighed before following Gertie to the door. She paused on the threshold. "Thank you for your hospitality, Mrs. Bingham. As you may have noticed, I have a turbulent relationship with my daughter, but I love her and my grandson dearly."

"I understand," said Gertie. "It's not always straightforward in families."

Lady Mary fixed her with a steady look. "Would you talk to Elizabeth, please, try to reason with her to let the boy come and stay with us? It's not safe in London, and I sense she might listen to you."

Gertie hesitated. She could see the desperation in her eyes, and yet Elizabeth was a grown woman who made her own choices regarding the welfare of her son. "I'm sorry, but I'm not sure that's my place, Lady Mary."

The woman nodded. "No. No, of course not. Well, goodbye, Mrs. Bingham."

"Goodbye."

As Christmas inched toward the new year, the ceasefire seemed to be holding and the world felt lighter somehow. Even Miss Snipp was in a good mood, having enjoyed Christmas with her sister, who not only managed to acquire a rabbit for dinner but who had gifted another to her to take home. Gertie was cautiously optimistic. The war still raged, but for the time being Hitler seemed to be leaving them be.

"I've heard he's turning his attention to Russia," said Mr. Reynolds, who was browsing a copy of *Martin Chuzzlewit.*

"I'm sure he'll receive the warmest of welcomes from Comrade Stalin," said Mrs. Constantine, handing a copy of *The Hound of the Baskervilles* to Gertie. She had exhausted Agatha Christie's oeuvre and was now turning her attention to Arthur Conan Doyle. "I must say, I do approve of your new book club choice, Mrs. Bingham," she said, nodding toward the window display for *Appointment with Death.* "I shall do my best to be here for the next air raid, although let's pray that the worst has passed."

"We can but hope," said Gertie, wrapping the book and handing it to her.

Gertie was preparing supper that evening when the siren screeched. Her first thought was of Hedy. She was at the cinema with her friend Audrey. Gertie had gifted her tickets to see the new Charlie Chaplin film for Christmas.

Hemingway stood waiting at the back door, as was his habit when he heard the siren.

"Hedy will be all right," she told him, picking up the basket containing her gas mask, ration book, and cake tin filled with the last remaining mince pies. "They'll either stay put or send them to the public shelter." Her heart was pounding in her ears as she hurried into the garden just as Elizabeth and Billy appeared through the side gate.

"Where's Hedy Fischer?" asked Billy. Gertie noticed he was wearing his tin hat and carrying his wooden rifle.

"She's at the cinema with her friend, but she'll go to the shelter. Don't worry, Billy," said Gertie, realizing she was saying this more for her own benefit.

"Should I go and escort her home?" he asked.

"No, you must stay here and protect us," said Elizabeth. "Hedy will be back soon."

"Good, because I want to hear the next chapter of Gertie and Arno's story."

They bundled into the shelter, and Gertie lit a candle. It felt strange to be here without Hedy. "Perhaps I shouldn't have let her go," said Gertie, staring at the flame.

"She's a sensible girl," said Elizabeth. "She'll be all right. The wardens will take care of them."

Gertie nodded, but her stomach was churning. It didn't matter how sensible you were or how kind or clever. Fate didn't care a jot about that. You could still be unlucky. All you could do was pray and hope that someone was listening.

They heard the familiar hum of aircraft increasing in volume on their path toward London and the thud of shells exploding in the distance. "That's our antiaircraft guns," said Billy with authority. "They stop the bad men from getting through."

It soon became clear that the bad men hadn't been stopped, as the far-off buzz quickly became a constant drone, which quickly grew into a petrifying cacophony above their heads. Gertie and Elizabeth exchanged glances as they were each hit by the realization that this raid was different. The sheer number of aircraft loaded with explosives was vast and terrifying. Elizabeth put an arm around her son and pulled him close.

A fizzing hiss followed by a flash of hot white light crackled somewhere nearby. Then there was another. And another.

"They sound like fireworks," said Billy.

"Then let's pretend that's what they are," said Gertie. "Nothing but great big fireworks."

They could hear them raining down all over London, some very close, some far away. "Actually, they are incen-dee-aries," said Billy carefully. "The bad men use them to light up their targets."

Gertie jumped as she heard one land nearby. Through a tiny gap in the shelter, she could see a green flame spitting into life. Before she had a chance to re-consider, she was on her feet and out of the shelter.

"Gertie Bingham!" cried Billy. Hemingway barked a similar protest.

Gertie grabbed one of her bigger flowerpots and dashed forward to empty the contents, daffodil bulbs and all, onto the flames, snuffing them out. Another incendiary landed three feet away, and she did the same again. "Not on my watch," she shouted at the sky.

"Stay there with Hemingway, Billy," called Elizabeth as she ran out to help her. Together they snuffed out three more before the droning stopped and the planes evaporated into the distance.

"Do you think that's it?" asked Elizabeth, staring

across the horizon toward the center of London. The sky was incandescent with hundreds of fires.

"No," said Gertie, as she caught the distant threatening murmur of yet more planes. "I think it's just the beginning. Come on. Let's get back inside."

"You were both so brave," said Billy in the earthy glow of the shelter. "I'm going to make you medals tomorrow."

Gertie stared at her trembling hands. A perfect storm of fear and anger pulsed in her chest. As they heard the first whistle and scream of bombs, Gertie's whole body twitched with rage. How dare they? This was her home. Her city. She had to do something.

"I need to look for Hedy," she told Elizabeth. "You stay here with Billy and Hemingway."

Elizabeth clutched her arm. "Be careful, Gertie."

Billy held out his tin hat. "You can borrow this, Gertie Bingham."

She plonked it on her head before grabbing a flashlight and hurrying out through the side gate. The road was pitch-black and silent, as if the street were holding its breath. Gertie kept to the shadows, taking care to shine her light downward so as not to attract attention. She coughed as the bitter tang of smoke caught in her throat and did her best to ignore the drama unfolding in the skies. Gertie had no idea where she was headed but knew she had to keep going. *Keep moving.* She heard the hiss and crackle of a fire and turned to see its flames leaping into the air. For some reason she made a move toward it.

"Trust Gertie. Out of the frying pan and into the fire," Jack would say as his sister received another telling-off from their father, usually for upsetting the governess with her smart remarks.

"Never miss a chance to stand up and fight, Gertie," Lilian told her time and again. "People will always give you a reason not to, which is precisely why you should."

Gertie amazed herself by breaking into a run. She couldn't remember the last time she'd felt so alive. So free. Even more surprisingly, she didn't feel the least bit afraid.

As she rounded the corner, Gertie could see the spire of St. Mark's engulfed in a funnel of crimson and amber. She spotted two firemen and two wardens doing their best to get the fire under control. Gertie recognized one of them immediately.

"Betty!" she shouted.

"Mrs. B! What are you doing here?"

"I'm looking for Hedy. She was at the cinema when the raid started."

"I'm sure they'll be in the public shelter. My friend Judy is a warden down there. I can try to find out what's happened as soon as we've got this under control."

"You shouldn't be out of your shelter," said the other warden to Gertie. "It's not safe."

"Let me help," she said.

"Has this woman had any formal training?" he demanded.

Betty scowled. "No, but then you hadn't either until two weeks ago, Bill." She turned to Gertie. "How are you with a stirrup pump? We've got a spare but no one to man it."

"Just show me what needs to be done," said Gertie, rolling up her sleeves.

It was hard work, but whether it was through fury or determination, Gertie kept pumping until they managed to bring most of the fire under control. "Cor, I reckon we should recruit you into the service, lady," said one of the firemen as they walked to the canteen where volunteers were serving hot tea and soup. "You're more use than Bill, that's for sure."

Gertie accepted a tin mug of tea with gratitude. She cast around the crowd, desperately searching for Betty returning with news of Hedy. The faces surrounding her were etched with soot-caked exhaustion. Volunteers sat by the roadside, drinking tea and smoking. There was an eerie silence about the place as if the assembled company was in shock, absorbing the same thought: How much longer could they endure this?

"Mrs. B!" called a voice.

Gertie looked up, spotting two recognizable forms waving to her through the darkness. As they moved into the light, Gertie leapt to her feet.

"Look who I've found!" cried Betty.

When Gertie saw Hedy's weary face, she was overcome. She darted forward, drawing her into a tight embrace as the realization hit. It was Gertie's duty to protect this girl for her mother, to keep her safe. Nothing else mattered. She knew this now. "Are you all right, Gertie?" asked Hedy.

"I am now," she said as they let go.

"I'm sorry for worrying you," said Hedy. "When the siren sounded we panicked and decided to walk back to Audrey's house."

"Oh my dear. Why didn't you go to the shelter?"

Hedy looked sheepish. "I don't know. I suppose we felt safer somehow."

"Well, it was a jolly good job you did," said Betty gravely. "There was a direct hit by the cinema. They're digging for survivors now."

Gertie and Hedy stared at one another as the realization of what might have been sank in. "Oh Gertie," whispered Hedy.

Gertie put an arm around her shoulder and pulled her close. "It's all right," she said. "You're safe. That's all that matters."

"Here you go, missus," said a kindly fireman, appearing at her elbow and holding out a hip flask. "Have a drop of this."

Gertie accepted, wincing against the sharp heat of alcohol. "Thank you," she said, handing it back to him.

"Nothing worse than when you lose sight of one of your nippers, eh?" he said, smiling at them both.

Gertie was about to correct him, but he had already gone, heading off into the darkness to wherever he was needed next. She felt Hedy rest against her shoulder and instinctively drew her closer.

"The city's getting a proper drubbing tonight," said one of the wardens. They turned to stare at the scarlet sky, fiery orange fingertips reaching heavenward as if praying for salvation.

My beloved London, thought Gertie. *How could they?*

Hedy linked an arm through Gertie's. "Let's go home."

"Shall I escort you?" asked Betty. "The bombers are concentrated over the city, but it's still dangerous."

"We'll be fine, won't we, Hedy?" said Gertie.

Hedy nodded. "We've got each other."

The streets were eerily quiet except for one black cat out on a nighttime stroll. The wind had picked up and was whistling around their ears. Gertie pulled up the collar of her coat and glanced toward the sky. The familiar thrum and drone had begun again, but the planes were all heading in the opposite direction.

"They've done their worst and now they're on their way," she murmured as they turned onto the street adjacent to hers.

"Maybe they'll sound the all clear soon," said Hedy, casting her eyes heavenward. She froze. "Gertie, look out!"

As Gertie followed her gaze, the world seemed to slow as if they were moving through treacle. She saw the underside of a German plane, backlit by the moon, a monstrous vulture above their heads. As she watched it open its hatch and hurl out a bomb, she struggled to grasp the nightmarish reality of what was happening. Gertie was familiar with the whistle and scream as these horrors hurtled toward the earth. However, she wasn't prepared for the silence. In the moment before the bomb struck, the world was muted. A split second. A gut instinct. Gertie grabbed Hedy and flung them both over the nearest garden wall, throwing herself on top of the girl in the process. She squeezed her eyes shut and held her breath. A heavy cracking thud. A heartbeat. Silence.

Gertie opened her eyes and hauled herself to a sitting position as Hedy uncurled beside her. They peered over the wall, blinking toward the large crater with its unexploded bomb poking out from the middle of it. A vast hissing monster.

"Are you all right, dear?" asked Gertie as they helped each other to their feet.

Hedy stared at her. "Yes. And you?"

"We're alive!" cried Gertie, shaking her gently. "We're alive, Hedy." They fell into each other's arms and wept for fear, for relief, for survival.

They were still clinging on to each other when the police arrived and began to evacuate the street. Shakily, Gertie and Hedy walked arm in arm, following the throng of people along the road back onto their own street. As the all clear sounded, the crowds echoed with a loud cheer.

"Gertie!" called Elizabeth, meeting them by their front gate with Billy and Hemingway in tow. "Are you all right?"

"Gertie Bingham and Hedy Fischer," cried Billy with wide, excited eyes. "There's an unexploded bomb on the next street."

"I know, dear. It missed us by a whisker."

"Gosh," said Billy with even wider eyes.

"Thank goodness you're both all right," said Elizabeth with a look of relief. She turned to her son. "Come along, Billy. We must let Gertie and Hedy go inside and you need to get to bed. That's quite enough drama for one night." She gave a cheerful wave before they disappeared.

Gertie was trembling but elated. They were alive. They were safe. They had survived another night. This was all that counted. They were fighting and would continue to fight. Gertie, Hedy, Bingham Books, and the people of Beechwood. This was her world. It was where she was meant to be, and she would defend it with all her might.

They had just reached the front door when a shout went up. Gertie turned to see Betty running along the road toward them.

"Perhaps she heard about our near miss with the bomb and wants to check we're okay," said Gertie.

As Betty reached them, she stopped in her tracks, shaking her head, her face drained of color.

"Whatever is it, Betty?" asked Gertie, with rising panic.

"I'm not sure how to tell you."

"Has something happened to Sam?" whispered Hedy.

Betty gave a vigorous shake of her head. "No. It's not that."

"Then what is it, dear? What on earth has happened?" asked Gertie.

Betty fought back tears as she spoke. "It's the bookshop, Mrs. B. It was an incendiary. The fire brigade was too late. I'm so sorry."

Hedy and Betty caught Gertie's arms as she sank to the ground. The world had pulled the rug out from beneath her yet again. After every pitfall of her life—losing Jack, her father, her mother, and then Harry—Gertie had tried to rise again, less like a phoenix and more like a wounded bird with patched-up wings. With Hedy's arrival and the reality of another war, Gertie had found new strength to fight on, to build something that helped others when they needed it most. But now that was gone forever. It was the end. Betty and Hedy tried their best to comfort her, but after years of stifling the nagging pain and sorrow, she gave in. Hedy pulled her close as Gertie buried her face in her hands and sobbed.

Chapter 13

1941

Sweet are the uses of adversity,
Which, like the toad, ugly and venomous,
Wears yet a precious jewel in his head.

—William Shakespeare, *As You Like It*

Appointment with Death. Gertie had to squint to make out the book's title from the scorched scrap of cover as she and Hedy cast around the empty charcoal shell, desperate for some grain of hope.

Gertie had seen photographs of a badly damaged bookshop not long ago with a boy sitting in the midst of the chaos reading. There was no front or back to the premises, but all the books remained intact. The thought of this photograph had persuaded Gertie to come today. Perhaps their stock would be salvageable.

They could sweep up the glass, repair the damage, and carry on as before. However, she had not fully comprehended the destructive power of an incendiary, nor its impact on a room lined with kindling in book form. The fire service had been overstretched to its breaking point that night. It arrived too late to preserve the books, and any that remained were then ruined by the jets of water that eventually quelled the fire.

"At least the sign isn't too damaged," said Hedy from outside the shop, gazing up at its singed edges and peeled gold lettering. "A little charred, but you can still read the words."

The gilt letters spelling "Bingham Books" no longer shone down at Gertie. They were as battered and bruised as she felt. The red background, which once seemed so warm and welcoming, was blackened as if the darkness of war had finally arrived in Beechwood. Gertie's eyes brimmed with tears as she cast her gaze up and down the high street. The clock that once hung proudly outside Robinson the Cobbler's had been blown clean from its fittings and smashed through the windows of Perkins's Confectioners. It was a blessing that the timing of the raid meant that no one was killed. The street was a mangled wreck of broken glass and scattered detritus. The shopkeepers were doing their best to clean up, sweeping and clearing, but it was a mammoth task. Only the Beechwood town sign remained untouched, its white horse galloping onward. Normally, Gertie would have found some crumb of hope in this, but today felt different. There was an air of resignation as young Mr. Piddock gave her a weary wave before returning to his sweeping. No one could offer comfort or optimism today. "I can't do this," she whispered.

Hedy clutched her arm. "You can, Gertie. You're strong."

Gertie shook her head. "No. I'm not strong. Not really. I have kept going all these years because I had to, but I don't want to keep going anymore."

Hedy squeezed her hand. "You're tired. We shouldn't have come here today. It was too much for you seeing the shop like this. Come on. Let's go home."

Gertie stayed in bed for a month. She left her room only for meals and air raids and accepted the latter under sufferance. What on earth was the point? She had lost everything she loved from her parents to her brother to her husband and now her beloved bookshop. If the Germans wanted her life as well, then they jolly well better come and take it. She knew what she was doing. She was stubborn enough to know when her mind was made up. Gertie Bingham had officially given up.

Hedy did all she could to coax her from this inertia. She took charge of the day-to-day management of the household, lighting a fire, preparing meals, and baking ginger biscuits, which she knew were Gertie's favorite. She plied Gertie with tea and sympathy and would read amusing extracts from Sam's letters to cheer her up.

"He said that he really enjoyed the P. G. Wodehouse book we sent him for Christmas. Apparently, there's a man in his squadron who reminds him of Gussie Fink-Nottle because he keeps newts."

"That's nice, dear," said Gertie, staring into the distance. She appreciated Hedy's efforts and knew she was being a terrible bore, but the simple fact was that Gertie had neither the desire nor the ability to rouse herself from this stupor.

In desperation, Hedy called on everyone they knew to try to lift Gertie's spirits. Mrs. Constantine visited, bringing a bottle of French brandy and the assertion that the dark clouds would dissolve because they always did. Uncle Thomas telephoned to commiserate and make the well-intentioned suggestion that Gertie was in good company, as twenty-seven publishers had similarly lost five million books on the same night thanks to "that mustachioed lunatic."

Gertie was grateful for their kindness but had no real desire to do anything except stay in bed and reread *Jane Eyre*. It was the only thing that seemed to console her, allowing her mind to bask in earlier, happier times when Harry was alive and the world shimmered with hope.

One day she was doing just this when there was a knock at her bedroom door. "Come in," she said, expecting Hedy. It was a surprise, therefore, when the door opened and Billy's small round face peered in. "Hello, young man. What are you doing here?"

He cast a furtive glance over his shoulder before inching into the room. "Mama is having tea downstairs with Hedy Fischer. She got a telegram from her mama today and is happy but also a bit sad."

Gertie felt a pang of guilt that she wasn't downstairs comforting Hedy as well. She turned to Billy. "Did your mother ask you to come up?"

"Not exactly," said Billy, toeing the carpet. "But she didn't say I couldn't either."

"Well, in that case, you better come in."

Billy marched around the bed and came to stand very close in front of Gertie, regarding her with bright eyes. "I've never been in a lady's bedroom before," he told her. "Except Mama's, of course."

"Of course. So to what do I owe the pleasure?"

He adopted a thoughtful expression. "I was very sad to hear about the fire at the bookshop. I am sorry."

"Thank you, Billy."

"And I wanted to give you this." He reached into his pocket. "Close your eyes and hold out your hand."

Gertie did as she was told. There was a jolt of warmth as he placed a small soft bag in her palm.

"You can open them now."

She stared at the red velvet pouch. "What is it?"

"Tip them out. You'll see."

Gertie upended the bag, and out scattered a collection of pennies, shillings, and a couple of shiny sixpence.

"I've saved it up. You can have it all so that you can buy a new bookshop."

Tears pricked Gertie's eyes. "Oh, Billy."

"And I collect stamps too. We could sell my collection if this isn't enough."

Gertie reached out and held him by the shoulders. "You are the kindest boy I have ever met. Thank you."

"Billy Chambers. Come down here at once!" cried his mother from the bottom of the stairs. He froze.

"It's all right, Elizabeth," called Gertie. "I said he could come in."

Billy recoiled at the sound of his mother marching up the stairs. "Gertie, I'm so sorry Billy disturbed you." She turned to her son. "Young man, you will go to bed without a story tonight."

"Oh but, Mama."

"William Chambers. You will not talk back to your mother."

William Chambers knitted his brow together in an indignant scowl.

Elizabeth caught sight of the money bag on the bed. "Is that yours, Billy?" He gave a slow nod.

"He offered it to me so that I could buy a new bookshop," said Gertie.

Elizabeth blinked in surprise. "Oh. Well."

"It's the most delightful thing I've ever heard," said Gertie.

Elizabeth's face softened. "You shouldn't have come up here, but it was nice of you to offer it to Mrs. Bingham."

"Does that mean I can still have my story please, Mama? I want to know what happens to Peter Rabbit and whether he ever gets out of the watering can."

"We'll see," said Elizabeth. "Now come along. Let's leave Mrs. Bingham in peace."

"Goodbye, Billy. Thank you for coming to visit me." Gertie put the coins back in the bag and held it out to him. "I think you should keep the money safe at home for now."

Billy gave her a sage nod. "All right, Gertie Bingham. You let me know when you need it."

"I will."

Elizabeth ushered Billy from the room and paused in the doorway. "You were so kind to us when we first moved here. Please let me know if I can return the favor."

"Thank you, dear," said Gertie. "Is Hedy all right?"

Elizabeth's eyes misted. "I think she's the bravest woman I've ever met. I may not be on the best of terms with my family, but I couldn't bear not knowing where they are or what's happening to them."

"Thank you for comforting her."

Elizabeth smiled. "As I said, Gertie, you've both always been so kind. Now it's our turn."

Gertie nodded, but her heart told her otherwise. Everyone was trying so hard to help, but she knew deep down that there was nothing to be done.

Only Charles seemed to understand how Gertie felt. "I wish I could tell you to pull yourself together, but I'd be a dreadful hypocrite if I did. I barely left the house for a year after returning from the last war," he told her as they took tea in the living room during one of her rare excursions downstairs.

"I remember." She recalled visits to his house with Harry as they desperately tried to coax him from his torpor. When he eventually emerged, something within him had changed. He was the same dear man, but there was a steeliness about him, an almost devil-may-care attitude.

"However, I have to tell you that I don't think this war is going to end anytime soon."

"So I need to keep on fighting?"

Charles shrugged. "What else can you do?"

Gertie stared at the collection of family photographs on the end table, the smiling, hopeful faces of the ones she'd lost. "I don't know, Charles. I'm not sure I have the strength to keep fighting. It would be different if Harry were still here, or Jack or Mama and Papa."

Charles nodded. He moved to the mantelpiece, plucking a small pewter frame from the shelf. "Wasn't this taken at the party when you opened the bookshop?" he said, taking his place beside her once more.

Gertie smiled as she took the picture from him. They were all there: her parents, Uncle Thomas, Jack, Charles, Harry, and her. Her mother was standing at her elbow, glowing with pride, while Gertie stared out with a look of wistful determination. "I insisted we have the party because we had virtually no customers, except Miss Crow, who visited in her official capacity as town busybody. I remember Harry asking if he could help her find something to read, and she looked at him as if he'd suggested they tango naked along the street."

Charles laughed. "Treasured memories, eh, Gertie?"

She nodded. "Although that was the night I heard Father arguing with Jack. They never saw eye to eye after that."

Charles stayed silent.

"Jack always had a boiling temper. Harry seemed to think it was about gambling, but I never did get to the bottom of it."

"Is that what Harry said?" asked Charles, his eyes fixed on her face.

Gertie nodded. "I don't suppose Jack ever told you what happened, did he? I know you spent quite a bit of time at his club back then."

Charles turned his gaze toward the fireplace. "I'm not sure. It was a long time ago."

"Indeed. It feels like a different life somehow. Anyway, it's all in the past, isn't it? These silly spats we have. They don't matter in the end, do they?"

"No," said Charles. "They don't matter a jot."

Gertie rested her head on his shoulder as they sat

side by side staring at the photograph. Two careworn friends wrung out by life and loss but comforted by these shared recollections.

"I'm going away in a few days," said Charles after a while.

Gertie turned to look at him. "Is this for work?"

He nodded. "I should be back in a week."

Gertie noticed he didn't meet her eye. "It's nothing dangerous, is it, Charles?"

"Gertie. We're living through a war. Walking down the street is dangerous, as well you know."

She grasped his hand. "Be careful. I couldn't bear to lose you too."

He leaned forward to kiss her cheek. "We're survivors, you and me. Never forget that."

"Clinging to the wreckage of life."

Charles smiled. "No one I'd rather cling to it with."

Chapter 14

The beginning is always today.

—Mary Shelley, *Short Stories, Vol. 2*

During her sixty-odd years, Gertie had come to realize that fate's messengers appeared in many guises. Sometimes it was obvious, as when she first met Harry in her father's bookshop. On other occasions fate needed a little nudge, as during the events leading up to Hedy's arrival. This time, it arrived unexpectedly on her doorstep at approximately quarter past three on a wet afternoon in February.

Hedy was at the pictures with Betty and Gertie was upstairs reading a Dorothy L. Sayers novel when there was a loud knock at the door. Gertie sighed and put down her book with reluctance. She checked her appearance in the mirror and wondered when her face had become so round. It might have something to do with Hedy's exceptional baking. She tidied her hair and went downstairs, meeting Hemingway in the hall. Gertie opened the door, half expecting it to be Hedy having forgotten her key. She was therefore rather surprised to be staring into the glowering face of Miss Crow.

"Good afternoon, Mrs. Bingham. Is this a convenient time?" she asked, casting a critical eye toward the biscuit crumbs on Gertie's blouse.

As Gertie surreptitiously brushed them to the floor, Hemingway fell upon the precious morsels with delight. "Of course," she said. "Would you care for some tea?"

Miss Crow looked momentarily unsure, as if no one had ever offered her tea before. "Yes. All right. Thank you."

"Go through to the living room. I won't be a moment."

When Gertie returned, Miss Crow was standing by the mantelpiece looking awkward. "Please. Do take a seat."

She did as she was told, perching on the edge of an armchair as Gertie handed her the tea. "Thank you."

"So," said Gertie, taking her place on the sofa. "What can I do for you?"

Miss Crow fixed her with a beady-eyed gaze. "You must open up the bookshop again."

Of all the sentences Gertie expected to come out of Miss Crow's mouth, this was one of the unlikeliest, along with *You're looking lovely today, Mrs. Bingham,* and *Let me share my rations with you.* "Beg pardon?" she said.

Miss Crow frowned as if addressing a half-wit. "Your bookshop," she said slowly. "You need to reopen it."

Gertie blinked at her. "But it's been destroyed."

"Well," said Miss Crow, fiddling with the handle of her cup. "The thing is, I've been talking to Eleanora."

"Miss Snipp?"

"Yes. We fell out, you see, after school. It was over a silly thing. A young man, actually."

Gertie's eyes widened at the idea of Miss Snipp and Miss Crow competing for the same beau.

"He ended up marrying someone else in the end, so it was all for nothing."

"I see," said Gertie, bewildered but relishing the story nonetheless.

"Anyway," continued Miss Crow. "After what happened to my nephew and that night when your shop was destroyed, I started to realize how foolish I'd been. So I went to see Eleanora and we've made amends."

"I'm delighted for you, but I'm still not sure what this has to do with the bookshop."

"It's fate," she said with a note of exasperation. "It's because of the bookshop that we rekindled out friendship. I came in to get that book for my nephew's boy. *Treasure Island.* He loved it by the way." She avoided Gertie's eye as she continued. "The thing is, I've never been very good at reading. Eleanora has been helping me so that I can read to young Fred."

"That's wonderful, Miss Crow."

"Yes, yes, but don't you see?" said the woman, flapping her hands with impatience.

"Not really."

"You have to reopen the bookshop."

Gertie shifted in her seat. "I'm afraid I can't."

"If it's the damage you're worried about, you needn't be. I've spoken to Mr. Travers. He says it's structurally sound. Everything can be repaired."

Except hearts, thought Gertie. "I'm grateful to you for taking the time to tell me all this, Miss Crow, but the answer is still no."

Miss Crow frowned. "May I ask why?"

Gertie sighed. "I built that business over twenty-five years with my husband. I can't start again from scratch."

"Well," said Miss Crow, putting down her teacup and standing up. "I suppose there's no more to be said."

"I suppose there isn't. I'm sorry you've had a wasted trip."

Miss Crow made for the door but paused as she caught sight of a photograph of Harry on the mantelpiece. It had been taken shortly after he qualified as a librarian and was one of Gertie's favorites. "It was a great loss to Beechwood when Mr. Bingham died," she said.

"That's kind of you to say."

"He was a nice man," said Miss Crow. "Kind."

"Yes. He was."

"I couldn't imagine him giving up on his community."

And there it was. Fate. Not stroking her cheek with a velvet glove but striking her in the face with an iron fist. Gertie boiled with indignant rage. She wasn't about to let Philomena Crow get the upper hand. This woman had no idea of the pain she'd endured. "How dare you?" she stammered. "I have lost everything."

"Have you?" said Miss Crow, her eyes flashing. "You still have this house. You still have that young woman who cares about you."

Gertie flushed with shame.

"She called on Eleanora, by the way, because she was concerned and wanted to know if anything could be done. She's the reason I'm here in the first place. But no, don't you worry. You've lost everything. Stay here feeling sorry for yourself." She straightened her shoulders and fixed Gertie with a cold stare. "Everyone has lost something. You're no different from the rest of us. And you're a coward if you give up now."

Gertie opened her mouth to protest, but much as it pained her, she knew Miss Crow was right. She was giving up. She was hiding. Avoiding the world. Feeling sorry for herself. It had to stop. She owed it to Hedy, to her parents, to Jack, to dear Harry. Most of all, she owed it to herself. She turned to Miss Crow. "You mentioned that Mr. Travers said everything can be repaired?"

The woman gave a brief nod. "Come to the shop at nine A.M. sharp tomorrow. You'll see."

Gertie couldn't have been more surprised if Clark Gable himself had offered his hand in marriage. As she and Hedy stepped through the doorway of the bookshop the next day, it felt as if every person who'd ever been welcomed across the threshold of Bingham Books was there. Miss Snipp's soot-blotched face was frowning at the wall she was scrubbing as if daring it to remain grubby. Elizabeth Chambers and Mrs. Wise were heaving sacks of rubbish out through the back door. Even Mrs. Constantine was there, adding a touch of glamour to the proceedings, her hair tied in a magenta silk headscarf, sweeping the floor with elegant care. "Good morning, my dears," she said, glancing up from her industry.

"Good morning," said Gertie, her voice cracking a little.

"Let me help you with that, Mrs. Constantine," said Hedy.

"Thank you, my dear. Mr. Reynolds and I were supposed to be taking turns, but he seems rather occupied at present," she said, nodding toward the old man, who was propped up in the corner on a chair, head nodding against his chest, a copy of Churchill's *Amid These Storms* dropped at his feet.

"Ah, Mrs. Bingham. Just the woman," said Gerald Travers, appearing from the back of the shop. "Now I hope you don't mind, but I've had a mate of mine who knows about these things check everything over to be sure. Belt and braces, if you like. Structurally, it's tickety-boo. And as luck would have it, the door to the shelter was closed and thick as a cement block, so . . ."

"The books?"

"See for yourself," he said, gesturing like a magician about to reveal a trick.

Gertie stepped forward and pushed open the soot-cloaked door. "They're still here," she whispered. It was like walking into a room of old friends. She spied Jane Eyre, Bertie Wooster, David Copperfield, Monsieur Poirot, the March daughters. They'd been there all the time, waiting for her. It didn't even matter that the stocks were low. The books were enough. She picked up a copy of *Winnie-the-Pooh* and flicked through the pages. She could smell the ash and sulfur, but behind them was the comfortingly fusty scent of books.

"I think with a bit of elbow grease, we should be able to get you up and running in no time," said Mr. Travers.

Gertie reached out to grasp his hands as she blinked back tears. "I'm very grateful to you."

He patted her hand. "And I was grateful to you for all your kindness when my Beryl was laid low, Mrs. Bingham. It's the Beechwood way."

The Beechwood way. Gertie smiled as she made her way back into the shop. "Thank you," she said to the gathered helpers. "Thank you all. I had no idea people cared so deeply about the bookshop."

"It is so much more than a bookshop, Mrs. Bingham," said Miss Snipp reproachfully. "It is a precious treasure trove of knowledge and imagination. Books have the power to change the very course of history, and they will help us win this war, you mark my words."

"Hear, hear," said Mrs. Wise, looking up from her sweeping. "My Ted wouldn't have the first clue about hanging a picture if it weren't for that book you recommended to him, Mrs. Bingham. By the way, he said he'll come after work and help repair the shelves whenever you need him to."

"Yes, and Mr. Reynolds said he had some old paint he could donate," said Mrs. Constantine. "Didn't you, Wally? Wally!"

Mr. Reynolds woke with a start. "What? Who's there? Try that again, Adolf, and I'll knock your block off!" He blinked at them in astonishment as he realized where he was. "Sorry, I must have dropped off."

"And I can repaint the Bingham Books sign," said Elizabeth. "I was thinking of a little gold phoenix to mark a new beginning."

"I don't know what to say," said Gertie, looking 'round at them all. "I can't thank you enough. Truly."

"You don't need to say anything," said Miss Crow, "but I do hope those aren't your best clothes." She held out a broom. "Your bookshop needs you."

Over the course of the next few weeks, Gertie watched with pride and gratitude as Bingham Books began to reemerge, reminding her of one of Harry's dormant magnolia buds and his assertion that "the world always begins anew." How right he'd been and how glad she was that she'd been persuaded not to give up and to accept help. This assistance came in many forms, some more useful than others. The Finch sisters turned up one morning to help with the painting but were soon sent away by their aunt when they proved to be nothing but a distraction for some of the younger male volunteers. Miss Crow surprised everyone with her eagle eye when it came to aligning shelves, and of course Mr. Travers was always on hand, bringing a handful of new ARP colleagues every day to fix, rebuild, paint, and varnish until all that remained to do was restock the shelves. A few days before the grand reopening, Gerald arrived early with a fellow warden, Evan Williams, a giant of a man who had impressed everyone by managing to move the large oak counter into place without breaking a sweat and whose wife made the best Welsh cakes this side of the River Severn.

"Thought we'd help you with the finishing touches,

Mrs. Bingham," said Gerald. "And Evan and I are keen to know what your next book club title will be."

"Oh gosh, I hadn't given it much thought. Any suggestions?"

"Well, you know I'll always plump for Mr. Steinbeck," said Gerald.

Evan reached a great paw-like hand into his pocket and pulled out a book. "May I humbly suggest this, Mrs. Bingham? It feels very appropriate. My wife and I both enjoyed it a great deal."

Gertie accepted the book with a smile. "Thank you, Mr. Williams. I look forward to reading it."

It was no surprise to Gertie that on the day they reopened, Mrs. Constantine was the first over the threshold. Hemingway greeted his old friend with tail-wagging delight before coming to sit before her like the most obedient dog in the world.

"I have missed you, my dears," she said, reaching into her bag and rewarding him with half a mutton chop.

"Are you talking to us or the books?" asked Gertie.

"Both," said Mrs. Constantine with a fond smile. "And now to business, Gertie. I am in need of a new detective if you have one. I couldn't get on with Sherlock Holmes. Far too arrogant. Reminded me of an uncle I particularly disliked."

"I think I may have just the thing," said Gertie, retrieving a copy of a Dorothy L. Sayers novel. "Lord Peter Wimsey. The author claims he's a mixture of Fred Astaire and Bertie Wooster."

"Sounds divine. I'll take it." She turned to Hedy. "And how are you, my dear? Any news?"

Hedy looked up from the orders book. "I had a letter from Sam last week. He's been promoted to corporal. He's also seen Betty since she joined the WAAF. He says she's as annoying as ever, but it was good to be able to keep an eye on her."

Mrs. Constantine chuckled. "He's a good boy. Anything from home?"

"Not since the telegram from Mother last month. Everyone was fine then."

Mrs. Constantine took her hand and squeezed it. "That's as good as it can be, my dear," she said. "And what is this?" She picked up a copy of *How Green Was My Valley* from a pile on the counter.

"It's our new book club title, recommended to me by one of the ARP wardens," said Gertie. "It's about a Welsh community helping one another through difficult times. The characters are wonderful."

"How apt," said Mrs. Constantine, placing it on top of her other book. "I'll take it."

Chapter 15

1943

Who so loves believes the impossible.

—Elizabeth Barrett Browning

Archibald Sparrow was a tall, shy man who had trained as a vicar at his mother's behest but left the calling when he stopped believing in the God who "allowed my two brothers to perish during the Great War." He had been exempt from conscription himself owing to astonishingly poor eyesight, which meant he was forced to read his beloved poetry through thick-lensed tortoiseshell spectacles that gave him an expression of constant surprise. He would spend hours at a time browsing the shelves of Bingham Books, usually when the shop was at its quietest. As soon as it became busy, he would either make a hurried purchase or scuttle away without buying anything. Gertie was rather fond of this slightly awkward fellow. He reminded her of Harry when they first met.

"Good morning, Mr. Sparrow. Are you after anything in particular today?" she asked as he appeared one day.

"G-G-Good morning, Mrs. B-B-Bingham," he answered in hushed tones. He had a soft, gentle way of speaking. Gertie noticed that instead of a barked greeting, Hemingway would always approach him with a benign tail wag. Archibald would lay his hand upon the dog's head in reply as if offering a blessing. "I am just b-b-browsing, thank you."

"Of course. Do let me know if there's anything you need."

He touched the brim of his hat in reply and made a beeline for the poetry shelves. The bell above the door to the bookshop rang and Gerald Travers crossed the threshold.

"*War and Peace*, Mrs. Bingham," he said by way of a greeting. "Do you have it, please?"

Gertie fetched three red cloth volumes from the shelf. Since his rekindled love of reading, Mr. Travers had become one of her best customers. "It's our most popular book at the moment, so you're lucky I have stock," she said. "It will keep you entertained for a good while."

"Gosh," said Gerald, eyeing the books as one might view the summit of Everest. "Well, this war seems to be never-ending, so I may as well choose something to keep me occupied."

"Ah, my dear Mr. Travers," called a voice so booming it nearly caused Mr. Sparrow to drop the volume of Keats's poetry he was perusing. They turned to see Margery Fortescue sweep in through the doorway, seeming to fill every nook and cranny with her personality as she did. She wore a bottle-green Harris Tweed uniform finished with a porkpie hat that barely clung to her immaculate cloud of dark gray hair. Cynthia followed in her wake, similarly dressed, carrying a clipboard.

Mr. Travers's eyes sparkled as he turned to introduce them. "Have you met Mrs. Fortescue?" he asked Gertie.

"Not formally," she said, offering her hand. "Gertie Bingham."

Mrs. Fortescue issued a beatific smile as she accepted. "Margery Fortescue, head of the local Women's Voluntary Service. Pleased to make your acquaintance. And this is my daughter and deputy, Cynthia."

Cynthia flushed beetroot red at the mention of her name.

"So," said Mrs. Fortescue, casting a critical eye around the shop. "Did Mr. Travers tell you the news?"

"I don't think so?" said Gertie, glancing at Gerald.

Mr. Travers looked nonplussed. "News?"

Margery frowned slightly. "About the WVS's need for new premises."

"Oh yes," said Gerald. "The Ministry for Food is taking over the village hall—"

Margery cut him off. "They're not taking over. We are vacating the premises. Our needs are somewhat different," she said through clenched teeth.

Cynthia gazed up at her mother in confusion. "Wasn't it because of the kerfuffle after the 'knitting with dog hair' demonstration, Mummy? Didn't it end up contaminating a batch of damson jam?"

"It took hours to sweep up that Pekingese hair," said Gerald gravely.

Mrs. Fortescue looked thunderous. "It had nothing to do with that. There was merely a clash in the time-tabling of our activities, and as the WVS is a vital cog in the machine of war . . ."

"Vital," echoed Gerald with a vehement nod.

". . . the powers that be deemed it necessary for us to have access to a space exclusively for our use. And as the premises next door have been vacant for some time, we are to be neighbors, Mrs. Bingham. A bookshop and the Women's Voluntary Service. Rather an incongruous mix, one might say, but I'm sure we won't get in each other's way." She issued this statement like a challenge.

Gertie straightened her shoulders. "I do hope not. Please call on us if you need anything."

"Oh, I very much doubt that we'll be calling on you. We're the ones who offer the help, you see," said Margery, raising herself to her full, not inconsiderable height.

"Well, perhaps we can offer some respite from your hard work with a reading recommendation," said Gertie, as Hedy appeared from the back of the shop carrying a pile of books.

Mrs. Fortescue frowned. "I've never been a reader myself. I prefer opera. Cynthia here always has her nose in a book, don't you, dear?"

Her daughter offered a small squeak in reply.

"Yes, I've seen you in the shop on occasion," said Gertie. The woman gave a timid nod. "This is Hedy Fischer, by the way. She works here."

Cynthia stared at Hedy in wonder as if she'd just been introduced to the Queen.

Hedy smiled. "Hello. This is our latest book club choice if you are interested."

Cynthia took the book with reverent awe.

"*The Code of the Woosters?*" said Margery, snorting with derision. "Sounds like some dreadful communist propaganda pamphlet."

"It's P. G. Wodehouse, Mummy. He's very funny," said Cynthia.

Margery Fortescue folded her arms and fixed her daughter with a long, hard stare. "War is not the time for levity, Cynthia. Now come along, we must show Mr. Travers what needs to be done next door. Good day, Mrs. Bingham, Miss Fischer." And with that, Margery Fortescue swept out as she had swept in, like a swan, dignified yet not to be crossed.

Gerald looked from Margery's disappearing form to his unpurchased volumes to Gertie.

"Don't worry, Mr. Travers, I'll keep them to one side for you."

"Thank you, Mrs. Bingham," he said, hurrying after the formidable woman.

Cynthia wavered, clearly wishing she could stay a little longer. "Cynthia!" called Margery from next door with surprising volume. "Where have you got to?"

"Goodbye," she said, hurrying toward the door.

"Excuse me?" The voice was so soft that Gertie was surprised Cynthia heard him. She turned to see

Archibald Sparrow walking toward her. "You d-d-dropped this," he said, holding out one of her mustard leather gloves.

"Thank you," said Cynthia in a similarly hushed tone.

Gertie and Hedy exchanged glances as the pair held each other's gaze for a heartbeat.

"Archibald Sparrow," he said.

"Cynthia!" bellowed Margery again.

"I have to go," said Cynthia. "Sorry."

Archibald placed a volume of Elizabeth Barrett Browning's poetry on the counter and sighed. "Just this p-p-please, Mrs. Bingham."

"Well," said Gertie after he'd gone. "I feel as if I've just watched a Shakespeare play. We've had love, drama, intrigue. And Margery Fortescue is certainly a force of nature."

Hedy laughed. "I wonder if Hitler knows what he's up against."

Gertie was certain she could have set her watch by Else Fischer's telegrams. They arrived every month at almost precisely the same time. Some people might think it was difficult to convey everything you needed to say in just twenty-five words, but Hedy's mother always managed it. Gertie often mused that when life was cruel, there wasn't much to say except "I love you." It was all you needed to hear. Today's telegram had a different tone, however.

"What do you think she means by 'traveling to the east'?" asked Hedy, frowning at the words as if willing them to offer the answers she craved.

Gertie could see the desperation in her eyes and longed to offer some nugget of hope, but her telephone conversation with Charles the previous week weighed on her mind. He had recently returned from another trip. Gertie didn't ask where he'd been. She thought it best not to somehow.

"How is Hedy?" he asked. "Has she heard anything from her family?"

There was a tone to his voice that suggested he knew something. "Only that they're still in Theresienstadt in Czechoslovakia after they were moved there last year. Why?"

He cleared his throat. "No reason. There are just a great number of rumors flying around at the moment."

"What rumors?"

"Only that, Gertie. Rumors. I wouldn't want to worry you or Hedy unnecessarily. Especially Hedy."

Gertie sighed. "Oh, Charles. This blasted war. When will it end?"

"I think the bigger question isn't when but how?"

Now, all Gertie could do was offer Hedy a reassuring smile. "I don't think you should worry. This proves that your family is well and able to send you messages."

"But where are they going?"

"I wish I knew, but war makes everything uncertain."

Huge tears formed in Hedy's eyes. "I want my mother, Gertie. I miss her so much."

Gertie wrapped her arms around Hedy as she sobbed. She remembered when Hedy had first arrived, how reticent she'd been to offer an embrace, and yet now, it felt like the most natural action in the world. Hemingway appeared by her side, resting his great soft head on Hedy's lap.

"I know you do, my dear," said Gertie. "I know. I wish I could wave my magic wand and bring them all here. Your lovely mama, your dear papa, your handsome brother."

"And Mischa?" said Hedy, stroking Hemingway's ears.

"Oh, of course Mischa. She would be guest of honor."

"You would like my family."

Gertie reached over to brush away Hedy's tears. "I feel as if I know them already from everything you've told me."

"Do you think I'll ever see them again?"

Gertie's mind churned as she searched for the right

words. "It's my dearest wish that you will. All we can do is hope and pray."

"I feel useless," said Hedy. "What can we do to bring an end to all this if we're not allowed to fight?"

Hedy had a point, and it frustrated Gertie to the core. They were urged to "Dig for Victory," save for the war effort, "Keep Mum," but what good would that do if the war rumbled on much longer?

"I think that if Margery Fortescue were running the show, we'd have the war done and dusted by teatime."

"Maybe we should join forces."

Gertie raised her eyebrows. "Maybe we should."

Margery Fortescue was proving to be something of a thorn in Gertie's side. It was clear that she deemed the bookshop to be small potatoes in the war effort. One day, an air raid caused their paths to collide.

"Could Mrs. Fortescue and her volunteers use your shelter please, Mrs. Bingham?" called Gerald from the bookshop doorway, as the siren sounded. "Theirs isn't properly set up yet."

"And whose fault is that, eh, Mr. Travers?" said Margery, sweeping through the door, scowling at the books as if they had caused her great offense. "This is highly irregular, but I suppose it will do. Come along, ladies. Follow me." She led them toward the back of the shop. Gerald gave Gertie a wincing smile before he left.

"Yes, it's this way," said Gertie, grudgingly impressed by this woman's ability to take charge of every situation she faced.

"Ooh, it's cozy in here," said Emily Farthing, one of Margery's champion knitters, as they all gathered in the shelter and Gertie closed the door.

"Usually we discuss a title from our book club during air raids," said Gertie. "This month's book is *The Code of the Woosters*, by P. G. Wodehouse. Has anyone read it?"

"Usually, we sing songs to rally our spirits during air raids," countered Margery.

"I've r-r-read it, Mrs. B-B-Bingham," said a voice from the corner of the shelter. Margery glared at the voice.

"Mr. Sparrow," said Gertie, throwing a relieved glance toward Hedy. "I didn't realize you were here. Would you like to tell us a little bit about it?"

Archibald looked as if he'd rather run out into the street and take his chances against one of Hitler's Messerschmitts than speak before this group of women, particularly Margery. She was regarding him with the flared-nostril disdain of a person who has recently encountered an unpleasant odor. "Um, well, I'm not sure . . ."

Another voice spoke up. "It all begins when Bertie Wooster's Aunt Dahlia instructs him to dupe an antiques dealer into selling her an eighteenth-century cow creamer. However, when Bertie arrives at the shop, he discovers that Sir Watkyn Bassett, a local magistrate, is there with Roderick Spode, the fascist leader of the Saviours of Britain. Sir Watkyn has used trickery to obtain the creamer for himself. Aunt Dahlia then sends Bertie to the Bassetts' house to steal the creamer. Things get jolly complicated when Bertie's pal Gussie Fink-Nottle asks him for help in the matter of his forthcoming marriage to Sir Watkyn's daughter, Madeline. However, due to various misunderstandings, Madeline thinks Gussie is being unfaithful and decides she loves Bertie instead. In the meantime, Aunt Dahlia steals the creamer and insists that Bertie hide it at his flat. Sir Watkyn wants to have Bertie imprisoned for theft, but luckily Bertie knows that Roderick Spode secretly runs a ladies' underwear shop called Eulalie Soeurs and persuades him to take the blame, otherwise Bertie will discredit him by revealing this information to his fascist followers. In the end, Bertie's butler, the ever-faithful Jeeves, helps to rescue Bertie from being engaged by mistake, and they embark on a cruise of Europe."

Only the thrum and drone of the overhead planes could be heard as everyone turned in amazement toward Cynthia Fortescue, whose cheeks were burning scarlet and who was a little out of breath after this plot summation. "Gosh," said Archibald.

"Bravo," said Gertie, exchanging a smile with Hedy.

"Put me down for a copy, Mrs. Bingham," said Emily. "You'll have one too, won't you, Mrs. Wise? You love a caper."

The woman next to her nodded. "I do, dearie. This Bertie Wooster sounds like a good lad."

"He's a bit of a dolt," said Cynthia, sitting up taller in her seat. "But the real hero is Jeeves. He's jolly clever and makes sure Bertie doesn't get into too many scrapes."

"What about Roderick Spode?" asked Hedy. "What did you think of him?"

"It's a b-b-brilliant piece of p-p-political satire by Wodehouse," said Archibald, directing his comment to the far wall. "To p-p-pillory fascism makes it less frightening somehow."

"And gives one courage to fight it too," said Cynthia, nodding.

Archibald risked a glance in Cynthia's direction. "I couldn't agree more."

Only Margery remained tight-lipped during this entire conversation, occasionally huffing with impatience like an old steam engine. When the all clear sounded, she leapt to her feet. "Right, come along, ladies. That's enough time wasted. Thank you for your shelter, Mrs. Bingham." She marched back out through the shop, throwing one final comment over her shoulder before she left. "Remember, we fight for victory, we save for victory, we dig for victory. We do not *read* for victory."

Gertie had always relished a challenge, particularly when she knew there was an opinion that needed to be changed. In her youth, she would have very likely strode right up to Margery Fortescue and set her straight. However, Gertie knew that sometimes people needed to be coaxed, and in her heart of hearts, she sensed that she and Margery might even share common ground in the wasteland of widowhood. Gertie also admired the way she went about her business. She organized her troops, as she called them, with the military precision of a field marshal. On Mondays, her volunteer knitters would arrive, the click-clacking of their needles filling the air with industry as they produced endless quantities of socks and scarves. Wednesdays were "Make Do and Mend" days, when her army of expert seamstresses would repair bag loads of uniforms sent from all over the country. On Fridays, they welcomed anyone who needed help as a result of the bombings. They would try to find them new homes if needed, offer bags of clothes or other essentials, and generally provide much-needed tea and sympathy. All the while, Mrs. Fortescue produced countless cups of refreshment from the "Old General," as she called the water boiler, which hissed in the corner of the room like a permanently deflating tire.

Gertie particularly enjoyed Fridays. The shop next door came alive with noisy children, weary mothers carrying babies, bewildered elderly people in need of help or just a good cup of tea. Margery was in her element on these days. Gertie noticed how she doled out bags of clothes, toys, and kindness with a gentle touch. Gone was the bossiness of Mondays and Wednesdays, and out came the simple care of a woman trying to help others.

One Friday, Gertie dared to step next door with a box under her arm. "I wondered if these might be of any use?" she said. "They're secondhand picture books. I thought the children might like them."

Margery regarded the offering with pursed lips, ready to refuse.

"Mama, look," said Cynthia, uncharacteristically bold as she lifted a copy of *Alice's Adventures in Wonderland* from the box. "You used to read this to me when I was a child. We loved looking at the pictures together. The white rabbit reminded us of Father."

Margery's face seemed to crumple as a maelstrom of emotions flitted across it. "Yes," she whispered. "I do remember." She straightened her uniform and picked up the box. "Thank you, Mrs. Bingham. Most generous. How are things at your bookshop?" She delivered the word "bookshop" as if inquiring after an illness.

Gertie refused to be deterred. "Oh yes. Jolly good, thank you."

"I'm so glad," she said, taking a seat and beginning to sort through a basket of clothes. "Well. We're rather busy, so if that's all?"

"How does one go about volunteering?" The words leapt from Gertie's mouth before she had time to stop them. "I'm asking for myself and Hedy as well."

Mrs. Fortescue rose, regarding her with a critical eye. She was taller than most men Gertie knew. She was certainly taller than Gertie. "Can you sew?"

Gertie pulled a face. "Not really. Miss Deeble, my sewing teacher at school, said I produced the worst blanket stitch she'd ever seen."

"Oh dear."

"Quite. But Hedy has inherited her mother's skills as a seamstress."

"Very good. Tell her to come and see me. If you can't sew, can you knit?"

"A little. Although I made my father a pair of socks once and he said he would only wear them on Sundays because they were so holey." One of the volunteers snorted with laughter.

"Miss Farthing. Please," said Mrs. Fortescue, who was clearly not a fan of idle humor. "Well, are you any good at making tea?"

"Oh yes. Olympic standard."

"Very well. We run mobile canteens for the civil defense operations every night. Shall I put you down for some shifts?"

"Absolutely."

Mrs. Fortescue held out her hand. "Welcome to the Women's Voluntary Service, Mrs. Bingham."

Chapter 16

We must go on, because we can't turn back.

—Robert Louis Stevenson, *Treasure Island*

Gertie heaved the Old General onto the counter of the mobile canteen and set about filling it with copious jugs of water. She checked her watch and frowned. It wasn't like Margery Fortescue to be late. Over the past few months they had served more than a dozen shifts together, and Margery was always there before she arrived, a bustling storm of efficiency. Gertie didn't find her the easiest person to be with. She was curt yet polite in their interactions, but whenever a weary member of the civilian defense service appeared in desperate need of a little cheer and a cup of sustenance, she was transformed.

Gertie recalled one particular night when a young ARP warden, who was around the same age as Hedy, appeared. He was returning from an incident at a pub around the corner—a direct hit where the whole building had crumpled like a tin can. They had spent hours searching for survivors, digging in vain through the wreckage. The boy's eyes were as wide as dinner plates as he approached the canteen. Gertie couldn't remember the last time she'd seen anyone look as pale or afraid. He was muttering under his breath. Gertie turned to point him out to Margery, but she was already out of the truck, wrapping a blanket around the young boy.

"We couldn't save them," he told her. "There was nothing left. Just arms and legs. And . . ."

"I know," said Margery in soothing tones. "It's ghastly, but there's nothing you could have done. You must rest now."

"Here, Mrs. Fortescue," said Gertie, holding out a mug of tea. "I've put three sugars in it for the shock."

"Thank you, Mrs. Bingham." She held the mug to the boy's lips. "You must drink this. It will make you feel a little better."

"Legs and arms," he said to her, voicing it like a question, stupefied with horror.

"Hush now, dear. Come with me. You can rest now. You need to rest," she said, leading him away.

Gertie watched them go. It was clear that beneath

Margery Fortescue's robust, tweed-clad exterior lay a large, soft heart.

Despite Margery's brusque ways, Gertie enjoyed her night shifts at the canteen. She had expected it to be a fairly rudimentary operation, rather like going on a camping expedition, but in fact, Margery always seemed to have the very best of provisions. Along with sufficient tea to quench the thirst of half of London and cigarettes, there were sandwiches, pies, sausages, Cornish pasties, cake, biscuits, and, on one occasion, a bread pudding.

"An army runs on its stomach," Margery would say with authority as she poured mug after mug of tea. "And this army needs us to feed it."

When Gertie saw the grateful ash-and-grease-stained faces of the men and women after a shift fighting fires or dealing with the mangled ruins of buildings and bodies, she knew Margery was right. A mug of tea, a slice of malt loaf, and a kind word didn't seem like much, but Gertie had lived long enough to know what a difference they could make, especially in dark times.

She had nearly finished laying out the tea mugs when Margery arrived red-faced and out of breath.

"Manifold apologies, Mrs. Bingham," she said, climbing into the truck. "I was sidetracked by a domestic issue."

"Not at all," said Gertie. "Is everything all right?"

"Oh yes. Quite all right, thank you," said Margery. "How's the Old General doing?"

"Wheezing into life as usual," said Gertie.

Margery snorted with uncustomary amusement. "Jolly good."

Gertie noticed her face was a little pink and there was a far-off expression in her eyes. "Mrs. Fortescue," she said gently. "Have you been drinking?"

Margery hiccupped and put a hand to her mouth. "Only a small sherry. I do it every year on this day."

"Oh," said Gertie. "Is it a special occasion?"

Margery's shoulders sagged a little. "It's my dear Edward's birthday," she said. "I always toast his memory with a small schooner of sherry, but I must have dropped off afterward, hence my tardiness."

Gertie lifted one of the tea mugs. "Happy birthday, Edward."

Margery gave a resigned smile. "He would have been seventy-two this year. I miss him every day." She stared into the distance for a moment before snapping back to the present. "Sorry, Mrs. Bingham. That's dreadfully ill-mannered, and after I was late as well. Forgive me."

"Nothing to forgive. I miss my husband every day."

Margery regarded her for a moment. "What was his name?"

"Harry."

Margery held up a tea mug. "To Harry and Edward."

"Harry and Edward," said Gertie. "Mrs. Fortescue?"

"Yes?"

"I was wondering if we might address each other by our first names. I do find the formality of Mrs. Bingham rather stifling sometimes. Please call me Gertie."

Margery straightened her shoulders and smoothed down her uniform. "It's highly irregular, but I suppose we could give it a try, Gertie."

"Thank you, Margery," said Gertie with a smile.

Gertie was so immersed in the task of earthing up her potatoes that she didn't hear the doorbell. It had been a particularly warm spring, and she was enjoying her Sundays in the garden with a tin mug of tea and Hemingway for company. If it weren't for the air-raid shelter, now decorated with a creeping marrow's form, and the line of barrage balloons in the distance, you could almost forget there was a war on. The sky was cornflower-blue with just the odd thread of cloud scudding in the breeze. Gertie inhaled and realized she was happy. In this moment, in her garden, with Hedy upstairs writing her letters and stories, she was happy. No one could predict what was around the corner, but if she had learned one thing over the past five years, it was the importance of seizing the day. After all, what was life but a series of moments to be grasped: meeting Harry, finding the bookshop, allowing Hedy into her life, and, now, joining Margery's war effort. Gertie sensed that she was moving forward once more, instead of being doggedly glued to the past.

It was Hemingway who first alerted her to the visitor, as he abandoned his sun-blanketed snooze and scampered back toward the kitchen. When Gertie heard Hedy's cry, she dropped her trowel and flew toward the house. *News. There must be news. Please. Let it be good.*

Gertie almost bumped into the news as it bowled out through the kitchen door in the form of Sam hand in hand with Hedy. "Sam has asked me to marry him," she cried.

"Oh, but that's wonderful, my dears," said Gertie, throwing open her arms. At that moment, she understood how it was for mothers, some watching their sons march off to war, others seeing their daughters left behind. Waiting. Hoping. Praying. Falling in love shouldn't be so perilous, so reliant on fate. Theirs should be a life filled with effortless happiness. Of marriage, a family, a life together. And yet the war made it impossible to plan or ever dare to hope for this. She recalled with shame how she'd taken Harry's love for granted to start with. Life was so fragile, and yet how quickly humans forgot this when events overtook them. How quickly they took everything for granted. "When will you marry?" she asked.

"Not until my parents know," said Hedy. "I've told them about Sam in my letters, of course, but this is different."

Sam curled an arm around his fiancée and kissed the top of her head. "When this war is over, we'll have the wedding to end all weddings."

"I'll start saving my rations for the cake," said Gertie. Part of her was relieved that they weren't marrying right away. She knew of too many young widows who'd done just that. As she, Sam, and Hedy celebrated with tea and slices of ginger cake, the talk was of the future, of wedding plans, of Hedy's family coming to England for the celebrations, of her mother making her dress. Gertie knew now this was the only way to survive a war: to keep going, to keep reaching forward to a bright horizon and whatever lay beyond it.

It was fast becoming apparent that Gerald Travers's admiration for Margery Fortescue was growing into something more than mere friendship and that the feeling was mutual. Hedy noticed it first and was quick to point it out to Gertie.

"You watch. He walks past the shop at ten to eleven on the dot every day on his way to see her."

"Are you sure you're not dizzy with romance yourself, given recent events?" said Gertie. "You were very insistent about our book club choice this month," she added, nodding toward the copies of *Gone with the Wind* that Hedy was arranging in the window.

Hedy shook her head. "I was helping at one of Mrs. Fortescue's 'Make Do and Mend' sessions the other day, and you should have seen her face when he walked through the door. It was Scarlett O'Hara and Ashley Wilkes all over again."

Gertie laughed.

"Excuse me, but surely there's been a mistake?"

Gertie looked up into the scowling face of a man whom she estimated to be around the same age as her uncle Thomas. "Mistake?" she asked.

"Yes," said the man, holding up a copy of *Gone with the Wind*. "Surely a bookshop wouldn't recommend a tome such as this?"

Gertie raised her eyebrows. "What exactly is it that you object to?"

His deepening frown coupled with a pair of small

round spectacles gave him the appearance of an angry mole. "It's not exactly literature, is it?"

Gertie folded her arms. "And how does one define literature?"

The man waved his arms expansively. "Tolstoy, Dickens, Henry James. Not this kind of emotional scribbling."

Gertie fixed him with a look. "Personally, I believe that a jolly good story is a jolly good story, and it would appear that half the reading world agrees with me on this one," she said. "It's one of our bestselling books."

The man gave a vexed sigh and placed a copy of *Moby-Dick* on the counter. "I'll take this, thank you." He placed a copy of *Gone with the Wind* on top. "And this. For my wife. She loves her silly romances."

"Well," declared Gertie after he'd gone. "What a pompous little man."

Hedy shrugged. "One man's meat is another man's poison."

"Gertie, do you have a minute?" called Margery, appearing in the doorway. "Could we perhaps go for a stroll through the gardens by the village hall? It's something of an emergency."

"Of course," said Gertie. She threw Hedy a wide-eyed look. "Back in a tick."

Gerald cared for the gardens surrounding the village hall with the doting tenderness of a new father. Sweetly scented wallflowers clustered with daffodils and tulips, all nodding in the gentle breeze. It was a glorious spring day with barely a wisp of cloud. In direct opposition to the beauty of the scene, Margery stood grim-faced with arms folded in front of an elder tree.

"Is everything all right?" asked Gertie.

Margery inhaled and exhaled. If she'd been a dragon, she would have definitely produced a plume of smoke. "We are friends, aren't we?"

"Of course."

"Then I can speak frankly with you?"

"Absolutely," said Gertie, with a rising sense of dread.

Margery spoke slowly, enunciating each word for emphasis. "Mr. Travers has invited me to tea. At his house."

"I see." Gertie waited for more information, but Margery remained tight-lipped. "Anything else?"

Margery stared at her in alarm. "Isn't that sufficient?"

Gertie narrowed her eyes as she tried to understand. "Forgive me, Margery, but what is the issue with you having tea with Mr. Travers?"

Margery threw up her arms. "I am a woman on my

own, and he is a gentleman on his own. It wouldn't be seemly," she cried.

"Oh, I see. You're concerned about the impropriety."

Margery's eyes bulged. "It would cause a scandal, Gertie."

"Oh. Oh dear." Gertie sensed that this matter required the softest of kid gloves. "Well, would you like to have tea with Mr. Travers?"

Margery's face softened. "I think I would."

"Then how would it be if I came with you? To act as chaperone."

"You would do that?"

"Of course, Margery. We're friends, after all."

Margery astounded Gertie by pulling her into an embrace. "Thank you, Gertie. You don't know what this means to me."

Gertie patted her on the back. "It's quite all right."

Margery pulled away and smoothed down her uniform. "Gosh. I apologize for that outburst. I'm not sure what came over me. Right. We'll never win this war if we stand around gossiping. Back to it."

"Back to it," repeated Gertie, ready to follow her. Before she left, she spied her disgruntled customer from earlier, sitting at one corner of the garden in the sunshine, a gentle smile on his face, his copy of *Gone with the Wind* open in front of him. "Everyone needs a little romance," she murmured.

A few weeks later, Betty was granted leave, and Gertie seized the opportunity to invite her for supper. She and Hedy were in high spirits as they prepared the table, laying out Gertie's best china and cutlery. Gertie had saved their rations so that three pork chops were waiting in the larder ready for the pan, and Hedy had made a plum cake using Gertie's preserved fruit from the previous year. She had also cut a few stems of blossom from the garden and was arranging them artfully in a vase when there was a knock at the door. They hurried to answer with Hemingway close on their heels.

"ASO Betty Godwin reporting for duty," said Betty with a grin. "I had to wear the uniform. It's a bit scratchy, but I think it's pretty stylish."

"Oh, Hedy, doesn't she look wonderful?" cried Gertie.

"Very smart," said Hedy. "That blue really suits you. Come in so we can get a better look at you."

Betty sashayed into the hall, striking a pose like a Hollywood starlet on the red carpet before dissolving into laughter and hugging them both. "It's good to see you," she said as they made their way to the kitchen.

"My brother is a prize plum, but I'm so glad we're going to be sisters," she told Hedy. "And I hear you're chumming up with Mrs. Fortescue and the WVS too, Mrs. B. Is she still as terrifying as ever?"

"She has her moments," said Gertie. "Now, tell us all about what you've been up to while I prepare supper."

Betty's eyes lit up as she spoke. "I'm having the time of my life."

"That's wonderful, dear," said Gertie.

"I mean, it's hard going, but I feel as if I'm actually doing something to help win the war."

"Is the work difficult?" asked Hedy.

"We're not allowed to talk about the nitty-gritty of it, but we get all the training. It's jolly interesting too. We've got a terrific group of girls in our station. Lots about your age, Hedy. We rub along very well and have some fun, going into town. There's a dance hall and a theater. Oh, and I've met a chap."

"What's he like?" asked Hedy, eyes glittering with excitement.

"He's an American. William Hardy. I told him I was coming to visit you, and he sent this." Betty produced a bar of Hershey's Tropical Chocolate from her bag.

Hedy stared at her. "Chocolate?"

"They've got tons of the stuff. And nylons and cigarettes. Speaking of which, do you mind if I smoke, Mrs. B?"

"Not at all," said Gertie, reaching into the cupboard for the ashtray she reserved for Uncle Thomas's expensive Cuban cigars.

"Our superior is a bit of a curmudgeon, but he likes me. Told me I was better than half the chaps he'd worked with," said Betty.

"It sounds so interesting," said Hedy.

"It's not all beer and skittles. We lost one of the girls during a raid the other night," Betty said, inhaling on her cigarette. "Every day you hear about someone's sweetheart being killed. It teaches you to live in the moment, that's for sure."

"Dinner is served," said Gertie, placing plates of chops, homegrown potatoes, cabbage, and carrots in front of them.

"Golly, this is a treat," said Betty. "Thank you, Mrs. B. Air force rations aren't bad, but there's nothing like a home-cooked meal."

They were poised with knives and forks when the siren wailed. "Supper in the shelter?" said Gertie. Hedy and Betty laughed as they picked up their plates and followed her out the door into the cool night air.

The next morning, Billy came to the bookshop early to help with preparations for the children's air-raid book club. Although raids had become less prevalent, there were still blackouts to contend with, and local mothers were grateful to Gertie and Hedy for providing any diversion. The children also liked to gather once a month in the bookshop shelter.

"It's so cozy," said one little girl called Daisy. "Much nicer than our shelter at home, and I love the smell of the books."

"I like it because it's dark and we can tell ghost stories," said a little boy called Wilfred, who invariably had a smut of soot on the end of his nose.

Today, Billy was helping Hedy fashion a dozen eye patches in readiness for their discussion on *Treasure Island*. He took his book club assistant role very seriously and had a keen eye for the details of the story. He was consequently very strict with his fellow book club members and sent Wilfred home once when he couldn't name Tom Sawyer's aunt.

"I didn't like the part with the skeleton," he told Hedy with a shiver. "I'm not sure I'd want to go on a voyage searching for treasure."

"But imagine if you found gold and could be rich beyond your wildest dreams."

Billy shrugged. "Grandpapa is rich, but I don't think he's very happy."

Hedy exchanged a look with Gertie.

"Although I don't see him much, so I can't ask him."

"Well, I expect he's a busy man. At least you see your grandmama sometimes," said Gertie.

"Yes, but I'd like to see them both more. And Papa. Although Mama says he's away on important business." Billy leaned forward to whisper. "I think he might be a spy."

Gertie was about to answer when the door of the bookshop burst open. Betty appeared looking frantic. As soon as their eyes met, Gertie knew it was bad news. The world seemed to stand still as Hedy moved toward her.

"It's Sam, isn't it?" she whispered. Betty nodded. "Oh, Gertie," cried Hedy, turning to her with imploring eyes.

Gertie rushed forward and placed an arm around Hedy's shoulders. She could feel her body trembling and sent up a silent prayer. *Please. Please let him be alive. Please don't steal every scrap of hope from this poor girl.*

Betty took hold of Hedy's hands, her voice cracking. "He was on a raid in Europe the other night when his plane was shot down. I'm sorry to have to tell you he's missing."

Gertie folded Hedy into her arms as she sobbed, while Billy placed a hand on her shoulder. "There, there, Hedy Fisher," he said. "Everything will be all right. You'll see."

Gertie stroked the cheek of this kind little boy and dearly hoped he was right.

Chapter 17

It is best to love wisely, no doubt:
but to love foolishly is better than not
to be able to love at all.

—William Makepeace Thackeray,
The History of Pendennis

Gertie took in the cozy living room with its blush rose—decorated rug, two plump sage-green armchairs, and the radio nestled in between. Her eyes traveled from the wedding photograph of Gerald and Beryl beaming at them from the dust-flecked mantelpiece, toward the small square dining table with two Windsor chairs facing one another and the pile of Gerald's gardening books, occupying the space where a couple used to share meals and tales of their day. The ghost of Beryl Travers couldn't have been more apparent if she'd drifted into the room and stood in the corner waving at them.

Margery sat bolt upright on the edge of the sofa next to Gertie while they waited for Gerald to return with the tea. They could hear him whistling away as he clattered teacups and opened and closed drawers. Gertie glanced at her, ready to make conversation, but Margery kept her eyes fixed forward, breathing deeply, staring grim-faced toward the matching porcelain Staffordshire spaniels perched on the mantelpiece, who stared back at her in astonishment. She had the air of a woman who was enduring a terrible toothache.

"Here we are," said Gerald, carrying the tray in through the door and placing it on the tea table. "I'll be Mother, shall I?"

Margery let out a high-pitched, nervous laugh that almost made Gertie leap from her seat. "Oh yes, jolly good."

"Milk, sugar, Mrs. Bingham?"

"Just milk, thank you, Mr. Travers."

"And for you, Mrs. Fortescue?"

"The same please," said Margery with an alarmingly toothy grin that Gertie couldn't recall having seen before.

He passed 'round the tea before opening a cake tin and offering it to Margery. "It was ever so good of you to bake these cakes, Mrs. Fortescue. I haven't had a rock bun since . . ." It was clear from his glazed expression that he was lost in a memory of Beryl. "Well, never mind. Please. Help yourself."

Margery threw a panicked look toward Gertie. "I don't suppose you have any small plates, Mr. Travers?" said Gertie, reading her mind.

Gerald put a hand to his head. "I'm dreadfully sorry, ladies. I don't entertain much these days. Back in a jiffy."

Margery turned to Gertie. "This is a terrible mistake."

"But why?"

"I shouldn't have come. This is all wrong. I can't stop thinking about dear Edward, and it's clear that Mr. Travers is still overwhelmed with thoughts of his spouse. Look around you, Gertie. She's everywhere."

"Well, you can't expect him to tidy away his wife. They were married for over forty years."

Margery grimaced. "Of course I don't expect that. It's just . . ."

"Here we are," said Gerald, returning and handing 'round the plates, napkins, and cakes with a triumphant air. "I had to dig around a bit, but I found them. I haven't had cause to use them for a while. I'd forgotten we had them, to be honest."

"Thank you, Mr. Travers," said Gertie, deciding to steer the conversation toward more neutral territory. "I must say your front garden is looking splendid. How do you get so many roses on one bush?"

"Horse manure."

"Beg pardon?"

"Horse manure," he repeated. "I know a farmer. He delivers me bags of the stuff whenever I need it. Works a treat."

"Gosh," said Gertie. "How marvelous."

"I tell you what are marvelous," said Gerald. "These cakes. Absolutely delicious, Mrs. Fortescue."

"Thank you, Mr. Travers. And I agree with you about the horse manure, although it does make for a pungent few days after you spread it."

Gerald chuckled. "Very true. Beryl used to tell me off because she had to shut all the windows. She did like to air the house every day."

Gertie felt Margery shift in her seat. "Harry was the same," she told him. "I can't bear a draft. He'd throw them all open in the morning and then I'd go 'round closing them."

Gerald nodded. "I remember your Harry helping me find a book for Beryl when she was ill. He always had a kind word when you needed it. I put great store in that."

Gertie smiled. "Your Beryl was the same. I wouldn't have had half the success with my runner beans if it hadn't been for her. Planting nasturtiums alongside them to stop the blackfly made all the difference."

"Ah, Beryl was an expert when it came to growing fruit and veg. Caulis as big as your head, and her black currants? Well. She made enough pies, jellies, and jams for the whole street."

"We've been lucky, haven't we?" said Margery quietly. Her face was glowing with gentle happiness. "To have met and married such people."

"Yes," said Gerald, catching her eye. "Very lucky indeed."

The car was waiting for Gertie and Hedy on their return from the bookshop one day. Gertie recognized it immediately from the time Sam drove them all to the beach. It felt like a different life. It wasn't Sam at the wheel, of course. It was an older version of him with neatly combed charcoal-gray hair. He had fallen asleep, his spectacles teetering on the end of his nose.

Hedy tapped lightly on the window. "Dr. Godwin," she said, her voice brimming with expectation.

Dr. Godwin woke with a loud snort, blinking at the pair of them as he tried to recall where the blazes he was. Gertie had met Betty and Sam's father only once or twice, but she could see how the daily agonies of a war in which his son was caught up had taken their toll. He had a weary, haggard appearance. Dr. Godwin rose from the car with some effort and turned to Hedy. "Betty gave me strict instructions to come 'round straightaway to give you the news. Samuel is in a prisoner of war camp in Poland." He held out a chit of paper. "Daphne wrote down the address for you."

Hedy stared at the piece of paper for a moment before throwing her arms around Dr. Godwin's neck. He glanced at Gertie in surprise before accepting the embrace with a gentle smile.

"There, there, my dear. No need to be upset. Everything is all right."

"Thank you," whispered Hedy. "Thank you so much."

"At least we know he's safe," said Dr. Godwin. "Now all we have to do is pray."

"I'm going to do more than that," said Hedy, with a determined look.

The next day, Gertie found herself standing outside the local recruitment office with Hedy at her side. "You're sure you want to do this?" she said. "You know they could send you to the Outer Hebrides."

Hedy gave an emphatic nod. "I want to do what Betty's doing. I want to make a difference, to help bring an end to all this."

Gertie longed to tell Hedy how much she'd miss her,

how the house would seem empty again without her, but she could see how determined she was. She recognized that fire, that need to fight. Gertie had been experiencing it herself of late. "Come along then. Let's get you signed up."

They pushed open the door of the stark, bare offices and followed the signs to a room where a bored-looking man of about Gertie's age was interviewing a young woman of about Hedy's age.

"I can offer you the Land Army or work in a munitions factory," he told her.

"I don't really like animals," said the girl. "But then I don't really like guns either."

The man sighed. "How about I send you to a potato farm where there are no animals?"

"Will I have to do the digging?"

The man raised his eyebrows. "A little."

"Hmm, all right then, although I don't want to lose a nail."

The man wrote something on her paperwork, stamped the form, and handed it back to her. "Next."

The girl grinned at Hedy and Gertie as she walked past. "Potatoes," she said cheerfully.

"Splendid," said Gertie.

"Name?" said the man.

"Hedy Fischer," she said, handing over her papers.

The man looked startled as he spotted the swastika, as if expecting the entire German army to march out from behind it. "You're German."

"Yes. That's right," said Hedy. "I am a German Jew who escaped Nazi persecution in 1939." Gertie's cheeks burned with pride.

The man slid the papers back across the table. "I'm sorry. We can't employ enemy aliens for war work. They pose too much of a risk."

Gertie fixed the man with a scowl. "Do you have any idea what this young woman has been through?"

The man wore a blank expression. "I'm sorry. I don't make the rules."

Hedy touched her on the arm. "Come on, Gertie. It's no use. Let's go."

As they walked back through the maze of corridors, Gertie noticed a room labeled "POW Parcel Centre." She stopped in her tracks and stared at the sign.

"What is it?" asked Hedy.

"I've had an idea," she said with a twinkle in her eye. "But I need to go home and find something first."

The letter was exactly where she thought it would be, in the burl walnut box with its secret drawer, which had so intrigued Gertie as a child, that had been left to her by her mother. It was where Gertie kept all her most precious treasures. "Here it is," she said, sitting on the edge of the bed next to Hedy. "Jack's last letter, sent in 1917."

"Your brother had terrible handwriting," said Hedy.

Gertie laughed. "He used to drive Father to distraction because he refused to practice his copperplate. Shall I read it to you?"

Hedy nodded and leaned against her, like a child listening to a story. Gertie cleared her throat.

My dearest Gertie,

I hope this finds you in good health. Thank you for your letter and parcel. I'm grateful to you for sending a copy of The Thirty-Nine Steps, as are the rest of the chaps here. It's a dash tedious being locked up for the war, although I know I shouldn't complain. I've heard about conditions in the Tommies' camps. The guards are all right provided you toe the line. The place is fairly basic and not all that clean. We do our best to keep up spirits. We put on plays or entertain ourselves with singing, but it's hard going, Gertie. I don't think I'll ever take my life as a free man for granted again. It makes a chap think about how he lived his life before. I know this will make you laugh, but I pledge to you now that I will be a better man when I get home. I know I've been selfish in the past, but I'm going to change, Gert. You can hold me to it. I keep thinking about that holiday in Suffolk when we were children. Do you remember? We met that farmer and he showed us his dogs and horses and pigs. Do you remember the pigs? We begged Father for weeks afterward to let us have a pet pig. Can you imagine? I often think back to that time as when I was happiest, when life was simple, when we didn't really have a care. I find being a man so bewildering sometimes. I know that's why I act the fool and drink too much. I'm putting up a front, pretending to be someone I'm not. Well, that will change when I get home. You'll see, Gertie. I'll be the man I'm supposed to be and maybe I'll live out my days on a farm in Suffolk. You can visit me and my dogs and pigs. Gosh, I'm giving myself goose bumps at the very thought of it. I'm tired, I think. The chap in the bed next to me is up coughing half the night, and I don't feel myself today. Probably the awful gruel they feed us in here. Don't worry. I'll be back bothering you and Harry as soon as this war is over. Give the old chap my best. I know I tease you about him, but he's a good man. You're lucky to have found each other. How are

Mother and Father? Mama writes every week,
but I never hear from Pa. Ashford wrote to me
the other week. He's still in the thick of it, poor
chap. I miss you, Gertie. Your letters are a real
tonic. I look forward to the day when we can dine
at the Savoy again with Harry and Charles. My
treat.

Ever your loving brother,
Jack

Hedy reached over with her handkerchief to wipe away Gertie's tears. "I think you and Jack are exactly like me and Arno," she said.

Gertie held her gaze for a moment. "I want us to help other POWs like I helped Jack. I want to help Sam and all the other poor chaps trying to get through this war."

Hedy nodded. "I think it's a brilliant idea."

"There's just one small problem," said Gertie.

"Miss Snipp?"

Gertie nodded. Hedy gave her a sage look.

"Leave it to me, Gertie. I know what to do."

Miss Snipp was already sorting through orders as Gertie and Hedy arrived at the bookshop the next day with Hemingway in tow. "Cup of tea, Miss Snipp?"

said Gertie. "Hedy's baked some ginger biscuits this morning."

Miss Snipp narrowed her eyes. "Do you require a favor, Mrs. Bingham?"

"I would welcome your advice, Miss Snipp. If you can spare the time." Gertie had known Eleanora Snipp long enough to understand that she needed to tread carefully. She was not a woman to embrace change with open arms. It had taken her a good five years to accept that women had been given the right to vote. She would still mention it with a shiver of disdain to this day.

"Very well," said Miss Snipp.

"Well, given the success of the Air Raid Book Club, I was considering extending this to prisoners of war."

Miss Snipp blinked. "Prisoners of war," she echoed.

"Indeed. But of course I wouldn't consider such an undertaking without speaking to you first."

Miss Snipp gave a grave nod.

"So I would welcome the benefit of your wisdom as to what type of administrative undertaking might be required for such a task?" said Gertie, knowing full well that she would have the answers at her fingertips.

"Well," said Miss Snipp with a labored sigh. "There is a great deal of paperwork and of course liaison with the relevant authorities—the Joint War Organisation, the International Red Cross, and so on—not to mention the additional packing materials required."

"Hmm," said Gertie. "That sounds like a lot of extra work. Perhaps it isn't worth the bother. Hedy, I know you would dearly like to be able to send books to Sam and his fellow POWs, but I think it's going to be too mammoth a task. You do understand, don't you, dear?"

Hedy bit her lip to suppress her amusement. "Of course."

Miss Snipp stared at Gertie as if she'd just suggested the Allies immediately surrender. "We will find a way," she said.

"Are you sure?" asked Gertie.

"Of course." She gestured toward Hedy. "Anything to help this poor girl."

Hedy rushed forward and threw her arms around Miss Snipp's neck. "Oh, my dear Miss Snipp. You're a peach. I will help you in any way I can. Thank you."

Miss Snipp blinked in amazement, offering Hedy a stiff pat on the back in reply. "Yes, well, dear. We must all do our bit. But we may need extra help parceling them up, Mrs. Bingham," she said with a reproachful stare.

"Leave it with me," said Gertie, heading for the door.

"The POW book club, you say?" said Margery as they took a turn around the village hall gardens.

Gertie nodded. "My brother was a POW during the Great War and was always grateful when I sent him books. He loved *The Thirty-Nine Steps,* so I thought we could make it our first choice."

"I didn't know you had a brother."

Gertie nodded. "He died in the camp. There was an outbreak of typhus."

Margery held her gaze for a moment before giving a grave nod. "Tell me what needs to be done."

"Well, I thought we could set ourselves up as a distribution center and send out books as part of the Red Cross food and recreation parcels."

Margery paused to admire a large rose bloom the color of a ripening peach. She inhaled, closing her eyes as the exquisite fragrance filled her nostrils. "I think it's a splendid idea, Gertie."

"I hoped you would." Gertie watched her friend for a moment. "I must say you're looking particularly radiant, Margery. May I ask if this has anything to do with Mr. Travers?"

Margery threw her a dreamy look. "He's asked me to a dance."

"A dance?"

She nodded. "On Saturday. I was wondering if you'd care to join us?"

"Oh, I don't know . . ."

"Come along, Gertie. Shouldn't we be grasping for these little moments of joy when we can? Who knows what tomorrow may bring."

"True."

"So you'll come?"

Gertie sighed. "Very well. I'll ask my old friend Charles Ashford to accompany me."

"Splendid," said Margery.

They turned out of the garden in the direction of the high street.

"Any luck at the recruitment office?"

Gertie shook her head.

"What utter tomfoolery," said Margery. "Aren't they always telling us to be up and at 'em? Surely we need all the brilliant young women we can muster to help with the war effort."

They had reached the bookshop when Margery noticed Gerald browsing through the window. She gestured for Gertie to follow her.

"Mr. Travers," she said by way of greeting, sweeping in through the door. "Aren't you in need of a new ARP warden?"

Gerald glanced up from the George Orwell novel he was perusing, apparently unsurprised by her direct line of questioning. "I am."

"Well, don't you think this young lady would be

perfect for the job?" said Margery, gesturing toward Hedy.

Gerald appraised her for a moment. "I do."

"Really?" cried Hedy. "But won't you get into trouble with the recruitment office?"

Gerald tapped the side of his nose. "What they don't know won't harm them. Training starts tomorrow at six sharp. Don't be late."

Gertie opened her wardrobe with an air of defeat. It had been years since she'd had cause to dress up, and she couldn't remember the last time she attended a dance. Surely she was too old to be gadding about anymore. She rummaged through the garments, stroking the smooth cool pleats of her turquoise silk ball gown and wondering why on earth she'd kept it. Gertie could only ever recall wearing it once to one of her uncle's literary dinners and that must have been at least twenty years ago. Really she should have donated it to the war effort. She could imagine Margery transforming it into at least a dozen handkerchiefs.

"Oh this is hopeless," she cried, staring at the columns of frumpy skirts and plain old dresses.

"Are you all right?" asked Hedy, appearing in the doorway, eyeing the curlers in Gertie's hair and the look of desperation on her face.

"What does one wear to dances these days?" said Gertie.

Hedy shrugged. "Nothing fancy. Just a nice dress and good shoes for dancing. Would you like me to help you?"

"Yes please. And if you could teach me the Charleston while you're at it, that would be splendid."

Hedy laughed. "I don't think you need to worry. You should just enjoy yourself." Gertie knew she was right and yet, the idea felt so alien. When was the last time she had done anything for the sheer joy of it? Was that even allowed when the world was in turmoil? Then she looked at Hedy with all her cares and worries. She kept cheerful, went to the cinema or out dancing with her friends. She kept going because, what else could you do? Life ticked along and all you could do was tick along with it. "I think you should wear this," said Hedy, retrieving a navy-colored tea dress with a tiny white apple blossom design. "It's so pretty."

"I'd forgotten I had that," said Gertie.

"Would you like me to style your hair?" she asked. "I used to help Mama prepare for her concerts so I know how to."

Gertie smiled. "I would like that very much. Thank you, my dear."

Charles was waiting for Gertie in the hall as she made her way down the stairs a while later. "I feel as if I'm watching a Hollywood star descend the red carpet," he said, framing his hands and pretending to take a photograph.

"It's all because of Hedy. She picked my outfit and styled my hair," she said, patting at her neatly coiffured curls.

"Bravo, Hedy," said Charles. "You look beautiful, Gertie." He took her hand and kissed it before offering his arm. "Shall we?"

"See you later," called Gertie over her shoulder.

"Have fun," said Hedy, waving from the doorstep with Hemingway sitting faithfully by her side.

Gertie needn't have worried about being too old for the Orchid Ballroom. Most of the couples dancing that evening were either in their sixties or young women in pairs. Regardless of this fact, the hall was buzzing with a certain carefree energy as people enjoyed a welcome escape from the drudgery of their wartime existence. A three-piece band complete with singer was playing "Don't Sit Under the Apple Tree" as they arrived, making it impossible not to be enticed immediately onto the dance floor. Fortunately for Gertie, Charles was similarly lacking in dance experience, but they made a passable attempt at keeping up with the assembled company, managing to move around the dance floor without crushing each other's toes. Gerald and Margery, on the other hand, proved to be extremely elegant dancers, receiving many admiring glances for their stylish waltz. Apparently, as well as being an aspiring opera singer in her youth, Margery had been a promising dancer, while Gerald and Beryl had danced together ever since they met at school at the age of twelve. Gertie soon forgot her lack of ability. She found herself following Hedy's advice as she fell into a fit of helpless giggling during her and Charles's failed attempt to keep up with "Pennsylvania Polka."

"I think this could be our cue for a rest," said Charles.

"Jolly good idea," said Gertie, allowing him to lead her to the plush red sofas at the side of the hall and sinking gratefully into the seat beside him. The band had struck up a Charleston, and they watched in surprise as the crowd parted to reveal Gerald and Margery and a handful of other dancers taking center stage. "Margery

Fortescue never ceases to amaze me," said Gertie to Charles, watching them swivel and kick their way back and forth.

"We rather missed out on the Charleston, didn't we?" he said.

Gertie laughed. "True. Harry had two left feet, so we never really went dancing, but I must say I'm having a wonderful time."

"Me too."

"It almost makes you forget there's a war on, doesn't it?"

"I think that's the only way to endure it sometimes."

"I've learned that trick from Hedy," said Gertie.

"She seems cheerful, all things considered."

Gertie nodded. "I'm proud of her. Gerald is training her up as an ARP warden. Don't tell her I said this, but I'm relieved she wasn't able to sign up for war work. At least I'll know where she is."

"You sound like a mother hen."

"Good."

Charles reached over and took her hand. "You know, I've made many mistakes in my life, but the one thing I will never regret is asking you to take in a child. It has transformed you, Gertie. I never thought I'd see you this happy again."

She regarded him for a moment. That kind, handsome face of a sweet soul, who reminded her so much of Harry. Whether it was the music or the sensation of his hand in hers, Gertie had a sudden flash of memory to what it was like to be young and in love. It made her heart rise with a tide of unexpected hope. "Neither did I," she said.

Chapter 18

His sorrow was my sorrow, and his joy
Sent little leaps and laughs through all my
frame.

—George Eliot, "Brother and Sister"

The two letters arrived within days of each other.
The first was from Sam. He would always send
Hedy a long letter during the first week of every month
followed by two postcards in the second and fourth
week. Hedy's face was transformed whenever she spied
one among that day's post. She would clutch the envelope to her heart, stealing away to read it alone in her
room. In the evening, she would sit with Gertie in the
living room recounting his anecdotes. Gertie was fond
of Sam and his amusing stories. He had a good friend in
the camp called Harris, and together they would stage
shows to keep everyone entertained. The pair would

dress up as a couple of aristocratic old women and sing songs in high-pitched voices. Apparently, even some of the German prison guards enjoyed these revues.

The second letter arrived two days later. Gertie's pulse quickened as she spotted the German script and Swiss postmark. "Hedy!" she cried. "Hedy, you must come at once."

Hedy hurried down the stairs with Hemingway close on her heels. "What is it?"

Gertie held out the envelope. Hedy accepted it with trembling fingers. "Arno," she whispered, staring at the letters as if daring to hope that he might materialize from within them.

"Do you want to read it alone?" asked Gertie. Hedy shook her head. "Come through to the kitchen then. We'll read it together."

They sat at the table with Hemingway bolt upright beside them, as if he understood the significance of this moment. Hedy unfolded the blue parchment paper and stared at the words in surprise. "He has written in English."

"Probably to stop too many prying German eyes from reading it," said Gertie.

Hedy took a deep breath. *"My dearest Hedchen."* She paused as the tears began to trickle down her cheeks.

"Would you like me to read it, dear?" asked Gertie gently. Hedy nodded. Gertie took the letter from her shaking hands and began:

My dearest Hedchen, my darling sister,

> *I can only hope and pray that this letter reaches you safely. I have entrusted it to someone who I am sure will not let me down, but you can never be certain in this war. I must be quick in my writing as I do not have much time. I am safe, working in a factory in Poland. I was lucky to get this job and am grateful for it. The last time I saw Mama and Papa was when we traveled east, and apart from hunger, they were both in good health. I hope you have found a happy life in England. I think about you often, about afternoons strolling through the Englischer Garten with you, eating Pfeffernüsse . . .*

Hedy let out a sob. Hemingway rested his huge warm head in her lap.

"Shall I stop, dear?"

Hedy shook her head, cuddling the dog to her as Gertie continued.

. . . talking about our plans for the future. I was going to build the tallest skyscraper in Europe, bigger than the Empire State Building, and you were going to write books, adventure stories of brave girls and boys beating the villains. I hope we still get those dreams, my dear Hedchen, and I hope the brave girls and boys beat the villains in the end. I miss you so much and I love you even more. I hope you are impressed by your lazy German brother's English. I expect your English is better than the Queen's by now.

Ever yours,
Your brother, Arno

Gertie's eyes were streaming with tears as she finished. She and Hedy clung to each other for a long time, weeping for the ones they couldn't protect. After a while, Gertie reached into her pocket and pulled out a handkerchief. Very gently, she wiped Hedy's eyes and kissed her on the forehead. "He's alive, Hedy. Your brother is alive," she said, folding her into a tight embrace.

Uncle Thomas did not like to travel south of the river. In fact, he didn't really like to travel beyond the confines of Cecil Court, but he made an exception for his niece's sixty-fourth birthday. The dinner had been Hedy's idea. She suggested that guests each bring a dish to make their rations stretch further.

"My parents used to have these supper parties at our apartment in Munich. I loved it when I was a child. The place was full of artists and musicians all drinking, smoking, and discussing art and literature," she told Gertie as they laid the table, decorating it with a vase of freshly cut roses and a silver candelabra.

Gertie smiled, setting down the bowls of salad made with homegrown produce. She had noticed a new confidence in Hedy over the past few weeks. Gerald declared her to be "more competent than any fellow I've ever trained," and her engagement to Sam and letter from Arno seemed to be giving her a renewed zest for life. She devoured every piece of news from the papers and radio and spent any spare hours scribbling furiously in notebooks. She hadn't shared her stories with Gertie yet. However, Billy had stuck his head over the fence one day for a chat and reliably informed her that "they're stories for children, so not really for you, Gertie Bingham. I've seen them when she showed Mama and me. They're very good."

Uncle Thomas was the first to arrive for the party. Gertie was intrigued to see what he'd bring. "Bacon and egg pie," he said proudly, handing over a cloth-covered dish.

"Gosh," said Gertie. "Did you make it yourself?"

He snorted with laughter. "Very good, Gertie. Yes. Highly amusing. Couldn't boil an egg to save my life. No, Mrs. Havers rustled it up for me. Potato pastry and dried egg, unfortunately, but needs must." He retrieved a brown paper parcel from his pocket. "Happy birthday, my dear old thing."

She unwrapped the package to reveal a small blue cloth poetry book with silver lettering. "George Eliot," she said, kissing his cheek. "Thank you, Uncle dearest."

"Just a token of my esteemed affection," he said. "Oh, and I found this for you, young lady," he added, pulling a book from his other pocket and holding it out to Hedy.

"*Emil and the Detectives*," she cried. "Arno and I used to love this book. Thank you."

Uncle Thomas nodded his approval. "I don't suppose you've got any of Harry's whisky squirreled away, have you, dear heart? You know how journeying this far south affects my constitution."

Gertie smiled. "I may be able to pour you a nip for medicinal purposes."

"Much obliged, Gertie. Much obliged."

Charles was the next to arrive with a tray of salmon fish cakes. "Made by my own fair hand," he said, passing them to Hedy.

"I had no idea you harbored such talents," said Gertie, kissing him on the cheek, catching the reassuring scent of cedar and spice.

"When you've lived alone for as long as I have and spent time in the army, you learn a thing or two," he said. "Happy birthday, dear Gertie." He held out a small red velvet box with a gold clasp.

"This isn't a proposal of marriage, is it, Charles?"

He laughed. "Not today. Open it."

Gertie pressed the button clasp to reveal a gold heart-shaped necklace decorated with a tiny ruby. "It's beautiful," she said, lifting it from the box.

"I'm glad you like it. Here, let me help you." As he fastened the chain behind her neck, Gertie's skin tingled at his touch. "Perfect," he said, standing back to admire her.

The last guests to arrive were Billy and his mother. "Happy birthday, Gertie Bingham," cried Billy, marching into the room. "Here is your present." He handed over a flat rectangular package, loosely wrapped in brown paper.

"Thank you, Billy. And what do we have here?"

She unfurled it and slid out a framed watercolor drawing.

"Mama did it," he said with glee. "Isn't she clever?"

"With apologies to Mr. E. H. Shepard," said Elizabeth.

Gertie stared at the picture. Elizabeth had drawn Gertie, Hedy, and Hemingway along with Billy and her sitting in their air-raid shelter with Winnie-the-Pooh and Piglet. "I adore it. Thank you," Gertie said, kissing her on the cheek.

Elizabeth gave a shy smile. "And this is our food contribution," she said, handing over a cloth-tied basin. "I made a summer pudding."

"My favorite," said Uncle Thomas with a satisfied grin.

After the meal, Gertie stood and raised her glass to them all. "Thank you, everyone, for making my birthday so special. Thank you, Hedy, for arranging this. It's been wonderful."

"I have one more surprise for you," said Hedy. She disappeared from the room and returned moments later carrying a sheaf of folded papers. "This is the first chapter. I've been working on it for a while. Elizabeth has done some wonderful illustrations too."

Gertie took the papers and held them to her heart. "I'll save it for bedtime," she said. "Thank you. Both of you."

"And may I be the first to offer you representation," said Uncle Thomas, reaching into his pocket for a business card and sliding it across the table. Elizabeth and Hedy exchanged grins.

"What's your story about, Hedy?" asked Charles.

Hedy's eyes glittered as she spoke. "It's about a brother and sister who have many adventures and always beat the villains."

"Could the boy be called Billy?" asked Billy.

"Perhaps. Although I did think that Billy might be a good name for their little black-and-white dog, who is excellent at sniffing out clues."

Billy considered this for a moment. "I wouldn't mind being a dog," he said, reaching out a hand to stroke Hemingway, who was asleep by his feet.

"Is the boy called Arno by any chance?" asked Gertie.

Hedy nodded. "And the girl is called Gertie."

Charles laughed. "Gertie Bingham. In print at last! What on earth will Miss Snipp say?"

"She's too busy complaining about all the extra work she has to do for the prisoner of war book club," said Gertie. "Apparently, *The Thirty-Nine Steps* is to blame for her sciatica flaring up again."

"John Buchan should be ashamed of himself," said Uncle Thomas with a twinkle in his eye.

"Well, it's a good effort, Gertie," said Charles. "I bet those chaps are grateful to have anything to help them pass the time."

"Sam says they're a godsend," said Hedy. "Apparently the copies of Maugham and Hemingway that we sent him have been shared 'round so much they're falling to pieces."

"Does he say much about what life is like?" asked Elizabeth.

Hedy shook her head. "Not really. They're grateful for the food parcels, as the rations aren't up to much, but they keep themselves busy."

"What else can you do in this blasted war?" said Uncle Thomas.

"True," said Gertie, patting his hand. "Now, who's for tea?"

"You shouldn't be making the tea on your birthday," said Charles, standing up.

"You can help me then."

The sky was awash with fading shades of peach and apricot as the sun descended behind the trees, cloaking the world in shadow. Gertie and Charles moved companionably around the kitchen, laying out cups and setting the kettle to boil. She hummed a little tune to herself as she fetched the milk.

"It's good to see you happy, Gertie."

She stared into his clear blue eyes, overcome with a sudden urge to tell him what she was feeling. Right on cue, the air-raid siren screamed. "Well, I always think that tea tastes better in the shelter," she said. "Come along, everyone. Chop-chop!"

"You see this is the reason why I don't venture over the river," said Uncle Thomas, hobbling toward the back door.

"I do believe they have air raids north of the river as well, Uncle," said Gertie, placing an arm under his elbow and steering him out into the garden.

"Shall we play a game?" asked Billy, his eyes shining as they huddled inside the shelter.

"Or what about a story?" said Hedy. "I used to play a game with my family where we took turns and told a few lines each."

"That sounds like fun," said Gertie, taking a sip of tea. "Who wants to start?"

"I will!" cried Billy.

"Very well, young man. Off you go."

Billy cleared his throat. "Once upon a time there was a girl called Gertie Bingham," he began. "She lived in a house full of books and was very brave . . ."

"I like the sound of her," said Charles, flashing a grin at Gertie. Billy scowled. "Sorry, Billy. Please continue."

"She lived in a house full of books and was very brave, but she was lonely."

Gertie felt Charles reach for her hand.

"Your turn, Mama."

"One day," said Elizabeth, "there was a knock at the door, and there, on the doorstep, was a gigantic egg."

"A dinosaur egg?" whispered Billy.

"Wait and see," said Elizabeth. "Hedy, you're the storyteller. I think you should continue."

Hedy thought for a moment. "Gertie carried the egg inside and placed it on a shelf in the airing cupboard to keep it warm. A few days later, she was preparing her breakfast when she heard a squeaking and a creaking from the cupboard and then a loud CRACK!" Billy squealed. Hedy stared at him goggle-eyed as she whispered, "Gertie crept to the cupboard and very slowly opened the door. Inside was . . ." She looked to Charles.

"What?" cried Billy, jiggling up and down. "What was in the cupboard?"

Charles hesitated for a moment before answering. "A baby dragon," he said.

"I love dragons," said Billy.

"This was a young girl dragon. She was willow green, and her scales were tipped with purple. As Gertie opened the cupboard, the little dragon sneezed. A tiny spark of fire flew from the dragon's nostrils so that Gertie had to jump out of the way to avoid getting singed. Most people would be scared to find a dragon in their airing cupboard, but not Gertie. She carried the little dragon to the kitchen and fed her kippers for breakfast." He grinned at Gertie, who rolled her eyes. "Over to you."

She smiled. "At first, Gertie wasn't sure about this little dragon," she said, glancing toward Hedy. "But she came to realize how much she needed her and was very glad that the dragon came to stay."

"Is that the end?" asked Billy with a note of disappointment.

"I think it's my go," said Uncle Thomas. "And then the dragon grew too big and started a colossal fire and burned down the whole house."

"Gosh," said Billy. "Was everyone all right?"

"Yes, everyone was fine. He was only joking," said Gertie, relieved as the all clear sounded. "And that's why it's better for you to sell books rather than write them," she told Uncle Thomas as she helped him from the shelter.

"I think I better get Billy home to bed," said Elizabeth. "It's very late."

Gertie kissed them both good night. "Thank you for coming. And for my beautiful picture."

"I'll be off now too, dear heart," said Uncle Thomas,

pecking her on the cheek. "Sparkling soiree. Haven't enjoyed myself so much in ages."

As they returned to the living room, Gertie spied the whisky bottle still on the side table. "One last toast?" she asked Charles, keen for him to stay a while longer.

"Why not?"

Gertie poured two glasses and handed one to him.

"Many happy returns," he said with a smile.

Hedy picked up Elizabeth's picture to admire it. "We should find a place for this."

Gertie gestured toward a small, framed pastoral scene next to the bookcase. "You could take that one down and put it there perhaps."

Hedy lifted the picture from the wall, and as she did, something slipped to the floor. She bent down to retrieve it. "I think this might be yours, Gertie," she said as she unfolded it.

As soon as Gertie saw the words "My dearest love," she knew what it was. The words swam before her, but she didn't need to read them. She knew them by heart. Each syllable hung heavy in her memory like the pendulum of a grandfather clock endlessly ticking with guilt and regret. That was why she'd hidden the letter for so long. She could neither bear to part with it nor be faced with the daily reminder of its contents.

"Are you all right, Gertie?" asked Charles as she sunk onto the sofa, her face drained of color.

"It was my fault," she whispered, clutching the letter to her heart as tears formed in her eyes.

When Harry first mentioned his cough, Gertie had dismissed it as a common cold. A week later, he took to his bed, and still, she didn't send for the doctor. Harry would be all right. She had lost Jack, her father, and her mother, but Harry? Harry couldn't possibly go anywhere. She simply wouldn't allow it. On the day she came home and found him collapsed in the bathroom, she knew she'd made a mistake.

"Didn't you know about his childhood condition?" asked the doctor accusingly.

Gertie nodded. "It was why he received medical exemption in the war."

"Well, he should have come to us a lot sooner. He's very sick."

Gertie had left the hospital and gone straight to Southwark Cathedral. A service was in progress as she crept in at the back. She sat in the sacred calm, turning her despairing face upward toward the angels and archangels.

Please. Not Harry.

It would seem that someone was listening, as Harry

started to rally. "He's been very, very lucky," said the same doctor in the same accusing tone.

As he began to recuperate, Gertie and Harry had agreed that daily visits were unnecessary and started to write letters to each other instead. Gertie wrote long tales of that day's events at the bookshop: Of Miss Snipp informing their publisher's representative, Mr. Barnaby Salmon, that it was a travesty that his publisher had let Florence L. Barclay's titles go out of stock. Of how sad Mr. Travers was now that his wife had died. Of how cross she'd been when Hemingway had chewed through a first edition of Thomas Hardy poems. In return, Harry wrote with tales of hospital life: of a patient who argued with his wife before she picked up his wooden crutch and hit him over the head with it, and of the kerfuffle when the police had to be called. He told her that the nurse called Winnie was his favorite because she reminded him of a kind aunt who had always given him biscuits. His least favorite was called Enid. She had a sharp tongue and made him think of a storybook witch on account of the hairy mole on her chin. Gertie's heart had danced with joy whenever the post arrived.

The letter she held in her hands now had been the last one she received. It had arrived on the day Harry was due to come home from the hospital. Gertie stared at the words through a blur of tears.

My dearest love,

Another night is over and all I can think is that I'm another night closer to being with you again. The doctors think I should be well enough by Thursday. I can't wait to be safe with you and Hemingway in our dear little house. Being stuck in hospital for too long makes a man realize how lucky he is, and I am desperately lucky to have you, my darling Gertie. The day I walked into Arnold's all those years ago was the happiest of my life. There isn't a single moment that goes by when I don't thank the god of fate for bringing us together. I've been thinking that we should take a little trip. Perhaps Paris to see the Bouquinistes? All I know is that we must live for the day, my darling. Life is fragile, and I want to relish every moment of mine with you.

Ever your loving husband,
Harry

"We still had so much life to live," she told Charles and Hedy with an anguished sob.

They came to sit on either side of her, offering murmured comfort as Gertie's grief surrounded her like a dense London fog.

"It was all my fault," she said, ignoring their gentle protestations. "I should have insisted he go to the doctor sooner. I could have prevented his death." She glanced at each of them in turn as she finally uttered the secret she had buried for so long. "Harry would still be alive today if it weren't for me."

Chapter 19

Time brought resignation, and a melancholy
sweeter than common joy.

—Emily Brontë, *Wuthering Heights*

The Christmas revue was Gertie's idea. "I think it's just the ticket to lift the spirits," she told Margery one day as they gathered to parcel up the Red Cross packages. "We could invite local residents to take part, deck the village hall with boughs of holly, fire up the Old General for tea. What do you think?"

Margery regarded Gertie in astonishment. "I think . . ." she began. The room held its breath. ". . . that I wish I'd thought of it first. Gerald?"

"Yes, my dear?" He glanced up from his newspaper. Following many weekend dances and country walks, Gerald and Margery had now reached the dizzying heights of first-name terms.

"Were you listening to Gertie's idea?"

Gerald narrowed his eyes with concentration. "Christmas revue. Village hall," he said. "I think it's a splendid idea. But only if you sing, Margery."

She looked a little coy. "Well, I don't know."

"Come along, Margery. Don't be shy," said Gertie, placing a pile of books at one end of the packing table.

"Oh please, Mrs. Fortescue," said Hedy. "It would be wonderful if you could."

"I'll give it some thought," said Margery, her eyes twinkling. "Now then. What have we got on the packing list today, Mrs. Chambers?"

Elizabeth cleared her throat and pointed to each item in turn. "One tin of service ration biscuits, one tin of cheese, one packet of chocolate, one tin of creamed rice, one tin of marmalade, one tin of margarine, one tin of pressed beef, one tin of milk, one tablet of soap, one tin of sugar, one packet of tea, one tin of peas, one packet of cigarettes, and one Christmas pudding."

"And one copy of *A Christmas Carol*," said Gertie, pointing at the books.

"Very good," said Margery. "Let's get to it."

There was a spirit of cheerful optimism in the air as they worked. People were starting to believe that the war would end next year. The idea of this being the last Christmas they would have to endure murkey for dinner and embargoes on bell ringing, alongside the ceaseless struggle of rations, air raids, and blackouts, was giving everyone quiet reassurance.

Despite Miss Snipp's initial misgivings and the logistical challenges, Gertie was convinced that they were making a difference to the war effort, and she knew the people in this room agreed with her. Many of them had personal reasons for wanting to ensure that the lives of the POWs were eased in any way possible. Emily Farthing's brother was in a camp in Italy, while Ethel Wise's grandson, like Sam, was a prisoner in Poland. As well as packaging the Red Cross parcels, they also served as a sorting point for the next-of-kin parcel. Today, Emily was repacking one for Gertie's neighbor Mrs. Herbert, whose husband, Bill, was a POW in Berlin. The woman stood before her as Emily checked the items one by one.

"Right, Mrs. Herbert. I'm going to separate the soap from the chocolate. We don't want Mr. Herbert having a taste of Sunlight when he's enjoying his treat, do we? Oh, aren't these hand-knitted socks lovely?" she added turning them inside out. "Just the ticket to keep him warm through the winter." She pulled out a paperback copy of *The Invisible Man*, by H. G. Wells, and gave it a shake.

"Here, you're not checking for contraband, are you?" said Mrs. Herbert, looking offended.

"I'm sorry, but it's the rules," said Emily. "We have to check for forbidden items to stop the Jerries from confiscating the whole lot. I just want to make sure this gets to Mr. Herbert."

Mrs. Herbert's cheeks seemed to flush slightly under the scrutiny. "What would be forbidden exactly?"

"Someone tried to send a jar of homemade cherry jam the other day," said Emily, checking the seal on a tin of boot blacking. "Only chocolate is allowed in next-of-kin parcels."

"Oh, well, that's all right then. I can't make jam for love or money."

It was Emily's turn to blush as she pulled out a pair of large woolen underpants.

"Thermals," said Mrs. Herbert. "They say the German winters are bitter."

"Hang on a minute," said Emily, holding up the underwear. "What's this writing?"

Elizabeth, Hedy, and Gertie glanced over in amusement.

"V for victory," said Mrs. Herbert, jutting out her chin. "Our boys are going to win the war any day, and I want to send that message to the Jerries loud and clear."

The assembled company all laughed and cheered except for Margery. "Mrs. Herbert, you know as well as I do that written messages of any kind are not allowed in these parcels," she said with a disapproving look.

"Oh, very well," said Mrs. Herbert, taking them back from Emily. "I suppose I'll have to wear them and show my backside to the Luftwaffe next time they fly over."

Emily snorted with laughter as Margery rolled her eyes. "Highly improper," she said, but not with much vigor.

"Can we talk about *Wuthering Heights*, please?" said Ethel Wise, turning to Gertie after Mrs. Herbert had gone.

"Ooh yes, it was a good choice, Mrs. Bingham," said Emily. "I'd happily get lost on the moors with Heathcliff."

"Miss Farthing. Please!" scolded Margery.

"Sorry, Mrs. Fortescue."

"You see I was a bit confused," said Ethel slowly.

"How so?" asked Gertie.

"Well, there were so many characters, and they all had the same name."

"There's Catherine Earnshaw, and she has a daughter called Cathy," said Cynthia, sitting up straighter in her chair. She had become a regular contributor to their book club discussions, and Gertie was invariably grateful for her vast literary knowledge.

"Is she the one who loves Heathcliff?"

"No. It's Catherine who loves Heathcliff."

"Oh, and so is Cathy their daughter?"

"No. Catherine marries Edgar Linton. Cathy is *their* daughter."

"I see. So Heathcliff doesn't marry?"

"He does. He marries Edgar's sister, Isabella Linton, and they have a son called Linton Heathcliff. He marries Cathy."

Ethel's brow was knitted into the deepest frown as she struggled to keep up. "So Heathcliff does marry Cathy?"

Cynthia threw a pleading look toward the others.

"It's Heathcliff's son who marries Catherine's daughter, but then his son dies and she marries Hareton Earnshaw," explained Hedy.

"And who on earth is he?"

"He's the son of Catherine's brother, Hindley."

Ethel threw up her hands. "It's too complicated. Why couldn't the author give them different names like Jim or Peg or Ethel?"

Hedy laughed. "I'm not sure, but did you enjoy it?"

"Oh yes," said Ethel. "It was a super yarn."

Gertie smiled to herself as she listened to their chat. When Charles asked her to take in a child all those years ago, she never could have imagined how it would transform her life. Theirs was a relationship carved from necessity that had bloomed into a bond of true friendship.

The night she shared her guilt over Harry's death, Hedy had offered her arms and held her close as she wept. Gertie hadn't felt such comfort since her mother was alive. It was as if love was holding her in the palm of its hand.

She knew that she would never have had the courage to take on the challenges of this war without Hedy: to fall and rise again, to support their community, to offer relief and comfort. Gertie had come to realize that wars weren't fought by generals and politicians. They were fought by armies of ordinary people battling, struggling, and holding one another up as they pushed onward. Ordinary people living through extraordinary times, making a difference through small endeavors and vast courage. It was Margery and her legion of knitters, Gerald and his ARP clan, and Bingham Books offering escape through the power of stories.

As Gertie returned home with Hedy and Elizabeth a while later, an icy wind nipped at their ears. Gertie wrapped her scarf more tightly around her neck and glanced up at the banks of white clouds with a shiver. "I wonder if we'll have snow for Christmas."

"We always had snow in Munich," said Hedy with a wistful air.

"A white Christmas, like in the song," said Elizabeth. "Speaking of songs, are either of you tempted to perform in the revue?"

"No fear, but I am looking forward to hearing Margery sing," said Gertie.

"I'm sure Billy would love to do some magic," said Elizabeth.

"He should," said Hedy. "His disappearing coin trick is very impressive."

As they rounded the corner onto their street, Elizabeth stopped in her tracks.

"Are you all right, dear?" asked Gertie.

"That's my father," she said, nodding toward the shiny black Daimler parked outside her house.

As they approached, a chauffeur appeared from the front. He didn't acknowledge any of the women as he held open the door for his employer. The figure who emerged from the car moved with the confidence of a man who was used to people obeying his will. With his neatly combed gray hair and dark mustache, he reminded Gertie a little of Neville Chamberlain. "Elizabeth," he said with a curt nod.

"Hello, Father."

"Where is the boy?"

Elizabeth narrowed her eyes. "By 'boy,' I take it you mean your grandson Billy."

Her father's gaze was stony. "You and the boy need to come home at once. Chivers will help you pack." He nodded at the chauffeur, who turned toward the house.

"We're not going anywhere," said Elizabeth.

Her father glanced toward Gertie and Hedy. "Perhaps we could have this discussion somewhere more private."

"There is no discussion to be had, Father. Now if you will excuse me, I need to get on with some chores before I collect Billy from school." Elizabeth turned her back and started to walk up the garden path.

"Your mother is ill." There was a slight tremble to his voice as he said this.

Elizabeth froze, her face still fixed toward the house. "What's the matter?"

"I will not discuss this in public, Elizabeth."

She turned briefly. "Then we will not discuss it at all."

Gertie touched her gently on the arm. "Why don't we go inside with your father? It's chilly out here. I can make us all some tea."

Elizabeth's father regarded Gertie with disdain. "Thank you, but we do not share our business with strangers."

Elizabeth scowled. "She's not a stranger. She's a dear friend who has been more support to me than my own family."

Gertie noticed a shadow of hurt flit across his face. "I'll tell your mother that you don't care then, shall I?"

"Goodbye, Father," said Elizabeth.

There was a moment's hesitation before his expression hardened. He gestured to the chauffeur, who opened the door for him, and within moments they had driven away.

Gertie exchanged a glance with Hedy. "That cup of tea is still on offer, my dear. Or something stronger if you need it?" she said, noticing Elizabeth's trembling fingers.

"Thank you," said Elizabeth, following them both inside. "I daresay you think me terribly cruel."

"If I've learned anything in my sixty-odd years, it's never to judge books by their covers," said Gertie. "Always wait until you've heard the full story."

"Well, I think it's time I gave you the full story."

"You don't need to explain anything to us," said Hedy.

"No. It's all right. I want to." Gertie placed a glass of whisky in front of Elizabeth, who took a wincing sip. "I expect you've guessed by now that Billy's father isn't away fighting in the war."

"I did think Billy might have tales to share if he was," admitted Gertie.

"You know him well," said Elizabeth with a fond smile. "The truth is that his father is a very eminent man. A friend of my father's in fact."

"Ah. I see."

"Yes. You can imagine how my father reacted to that little scandal." Elizabeth took another sip of whisky before continuing. "At first he wanted to throw me out, but then Mother made him see that this would cause even more of a fuss. It doesn't help that my sisters have always done exactly as they were told. Married into wealthy families, produced grandchildren. Unfortunately, I decided to fall in love with a married man and have a child out of wedlock. You probably noticed from my father's demeanor that he's used to people doing what he tells them. So, he got in touch with all the newspaper owners he knows, and the story was suppressed. He only cares about the reputation of the great family name. He doesn't give a fig for Billy or me."

"But what about Billy's father? Does he ever see him?" asked Hedy.

"He's met him once. In a park. When he was a baby. Not exactly a memorable experience which forges a lifetime of fatherly love. He does pay for the house, however. He and my father came to an arrangement."

"I'm so sorry, Elizabeth," said Gertie. "For you and Billy to be pawns in all of this."

Elizabeth shrugged. "It's what happens when you get caught up with powerful men. I count myself as one of the lucky ones. I have Billy and I have a roof over my head. And I have you. What else do I need?"

"What about your mother?" said Gertie, leaning forward. "I don't mean to speak out of turn, but I could see how much she loves Billy when she called 'round that Christmas. And how much he loves her too."

Elizabeth folded her arms. "She sides with Father. She comes to see Billy, but it's always in secret as if she's ashamed of us."

Gertie placed a hand on Elizabeth's. "I understand your anguish, but I can also see how hard it is for your mother. She clearly cares about you both."

Elizabeth shifted in her seat. "You think I should go to her?"

"You might regret it if you don't," said Hedy.

Elizabeth stared at her. "I'm sorry, Hedy. You must think me a monster. I know you would do anything to see your own mother."

Hedy shook her head. "Everyone is different. My mother used to infuriate me at times, but no one loves me more than she does. I think this is the same for your mother. I saw how she was with Billy. She wants to make things better but doesn't know how to."

Elizabeth's eyes brimmed with tears. "You're right.

Of course I know you're right. I've just felt so alone. Until now."

"Perhaps that's how your mother feels," said Gertie.

Elizabeth nodded. "I must go to her. I'll take Billy. To hell with what Father thinks. Thank you. Both of you. I was worried you might think badly of me."

"There are plenty of people doing terrible things in the world at the moment," said Gertie. "I can assure you that you are not one of them."

Margery Fortescue had pulled it off once more. The village hall was laced with the delicious scent of the fir tree she had instructed Gerald to cut from her garden that morning. It sat proudly in the corner of the stage decorated with whitewashed pinecones and homemade bows fashioned from scraps of material. Garlands of holly and ivy, which sparkled thanks to an ingenious idea from Emily Farthing to dip them in a strong solution of Epsom salts, were draped from corner to corner. The Old General hissed and wheezed from the far end of the room, ready to serve tea to the audience, which was now gathering with a murmur of excited anticipation. Gertie and Hedy took their places next to Elizabeth and Billy, who looked extremely smart in his magician's cape and bow tie.

"Mama, do I have to do my tricks?" he whispered.

Elizabeth ran a hand through his hair. "You've been practicing all week, Billy."

"I would really like to see your show," said Hedy.

"Will you be my assistant?"

"It would be my honor."

"We went to visit my mother last week," whispered Elizabeth as Margery strode onto the stage.

"How is she?" asked Gertie.

"Much better, thank you. It was a good visit," said Elizabeth.

"I'm glad, dear," said Gertie, patting her hand.

"Good evening, everyone," cried Margery in resounding tones. "Welcome to our Christmas revue. We have a wonderful program full of surprising talent. And to start our show, may I present Miss Eleanora Snipp, who will perform 'Ave Maria' on the saw."

Gertie watched in amazement as her orders clerk, whom she had known for over thirty years, began to play this most eccentric of instruments, her expression fixed in serious concentration. It was mesmerizing and oddly charming, and one in a succession of many entertaining surprises that evening. Mr. Travers proved to be a dab hand on the harmonica, Emily Farthing entertained them with a song and comedy act that reminded Gertie of Gracie Fields, and one man rode a unicycle, another balanced bricks, and a woman tap-danced and played the banjo in perfect unison. Gertie found it all utterly delightful. When it came to Billy's turn, his mother kissed his cheek and Hedy held out her hand.

"He's very nervous," whispered Elizabeth to Gertie. There was a creak behind them as the door to the hall opened. Gertie glanced over her shoulder to see Elizabeth's mother and father appear. When Gerald stood up to let Lady Mary sit down, she accepted with a gracious tilt of her head, while her husband stood stone-faced at the side of the room. Gertie glanced at Elizabeth, who was transfixed by her son and hadn't noticed her parents' entrance. Billy already had the audience in the palm of his hand as he pulled a string of flags from Hedy's pocket. Hedy was playing the perfect assistant by reacting to his actions with a mixture of astonishment and delight. Gertie and Elizabeth laughed along with everyone as Billy requested that Hedy cluck like a chicken while he waved his magic wand over an empty black felt bag. When he produced two eggs from the bag, the crowd roared. For his finale, he brought down the house by pretending to throw a jug of water, which turned out to be full of silver streamers, over the spectators. Elizabeth and Gertie leapt to their feet, whooping and cheering with the rest of the audience. Gertie stole a glance behind her and noticed that Elizabeth's mother was doing the same, while her father's serious expression had lifted to one of bright-eyed amusement. Billy and Hedy took several bows before he led her from the stage.

"Grandmama!" he cried, running toward the back of the hall as soon as he spied her. Elizabeth looked on in amazement as Billy flew into her mother's arms. She turned to her father, who acknowledged his daughter with a courteous nod.

Margery appeared on the stage once more, waiting for the audience's hush. "I would like to thank all our performers," she said. "I hope you will agree that this has been a most uplifting evening. I must thank Mrs. Gertie Bingham for coming up with the idea in the first place." There were cheers of agreement as she led the audience in a round of applause. Margery waited for the clamor to die down before continuing. "We are all facing difficult, dark times, but I believe that we are able to keep going because of the people around us." She caught Gertie's eye as she said this. "We gain strength from one another when we need it most, and I for one am grateful for that. I would like to finish this evening with a song. A friend told me that I had to sing tonight, but I would ask you to join in, because I think we all know the words. Gerald, if you would be so kind."

Gerald took his place at the piano and played the

opening bars to "We'll Meet Again." Margery started to sing, impressing everyone with her clear, sweet tones. Slowly the whole room joined in for a rousing chorus of the song that was so familiar and poignant to them all. By the end, there wasn't a dry eye in the place.

"What a splendid evening," said Gertie as they left the hall. "And we managed to get through the whole show without an air raid."

"Can Grandmama and Grandpapa come and stay at our house tonight?" asked Billy.

"Not tonight," said Elizabeth.

"But we'll see you at Christmas," said Lady Mary.

"Really?" said Billy. His mother nodded.

Billy hugged his grandmother and then, instinctively, his grandfather, who looked astonished before his face softened. "There's a good lad," he said, patting his grandson's head.

Lady Mary grasped Gertie by the hand. "Thank you," she whispered. "For persuading Elizabeth to come to see us. I know you had a hand in it and I'm grateful."

Gertie caught sight of Elizabeth kissing her father good night. "Families need to look after one another if they can," she said. "Merry Christmas, Lady Mary."

"Merry Christmas, Mrs. Bingham."

Christmas was a quiet affair. With Elizabeth and Billy away and Mrs. Constantine at home nursing a cold, it was just Gertie, Hedy, and Charles for Christmas dinner. Even Hemingway didn't seem enthusiastic about the festive delicacies on offer this year. Mutton followed by tinned pears hardly seemed like a recipe for cheer, and yet as the three of them sat around the table, Gertie knew she had a lot to be grateful for. A stranger looking in at them now might presume that they were a family, and in many ways, for Gertie, that was precisely what they were. She watched as Hedy laughed at something Charles said and wondered at the circumstances that had brought them together. To think she might have missed all this by retiring. She couldn't picture a life beyond the war, but more important, she couldn't picture a world without these two people. Of course, she missed Harry every day, but life without him had become more bearable since the war had gifted her new purpose.

As they cleared the dishes away later, Charles seemed quieter than usual. "Penny for them?" said Gertie, handing him a plate to dry.

"Sorry," he said. "The older I get, the more melancholy I find Christmas. Too many years and too many memories."

"Happy ones, though."

He nodded. "Very. That's the problem. It must be the same for you."

"Yes, but I seem to be creating new memories these days, and the old ones bring me comfort."

"Gosh, Gertie. You sound positively grown-up."

She laughed. "At the grand old age of sixty-four." She stole a glance at him. "May I ask you a question?"

"Of course."

"Why did you never marry? Was it simply because the right person never came along?"

He stared out the window into the darkness. "Something like that."

The telephone began to ring in the hall. "I'll answer it," called Hedy.

Gertie touched him on the arm. "It's all right, Charles. You can tell me. We've been friends for long enough. I won't be shocked."

Charles opened his mouth to respond as Hedy let out an anguished cry. Gertie threw down her dishcloth and rushed to the hallway. "What is it, my dear? Whatever has happened?"

Hedy turned, tears brimming in her eyes. "Sam and Harris tried to escape from the camp, but Harris was shot by a guard. He's dead."

Gertie touched her gently on the arm. "What about Sam?"

"He's missing, Gertie." Hedy stared wildly at her. "He's on the run. If they find him, they'll kill him."

Gertie looked to Charles as she folded Hedy into a tight embrace. It was all you could do: to comfort and reassure, to murmur that everything would be all right whilst clinging onto the hope that this would turn out to be true.

Part Three

1944

Chapter 20

I'm not afraid of storms, for I'm learning
how to sail my ship.

—Louisa May Alcott, *Little Women*

Margery and Gerald's registry office wedding was a bolt from the blue. For a woman whose conservatism could challenge Churchill's, it was surprisingly impulsive. The bride looked radiant in an air force–blue utility suit, eschewing her usual WVS headwear in favor of a matching feather-adorned tilt hat. The groom wore his best suit, a pink Christmas rose from his garden, and the biggest grin Gertie had ever seen. The women of the WVS, Gertie and Hedy among them, turned out to form an honor guard with knitting needles, while Gerald's ARP wardens rang their "all clear" bells in celebration. At the lunch party held at Margery's house afterward, there were pilchard sandwiches, cheese and potato flans, all manner of vegetable salads thanks to Gerald's abundant harvest, and a fruitcake made with the combined rations of Margery, Mrs. Constantine, Gertie, and Miss Snipp. Gerald had managed to buy a barrel of beer from a local publican friend, adding to the joyful party atmosphere. Archibald Sparrow, who had been quietly courting Cynthia since the Wodehouse book club discussion, had revealed himself to be a talented pianist and was more than happy to entertain the gathering rather than engage with them socially. Cynthia sat beside him on the piano stool, smiling and occasionally reaching over to turn the page for him.

"Perhaps we should advertise Bingham Books as the place to fall in love," said Gertie to Hedy as they watched the lovestruck pair.

"Maybe it's you, Gertie," said Hedy. "After all, I wouldn't have met Sam if it weren't for you."

Gertie squeezed her arm. There had been no news of Sam since his escape. Hedy bore it all with the stoicism that she'd learned to wear like a cloak since the war began. She no longer ran for the post or asked if there had been any telegrams. Gertie knew that Hedy pored over the news and would have heard the rumors about the plight of the Jews. There was a time when she would have tried to protect her from this, but Hedy was an adult now. There was no hiding the awful truth of war when you were living through it. The only thing they could do was cling to the fact that no news was good news. It seemed strange to live in a world where your hope existed purely because no one had given you the news to extinguish it, and yet what choice did they have? If no one quashed that hope then it remained, a tiny seed, waiting to be nurtured.

"Fruitcake?"

Gertie turned to see Margery holding out a plate. "Thank you. How are you?"

"Never been happier, my dear Gertie. By the way, I meant to tell you. I read *Jane Eyre*."

Gertie stared at her. "Margery Fortescue read a book."

"Margery Travers if you please," she said with a smile. "Well, you know how Gerald loves to read, and you said it was a good story."

"And? What did you think?"

Margery gave an approving nod. "I admire Jane's backbone. She'd make a jolly fine recruit for the WVS."

Gertie laughed. "This is a splendid celebration, Margery. I'm delighted for you and Gerald."

"Carpe diem, my dear Gertie. We could all be blown from our beds at any given second. You have to grab these chances of happiness by the throat while you can."

Gertie wondered how happiness felt about being grabbed by the throat but guessed that it would comply with Margery's wishes, as most people did. "You make a wonderful couple."

Margery astonished Gertie by kissing her on the cheek. "It never would have happened if it hadn't been for you, my dear. Gerald and I call you our little cupid. He's a darling man. There will never be another like my Edward, but there will never be another like my Gerald. I count myself very lucky to have been blessed with two such fine husbands. You know you should really think about it, Gertie."

"If I chance upon Clark Gable on my way home, I'll be sure to pop the question."

"I'm serious. It's never too late for a second chance at happiness."

Whether it was Margery's encouragement or the fact Gertie had drunk a glass of beer to toast the happy couple, she made a snap decision to telephone Charles that evening. They hadn't spoken since Christmas. Gertie recalled their unfinished conversation and decided that it was time to pick up the thread.

"Gertie? Is everything all right?" He sounded weary.

"Everything's fine. I wanted to talk to you about what was said at Christmas."

"I'm not sure this is a good time."

Gertie was determined not to be fobbed off. "When is a good time, Charles? When this cursed war is over? Because who knows when that will be. Surely we need to live for the day. Or seize the day or something."

"Have you been drinking, Gertie?" His voice was gentle, teasing. The Charles of old. The Charles with whom she could share her deepest feelings.

"A little. Margery and Gerald got married today, and I may have had a small beer to toast their happiness."

"Good for you, Gertie."

"And consequently, I am feeling rather loquacious."

"I'm impressed you can still say the word."

Gertie laughed. "I love you, Charles Ashford."

"I love you too, Gertie Bingham."

"No. I mean I love you like Margery loves Gerald. Well, probably not precisely like that. I wouldn't boss you around like she bosses Gerald, but I do love you, and I think it's time we got married." There was silence on the other end of the line. "Charles? Are you still there? Did you hear what I said?"

"Yes."

"Oh," she said. "You don't love me in that way."

"Gertie . . ."

"No. It's all right, Charles. I've been a perfect fool. Please forgive me."

"Gertie, please listen. It's all right. I'm flattered. Very, very flattered, but the truth is I could never make you happy. I could never make anyone happy. I love you dearly, more than any wife in truth, but I'm not the man for you. I'm sorry."

Gertie was relieved he couldn't see her face, which she was convinced was now the color of one of Gerald's prize beetroots. "It's quite all right, Charles. I understand. It's just that you mean the world to me, and I thought there might be more to it. We're still friends, aren't we?"

"Of course. Forever and a day. I do love you, Gertie Bingham."

"I know you do. Good night, Charles." Gertie hung up the phone and sank into her armchair, clutching her forehead in her hands. Hemingway lolloped over and plonked his head in her lap. She stroked his downy fur and sighed. "Your mistress is an utter chump."

The flying bombs brought a fresh terror that Gertie hadn't experienced since the London Blitz. They were relentless and deadly, falling all night and every night for weeks on end. Even if Gertie had wanted to sleep, she wouldn't have been able to, particularly on the nights when Hedy was on ARP duty. She sat up in the shelter with Hemingway curled but alert at her feet. She missed the Chamberses' reassuring presence but was glad that Elizabeth had decided to take Billy to stay with her parents. At least they would be safe there.

On these nights, Gertie would distract herself with a book. The air-raid and POW book clubs had gone from strength to strength over the course of the war. Much to Miss Snipp's mock annoyance, they now sent books to every corner of the globe. This month's book had been suggested by Cynthia. She approached Gertie one day when the shop was quiet, sliding a copy of *Little Women* across the counter.

"I thought this might perhaps make a good read for the book club," she said, avoiding Gertie's gaze. "I found it very comforting after Father died."

"I think it's a wonderful idea," said Gertie. "Marmee always reminds me of my mother."

Cynthia smiled at the floor. "Laurie reminds me of Archie."

Gertie was lost in the world of the March girls when she heard the first ghostly bomb fall. A deadly robot grinding its teeth. A moment's deathly silence. A screeching rush of a steam train followed by splintering, smashing, falling, thudding. Chaos. Carnage. Whole streets flattened. Bodies ripped apart. Children buried alive. Hell on earth.

When Hedy returned from nights like these, as the sun was inching its way through the clouds, transforming the sky from scarlet through fiery orange to ripe lemon, Gertie was always waiting for her at the kitchen table. She would make tea and listen to Hedy's stories with tears in her eyes, grateful for her safe return. Gertie was glad she shared these tales rather than swallowing them down to remain in her heart. Better to recount and sob for the family whose baby had been blown clean from her cot, and whom Hedy had covered with her coat and carried to the ambulance, or the elderly couple who were found in the rubble still clinging to each other in the marital bed they'd shared for over fifty years. Better to look horror and inhumanity squarely in the eye, staring them down so that they couldn't drag you to their dark pit of despair, so you could rise again and face another day.

Gertie always rested easier on the nights when Hedy was at home. It wasn't only the company; it was the reassurance that she knew where she was. *If I keep her close, I can keep her safe,* she would tell herself. Gertie knew that sometimes her fussing irritated Hedy. Five years of war had taken its toll and it was hard not to lose patience. One night, the siren wailed at a little past midnight and Gertie hurried from her bed.

"Come along, Hedy. Let's get down to the shelter,"

she called, knocking on her door. There was a groan from inside. "Come along, dear. We must hurry."

"Not tonight, Gertie. Let me stay in my bed. Please."

Gertie pushed open the door, her mind whirling with panic. She yanked back the covers of Hedy's bed. "You must come at once. It's too dangerous to stay inside."

Hedy snatched the covers back and pulled the pillow over her head. "Go away, Gertie. I don't have to do what you say. You're not my mother."

Gertie took a step back as if she'd been stung. "No, I'm not your mother, but I'm sure she wouldn't want you to stay in your bed while Hitler's bombs rain down around your head."

There was a moment's silence before Hedy gave a resigned groan. "All right. I'm coming."

The atmosphere was tense as they settled into the shelter. Gertie lit the candle while Hedy curled herself onto one of the bunks and took out her notebook. "How are you getting on with your story?" Gertie asked.

"Fine," said Hedy, scribbling away.

"I'm sorry if you think I make a fuss, but I have to keep you safe for your mother, you see."

"I know." Hedy continued to write, so Gertie took out her book and began to read. "Gertie?" said Hedy after a while.

"Yes, dear?"

Hedy looked up from her notebook. "I'm sorry for what I said."

"It's all right."

"I get grumpy when I'm tired."

Gertie smiled. "So do I. You carry on with your writing. Hemingway and I are used to—" She froze. "Oh no." Gertie cast 'round in a panic. "He must not have heard the siren. He's a little deaf these days. I'm so used to him following me out here."

"I can go and get him," said Hedy.

Gertie shook her head. "You stay here. I'll only be a moment. Perhaps you could read me some of what you've written when I come back. I want to know if Arno and Gertie escape the shellycoat."

"Yes please," said Hedy. "I need some advice about the next part of the story."

The sky was a clear canopy of blue silk peppered with silver stars as Gertie made her way back to the house, the moon illuminating her path. On nights like these, it was easy to forget there was a war on. Gertie let herself in through the back door.

"Hemingway? Hemingway?" she called. She padded through the kitchen to the hall, peering into the living room, but he was nowhere to be seen. "Hemingway?" she cried with increasing alarm as she climbed the stairs.

The moon threw a shard of milky light onto the landing where Hemingway lay, his great hearthrug body spread between the two open doors of Gertie's and Hedy's bedrooms. A chill of terror spread through Gertie's veins as she peered at his fur, unable to detect the rise and fall of his breathing.

"Hemingway?" she whispered, tears springing to her eyes. She reached out a tentative hand toward his large, soft head. "My dear sweet boy. Not you as well. Not my darling Hemingway." As soon as she made contact with his fur, the dog opened one eye and gazed up at her quizzically. Gertie clutched her chest. "Oh thank goodness," she cried, burying her face in his neck. "Thank goodness. Come along, my boy. We must get back to Hedy. She'll be worried about you."

They were descending the stairs when Gertie heard the pulsing buzz. It seemed to come from nowhere, but all at once it was as if a thousand wasps were swarming above the house. And then silence. Gertie glanced toward the kitchen. There was no time to reach the shelter. No time to run. No time to do anything but pray. She threw her body over Hemingway's and held her breath. The world exploded. Darkness fell.

Chapter 21

Do the wise thing and the kind thing too,
and make the best of us and not the worst.

—Charles Dickens, *Hard Times*

Gertie wouldn't leave. She couldn't. As long as
Hedy was trapped under the mountain of rubble
from the house that had backed on to her garden, she
would stay and she would search. The firemen tried
to reason with her ("It ain't safe, missus") and then
Gerald did his best to persuade her ("I beg you, Mrs.
Bingham. Why don't we wait for the rescue team?").
Finally, they sent for Margery Travers.

"If you've come to tell me it's too dangerous for a
woman like me, you can save your breath to cool your
porridge," said Gertie, lifting another brick from the
vast pile covering the shelter.

"I wouldn't dare," said Margery. "I've brought some tea and an extra pair of hands if you'll have me."

Gertie blinked into the face of this ferociously kind woman and felt her lip tremble. "I told her to stay in the shelter, Margery," she whispered. "I thought she'd be safe there. I went back for Hemingway." She glanced over at the dog, who was lying close by, watching the drama unfold with forlorn eyes.

"Now, now, Gertie. There's no time for all that. You did what you thought was right. That's all we can ever do. Now, we must concentrate all our efforts on the rescue." She reached out a hand and squeezed her arm. "We will find her."

They worked all night and into the next morning as the day dawned pink and orange in a sky still thick with smoke and plaster dust. Gerald appeared after his warden shift, bringing another flask of tea and an air of quiet purpose. Together the three of them heaved and hauled the filthy debris until their hands were raw. The task seemed impossible, like trying to shovel snow in the middle of an avalanche. Gertie looked from the pile they'd cleared to the mountainous heaps remaining and felt her shoulders sag.

"We thought you might need some help," said a familiar voice. Gertie turned, blinking through the rubble dust at Miss Snipp, standing with Miss Crow, Cynthia, and several of Margery's WVS volunteers including Emily Farthing. For once in her life, Gertie Bingham was lost for words.

"Jolly good," said Margery, rolling up her sleeves. "Just what we need. Right. Miss Farthing, you start to clear from this side with Miss Crow; Cynthia, you come with me and Miss Snipp. Gertie, Gerald, the rest are with you."

Hemingway circled the group as they worked, sniffing the air for his beloved Hedy. After more hours of clearing, a shout went up. "I see corrugated iron here!" cried Emily. Hemingway made a beeline for the spot and began to bark.

"Here!" cried Margery. "We need to dig here."

They hurried over and redoubled their efforts to the one spot, clearing as quickly as they could until everyone was covered in dust and the door to the shelter was visible.

"Right," said Margery. "Put your backs into it."

They heaved at the door, which was bent out of shape and wedged fast.

"Again," she said, jutting out her chin. "Imagine we're playing tug-of-war with Hitler himself."

They shot one another steely nods.

"On my count. One. Two. Three!"

The door gave way with a metallic shriek as they wrenched it from its hinges. They peered into the inky darkness.

"We need light," called Margery.

Gerald passed his flashlight to Gertie, whose fingers were trembling as she took it. Margery placed a hand on her shoulder as she directed the beam inside. The shelter looked almost exactly as she'd left it. There were the mattresses, blankets, her tea and book from earlier, the candle knocked to the floor. Gertie narrowed her eyes, desperate and fearful of what she might see as she darted the light from left to right.

It was the locket she caught sight of first, glinting like lost treasure. The locket Sam had given Hedy on her sixteenth birthday when the world was still intact, when life had been full of light. She followed the beam and there, tucked in the corner, her eyes closed as if she was fast asleep, was Hedy.

"I see her!" she cried. "Help me down. Please. Someone help me down."

Strong hands reached out to lift Gertie into the darkness. Margery shone the flashlight as Gertie inched toward Hedy, her heart thundering in her ears. *Please,* she prayed. *Please let her be alive.* She crept nearer, whispering, "Hedy? Hedy, can you hear me?" The silence was suffocating.

"Check her pulse, Gertie. Feel her wrist," urged Margery.

Gertie knelt beside her and reached out through the dank darkness. She took hold of her hand. It was freezing cold. "I'm so sorry, my darling Hedy," she whispered, tears springing to her eyes. "I'm so, so sorry." She felt her wrist, tracing the veins with her fingertips, desperately hoping, willing there to be the smallest beat of life. Gertie began to shake her head as she realized it was useless. "No. No, no, no."

"Try her neck," urged Margery. "Just under the back of her jaw."

Gertie did as she was told, sniffing back her tears. "Please, Hedy. Please. The world needs you. I need you." She closed her eyes as thoughts of all those she'd loved and lost flooded her mind. She hadn't been able to save them, and now this precious girl, entrusted to her by her mother, would be lost too. A vision of her loved ones' bright faces danced before her: Jack teasing Gertie at her wedding, Lilian comforting her when she was ill, her father smiling proudly, and Harry. Dear Harry. Her true and only love. That was the moment Gertie felt it. Her own heart skipped in unison. A flicker of life. A tiny pulse. Very faint but very certain. She opened her eyes and jumped to her feet. "She's alive!" she cried. "I can feel a pulse. It's very weak. Send for an ambulance. Quickly! She's alive!"

The prognosis from the doctor was grim. "She's lucky to be alive and she's not out of the woods yet. She inhaled a great deal of plaster dust while trapped under the rubble. Her lung function is severely compromised. For now, she needs rest and recuperation."

Gertie visited every day. There were strict visiting times, but depending on which nurse was on duty, she was sometimes allowed to flout the rules and stay a little longer. Nurse Willoughby was her favorite. She had a daughter the same age as Hedy.

"You'd do anything to make sure they're all right, wouldn't you?" she said. Hedy was yet to open her eyes or communicate with more than a gentle sigh.

Gertie kept her eyes fixed on Hedy's face. "Yes," she said. "Anything."

Nurse Willoughby smoothed down the covers of her bed. "She'll be right as rain and driving you potty before you know it, Mrs. Bingham. Girls are made of stern stuff."

Margery had given Gertie strict instructions not to worry about the bookshop. "We'll take care of it in your absence. Miss Snipp can show us the ropes, and Cynthia is giddy at the prospect of working there. You just concentrate on getting Hedy better."

Gertie was grateful. In truth, she hadn't given the shop a second thought. There was only one thing on her mind, and it took up her every waking hour. Hedy was the last thought before she went to sleep at night and the first to occupy her mind in the morning. When she was at the hospital, her whole focus was Hedy, and whenever she left, all she could think about was the next visit.

By some fortune or miracle, the damage to Gertie's house had been minimal. The glass from her blown-out windows was soon swept up, the panes replaced by Gerald. When Gertie was home, she would spend hours in Hedy's room. She sat at the dressing table Hedy had commandeered as a desk, pressing a hand over her notebooks, gazing out the window toward the space beyond the mound of debris in her garden where a row of houses once stood. Hemingway barely left her side. He would meet her by the door when she returned as if eager for news and follow her 'round the house, sleeping at the end of her bed every night.

One day, Gertie caught sight of the pile of books beside Hedy's bed and one particular volume gave her an idea. For the next week or so, she was transported to 1920s Berlin with Emil, Gustav and his detectives, Pony Hütchen, and the villainous Herr Grundeis. As she read aloud, Gertie would glance over at Hedy from time to time to see if there was any flicker of recognition. She had heard stories where people who were unconscious could hear and decided that this of all books might be the one to rouse Hedy. As she reached the last page of the story, Gertie couldn't help but feel discouraged. Her eyes misted as they fixed on the final words. It was then that she heard a murmuring sound. She looked over and was amazed to see Hedy's lips moving.

"What is it?" she cried. "What are you trying to say, my dear?" Gertie leaned toward her, doing her best to pick out the words.

"*Money . . .*" whispered Hedy.

"Money?"

Hedy nodded. ". . . *should always be sent through the post.*"

Gertie glanced down at the page. "That's what Grandma says to Emil," she cried. "Oh, Hedy, you remembered the line."

"*Three cheers,*" whispered Hedy.

Gertie caught sight of the final line of the story. "Yes! That's right. Three cheers indeed."

Little by little, Hedy's health began to improve. Gertie visited every day, bringing more books. They read Jane Austen, John Steinbeck, Emily and Charlotte Brontë, and, at Uncle Thomas's insistence, Charles Dickens. "First class for rebuilding the constitution is Dickens," he told Gertie on calling to inquire after Hedy.

Hedy had a steady stream of new visitors now. Mrs. Constantine, Miss Snipp, Margery, and Cynthia all came to spend time with the patient. One day, Charles appeared while Gertie was there. He had been away but still telephoned from time to time. Their exchanges had been overly cheerful, bordering on awkward. Gertie's neck grew hot with shame now as she recalled their conversation after Margery and Gerald's wedding.

"Charles," said Hedy, her eyes lighting up at the sight of him. Her voice was hoarse and she was still weak, but Gertie noticed the color returning to her cheeks with each passing day. "It's good to see you."

"It's good to see you too. You gave us all quite a fright," said Charles, glancing at Gertie. "But I can see you're in the best possible hands."

"Gertie has been reading to me," said Hedy.

"The healing power of books, eh?" said Charles.

"Indeed," said Gertie, rising from her chair. "Well. I think it's time I went home. I don't want to wear you out, Hedy."

"Please. Don't go on my account," said Charles.

There was something imploring about the way he said this that made Gertie sit back down again. After half an hour, Hedy started to cough.

"Here, Hedy. Have some water," said Gertie, pressing a tin cup to her lips.

"Now then. I think visiting time is over," said Nurse Willoughby, breezing into the room. "This young lady looks to me as if she needs her rest."

"Yes, of course," said Charles, standing up. "Goodbye, Hedy."

"See you tomorrow," said Gertie.

"Thank you for coming," said Hedy in a faltering voice.

"She seems to be doing well," said Charles as he and Gertie walked along the winding corridor toward the exit.

"It's a long road to recovery, but she's making good progress. I only hope the same can be said for these poor fellows," she said, pointing toward the wards full of recuperating soldiers, their bandaged, war-weary faces staring back at her with vacant expressions. They passed one man limping on crutches and one leg, his other missing at the knee.

"Poor blighter," said Charles. "And he's the lucky one. He'll just have to live with the recurrent horror for the rest of his life."

Gertie noticed his expression, set hard with bitterness as he said this. "Is that what you've done since 1918?"

Charles slid his gaze toward her. "I try not to dwell, but it's not always possible. It's the nightmares, you see. You can't stop them."

"You know you can always talk to me, don't you?"

Charles swallowed. "Actually, do you have a moment now?"

"Of course."

They took a stroll around the hospital grounds, a wide-open expanse of green punctuated with oak, ash, and chestnut trees. "I feel I owe you an explanation after our last conversation," he said.

"There's really no need," said Gertie, avoiding his gaze. "I'm very embarrassed by the whole thing. It was a moment of madness. I don't know what came over me."

Charles took her hands. "No, Gertie. It wasn't. It was a kind and wonderful offer, and I was deeply flattered. You mustn't be embarrassed. If circumstances were different, I would have jumped at the chance."

"What circumstances?"

Charles stared at the ground. "I love someone else."

"Oh, but that's wonderful. Who is it? Do I know her? I'm so happy for you." She darted forward to kiss his cheek. It was then that she realized he was crying. "Charles, whatever is it?"

"The person I love died," he whispered. "A long time ago."

Gertie's face crumpled with sympathy. "Oh, Charles. I'm so sorry. How awful for you to carry the sorrow alone. And for so many years."

"That was it for me," said Charles through his tears. "No one ever came close."

"Oh my dear," said Gertie. "I do understand, but why the secrecy? Why didn't you tell me this earlier? Was she married?" Her mind flitted to Elizabeth's revelation. "Don't worry, I won't be shocked."

Charles shook his head, a look of fear creasing his face. "I can't tell you, Gertie. I thought I could, but now I don't think I can."

Gertie looked him in the eye. "Charles. You told me once that we were the survivors, the ones left behind. You have been a rock to me when I needed you most. You can tell me anything, so please. Who was it?"

Charles stared at her sorrowfully. "Jack," he whispered. "Your brother, Jack."

Gertie felt her body sway like a boat caught by a sudden wave. "Jack," she said. Charles nodded. "You loved Jack."

"Yes. I still do."

"I'm sorry, Charles, but could we sit down for a moment please?" she said as the world seemed to spin around her.

"There's a bench over here," he said, guiding her toward it.

Gertie felt as if she were watching herself from above as Charles's news began to sink in. She knew what the law said, what society said, and yet none of this mattered to her. She knew Charles and she had known her brother. Slowly, the memories from history started to piece together in her mind. Jack's argument with her father. Harry's suggestion that it might be something to do with gambling. Charles's insistence that he simply wasn't the marrying kind. It all made sense now. She felt like a fool for not seeing it before. She could have been a friend to Charles, offered comfort when he needed it. Instead, he had lived with his secret for years, unable to discuss how he truly felt after Jack died. Imagine losing the person you love most in the world and never being able to tell another soul. When Gertie thought back to the aftermath of Harry's death and how much Charles had helped her, she felt nothing but shame.

"Gertie. Please say something."

"I'm sorry," she said.

"I beg your pardon?"

She turned and took his hands in hers. "I said I'm sorry."

Charles looked confused. "What on earth for?"

She gazed into his clear blue eyes. "For you, having to face all this alone. Grief is a beastly place. Lonely and desolate. I have only been able to cope with losing Harry because you were there. I cannot imagine what it must have been like not to be able to tell anyone."

Fresh tears formed in Charles's eyes. "You're not appalled?"

Gertie kissed his hands. "The world is on fire, people are dying every day in a war that feels as if it will never end, human beings are turning into monsters out of sheer hatred for their fellow men and women. You have shown nothing but love and kindness throughout your whole life. You love my brother, who was dearer to me than life itself. What on earth could I find appalling in that?"

Charles stared at her for a moment before falling into her arms. Gertie held him close as they both sobbed, united in love and loss.

Hedy's recovery was slow but steady. The doctors seemed optimistic that she would be able to come home within a week. Gertie started to make preparations for her return, airing the house from top to bottom, banishing every speck of dust, making a fresh bed, and buying her a brand-new notebook. The news from Germany was grim. Despite the Red Cross's assertion that the camps that housed many Jews were benign, the rumors leaking from the east were of unimaginable horror. There were no telegrams. No letters. It was difficult to know what to do except wait and hope as they had been waiting and hoping for so many years. Gertie would have given her eyeteeth for a scrap of good news, and then one day it arrived.

She was out in the garden, harvesting her potatoes, when she heard the telephone ring. She set the fork in the soil and pulled off her gloves, satisfied with her work so far. The shelter and the area behind it had been covered in rubble after the blast, but the vegetable patch had remained untouched. She hurried to the hall.

"Beechwood 8153?"

"Mrs. Bingham?"

The female voice at the other end of the line was familiar, and yet Gertie couldn't immediately place it. "Yes?"

"It's Daphne Godwin here. Samuel and Betty's mother."

"Oh, Mrs. Godwin. How are you?" asked Gertie with a jolt of alarm.

"Well. In actual fact, I'm rather well. Samuel is home."

At first, Gertie thought she'd misheard. All the waiting and hoping made it difficult to accept without question. "I'm sorry. Could you repeat that please?"

Daphne laughed. "Yes, I was exactly the same when they told me. It's true. Samuel is home. I wanted to let you know so that you could tell Hedy. I trust she's making a good recovery?"

"She is indeed, and you have no idea how much this is going to speed it along. Thank you. Is Sam all right?"

Daphne hesitated before she answered. "Well, you know how this dreadful war takes its toll. The nighttimes can be difficult."

Gertie's mind cast back to her conversation with Charles. "Poor Sam."

"He's rather frustrated at the moment, his father has prescribed bed rest for the next week or so, and as you can imagine, he's desperate to see Hedy."

"Of course. Well, I'm hopeful that she'll be home in the next few days. I'll telephone you as soon as I know, shall I?"

"Thank you, Mrs. Bingham. Do give Hedy my best wishes, won't you?"

"I shall. Please send mine to Sam. And thank you, Mrs. Godwin. I'm going to visit Hedy this afternoon and I can't wait to tell her the good news."

Gertie practically skipped along the corridor of the hospital later that afternoon. She could already picture Hedy's happy face when she told her about Sam. She hoped that Nurse Willoughby was on duty since she knew she would delight in hearing that he was home safe, but as she walked onto the ward, she froze. Hedy's bed was empty. There were no nurses in sight. She hurried back to the corridor and almost bumped into Nurse Willoughby walking the other way.

"Oh, Mrs. Bingham. I tried to telephone you earlier, but there was no reply."

"Is something wrong?" asked Gertie, noticing that her usual genial demeanor was laced with concern.

"I think you better come with me," she said. "Dr. Fitzroy will want to speak to you."

"All right," said Gertie, her heart thundering in her chest as she followed.

"Mrs. Bingham," said the doctor. He looked even graver than usual. "I'm sorry to tell you that Miss Fischer is seriously ill. You may remember I told you that her lungs were badly damaged. I'm afraid to tell you that she has contracted pneumonia."

"But she was recovering," Gertie protested. "I thought she'd be coming home soon."

"I'm sorry," said the doctor. "Her immune system was weakened, which made her very susceptible."

"I saw her yesterday and she seemed fine. She had that blasted cough, but she was talking to me." Gertie's tone grew desperate. This couldn't be happening again. First Harry. Now Hedy. An endless cycle of loss and despair.

"Her condition worsened overnight. I am very sorry."

"But she'll get better. She has to get better."

Nurse Willoughby put an arm around Gertie's shoulders.

The doctor sighed. "She is very sick. We don't know anything for certain at this stage, but you should prepare for the worst."

Chapter 22

There is nothing I would not do for those
who are really my friends. I have no notion of
loving people by halves; it is not my nature.

—Jane Austen, *Northanger Abbey*

Margery had made beetroot and cabbage soup. Even if Gertie had been hungry, she doubted she would have had the stomach for it. The smell and color were both alarming. She had been worried that her friend would insist on standing over her while she ate a bowl. Instead, Margery placed the dish on the side and set about making tea and toast, spreading it thickly with Gertie's homemade plum jam. Gertie sat at the table, watching her move around the kitchen with comfortingly familiar efficiency.

"What if she dies, Margery?"

Margery froze as the question hung in the air. She

turned to Gertie, her usual stoic expression softening into something approaching sympathy. "It doesn't do to think about such things," she said, placing a cup of tea in front of her along with a plate of toast.

"She means everything to me," said Gertie. "Everything."

Margery slid into the chair opposite. "I know, dear, which is why you must keep yourself strong for her, Gertie. It's no good to Hedy if you fall apart."

"I should never have left her in the shelter alone."

"Would it have been better if you'd been buried down there with her?"

Gertie blinked. "I suppose not."

"I suppose not too," said Margery. "Really, Gertie. I will allow you this moment's self-pity because you are my friend, but I will not entertain it again. It is simply not helpful in these dark times, my dear. Hedy needs you. We all do." Gertie met her gaze with a barely discernible nod of the head. Margery patted her hand. "Jolly good. Now eat your toast before it gets cold."

Gertie did as she was told. She knew Margery was right, and yet she felt the responsibility for Hedy yoke-like on her shoulders. She cast her mind back to when she had contracted scarlet fever as a child. Her parents never told her, of course, but Jack was quick to report, with ghoulish eyes, that he had heard their mother crying because she'd nearly died. Gertie remembered Lilian reading *Little Women* to her while she recuperated. For a week, they had escaped into the world of the March family. They feasted on their theatrical capers, gasped when Jo cut her hair, and held their breath when Amy fell through the ice. When they reached the part where Beth died, Lilian wrapped her arms around her daughter as they both sobbed.

"But why did Marmee let Beth go to that house with the sick children?" Gertie had wailed.

Lilian reached over to wipe Gertie's eyes with a handkerchief. "Mothers do all they can to protect their children, but you can't always see what's coming. You can only do what you think is best at the time."

Gertie nodded, leaning against her mother's warm, soft body. "I'm all right now, Mama. You don't have to worry anymore. I'm all better."

Lilian had folded her daughter into her arms and held her close, weeping silent tears. Only now did Gertie truly understand how her mother had felt.

Sam visited Hedy in the hospital as soon as he was able. Gertie prayed for a Sleeping Beauty moment, where the handsome prince would wake the princess from her slumber, but the hellish backdrop of war didn't give rise to fairy-tale endings. When Gertie arrived to visit, Sam was sitting at Hedy's bedside, holding her hand, gazing, hoping. She opened the door quietly, and as he turned, Gertie had to swallow down her shock. Sam's young face was drawn and weathered. There was still a twinkle in his eye, but it was fainter, like a dying star in the night sky. *Curse this war*, thought Gertie. *How dare it leave these young people so battered and bruised.*

"Mrs. B," said Sam, his voice laden with fatigue. "It's good to see you."

Gertie opened her arms and pulled him into a tight embrace. "Oh, Sam. It's good to see you too. I just wish the circumstances were happier."

Sam drew back and nodded. "I keep watching her face for a sign. We have to keep hoping, don't we?"

Gertie followed his gaze to Hedy's gentle face. "Yes, Sam. We do."

The days melted into weeks. Gertie and Sam took turns to visit Hedy every day and would telephone each other with evening updates. Each day that Hedy lived felt like progress to Gertie. It was as if this whole war had become a constant battle to stay alive. If you survived another day, you had reason to celebrate.

One day the doctor greeted Gertie with less encouraging news. "We need Hedy to wake up soon.

The longer she is unconscious, the weaker she becomes."

Gertie stared down at Hedy as she took her usual place at her bedside. She peeled off her gloves and pressed a cool hand to Hedy's burning forehead. She looked so peaceful, so at ease. It didn't seem possible that she could be teetering on the brink between life and death. Gertie took a deep breath, ready to begin her daily news report.

"Hemingway seems to have got his appetite back. I caught him stealing a slice of madeira cake from the kitchen counter yesterday." She gave a small chuckle. "He's taken to sleeping in your room every night." Gertie didn't mention the fact that he was pining for her, wandering around the house like a lost soul. They both were in truth. "And Miss Snipp has a new admirer. Mr. Higgins. He's a taxidermist of all things. According to Emily, they're rather sweet on each other." Gertie searched Hedy's face for a flicker of reaction. *Please come back to me,* she thought. *Please, Hedy. We're running out of time.* Gertie took a deep breath. "Margery is planning another Christmas revue. I spoke to Elizabeth yesterday. She sends her love of course. I think they're enjoying life in the country. She says that Billy wants to give a reprisal of his magic show, but only if you'll be his assistant again." Gertie's eyes pricked with tears. She brushed them away. "What else? Oh yes, Betty is engaged! To her American GI. She's over the moon, as you can imagine. Daphne Godwin says she's already saving her rations for the cake. She's hoping that she'll need enough for two." Gertie took hold of Hedy's hands. "I want her to need enough rations for two cakes, Hedy. There's nothing I want more than that." She bowed her forehead. "You know, when Charles first asked me to take in a child, I had my reservations. I thought I was too old, too tired, too sad after Harry died. But having you in my life has been nothing short of a miracle. You've taught me so much, but most of all you've taught me how to live again. I could never have got through this war without you. Never. You've been a daughter, a sister, a mother to me. Please don't leave me now. You have so much to live for. Sam loves you. I love you. Everyone loves you, Hedy. Please. Please don't leave us." Gertie sobbed as she stared into Hedy's face, praying for a flicker of life.

The door opened and Nurse Willoughby appeared. "Good afternoon, Mrs. Bingham. I'm afraid I need to take Hedy for more tests."

Gertie nodded, wiping her eyes with a handkerchief as she rose to her feet. "Of course."

As she trailed along the corridor, it was as if her shoes were weighed down by boulders and hope was dissolving to quicksand, disappearing with every step. She had almost reached the door when there was a shout behind her.

"Mrs. Bingham!" cried Nurse Willoughby. "Come quickly. Hedy's awake."

Gertie sped along the corridor as if she were five years old again. Hedy's face was radiant with joy as she burst into the room. "I've just had the most wonderful dream, Gertie," she said. "We were walking through the Englischer Garten with my mother on a beautiful sunny day, and the pair of you had become the very best of friends. It made me so happy."

Chapter 23

1945

We have inherited the past;
we can create the future.

—Anonymous

Hedy and Sam were married in the spring. Gertie dusted off her best tweed suit and glowed with pride as she watched the pair of them make their vows.

As soon as the date was set, Gertie had climbed into the loft, batting away the cobwebs with her feather duster to retrieve a large, faded cream box. She carried it downstairs, placing it before Hedy, who was lying on the sofa, writing in her notebook. "I know you'd rather your mother was here to make it for you, but as that's not possible, I thought this might do."

Hedy lifted the lid and peeled back the pearl-white tissue paper to reveal an ivory wedding gown with lace sleeves. She stared down at the dress and then up at Gertie.

"It might need some adjustment, but I'm sure Margery's seamstress army can help. Of course if you'd rather wear something more up to date . . ."

Hedy leapt up and threw her arms around Gertie's neck. "Thank you," she whispered. "Thank you, Gertie."

"I hope you are as happy on your wedding day as I was on mine, my dear," said Gertie, holding her close.

Margery's seamstress army did indeed work wonders to adapt the gown, adding the odd flourish and ensuring it fit Hedy as if it had been made for her. She wore a headdress that Betty fashioned from cherry blossom and ivy and looked as radiant as a Greek goddess. Sam gazed at her with such adoration that Gertie thought her heart might leap from her chest. *This is how mothers feel,* she thought as she stood beside Daphne, watching while they posed for photographs.

The wedding reception was held at the Godwin family home and felt to Gertie like the first of many celebrations to come. The world was alive with anticipation as every day inched closer toward the possibility of peace. News that the Rhine had been crossed gave everyone cause for great excitement. The dark cloud of fascism had spread across Europe like a virus, but now it was starting to dissolve.

Daphne and Margery had known each other through the Beechwood Operatic Society, so it didn't surprise Gertie to note that Margery had taken full charge of the catering arrangements. Thanks to Betty's GI fiancé, they were able to enjoy Spam in almost every form, along with potatoes prepared three different ways. The wedding cake was encased in a cardboard outer ring and decorated with blossom and ivy. Gerald had managed to secure another barrel of beer, and Margery and her WVS colleagues made gallons of tea.

"Wizard wedding, isn't it, Mrs. B?" said Betty, appearing by her side as Sam wheeled out the gramophone and started to play "On the Sunny Side of the Street."

"It's wonderful," said Gertie. "It'll be you next."

Betty glanced over at her fiancé, who was leading her jubilant mother around the impromptu dance floor. She grinned. "I can't wait. And what about you, Mrs. B? What will you do when all this is over?"

Gertie hesitated. She hadn't given the question much thought until now. The years had been taken up with surviving, hoping, waiting. There had been little time for anything else. Now that they were on the brink of peace, she had no idea what she would do. Sam and Hedy were going to live with her for the time being, but she knew they wouldn't stay forever. Sam had continued his law degree while in the prisoner of war camp and hoped to qualify soon. They would set up their own home. They would look to the future, and Gertie must look to hers. The problem was that she had no idea what it might be. It was as if she were standing on the shoreline, peering into the mist, unable to see what lay ahead. Before the war she had been set on retirement. During the war, the bookshop had given her purpose. Now, though, she had no idea what the promise of a life beyond it would bring. "Carry on as before, I suppose," she said, although the idea of this left her feeling oddly dissatisfied. "Are you excited about the prospect of moving to America?"

Betty grinned. "I'm fit to burst, but don't talk about it in front of Mother. She breaks down into tears at the mere mention." She glanced over at her fiancé and mother, laughing together. "Sometimes I think she's going to miss William more than me."

"Well, I know I'm going to miss you very much," said Gertie.

"We've had some rare old adventures, haven't we?"

"We certainly have, my dear."

"Pardon me," said William, bowing to them both. "But I was wondering if I could borrow my fiancé for a dance?"

Betty grinned. "I thought you'd never ask. See you later, Mrs. B."

Gertie gave them a jovial wave and decided to get some air. She'd enjoyed a glass of Gerald's beer and felt the need to clear her head a little. She pushed open the doors leading to the garden and immediately spotted Hedy sitting under the apple tree.

"Don't sit under the apple tree with anyone else but me," she sang, making her way across the lawn to join her.

"Gertie!" Hedy's face lit up. "I was feeling a little tired and thought the fresh air would do me good."

"Great minds think alike," said Gertie, sitting down beside her. She could see that Hedy's eyes were tinged with red as if she'd been crying. Instinctively she placed a hand over hers as they sat in companionable silence.

After a while Hedy spoke. "Today is my mother's forty-seventh birthday."

The words hung in the air, laced with sorrow. Gertie burned with frustration that she couldn't magic Else

Fischer into this moment or offer sufficient words to console. There were no words that could do this. She squeezed Hedy's hand in a gesture that felt woefully inadequate.

"I just want to know, Gertie. One way or the other, I want to know what's happened to them."

Gertie nodded. "I'll do all I can to help you. I promise."

There was a burst of the Andrews Sisters from the dining room as Sam opened the door. "Hedy, my love. Mother thinks we should cut the cake."

"I'm coming," she called, rising to her feet. Hedy turned back to Gertie. "You know I heard what you said to me in the hospital when I was ill."

"You did?"

Hedy nodded and offered her hand. "I feel exactly the same."

Back inside, Gertie found Charles by the buffet. "I feel like a proud mother hen today," she told him.

He looked over at Hedy laughing with Sam. "And I feel like a doting father."

Gertie touched him on the arm. "We have to help Hedy find out what's happened to her parents and brother. Is there anything you can do?"

Charles's face grew serious. "Leave it with me. It may take a while, but I'll do whatever I can."

There were cheers as Hedy and Sam sliced into the wedding cake. Charles offered Gertie his arm. "Come on," he said. "Let's risk a dance. It is a celebration, after all."

"Are you sure your toes can take it?"

"I wore my steel-capped shoes on the off chance."

Gertie laughed. "In that case, Mr. Ashford, I'd be delighted."

The first reports from inside the death camps came a few weeks later. It was broadcast as part of the news one evening.

"Are you sure you want to listen?" asked Sam as he, Hedy, and Gertie gathered around the radio in the living room.

"Of course," she replied.

As Richard Dimbleby delivered the facts in clipped, urgent tones, Hedy's eyes remained fixed forward. No one seemed to breathe while they tried to comprehend this *world of a nightmare*, where typhus, typhoid, and dysentery raged, where *living skeletons* teetered on the brink of death, where ghosts wandered dazed and lost, where civilization had left long ago and monstrous evil had taken hold. There were no words of consolation, no glimpses of hope, no chinks of light in the terrifying darkness. The world had closed in on itself. Humanity was dead. As the broadcast ended, the silence was deafening. Hedy's gaze hadn't moved from the same spot, while Sam's eyes were fixed on his wife with a look of despair and longing. Gertie understood how he felt. She would do anything to take this horror away from Hedy.

"They're dead, aren't they?" whispered Hedy after a while. "Mama. Papa. Arno. They're all dead."

"We don't know that," said Gertie, clasping her hands together. "There are survivors. The soldiers are doing all they can to help them."

"They burned ten thousand people alive," said Hedy. She looked from Gertie to Sam. "How are human beings capable of such hatred?"

"I don't know, my love," said Sam, his voice rippling with anger. "But they will be brought to justice. They won't be allowed to get away with it."

She reached out a hand to stroke his face. "Darling Sam. They already have."

Gertie had never seen so much bunting, not even after the end of the Great War. Every street, house, and lamppost was adorned in red, white, and blue flags, fluttering in the May sunshine. Margery had promised the biggest and best VE Day party in the country and requisitioned the village hall for the purpose. Thanks to Gerald, two loudspeakers had been mounted on the stage, and a catalog of wartime favorites, from Gracie Fields to Vera Lynn and others, were drifting through the town. Emily Farthing had painted a large sheet with an image of Britannia and the words "There'll Always Be an England" and draped it like a curtain at the back of the stage. But the highlight was the food. The women in charge of the households had saved up their ration stamps and worked together to serve up a feast. Half a dozen trestle tables groaned with all kinds of sandwiches, cakes, jellies, and blancmanges.

Gertie wasn't sure if Hedy would want to join the party. The end of the war brought peace, of course, but the word "victory" seemed ill fitting when so many had suffered and continued to suffer. There was nothing triumphant about the growing number of stories filtering from the east as death camp after death camp was liberated. It wasn't the ending to a story. It was only the beginning.

She was surprised, therefore, when Hedy appeared

on the day of the party wearing a blue skirt, white blouse, and red silk scarf. Sam stood beside her, smart in his demob suit. "We have to honor those who fought and those who are no longer with us," she said.

"I'll get changed," said Gertie, wiping her hands on her apron.

It seemed to Gertie as if the whole town had turned out for the party. Miss Snipp was looking positively radiant, dressed as Britannia, with Mr. Higgins beside her, cast as a very convincing Churchill, offering victory signs to all and sundry. Elizabeth and Billy had come back for the celebration too, along with Lady Mary.

"I couldn't think of a better place to celebrate than here," she told Gertie.

Billy was delighted to be reunited with Hedy, although it soon became clear that he was a little peeved with Sam. "I was going to ask Hedy Fischer to marry me before you came along," he told him with a scowl.

"Billy!" scolded his mother.

Sam put a hand on Billy's shoulder. "Then I'm just glad I asked her before you, as I can see I wouldn't have stood a chance."

Billy scrutinized Sam's face for a moment as if assessing his rival before nodding with satisfaction. "Would you like to see a coin trick?"

"Very much," said Sam.

Billy stayed close to his new friend and Hedy for most of the day. Gertie smiled as she watched them together, thinking what fine parents Sam and Hedy might make one day.

As darkness fell, a bonfire was lit in the gardens surrounding the hall, and everyone trooped outside to continue the party, baking potatoes in the flames, dancing and singing. Some of the children had made effigies of Hitler to throw onto the fire. As soon as Hedy saw the burning pyre, she turned to Sam. "I think I'd like to go now," she said.

"Of course. Shall we see you at home, Mrs. B?"

Gertie saw the horror in Hedy's eyes and understood. "No. I'll come too," she said, linking an arm through Hedy's as they walked into the night, leaving the whoops and cheers far behind them.

The world emerged blinking into the postwar sunlight, and Gertie followed, unsure of what to expect. After six years it was difficult to remember what peacetime looked like. Life without nightly blackouts, sirens, and air raids was cause for great celebration, but rations remained and continued to be the bane of people's lives.

"What have we been fighting for if not to finally say goodbye to these infernal queues and coupons?" complained Miss Crow as she arrived for the book club meeting. If Gertie needed confirmation that the world really had turned on its head, she need look no further than Miss Crow, who under Miss Snipp's tutelage had discovered a newfound love of reading.

"Oh, hush now, Philomena. The war is over. Can't you at least be grateful for that?" said Miss Snipp. Gertie had noticed that she'd recently developed a more positive outlook on life and put it down to the influence of a certain Mr. Higgins.

"Hmph," said Miss Crow, uncharacteristically chastened. "I suppose you're right." She retrieved a book from her shopping basket. "Now, this *Animal Farm*. I liked it as I greatly admire the pig—very intelligent animal by all accounts. My mother used to keep them when I was a child. However, I haven't got the foggiest clue what this is all about."

"I hope you're not starting without me," said Mrs. Constantine, sweeping in through the door. "I am deeply enamored by this novel. Such a clever satire of the Russian Revolution and that monster, Stalin. I do declare Mr. Orwell to be a genius."

"Oh," said Miss Crow, agog. "So Napoleon?"

"Is Stalin," confirmed Miss Snipp.

"Well, I never."

Mr. Reynolds appeared a short while later, along with Miss Snipp's nieces and Emily Farthing. Gertie sat on the sidelines, listening. Emily Farthing was greatly impressed when Mr. Reynolds told her that he had once met Karl Marx, while Sylvie and Rosaline confessed that they hadn't actually read the book but that their mother had sent them along as they were getting under her feet. It was a lively and engaging discussion, but Gertie found her mind wandering to thoughts of the future.

Bingham Books was managing to tick along as it had always done. Her regular customers still frequented the shop, and there were enough postal orders and the book club to keep Miss Snipp busy for the time being.

For Gertie, however, it felt as if something was missing. Every day she would pass the now empty shop where Margery and her WVS army had held fort and gaze inside with a pang of longing. They hadn't fought on the front line, but their work felt important. This was borne out by the letters they now received from grateful POWs. There was one in particular that struck a chord with Gertie.

I don't think I'm overstating it when I say that the books you sent saved me. I was in a pretty dark spot, and reading these comical stories of Jeeves and Wooster made me forget where I was. To be able to escape the grim reality and spend a few hours chuckling to myself was a balm to my soul.

Gertie had carefully refolded the letter and stored it between the pages of her own treasured Wodehouse volume.

"MRS. BINGHAM!"

Gertie flicked her gaze back to Miss Snipp, who was frowning at her over the top of her spectacles. "Sorry, Miss Snipp. What did you say?"

"Our discussion is over and people want to know what the next book club title will be."

Gertie glanced around the assembled company, unsure of what to say, unsure if she was the right one to answer.

"If you haven't selected anything, I'd be delighted

to lead a discussion on *Jude the Obscure*," Miss Snipp offered.

"Actually I read a super book recently," said Emily. "*The Pursuit of Love*, by Nancy Mitford. Very funny."

"Ooh, that sounds like just our thing," said Rosaline, nudging her sister.

"Yes, we might even read this one," said Sylvie with a giggle.

"*The Pursuit of Love* it is then," said Gertie, ignoring Miss Snipp's glare. "Thank you, Emily."

As she walked home that evening, Gertie realized that it wasn't just the WVS she missed. Hedy was still very frail after her illness and tired easily. She worked only a couple of mornings at the shop and spent the rest of the time at home, writing her stories. Sam was working hard to complete his studies and was planning to apply for a post as a trainee solicitor when he finished.

"I always fancied myself as one of those chaps in the fancy wigs," he told them over dinner one night. "But now I realize I'd rather work in a job where I can be close to home." He glanced over at Hedy with a look of tenderness as he said this. "Of course, we'll need to find that home soon. You don't want us in your hair forever, Mrs. B."

Gertie's heart dipped with secret dread. "You can stay as long as you need to," she said, trying to sound breezy. "But I appreciate you needing your own place. All married couples do."

"We'll still see each other," said Hedy. She phrased this like a question, as if seeking reassurance.

"Of course," said Gertie. They had been through so much together, more than most people experienced in a lifetime. Gertie couldn't think of a person other than Harry who meant as much to her as Hedy did. She also couldn't imagine what her life would look like without her. Gertie wasn't sure if she wanted to go back to the same world as before the war. Bingham Books. This house. A day-to-day existence on her own with just Hemingway for company. It was time to make a decision. The world had shifted again, and Gertie would have to find a way to shift with it.

As was their usual habit, Hedy and Sam insisted on clearing away the dinner things, while Gertie relaxed in the living room. She picked up the newspaper and tried to focus on a story about the arrest of Lord Haw-Haw but couldn't seem to settle.

"I'm just taking Hemingway for an evening walk," she called. "I won't be long."

The dog glanced up, having heard one of his favorite

words but unsure if he wanted to leave the comfort of his equally favorite rug.

"Come on, lazy dog," said Gertie, clipping on his lead. "Let's take the air."

The sky was alive with shades of lavender and mulberry as Gertie and Hemingway made their way out the front door. Hemingway turned his nose toward town. "Not tonight, boy. We're going somewhere different," said Gertie, leading him in the opposite direction. The residential streets soon gave way to more rural surroundings. Gertie had always loved that about this part of London. One moment you were in the town, the next in the Kent countryside. They strolled for a while beneath a canopy of enfolded beech trees before coming to a halt in front of a long drive leading toward a large house, its sign partly concealed by ivy: "The Dorcas Fitzwilliam Domicile for Genteel Women."

Gertie had been astonished the day her mother told her that she would be moving to "Auntie Dorcas's," as it was affectionately known. She had always assumed that Lilian would live out her days in the family home she'd shared with Gertie's father for almost fifty years. Arthur Arnold had died ten years previously, never properly recovering after the death of his son. "The simple fact is that I'm lonely," she said to Gertie one day. "And the upkeep of the house is so costly. I shall be fed and watered, which is all I need. And it does have the most magnificent library," she added, her eyes twinkling.

Gertie had relished her Sunday lunch trips to see her mother. She remembered one particular visit when they were served the tenderest roast beef along with Yorkshire puddings as light as clouds. It was a sublime meal, and yet for some reason, Gertie couldn't bring herself to enjoy it.

"Is everything all right, dear?" asked Lilian, glancing at her barely touched meal.

Gertie gazed at her mother. She had always been able to talk to her, to share the innermost affairs of her heart. "I feel . . ." Her voice trailed off as she fumbled for the right word. ". . . different."

Lilian raised one eyebrow. "Different? In what way?"

Gertie shifted in her seat. "It's difficult to say. I suppose I feel restless."

"How is Harry?"

Gertie shrugged. "Harry is Harry. You know how he is. Steadfast. Reliable."

"You say these things as if they are bad qualities."

Gertie sighed. "I don't mean to. He's such a dear man. I just feel as if life has got a little humdrum of late."

Lilian reached for her daughter's hand. "Do you know what I have learned over my seventy-odd years?"

"Tell me."

"To appreciate the calm. There is always a storm coming, always a battle on the horizon. You need to learn to enjoy the peace before it disappears."

"Am I being foolish?" asked Gertie.

Lilian shook her head. "No, my darling. I felt very similarly at your age."

"And what did you do?"

Lilian looked wistful. "I got a dog."

Gertie laughed. "You mean Pip?"

Lilian nodded. "He saved my marriage, Gertie."

"Gosh."

Lilian turned to her daughter. "We must learn to be content in our lives, but we don't need to put up with them if we're unhappy. The ground is hot. It's advisable to keep moving."

Hemingway gave a half-hearted whine, drawing Gertie back to the present. She ruffled the top of his head. "You're absolutely right," she said, leading him away. "We should keep moving. Clever boy."

Chapter 24

It's no use going back to yesterday, because I
was a different person then.

—Lewis Carroll, *Alice's Adventures in Wonderland*

The woman at the Red Cross Committee offices was
extremely apologetic.

"We simply don't have the information at the
moment. I'm so very sorry," she told them.

Gertie stared at her and then back to Hedy's ashen,
pinched face. Where the end of the war had brought
peace to so many people, it brought nothing but uncertainty for Hedy. Whomever they asked and however
hard they tried, no one seemed able to provide a defini-
tive answer as to where her family had ended up and
whether they were still alive. All Gertie wanted was to
be able to help her discover the truth. She had watched
Hedy grow from a spirited young girl into a fearless

young woman. Now, it felt as if Hedy's fight was draining from her, and all the hope she'd nurtured for so many years was fading like a photograph in the sun.

"Well, when do you think you will have the information?" asked Gertie, longing to reignite some of that hope.

The woman shook her head. "I don't know. You can of course submit a request and I will do my very best to help." She slid a form toward Hedy. "I'm desperately sorry."

"Thank you," said Hedy in a small voice. Gertie's heart clenched with frustration. Everyone was sorry. An apology. A note of sympathy. A sorrowful expression. As the horror of the Jews' systematic persecution became public knowledge, it was all anyone could offer. It wasn't enough. It would never be enough. Gertie knew this and could see how it weighed upon Hedy.

As they sat by the bank of the Thames later, staring out toward the barges and boats punting their way back and forth, Hedy asked, "Do you think I'll ever find out what happened to them?"

Gertie took her hand. "I can't say for sure, but I do know that they wouldn't want it to stop you living your life."

Tears sprang to Hedy's eyes, and Gertie wrapped an arm around her shoulders as they sat in silence, gazing out across the silty gray water. When Hedy began to cough, Gertie handed her a handkerchief and patted her back until she recovered, staring grimly at the billowing chimneys and smog-blanketed sky.

"I think you should consider moving out of London," she told Hedy and Sam later that evening. "It would be much better for Hedy's health." She thought of Harry and the rasping cough that eventually led to his death.

Sam gazed at his wife. "What do you think, my love?"

"But what about the bookshop?" she said. "I can't leave Gertie in the lurch."

Gertie waved away her concerns. "Your health is far more important. I'll be fine. Don't you worry."

After they said good night later, Gertie was tidying up in the kitchen when she heard a sound behind her. She turned to see Hedy standing in the doorway. "Is everything all right, dear?"

Hedy didn't reply. She just threw her arms around Gertie's neck and hugged her. Gertie held her close as they stood for a long moment, the pale moonlight kissing their cheeks through the window.

The little white house with its brilliant blue front door was perfect. It was one of half a dozen old fishermen's cottages just a stone's throw away from the pebble beach. The garden surrounding it was filled with rosemary, crocosmia, and sea holly, and the sea could be glimpsed from the top window. Sam had been insistent that Gertie come with them to see it. The Sunday drive had transported her back to that perfect day trip just before the war started. How much had happened in those six years, how the world had turned on its head, displaying the very best and absolute worst of humanity.

"What do you think?" asked Sam after the agent had shown them 'round. "It's only ten minutes from the town where my offices will be, and we're so close to the beach. Lots of sea air will do you the power of good."

"I think it's wonderful," said Gertie.

Hedy gazed at them both. "As long as there's space for Gertie and Hemingway to stay, I'm happy."

A week or so later, Miss Snipp approached Gertie wearing a grave expression. "I have a pressing matter which I need to discuss with you, Mrs. Bingham," she said. Despite their long association, the pair had never quite vaulted the precipice from last to first names. In some ways, Gertie found this reassuring. Too much was changing, and she had come to rely on the punctilious presence of Miss Snipp.

"Of course," said Gertie. "But I do hope you're not about to hand in your notice. I'm not sure I could bear it."

Miss Snipp looked stricken. "Did Philomena tell you?" she said.

"Oh," said Gertie. "No. No, she did not. I was joking but now I see."

"Yes," said Miss Snipp, surprising Gertie as a bloom of pink spread across her cheeks. "Mr. Higgins has proposed, you see, and I thought it only appropriate that I give you sufficient notice."

Gertie stared at her for a moment before darting forward and kissing an astonished Miss Snipp on both cheeks. "Oh, but this is wonderful, wonderful news. I'm delighted for you both."

Miss Snipp offered a rare smile. "Thank you, Mrs. Bingham. I must confess that I am very happy."

"I'm not surprised. Mr. Higgins is a fine man."

"Indeed," said Miss Snipp with sparkling eyes. "Thank you." She was about to retreat when she stopped. "May I say something else?"

"Of course."

Miss Snipp paused before she spoke as if picking over her words like shells on the beach. "I wanted to tell you what a pleasure it has been to work for you and your dear late husband."

"Oh," said Gertie. "I'm very pleased to hear it."

Miss Snipp nodded. "And you know it's never too late, Mrs. Bingham."

"Too late?"

"To find happiness." She held Gertie's gaze for a second before plucking a copy of *The Pursuit of Love* from the bookshelf to send to a customer. "You just have to know where to look," she said over her shoulder.

The weeds had spiraled into a chaotic tangle around Harry's grave since Gertie's last visit. She pulled out the sticky goosegrass and cleared as many of the oxalis and dandelions as she could before replacing the previous week's flowers with sweet-smelling peach roses. "Cut for you this morning, my darling," said Gertie as Hemingway lay panting in the sunshine. She had noticed him slowing down of late and felt herself slow with him.

He didn't come to the bookshop much now, preferring to stay at home, sitting beside Hedy while she wrote. She had completed her first book and given a copy to Elizabeth, who was working on the illustrations. She had kept another copy and passed it to Gertie to read. Gertie had been captivated by the story. It was an exquisite mixture of adventure and magic, which she knew children would love. According to Billy, it was "better even than *Winnie-the-Pooh*." Without mentioning it to Hedy, Gertie had sent it on to Uncle Thomas to show to his publishing associates.

"No obligation, you understand," she said. "It is her first book, after all."

"Understood, dear heart," said Thomas. "Publishers are as fickle as the wind, so don't pin any hopes."

He telephoned a day later. "They want to know if she can write another this year and possibly two more next. Think it would make a first-rate series for youngsters. Tell Hedy I'm happy to represent her. My rates are twenty percent." Gertie gave a loud cough. "Oh, very well. Ten, but only as you're my favorite niece."

"You'll waive all fees and be grateful to act as conduit for a talented young woman," said Gertie.

"Saints preserve me from difficult women," said Thomas. "So be it. I'll be in touch."

Gertie wiped the dirt from Harry's headstone with her handkerchief and ran her fingers over the lettering. "So you see, there's been much excitement in the household over the last few weeks, my love, what with Hedy's book and Sam's new job and their cottage by the sea . . ." Her voice trailed off. "And of course with Miss Snipp getting married and leaving us, it's all change again." She sighed. "Oh, Harry, I'm not sure what I'm going to do to be honest." Gertie thumbed away a stray tear. "What a silly old fool. I just feel as if I'm getting left behind. I even had Miss Snipp telling me it's never too late. That's all very well, but it's not as if these things pop up in front of you like a jack-in-the-box."

She cast 'round, remembering the fluttering newspaper article that had brought Hedy into her life many years before. All was quiet today. There was hardly a breeze, just a peaceful azure sky with bees and butterflies flitting above her head.

"No divine intervention today then, my love," she said, patting the headstone one last time before hauling herself to a standing position, wincing against her aching joints. "Well, I shall love you and leave you. Come on, boy," she said to Hemingway, who staggered to his feet with similar effort. They walked companionably together in the late-summer sunshine.

As Gertie let herself in through the front door, the telephone began to ring.

"Beechwood 8153?"

"Mrs. Bingham?"

"Speaking."

"Good afternoon, Mrs. Bingham. This is Alfreda

Crisp. We haven't spoken for a good while. I'm getting in touch to ask if you're still interested in selling your bookshop."

Gertie was momentarily caught off guard. "Oh gosh, I'm not sure . . ."

"It's quite all right. You don't need to decide now. It's merely that I have a young couple who are looking for a bookshop to run, and naturally I thought of you. Would you like to meet them? No obligation of course."

Gertie glanced toward the living room at Harry's photograph, smiling his encouragement. "Do you know, Miss Crisp, I would very much like to meet them."

"Splendid. Could we say tomorrow at ten?"

"Ten o'clock is perfect."

When Gertie saw Flora and Nicholas Hope walk through the door of Bingham Books, she felt as if she were stepping back in time. Flora's bright eyes as alert as a robin's and Nicholas's loping gait brought her squarely back to Arnold's Booksellers at the turn of the century.

"Oh look, Nicky, P. G. Wodehouse," said Flora, plucking a volume from the shelf. She grinned at Gertie. "I prefer Nancy Mitford, but Wodehouse is Nicky's absolute favorite, isn't he, darling?"

"No one better than Plum," said Nicholas. "Apologies for my wife. She gets rather excited when she enters a bookshop. Good morning, Mrs. Bingham. Nicholas Hope at your service." He offered his hand with a small bow.

"It's quite all right," said Gertie, moving around from the back of the counter to shake their hands. "I understand that sentiment entirely."

Chapter 25

1946

Gertie knew she was the only one who could
save Arno. She needed to be braver than she
had ever been in her life. She grasped the
enormous red velvet book with both hands,
lifted the cover, and let the magic catapult into
the air like fire from a dragon's nose.

—Hedy Fischer, *The Adventures of Gertie and Arno*

Gertie gazed at the book-lined shelves and closed
her eyes, breathing in that treasured aroma for
what would be her last morning as proprietor of Bingham Books. She opened them and ran her fingertips
over the cherished spines. There was nothing more
thrilling than an empty bookshop early in the morning,

with the sun streaming through the window, making the gilded type glimmer with promise.

The decision had been a straightforward one in the end. It didn't feel like giving up, more like passing on the mantle. She had become rather fond of Flora and Nicholas over the past few weeks. They were coming along to the party tonight. Gertie could hardly wait. She plucked a copy of *The Adventures of Gertie and Arno* from the counter, admiring its pale green cover adorned with Elizabeth's delightful illustration of the two characters. She opened the cover and read the dedication with a dip of sadness.

For Mama, Papa, and Arno, forever in my heart.

Where Hedy and Gertie's inquiries had proved fruitless, Charles had been more successful. He called 'round one Sunday while Gertie was tending to her roses in the front garden. As soon as she saw his face, Gertie knew. "You have news?"

He nodded, following her inside. "Is Hedy at home?"

"No. She's gone for a drive with Sam. It's not good, is it?"

Charles retrieved a document from his pocket and held it out for her to read. Gertie saw the names Johann and Else Fischer. "What is it, Charles? What are all these columns?"

Charles swallowed. "It's from a Totenbuch—a book of deceased prisoners."

Gertie put a hand to her mouth. "But how did you get hold of this?"

"Through my Red Cross contacts."

She stared at him for a moment, noticing that enigmatic side to Charles once more, sensing not to pry. "What else does it say?"

"Enough to know that they died in 1943 in Auschwitz. One of the prisoners kept this log and hid it on pain of death. They found it a few months ago concealed in a septic tank at the camp."

Gertie took the papers from him and sank into a chair. "What about Arno?"

Charles slid into the seat opposite her and rubbed at his temples. "All I know is that the factory where he worked was closed by the Nazis, but I haven't managed to find out what happened to the Jewish workforce."

Gertie sat up straighter in her chair. "But he's not in this book, is he? So there's still hope?"

"Most of the records of the deceased were destroyed," said Charles gravely. "I hate to say it, Gertie, but it's very likely that he ended up in a camp."

"So you think he's dead as well?"

"I'm sorry." He reached out his hand and she squeezed it tightly. "Would you like me to tell Hedy?"

Gertie shook her head. "No. I think she should hear it from me."

In the absence of a proper resting place, the dedication was Hedy's tribute to her family. Gertie couldn't think of a better way to remember the ones you'd loved and lost than to have them immortalized forever in the pages of a story. She was unpacking more copies of Hedy's book when there was a tap at the front door. She glanced up to see Betty grinning at her through the glass. Gertie unlocked the door and Betty bounded into the shop like a puppy let off its leash.

"Ready for one last hoorah, Mrs. B?" she cried.

"Ready as I'll ever be, dear."

For Gertie, the whole day was like sifting through her memories from the past thirty-odd years. Betty and Miss Snipp were there, of course, and all her best and favorite customers called in to say goodbye. Mr. Reynolds had to blow his nose several times, overcome by the thought that she would no longer be there to help him find his next thrilling volume of military history.

Mrs. Constantine was her customary stoical self and nearly moved Gertie to tears when she gifted her the emerald brooch that had belonged to her mother. "Because you have become like a daughter to me," she told her.

"You will come to Hedy's party later, won't you?"

Mrs. Constantine gave her a radiant smile that reminded Gertie of her mother. "I wouldn't miss it for the world, my dear."

Margery arrived at a little after four with her usual team of volunteers and delighted Gertie by wheeling out the Old General for tea-making duties. "Now then, Gertie," she said as they began to decorate the shop with paper streamers recycled from the previous year's VE celebrations. "What are your plans after Hedy leaves?"

Gertie was used to Margery's bluntness, but even this question caught her off guard. "Well, I suppose I'll retire."

"Retire?" Margery raised her eyebrows.

"Yes."

"And do what? Sit under a blanket all day?"

"No. I shall tend my garden."

"Hmm."

Gertie put her hands on her hips. "Come along, out with it. What do you think I should do?"

Margery inhaled, regarding her with a knowing air. "I'm just a little surprised you're not moving closer to Hedy."

Gertie folded her arms. "Margery. Poor Sam and Hedy have been living under my roof for over a year now. They are a married couple. I hardly think they want me moving to the same town."

Margery shrugged. "I just wouldn't let my Cynthia move away from me."

"Cynthia is your daughter. Hedy is my . . ."

"Your what?"

Gertie fixed her with a stern look. "She's not my daughter, Margery."

"Yes, but you've been a mother to her all these years."

"I am not her mother."

Margery held up her hands. "Very well. Very well. I shall save my breath to cool my porridge, as you like to say."

"Thank you."

"Besides, I would miss you, Gertie Bingham."

Gertie laughed. "And I'd miss you, Margery Fortescue."

"Travers."

"You'll always be the great, imperious Margery Fortescue to me."

Margery nodded with satisfaction. "Jolly good. Now let's get on, shall we? People will be arriving soon."

The party was as joyous as Gertie hoped it would be. Hedy and Elizabeth's editor, Eleanor, gave a short but heartfelt speech about the book and how she couldn't wait for readers to discover the world of Arno and Gertie. Everyone applauded, and Sam's eyes glittered with pride as he kissed his wife, while Billy spent most of the evening holding up a copy of the book and telling everyone "my mother drew the pictures and that's the real Gertie over there."

Gertie drank it all in like a final delicious cup of Margery's tea: Miss Snipp whispering with Miss Crow in the corner, Uncle Thomas inviting Mrs. Constantine for lunch at his club, Mr. Higgins regaling Betty and William with a tale of the time he stuffed an armadillo as part of his taxidermy training.

"Penny for them?" asked Charles, appearing at her elbow.

"Oh, just savoring my last moments as a bookseller."

"Any regrets?"

She gazed up at him and then back toward the merry throng. "Not a single one."

"Could I have your attention please?"

Gertie looked 'round in surprise to see Hedy addressing the room. She smiled as the collective hushed.

"Every story has a beginning, a middle, and an end, and so it is with Bingham Books." She turned toward Gertie. "There has been one woman who has lived its story for over thirty years. And I know she wanted this to be a party to celebrate my and Elizabeth's book, but this is Gertie's last day at the bookshop, and I think we should all toast everything she has done for us."

"Three cheers for Gertie Bingham!" cried Billy. The response echoed loud and heartfelt into the night. Gertie blinked back tears as she looked around at the joyful faces, wishing she could photograph this moment. Even Miss Snipp had to borrow Mr. Higgins's handkerchief.

Gertie sent up a murmured prayer to Harry. "We did it. And didn't we do it well, my darling?"

Hedy and Gertie were the last to leave the shop, as Sam had offered to escort Mrs. Constantine home. As she locked the door to Bingham Books for the final time, Gertie paused for a moment, gazing up at the sign. "You know Flora and Nicholas have decided to keep the name."

Hedy smiled. "The story continues."

"With a new chapter," said Gertie, as Hedy looped

an arm through hers. "Thank you for staying with me to the end, dear."

"Actually, Gertie, I have a secret I want to tell you."

Gertie noticed the sparkle in her eyes. "You're having a baby."

Hedy grinned. "You see, Gertie? New stories are being written all the time."

Chapter 26

West Sussex, 1947

We can never give up longing and wishing
while we are thoroughly alive. There are
certain things we feel to be beautiful and good,
and we *must* hunger after them.

—George Eliot, *The Mill on the Floss*

The baby was named Else Gertrude Godwin, and she was as delicious as a peach. Hedy had been telephoning Gertie every day. Shortly before the baby was due, she called in some distress.

"I need you, Gertie. Please, can you come and stay? I can't do this without you."

"I want you to take note of the fact that I have resisted the urge to say I told you so," said Margery as she and Gerald drove her to West Sussex two days later.

"Until now, my love," said Gerald, raising his eyebrows at Gertie, who sat in the back with Hemingway.

"A girl needs a mother when she's expecting."

"I've told you before, I'm not her mother, Margery," said Gertie.

Margery flapped her arms expansively. "Yes, but you've fulfilled that maternal role for a long time. Not all families need to be blood related, you know. Look at how Gerald has become a father figure to my Cynthia. He's always going 'round to help her and Archie make home improvements."

"Taught the young man how to put up shelves for all their books the other day," said Gerald proudly. "And I helped Cynthia make a frame for her runner beans. I'm going to build them a greenhouse next."

"You see?" said Margery. "Look at everything you've done for Hedy. You've been precisely like a mother to her."

"Well, perhaps," said Gertie. "But I would never presume to usurp Else Fischer."

"No one is asking you to, Gertie. Goodness me, for an intelligent woman, you can be rather dim sometimes."

"Margery," said Gerald in a mildly scolding tone.

Margery dismissed him with a flick of her hand.

"Oh, hush now, Gerald. Gertie's used to my forth-right ways."

"I couldn't imagine a world without them, Mar-gery," said Gertie, gazing out at the sweeping Sussex countryside.

Hedy's labor started one evening as they were finish-ing supper. She let out a loud gasp and clutched her belly. Sam's face went ashen as he rushed to her side. "Are you all right, my darling?"

Hedy nodded once the pain subsided. "It's starting," she said.

The district midwife was called Nelly Crabb, and she smoked Player's Navy Cut cigarettes during her tea breaks. "We're in for a long night, dearies," she told them on examining Hedy. "First babies are always a bit reluctant to leave." She bundled Sam out of the room. "Best you stay downstairs and keep that teapot topped up, young man. The mother and I will look after your wife, don't you worry."

Gertie caught Hedy's eye, but they didn't contra-dict her.

Hedy faced labor and childbirth with the same deter-mined courage she had shown toward everything else she'd had to face over the past eight years. Gertie kept hold of her hand, offering words of encouragement, soothing her brow with a cooling flannel, and watching in reverent awe as this young woman did what thousands of women did every day. When baby Else emerged, announcing her arrival with a bold, powerful cry, Gertie sensed the world around her shift again. New life. New hope. The future opening up before them.

"That's a voice that demands to be heard," said Nelly Crabb, as she cut the cord. "This girl is ready to take on the world."

Gertie and Hedy grinned at each other before gazing down at Else, who looked up at them and then immediately closed her eyes as if reassured that all was well. Nelly opened the door and Sam practically fell into the room. "In you come, Father," she said. "Congratulations."

Gertie stood back to let Sam embrace his wife and new daughter. "Oh, Hedy," he said. "She's perfect. Well done, my darling."

"I couldn't have done it without Gertie."

"Thank you, Mrs. B," said Sam.

"Right," said Nelly, bustling back into the room. "I need to tend to Mother, so if you could take the baby downstairs, but stay in the kitchen to keep her warm."

Tears brimmed in Gertie's eyes as she watched Sam take his daughter from Hedy, gazing down at her with such tenderness. "Hello, my beautiful girl," he said.

Gertie put on the kettle as Sam sat with Else in his arms. Hemingway sniffed the bundle before sitting bolt upright beside them as if ready to guard this precious being with his life. "Do you know, Mrs. B, my daughter is the best thing to come out of this blasted war. She gives me hope after I'd nearly run out of the stuff."

Gertie put an arm around his shoulders and gazed down at the baby. Else opened her eyes for a moment, staring up at them in surprise. "I know precisely what you mean, Sam. I'm over the moon for you both. It'll be quite a wrench to go home."

"Then don't."

"I beg your pardon?"

"Don't go home, Gertie. Please stay. We'd both like it if you did."

"Are you sure?"

Sam nodded. "I didn't mention it before because I thought you'd want to enjoy your retirement, but now, seeing you here with Hedy, it all makes sense."

"I don't want to be in the way," said Gertie.

"We've got three bedrooms, and I know Hedy would appreciate help with the baby. Why don't you stay for a while and see how you feel? I know the estate agent in town. I'm sure he could find you a house you'd like."

Gertie's mind buzzed with possibility. Sam was right. It all made sense, and yet she wasn't sure she could imagine leaving the place where she'd lived with Harry, where they'd built Bingham Books, where they'd been so happy. The baby squeaked as if offering a different point of view. Gertie smiled. "I'll stay for a while. Thank you, dear."

They quickly fell into a routine. Hedy would feed Else as soon as she woke, Sam would leave for work, and Gertie would tend to the household tasks and breakfast with Hedy while the baby slept. If Else was fractious, Gertie would take her for a walk and marvel at the way the sound of the sea would soothe her into slumber. The three of them spent joyful days in the garden or on the beach, taking pleasure in watching Else grow. Her first smile. Her first chuckle. The way she grabbed Gertie's finger and refused to let go. The way she gazed at Hedy as if she were the only person in the world. Gertie had the strongest sense that she was exactly where she was supposed to be.

She spoke to Margery once a week on a Tuesday at precisely six o'clock. "I have a proposition for you, Gertie," said her friend a few months after Else was born.

"Oh yes," said Gertie with a rising sense of dread. Margery's propositions invariably led to wherever Margery needed them to go.

"Gerald and I would like to buy your house."

"I beg your pardon?"

"Your house, dear. It's perfect. Since Cynthia has married, I'm rattling around this old place like a marble in a drainpipe, and Gerald has always admired your garden."

"I see. And do I have any say in the matter?"

Margery sighed. "Gertie, are you honestly going to tell me that you plan to return here and leave Hedy and the baby behind?"

"Well. I don't know."

"Precisely. As I said, it's a proposal, but I think we all know it's for the best."

"I'll give it some thought."

"You do that. Give my love to that divine family, won't you? Cheerio, Gertie."

"Cheerio, Margery."

Gertie first saw the man at the far end of the beach but didn't think anything of it. She was walking with Else while Hedy took a nap. The baby was teething, her gums red raw, and it had been a long night. Now, thanks to a miracle balm gifted to them by the wondrous Nelly Crabb, the baby was asleep, and Gertie was enjoying an early-morning stroll. She paused to take in the view, inhaling fresh salty sea air as the seagulls ducked and wheeled overhead, following a fishing trawler heading inland. The bulky clouds that had blanketed the sky when she woke were starting to lift, revealing the first glimmers of sun. Since moving here, Gertie had come to the conclusion that along with the heady scent of books, the best aromas were the sweetly intoxicating smell of a baby's head and an invigorating breath of sea air.

She turned her gaze to the far end of the beach and noticed the man walking toward her. It was difficult to discern his age at that distance, but he had a slightly wild air about him, with a headful of curly hair and a broad, bushy beard. Gertie's heart beat faster as she noticed him make a beeline for her. Instinctively, she placed a protective arm around the baby before walking quickly in the opposite direction. *There's nothing to fear,* she told herself. *You're so close to home.* Glancing over her shoulder, she noticed him quicken his step in response to her movement. Gertie panicked. She began to hurry up the beach toward the path leading to the house.

"Please! Wait!" called the man.

Gertie didn't look back. She picked up her pace as soon as she reached the verge, pulling Else close. The path was narrow, flanked on either side by overhanging cow parsley and arrow grass, making it difficult for Gertie to hurry, and with Else in her arms, she certainly didn't want to run.

"Please," cried the man as he reached the path. "I only want to talk to you."

There was something about his voice that made Gertie stop. He spoke English with a German accent. She spun 'round, doing her best to invoke the domineering tones of Margery Travers as she addressed him. "What do you want?" she demanded.

The man approached her breathlessly. Beneath his beard and baggy clothes, she discerned a slight frame and sallow complexion. He regarded her with desperate eyes that at once seemed familiar. "Do you know where Hedy Fischer lives?" he asked.

A thrill of recognition squeezed Gertie's heart. "You're Arno."

The man raised his eyebrows in astonishment before a thought struck him. "You're Gertie Bingham." Gertie nodded. His eyes traveled from her face to the baby in her arms. "And this is . . . ?" His voice trailed to a whisper.

Gertie held out the baby for him to see. "This is Else."

Arno yelped with a mixture of soaring happiness and deep heartache. He clutched his chest and gazed at the baby's face. "Can you take me to Hedy? Bitte?" he whispered, as if not daring to believe that this might be possible.

Gertie led him along the path and stopped outside the garden gate that led to the house. Arno stared at her for a moment. "Go and knock," she said. "I'll stay here."

He gave a brief nod before making his way to the front step. Gertie watched as he rang the bell and waited. When Hedy opened the door, she froze at the sight of him. Brother and sister stared at each other in silence, unable to believe that it was real. Then Hedy rushed forward, pulling her brother into her arms, and they collapsed to the ground in a reunion that was alive with joy, sorrow, and love.

As they sat around the kitchen table later, Gertie noticed a new spark in Hedy's eyes. She nestled close to her brother and hung on his every word as if fearful that he might disappear again at any second. "When did you last see Mama and Papa?"

Arno's face clouded at the memory. "1943. We were at Theresienstadt before being sent east. They wanted young men to work in the factory, so I was chosen. We knew it would probably be the last time we saw one another." He stared at the cup in front of him. Hedy grasped his hand. "Mother wrote letters." He looked from Hedy to Gertie. "For each of you." He reached into his pocket and retrieved two faded brown envelopes. "She told me I had to survive so I could find you and deliver them. I think that gave me courage. She said that if we found each other again we must remember that she and Papa are always with us, that all we have to do is look up at the night sky and find them."

Hedy nodded through her tears as she took the letter. He handed the other to Gertie.

"Thank you for taking care of my sister," he said.

"Your sister has taken care of me," she told him.

Gertie waited until she was home before she read the letter. Her cottage was just along the path from Sam and Hedy's with a magnificent view of the sea. The orange sun was kissing the horizon as she and Hemingway let themselves in through the front door. Gertie made some tea and carried it out into the garden, enjoying the still cool of the early-evening air. Breathing in the scent of lavender, she paused to enjoy a new pink rose, freshly bloomed that day, then sat on the bench that Sam had set up for her in the perfect spot looking out to sea. As the sky darkened, Gertie gazed upward, noticing two vivid stars in the distance. She thought back to Else's promise and smiled as she began to read.

Theresienstadt, 14 January 1943

My dear Gertie,

I hope you don't mind me addressing you in such an informal way. It is just that after Hedy's letters I feel as if I know you like a friend. I'm not sure when or how this letter will reach you, but I have entrusted it to my dear son, as I know that if anyone will bring it to you, he will. I sense that these letters will be the last I am ever able to write. My hands are shaking at this thought because it means that I will never see my darling daughter again. It pains me deeply to think that I will never catch sight of her beautiful face or hold her in my arms or kiss her soft cheek once more. I pray that one day she will become a mother so that she understands the strength of feeling I have for her. Hedy and Arno have brought my husband and me untold joy and love. I have never felt love quite like it. It is as wide as the ocean, as constant as the night sky, and it lives with you forever, regardless of what happens. It is also the reason we decided to send Hedy to England. I need you to understand how difficult it was to make this decision. I spent many sleepless nights questioning if it was the right thing to do and drove poor Johann mad with my fretting. On the day Hedy left, I was inconsolable. I would remember her sweet face gazing out the train window, so brave, so stoical. Every night in my dreams, I saw her crying out, begging us to let her stay. I would wake in a cold sweat, fearful of what had become of her. But then Hedy's letters started to arrive, and she told us about you and how kind you are. I could picture you both sitting in the garden with Hemingway. It made me think of our darling Mischa. I knew then that we had made the right decision. To lose your child and know you will never see her again is a living nightmare, but the thought that you were taking care of her, acting as the mother that circumstances prevented me from being, is everything to me. I can never thank you enough for what you have done. It is an endless comfort to me as a mother to know that my daughter is surrounded by love and kindness. In hopeless times, when there is nothing but darkness in the world, they are all we need.

Ever yours,
Else Fischer

Christmas 1952

Warmest greetings to all our book club members, old and new.

As you know it's been a busy year with two new branches of Bingham Books opening in Hoxley and Meerford. We are pleased to report that Cynthia and Archibald Sparrow have assumed the roles of manager and assistant manager, respectively, for the original Bingham Books in Beechwood.

We've had a wonderful selection of book club reads and meetings to enjoy, organized by our newest Bingham Books employee, Will Chambers (son of children's illustrator and local resident Elizabeth Chambers). Notable highlights have been the visit of Miss Barbara Pym to discuss her book *Excellent Women* and the children's book club meeting to discuss *Charlotte's Web*, where all the children made pig masks!

We were saddened to hear of the death of

Thomas Arnold, who ran Arnold's Booksellers for over fifty years and was greatly respected by everyone in the book world. Our old friend and niece of Mr. Arnold, Gertie Bingham, asked us to convey how grateful she has been for your messages of condolence. She is still enjoying her retirement on the Sussex coast living close to our favourite children's author, Hedy Fischer. We are excited to report that none other than Walt Disney is planning to adapt her bestselling *Adventures of Gertie and Arno* (illustrated by the aforementioned Elizabeth Chambers) into an animated film.

In other news, we send congratulations to former Bingham Books assistant bookseller Betty Hardy and her husband, William, who moved to Florida after the war and have recently welcomed their second child, Jimmy, a brother for Scarlet, into the world. We also send best wishes to former Bingham Books orders clerk Mrs. Eleanora Higgins, who recently opened a taxidermy business with her husband, Mr. Horatio Higgins. We wish many happy returns to Mrs. Constantine and Mr. Reynolds, two of our most loyal book club members, who both celebrated their ninetieth birthdays this year. Last but by no means least, congratulations to Mr. Gerald Travers, another book club regular, who won the 1952 Kent Best Allotment Award, and to his wife, Mrs. Margery Travers, who was recently appointed to the national chair of the Women's Institute. She is looking for someone to take over on a local level and asks that interested parties contact her directly at Beechwood 8153 to arrange an interview.

We look forward to welcoming you to the next meeting of Bingham's Book Club at our Beechwood branch on Thursday, 15 January, at seven o'clock. We will be discussing the new spy novel *A Shot in the Dark*, by Philip du Champ, which, as many of you know, is the pen name of Gertie Bingham's old friend Charles Ashford.

We would like to take this opportunity to wish you all a happy, blessed, and peaceful Christmas.

Yours,

Florence and Nicholas Hope

Bingham's Book Club
Recommends

TREASURED CLASSICS

The Arabian Nights

Pride and Prejudice by Jane Austen

The Tenant of Wildfell Hall by Anne Brontë

Jane Eyre by Charlotte Brontë

Wuthering Heights by Emily Brontë

The Good Earth by Pearl S. Buck

A Christmas Carol by Charles Dickens

Great Expectations by Charles Dickens

Middlemarch by George Eliot

Regency Buck by Georgette Heyer

Grimm's Folk Tales by the Brothers Grimm

Tess of the d'Urbervilles by Thomas Hardy

Little Women by Louisa May Alcott

How Green Was My Valley by Richard Llewellyn

Moby-Dick by Herman Melville
Gone with the Wind by Margaret Mitchell
The Pursuit of Love by Nancy Mitford
The Grapes of Wrath by John Steinbeck

THRILLING STORIES
The Thirty-Nine Steps by John Buchan
Appointment with Death by Agatha Christie
The Hound of the Baskervilles by Arthur Conan Doyle
Rebecca by Daphne du Maurier

EXCELLENT CAPERS
The Lord Peter Wimsey detective series by Dorothy
    L. Sayers
The Code of the Woosters by P. G. Wodehouse

CHILDREN'S FAVORITES
Peter and Wendy by J. M. Barrie
Alice's Adventures in Wonderland by Lewis Carroll
The Adventures of Gertie and Arno by Hedy Fischer,
    illustrated by Elizabeth Chambers
The Secret Garden by Frances Hodgson Burnett
Emil and the Detectives by Erich Kästner
Treasure Island by Robert Louis Stevenson
Winnie-the-Pooh by A. A. Milne
    Mary Poppins by P. L. Travers

Historical Resources

This story was inspired by a wealth of research, most of which was carried out remotely because of the pandemic. The following proved particularly useful:

BOOKS

Millions Like Us: Women's Lives in the Second World War by Virginia Nicholson (Penguin, 2012)

The Truth About Bookselling by Thomas Joy (Pitman, 1964)

1939: A People's History by Frederick Taylor (Picador, 2020)

Blitz Spirit: Ordinary Lives in Extraordinary Times, compiled by Becky Brown from the Mass Observation Archive (Hodder and Stoughton, 2020)

FILMS/TV

WW2: I Was There (BBC Studios, 2019)

Blitz Spirit with Lucy Worsley (BBC, 2021)

Into the Arms of Strangers: Stories of the Kindertransport, written and directed by Mark Jonathan Harris (Sabine Films / Skywalker / United States Holocaust Memorial Museum, 2000)

WEBSITES

Imperial War Museums (iwm.org.uk)

WW2 People's War (bbc.co.uk/history/ww2peopleswar)Acknowledgments

Acknowledgments

Thank you to my agent, Laura Macdougall, who when I told her about the idea for this book said, "How quickly can you write it?" She is always supportive, always honest, and always brilliant. Thanks also to Olivia Davies for her wisdom and encouragement. Huge thanks to the wider team at United Agents for their help in bringing this book to life, especially Lucy Joyce for answering my many questions and Amy Mitchell and the brilliant foreign rights team.

Thank you to Emily Krump and the team at William Morrow in the U.S., who published Eudora with such love and care and are now showing the same for Gertie and Hedy.

Thank you to Sherise Hobbs for sharing my vision

for this book and to everyone at Headline for their enthusiasm and passion.

Thank you to my publishers around the world who read Gertie and Hedy's story and got it straightaway. You are all now official members of Bingham's Book Club.

Many thanks to Catherine Flynn, senior archivist at the Penguin Random House Archive, who sent me an incredible amount of valuable information about the history of bookselling; to Lindsay Ould, borough archivist at the Museum of Croydon, who pointed me toward the wonderful local Ward's Directories, which led me to find the equally wonderful local Kelly's Directories; to Raphaelle Broughton at Hatchards, who recommended Thomas Joy's fascinating book *The Truth About Bookselling*; to Melissa Hacker, the president of the Kindertransport Association, who gave me lots of information and further resource references; and to the Bromley Gloss Facebook page community, who offered photos and facts about local history and bookshops.

Love and gratitude to my fellow writers who are always generous with their support and wise with their advice, especially Celia Anderson, Kerry Barrett, Laurie Ellingham, Fiona Harper, Kerry Fisher, Ruth Hogan, Andi Michael, Helen Phifer, and Lisa Timoney.

Thank you to the booksellers, librarians, and online community who tirelessly read, review, and share their love for stories and reading. This book is inspired by your passion.

Special thanks to Jenna Bahen (@flowersfavourite-fiction), who is kind, generous, and has been an incredible cheerleader for my books among the Bookstagram community.

Thank you to my friends who encourage, support, and cheer me every step of the way. To Carol for the blackberry jam, lychee martinis, and trips to author talks; to Jan for all the chats and laughs on and off the tennis court; to Melissa for daily Wordles, kindness, and excellent cultural recommendations; to Nick, Becs, Eva, and James for all their love (cheersn); to Julia for kind words and laughter; to Helen (and Kobe) for head-clearing dog walks in all weathers; to Gill, who believed in me from the day she read my first book nearly a decade ago; to Pammie and Rip for games of Perudo and kindness; to Sal for plot walks and excellent taste in wine; to Sarah for always sending me a message when I need it most and, more importantly, for taking the time to tell me about her family's experience of fleeing Germany in the 1930s.

All my love and gratitude to my dear friend Helen Abbott, who died in June 2022, just as I was finishing this book. She gave me endless encouragement with my writing over the years, and I am proud to dedicate this book to her memory.

Heartfelt thanks to my late parents, Margaret and Graham, who gifted me a lifelong love of books and reading.

A final huge note of thanks to my favorite people— Rich, Lil, and Alfie—for the love, laughter, and countless episodes of *Taskmaster* and *Better Call Saul*. And thanks to Nelson for all the plot walks.

HARPER
LARGE PRINT

We hope you enjoyed reading
our new, comfortable print size and found it
an experience you would like to repeat.

Well – you're in luck!

Harper Large Print offers the finest in
fiction and nonfiction books in this same larger
print size and paperback format. Light and easy to read,
Harper Large Print paperbacks are for the book lovers
who want to see what they are reading without strain.

For a full listing of titles and
new releases to come, please visit our website:
www.hc.com

HARPER LARGE PRINT